Simon Beckett has worked as a freelance journalist, writing for national newspapers and colour supplements. He is the author of four No. 1 international bestselling crime thrillers featuring forensic anthropologist Dr David Hunter – *The Chemistry of Death*, *Written in Bone*, *Whispers of the Dead* and *The Calling of the Grave* – and five stand-alone psychological thrillers, most recently *Stone Bruises*, also international bestsellers.

Where There's Smoke was originally published nearly twenty years ago and was made into an ITV drama. Simon has now revised his novel, bringing the story up to date.

To find out more, visit www.simonbeckett.com

D1148317

Where There's Smoke

Simon Beckett

BANTAM BOOKS

LONDON • TORONTO • SYDNEY • AUCKLAND • JOHANNESBURG

TRANSWORLD PUBLISHERS
61–63Uxbridge Road, London W5 5SA
www.transworldbooks.co.uk

Transworld is part of the Penguin Random House group of companies
whose addresses can be found at global.penguinrandomhouse.com

Penguin
Random House
UK

First published in Great Britain in 1997 by Hodder and Stoughton
Revised edition published in 2015 by Bantam Books
an imprint of Transworld Publishers

A CIP catalogue record for this book
is available from the British Library.

ISBN
9780857502766

Typeset in 11/14pt Sabon by Falcon Oast Graphic Art Ltd.
Printed and bound by CPI Group (UK) Ltd, Croydon, CR0 4YY

Penguin Random House is committed to a sustainable
future for our business, our readers and our planet. This book is made from
Forest Stewardship Council® certified paper.

MIX
Paper from
responsible sources
FSC® C018179

1 3 5 7 9 10 8 6 4 2

For Hilary

Author's Note

Where There's Smoke was first published in 1997. The idea for it came after I read a news item about a surrogate mother who refused to hand over her baby to the couple who'd paid her to become pregnant. That started me wondering what might happen if a woman hired someone to be the *father* of her child. It seemed to me that under the right – or wrong – circumstances, there was potential for a dramatic story.

Where There's Smoke was my third novel but the first I'd written that required extensive research. It also had a female central character, which was another first for me. But my aim was still to write a gripping thriller about a normal life descending into nightmare and chaos, and one that would hopefully appeal to men as much as women.

Although I carried out some editing for the new German edition in 2009, at the time I decided against changing it to a contemporary setting. For one thing, the law on donor anonymity had changed in the intervening years. And when *Where There's Smoke* was first written, the internet, email and mobile phones were still new technology, while social media didn't exist. Those elements would have a radical impact on the events in the story, and integrating them without drastically changing it would be no easy task.

So when my editor at Transworld, Simon Taylor, asked if I could update the novel, I was initially sceptical. Once I started working on it, however, I soon changed my mind. I realized this was an opportunity to not only bring one of my early novels up to date but to improve it and create a topical thriller as well.

I think it was worth the effort. I hope you feel the same.

Simon Beckett, July 2015

Prologue

Some moments burn in the mind for ever.

The landing is dark. Light comes from a window at the far end, enough to run by. Breath comes hard. From the stairs sound heavy footfalls of pursuit. The landing ends in a last doorway. There is no more running, only the need to hide.

Inside the room it is even darker. It is like walking in ink. Blind, she feels her way through the half-familiar landmarks of beds and bookshelves. And then there is the wall. She presses against it, trying to stifle the breaths that tear at her throat. Her heart thuds. Blood from the wound is sticky, and at her touch there is a white leap of pain that lightens the darkness.

She hears the footsteps now, drawing closer. Along the corridor, doors are opened, one at a time, until there is only hers left. The smell of petrol is sweet and heavy in its threat. She hugs her stomach, feeling the small pulse of new life inside, curled and vulnerable. The footsteps stop. A whisper of the door opening. Her name.

'Kate.'

The light is turned on.

Some moments burn in the mind for ever.

1

The warehouse had been burning all night. Smoke roiled into the sky, a darker cloud in an overcast morning. The bonfire smell of it thickened the air, giving the spring day a premature flavour of autumn.

The rush-hour faces outside King's Cross were turned to the dark column as Kate came up the steps from the Underground. The smoke rose above the rooftops in front of her, then the buildings closed in and blocked it from view.

Kate barely noticed. A tension headache was creeping up her neck. She tried to ignore it, hoping it would go away, and then she turned a corner and found the fire dead ahead.

She halted, startled to find it so close, but carried on when she saw the street wasn't cut off. The roar and crackle of the blaze grew as she approached. Set back from the road, the warehouse was surrounded by a confusion of uniforms and yellow helmets, white cars and red engines. Hoses snaked across the ground, flinging streamers of water into the smoke. The flames licked out in random snatches of colour, indifferent to them.

A hot breath of wind brushed her face, dusting it with ashes. She turned away, eyes stinging, and realized with surprise that she had slowed to a standstill. Irritated with herself for gawking, she walked on, skirting the small crowd that had gathered by the police cordon.

The warehouse was left behind. By the time she reached the Georgian terrace several streets away, Kate had forgotten it. Most of the buildings in the terrace were run down, some boarded up with skips outside. But one, cleanly painted, stood out like a raised hand in a classroom. Embossed in gold letters on its downstairs window were the words *Powell PR & Marketing*.

Kate went in. Three desks were fitted into the small office, angled to face each other. Standing behind one of them, a tall Afro-Caribbean man with a shaved head was pouring water into a coffee machine. He gave her a grin.

'Morning, Kate.'

'Hi, Clive.'

The machine hissed and gurgled. He tipped the last of the water into it and set down the jug. 'Well. The big day.'

His voice had a faint Geordie lilt. Kate went to one of the two big filing cabinets and slid out a drawer. 'Don't remind me.'

'Nervous?'

'Let's say I'll be glad to find out one way or the other.' The coffee machine had subsided to low hisses. Clive poured two cups and handed her one. He had worked for her almost since she had started the agency, over two years earlier, and if ever she made anyone a partner, it would be him.

'Did you pass the fire on your way in?'

'Mm.' Kate was flicking through the folders inside the cabinet.

'Been burning half the night, apparently. Bad about the kid, wasn't it?'

She looked at him. 'What kid?'

'The baby. A group of squatters were living there. They all got out, except for the baby. It said on the news the mother got burned trying to go back for it. Two months old.'

Kate put down her coffee cup. She was aware of the stink of smoke still clinging to her and looked down to see tiny flecks of grey ash dotting her clothes. She remembered its feathery touch on her face, the tickle as she had breathed it in. She felt the sting of it again.

She closed the filing cabinet without taking anything out. 'I'll be upstairs.'

Her office was on the first floor. Kate closed the door and batted the grey specks from her Chanel-style skirt and jacket. She knew she wouldn't feel comfortable in the suit again until she'd had it cleaned. Hanging her jacket behind the door, she went to the room's single window. Her reflection showed faintly in the glass as she looked out. Beyond it, the smoke was a spreading stain on the sky, against which her dark hair was invisible. Only her face was clear: a pale oval hanging in space.

She turned away and went to her desk. Downstairs, she could hear voices as the others arrived. The front office was too small for Clive and the two girls, but the only other spare room needed redecorating and a new ceiling before anyone could work in it. It wouldn't be cheap. Kate sighed and switched on her computer. As she waited for it to start, she checked the company's Facebook and Twitter pages to see how much activity there'd been overnight. The answer was depressingly little, although the blog review for the new restaurant they'd posted the day before had gained five more 'likes'. Better than nothing, she supposed, as there was a tap on the door.

'Come in.'

A girl entered, carrying a cellophane-wrapped bunch of red roses. Her plump face was openly curious as she handed them to Kate. 'These have just been delivered.'

A small envelope was tucked into the stems. Kate opened it and slid out the plain white card. A short note was written on it in swooping, forward-slanting script. She read it, then replaced the card in the envelope. She handed the roses back to the girl. 'Thanks, Caroline. Take these outside and give them to the first old lady you see, will you?'

The girl's eyes widened. 'What shall I say?'

'Anything. Just say they're with our compliments.' Kate gave a tight smile. 'And the nearer to ninety she is, the better.'

She stopped smiling as soon as the door closed. She took out the card and read it again. '*Commiserations in advance. Love, Paul.*'

Carefully, Kate tore it in half, then in half again before throwing it into her waste bin. Her entire body had tensed. She forced herself to relax.

She started going through the first of the day's emails,

but the sudden beep of her office phone stopped her. She picked it up.

'Yes?'

It was Clive. 'Paul Sutherland from CKB Marketing's on the line.' His tone was neutral. 'Do you want me to tell him you're busy?'

Kate hesitated. 'No, it's OK. I'll take it.'

There was a series of clicks. She closed her eyes briefly.

A second later she heard the familiar voice.

'Hello, Kate. Thought I'd ring and see if you'd got the flowers.'

'Yes. A little bit premature, though, I think.' She was pleased to hear her voice was steady.

'Oh, come on. You don't seriously think you're still in with a chance, do you?'

'Let's just wait and see what happens, shall we?'

She heard him sigh. 'Kate, Kate, Kate. You *know* what's going to happen. You've done well to get this far, but don't kid yourself.'

'Is that all you wanted to say? Because if it is, I've got work to do.'

There was a chuckle. 'Now don't be like that. I'm just giving you some friendly advice, that's all. For old times' sake.'

Kate clenched her jaw.

'Kate? You still there?'

'You've not changed, Paul. You always were a prick.' She regretted the words immediately. The amused laugh came down the line again, this time unmistakably pleased with itself.

'And didn't you just love it? But I can see I'm wasting my time trying to talk sense to you. Poor little Kate's got to do things her way, even if it means getting her fingers burned. Just try not to be too disappointed.'

The line went dead. Her knuckles were white as she banged down the receiver.

The bastard.

Kate could feel herself shaking as all the old feelings welled up in her. She realized her hands were clenched into fists: opening them she took first one deep breath, then another, trying to focus on the calming exercises she'd learned. Gradually her breathing slowed and became more natural.

The shakes had gone, but her headache was back, fingering its way across her scalp. Kate wished she'd not tied her hair back so tightly that morning. She kneaded her temples gently. *Is it worth it*?

When the invitation to tender for the Kingsmere Trust account had landed on her desk six weeks earlier, she had gone into the pitch without any real expectation. The Trust specialized in low-profile investments to allow its funding of a select few 'Worthy Causes' (the words had been capitalized in their brief) it deemed suitable. She had been surprised that they had even heard of Powell PR, let alone were prepared to consider them for a long-term, expensive campaign.

Then, amazingly, she had been shortlisted. The shock of that still hadn't worn off when she discovered who the other shortlisted agency was, and who she would be pitching against.

From then on, the pitch had ballooned until it filled

her entire horizon. Clive joked that she might as well install a bed at the office, to save going home at all. You're not happy unless you're working, he'd said. She had smiled, but behind it had been a dark stirring of panic. *Happy?* That night at the gym she had trained until her muscles screamed, trying to burn off her restlessness like calories.

Now the waiting had concertinaed into the final hours. Redwood, the chairman of the board of trustees, had told her he would let her know the Trust's decision before noon. Winning would mean financial security, perhaps eventually bigger premises. It would establish the agency's reputation, opening the way to bigger and better accounts.

Kate didn't let herself consider what losing would be like.

She found she was clicking her ballpoint pen aimlessly in and out. She stopped, put it down and determinedly started going through her emails. Soon she was engrossed in the work, though every few minutes her eyes would still stray to the clock on the wall.

The morning passed slowly. Each time a call came through she stiffened, expecting it to be from the Trust. None was. At five to twelve she gave up even the pretence of trying to work. She sat in the silence of her office, looking at the clock and waiting for the phone to ring. The second hand crept round the dial, bringing the noon deadline closer. She watched as it converged with the other two. The three formed a single, vertical finger, poised for a moment, and then the second hand ticked indifferently into its downward sweep.

Kate felt the anticipation leak out of her. In its wake was a heavy residue of disappointment. The Kingsmere Trust were almost obsessively punctual. If she'd won the pitch, she would have heard by now. She didn't move as the fact of failure sank in, no longer a possibility but a reality to be faced. Abruptly, she shook herself. *So you didn't get it. It's only a pitch. There'll be others.*

She sat straighter in her chair, doggedly went back to her emails.

The phone beeped.

Kate started. It beeped again. She picked it up. 'Yes?'

Caroline answered. 'It's Mr Redwood from the Kingsmere Trust.'

Even though she knew what he was going to say, Kate felt her heart bump. She cleared her throat. 'Put him through.'

There seemed to be more clicks than usual as the transfer was made. The line hummed hollowly. 'Miss Powell?'

'Good afternoon, Mr Redwood.' She allowed a faint emphasis to creep into the 'afternoon'.

'I apologize for the tardiness of the call. I realize you would have been expecting to hear sooner.'

The voice gave an accurate picture of the man. Scottish. Thin, dry and humourless. Clive had called him anal, and Kate hadn't been able to argue.

'Yes,' she said simply.

'Yes, I'm sorry about that.' He didn't sound it. 'It's our policy to inform the unsuccessful party first,' he went on, 'to put them out of their misery, as it were, and it took a little longer than we anticipated.'

It took a moment for the implication to register. Suddenly confused, Kate floundered. 'I'm sorry . . . You've spoken to CKB?'

She heard Redwood give an exasperated sigh. 'Perhaps I'd better start again. I'm pleased to tell you that your tender has been successful. The board of trustees has decided to invite your agency to handle our campaign.'

Kate felt an almost out-of-body detachment. Outside, a siren Dopplered in and out of existence.

'Miss Powell? Is there a problem?'

'No! No, I . . .' She made an effort. 'I'm delighted. Thank you.'

'Again, I apologize for the delay.' His voice became tinged with disapproval. 'I'm afraid the other tender was reluctant to accept our decision. The individual we were dealing with became quite . . . insistent.' Redwood brought himself up short. 'Well. Congratulations, Miss Powell. We look forward to working with your agency.'

Kate said something, she wasn't sure what. They agreed to meet later in the week. He rang off. She listened to the purr of the dialling tone before setting the receiver back in its cradle. From downstairs she could hear the rhythmic shuttling of a printer, the peal of someone's laughter. She stared blankly out of the window. For a moment she thought the patch of darkness outside was a raincloud. Then she remembered.

After a while she got up to tell the others.

The bus stopped outside the shops near her flat in Fulham. As Kate stepped off, it occurred to her, belatedly, that she could probably afford to get a taxi from the tube station now. Old habits died hard. She went into the convenience store and bought a pint of milk and a packet of rice. After a moment of indecision she added a bottle of Rioja to the wire basket.

There was a chill in the air as Kate left the shop, a reminder that spring had yet to reach further than the calendar. A drizzle had started, and she began walking faster, hoping to get home before it grew heavy enough to merit an umbrella. She almost trod on the child's mitten lying at the edge of a puddle. It formed a vivid splash of red against the dirty brown pavement and couldn't have been there long because it still looked new and clean.

Kate picked it up, glancing up and down the street for the pram or buggy it must have dropped from. No one was in sight, so she cast around for a wall or window ledge to put it on. There was nowhere, except back on the muddy pavement. Reluctant simply to discard it, she looked at the forlorn little object in her hand. The mitten was no bigger than her palm, and suddenly the memory of the warehouse fire came back to her. Kate felt her throat constrict, and before she knew what she was doing she had tucked the mitten into her pocket and walked on.

The drizzle had stopped by the time she reached her flat. The wrought-iron gate in front of the Victorian terraced house was open, as it always was since the hinges had dropped and wedged it against the path. The tiny garden, no bigger than a large rug, had been flagged over by a previous occupant, but a gap had been left in the centre for a thorny huddle of rose bushes. They needed pruning, Kate noticed absently. She went into the small open porch and unlocked the front door.

Envelopes were splashed on the tiles in the cramped hallway. She bent and picked them up, shuffling through for those addressed to her. There were only two: one a bill, the other a bank statement. The rest was junk mail. She divided it up and put half on her ground-floor neighbour's coconut-fibre welcome mat. As she straightened, the door opened and the old lady who lived there beamed out at her.

'I thought I heard someone.'

Kate mustered a smile. 'Hello, Miss Willoughby, how are you?'

Her heart sank as the woman emerged further, leaning heavily on her walking stick. The dark-green woollen dress was immaculately pressed, as usual, and the blue-grey wig sat incongruously on top of the wizened face, like a hat.

'Very well, thank you.' She looked down at the circulars on her mat. 'Are they for me?'

Kate picked them up again and handed them to her, resigned to seeing the routine through. 'Nothing exciting, I don't think.'

As far as she could tell, Miss Willoughby never received any letters. But she always came out to check when Kate arrived home. Kate knew she was only using the post as an excuse and usually didn't mind chatting to her for a few minutes. That evening, though, it was an unwelcome effort.

Miss Willoughby peered through her gold-rimmed spectacles at the flyers and special offers, and for a moment Kate thought she might escape easily. She started drifting towards her door, but then the old lady looked up again.

'No, nothing there for me. Still, you never know, do you?'

Kate forced a smile of agreement as Miss Willoughby leaned both hands on her walking stick, a sure sign that she was settling herself for a lengthy conversation. But before she could say anything else, a grey shape emerged with a clatter through the cat-flap in the front door.

The tomcat miaowed and rubbed around Kate's legs, then darted towards the old lady's doorway.

'No you don't, Dougal,' Kate said, grabbing it. The cat, a big tabby, squirmed to be put down. 'I'd better take him in. If he gets in your flat we'll never get him out,' she said, seizing the opportunity.

Miss Willoughby's smile never wavered. 'Oh, that's all right. But I won't keep you. I expect you'll both be hungry.'

With a final goodnight, she went back inside as Kate unlocked her own door. There was a cat-flap in that as well, but Dougal saw no reason to use it when Kate was there to let him in. She closed the door behind her before letting the cat jump down. His miaows receded as he ran up the carpeted stairs and towards the kitchen. Kate followed more slowly, feeling churlish now for dodging the old lady. Sighing, she took off her jacket, wrinkling her nose at the lingering smell of smoke. She put it on a coat-hanger, ready to take to the cleaners, and it was only when she saw the bulge in one pocket that she remembered the mitten.

The irrationality of the impulse that had made her keep it disturbed her. Decisively, she took it out and went to the bin in the kitchen. The lid sprang open when she stamped on the foot pedal, releasing a faint, sweet smell of rot. Kate looked at the hash of eggshells and vegetable peelings, holding the mitten poised above them. But she was no more able to throw it away now than before. She took her foot from the pedal, letting the lid slap down, and went back into her bedroom. Pulling open a drawer, she thrust the mitten far into the back under a pile of towels, then pushed the drawer firmly shut.

Kate went back into the hall, untying her hair with a sigh of relief. The light was flashing on the phone. She played the message, but whoever it had been had hung up without speaking.

Barefoot, she went into the lounge. Like the rest of the flat, its walls were plain white, partly because she preferred the simplicity of such a colour scheme and partly because the house faced away from the sun and was quite dark. Even now, when it was still light outside, the white walls did little to lift the gloomy twilight.

Kate switched on a table lamp. The furniture in the room was clean-lined and modern, except for an old pine seaman's trunk that served as a coffee table. On the wall was an abstract oil she'd bought from an exhibition, the only splash of colour on the otherwise blank back-drop. The flat was much cosier in winter, when the long nights came and she could draw the curtains and fill the corners with artificial light. Now, though, dark as the flat was, there was something not quite right about having a lamp on when it was still daylight outside.

She turned it off again and switched on the TV instead. Idly, she flicked through the channels. There was nothing on that interested her, but it illuminated the room a little, and the sound of voices gave the flat a less empty feel.

There was a miaow as the cat wrapped himself around her legs, butting his head against her ankles.

'You hungry, Dougal?' She picked him up. He was big, even for a tom, with close-set eyes that gave him a perpetually surprised expression. He had come with the flat, an extra that hadn't been mentioned by the estate agent when she'd bought it. The middle-aged couple who'd lived there before hadn't bothered to take their pet with them when they left. Kate hadn't wanted a cat, but Dougal had been either too stupid or too determined to accept that.

He wriggled free and jumped on to the floor, miaowing.

'All right, I know it's dinnertime.' Kate went into the kitchen and took a tin of cat food from the wall cupboard. The cat jumped up on to the work surface and tried to eat the meat as she was forking it into the dish. She pushed him back down. 'Just wait, gutbucket.'

Kate set the dish on the floor and watched as the cat began to gulp at the food. She considered getting something to eat herself. She opened the fridge, stared inside, then closed it again. False laughter came from the lounge. Kate went back in. A game show was on the TV, noisy and colourful. She switched it off. The laughter was abruptly severed as the screen went blank.

Silence crowded into the room. It seemed darker than ever, but she made no move to turn on the lamp. From the kitchen she heard the faint sound of the cat's dish softly scraping on the kitchen floor.

What's wrong with me?

Winning the Kingsmere Trust account was the biggest coup of her career. She should have been euphoric. Instead she felt nothing. There was no satisfaction, no sense of having achieved anything. Nothing, after all, had changed. She looked around the darkening lounge. *Is this it? Is this all there's going to be?*

The sound of the cat-flap slapping shut came from the hallway. Dougal had eaten his fill and gone out again. She was alone. All at once the darkness, the quiet, was oppressive. She turned on the lamp and randomly started the Bose music system without caring what was selected.

The sound of Tom Jones belting out 'It's Not Unusual' filled the room. Kate picked up her phone. She had made no arrangements to go out that evening, knowing that if she had lost the pitch she wouldn't want to. Now, though, the thought of staying in alone appalled her. The phone rang only twice at the other end before a woman's voice answered.

'Hello?'

'Hi, Lucy, it's Kate.'

'Oh, Kate, hi! Hang on.' There was a hollow *clunk* as the handset went down. Kate heard Lucy raising her voice in the background. There was a childish objection that she overruled, then she was back. 'Sorry about that. Slight disagreement over which programme we want to watch.'

'Who won?'

'I did. I told her she could either watch *EastEnders* with me or go to bed. So she's suddenly an *EastEnders* fan. Anyway, how did it go?'

'We got it.'

'Oh, Kate, that's *fantastic*! You must be over the moon!'

'Well, I don't think it's really sunk in yet.'

'It will! So you're off out celebrating tonight, then?'

Kate transferred the phone to her other ear so she could hear better over the music. 'Er, no. Look, I wondered if you fancied going out somewhere? My treat, so long as Jack doesn't mind babysitting.'

'Tonight? Oh, Kate, I can't! Jack's not going to be in till later.'

Kate kept the disappointment from her voice. 'It doesn't matter. It was pretty short notice.'

'I *know*, but we've not been out together for ages! Tell you what, why don't you come over? Bring a bottle of wine, and with a bit of luck we can be pissed by the time Jack gets home.'

Kate felt her spirits lift. 'Are you sure?'

'Of course. So long as you don't mind playing aunty again if the kids aren't in bed.'

Kate smiled at the thought of Lucy's children. 'I'd love to.' She told Lucy she'd be over in an hour and hung up, her melancholy gone. She was busy again, with somewhere to go and something to do. She would laugh and play with Emily and Angus, get a little drunk with Lucy, and kick herself out of any self-indulgent blues. She did a hip-twitching dance as Tom went into overdrive.

She phoned for a cab, then poured herself a glass of wine from the fridge. 'Cheers,' she toasted herself. She took the glass into the bathroom and put it on the edge of the bath while she undressed. She studied herself briefly in the mirror as she waited for the water to run hot, wishing as usual that she was tall and elegant instead of small and trim. But, on a high now, she didn't let it worry her.

She showered quickly, humming as the stinging water sluiced away the day's events. She had dried herself and was just beginning to dress when the doorbell rang. The cab was early. *Damn*. Kate hesitated, debating whether to throw on more clothes before going to answer it. A second, longer ring decided her. Pulling on a towelling robe, she ran downstairs.

The blurred silhouette of a man was visible through the coloured diamonds of the stained-glass panel. Kate unlocked the door and opened it a crack.

'Sorry, you're too—' she began, and stopped.

Paul was standing in the porch. He grinned at her. 'Too what?'

The sight of him froze her. She tried to kick-start herself over the shock.

'What are you doing here?'

'I've come to offer my congratulations.'

He lifted up the bottle of champagne he was gripping

by the neck. Kate could smell the beer on his breath, sour and mingled with a waft of cigarette. There was something about his smile that she didn't like. She kept hold of the door, barring him.

'I'm going out.'

His grin broadened as he slid his gaze down her body. She resisted the impulse to clutch the robe tighter. 'The taxi'll be here any minute. I've got to finish getting dressed.'

He moved his eyes from her breasts. 'Don't mind me. Won't be anything I've not seen before, will it?'

He stepped forward as she began to protest, and she instinctively moved away from him. That was all the space he needed to wedge his shoulders in the doorway, levering the door open against her pressure. He forced her back another pace, and then he was inside.

'Paul!' she began, but he brushed past her.

'Come on, Kate, I thought you were in a hurry?'

He went heavily up the stairs, bumping off the wall as he stumbled against it. Kate stood in the small hallway as his footsteps clumped into the lounge. *Don't go up, leave him, don't go up!* a small voice shrilled. But she didn't know what else she could do. Closing the front door, but not the one to her flat at the bottom of the stairs, she ran after him.

Paul was sprawled on the sofa, arms spread across its back. His face was flushed. He hadn't changed much since the last time she had seen him. His dark-blond hair was a little longer, and she noticed the slight tightness of shirt against gut. But the condescending arrogance with which he greeted the world was still the same.

He smirked at her. 'Nice place you've got here.'

'How did you find out where I live?'

'If you wanted to keep it a secret, you should go ex-directory. And I'd change the message on your answerphone, if I were you. You sound really bored on it.'

Kate stood by the doorway. 'I want you to leave.'

'Aren't you even going to offer me a drink?' He waggled the champagne. 'No?' He let the bottle drop on to the sofa. 'So much for congratulations.'

'Why've you come, Paul?'

A look of uncertainty touched his face, as though he didn't know himself. Then it was gone. 'To see you. What's the matter – too good to talk to me now?'

'There's nothing to say. And I've told you, I'm going out.'

'Where?'

'To Lucy's.' The reflex to tell him came before she could stop it. She hated herself for the automatic surrender.

The unpleasant smile was back on Paul's mouth. 'So you're still seeing that cow?'

'She isn't a cow, and who I see isn't any of your business anyway.'

His smile died. 'I'd forgotten how fucking smug you are.'

Kate didn't say anything.

'Oh, spare me the injured look!' Paul regarded her sourly. 'Christ, you haven't changed, have you? St Kate, still acting as if butter wouldn't melt in your mouth.'

He sat forward suddenly. 'Come on, don't pretend

you're not enjoying this! You did it! You beat me! You can crow about it, I don't mind.'

'I just want you to go.'

'What, just like that?' He looked at her with mock surprise. 'This is your big chance! You finally gave that bastard Paul Sutherland his comeuppance! Don't you want to rub my face in it?'

Kate felt the old guilt working. Beating him hadn't given her the lift she'd expected, but she couldn't deny it had been an incentive. The strength of her desire to apologize, to say he was right, maddened her. 'What makes you think you're important enough for me to be bothered?'

He grinned, pleased to have provoked her. 'Because I know you. I know what you're like. Christ, I should do, I lived with you long enough.' The thin veneer over his anger was beginning to crack. 'God, look at you. Miss Superior. You think you're better than me now?'

'I prefer not to think about you at all.'

'No?' He snorted. 'You always were an ungrateful bitch. Just remember who gave you your first fucking break.'

The retort came before she could stop it. 'That wasn't all you gave me, was it?'

'What's that supposed to mean?'

Kate looked away. 'Look, Paul, this is pointless. I'm sorry you're disappointed, but—'

'Disappointed? Why the fuck should I be disappointed? Just because some back-stabbing bitch screws me out of an account I worked my balls off for?'

'I didn't screw you out of anything.'

'No? Who did you screw, then? The whole board, or just Redwood?'

She held open the door. 'I want you to go.'

He laughed, but there was no humour in it. 'Come on, Kate, you can tell me. Did he touch your spot like I used to?'

'Get out! Now!'

He was up off the sofa before she could move. He grabbed her around the throat with one hand. The other pressed against her chin, forcing her head back.

'*Don't fucking tell me what to do!*'

Kate felt his spittle fleck her face. His breath was thick with alcohol. She tried to prise his hands from her, but he was too strong. His face worked.

'Think you're so fucking clever, don't you?'

He jammed her back against the door. The handle dug painfully into her spine. Then she saw the expression in his eyes alter, and suddenly she knew what was going to happen. As though the thought had prompted the action, he dropped one hand and wrenched aside the bathrobe, ignoring her struggles as he grabbed her breast. He dug his fingers into her.

'Paul – *no!*'

The hand on her throat choked her, stopping her from screaming. His leg went between hers, forcing them apart, pinning her. There was no space to kick or knee him. She tore at his wrist. Tiny points of light began to spark her vision. She felt his hand at her waist, yanking at the belt that still held the robe closed. *No! God, no!*

Abruptly, she stopped struggling. Feeling the lack of

resistance, Paul looked up. She forced herself to smile at him over his hand.

'Bedroom . . .' she croaked.

For a moment he didn't move, and she thought he was too far gone to listen. Then a grin touched his mouth. He stepped back, and as the pressure on her throat relaxed and his leg slid from between hers, she shot her knee up at his groin and pushed out as hard as she could.

It was too soon. Her knee skidded off his thigh, and even as he reeled away, he was already grabbing for her again. She lunged through the doorway, feeling him close behind her as she stumbled down the hall. He caught hold of her bathrobe as she reached the top of the stairs, dragging her back in an unequal tug of war. She could see the door standing open at the bottom, and in desperation spun round and wrenched the robe from his fingers.

She pitched back against the wall as it ripped free, her teeth snapping together painfully. Paul toppled the opposite way, into the open stairwell. He caromed off the banister and tumbled untidily to the bottom, crashing into the door and knocking it back against the wall before sprawling on to the tiled floor of the entrance hall.

Breathless, Kate ran down after him. His eyes were screwed shut, mouth frozen in a pained 'O' as she stepped over his legs and opened the front door. Dazed, he didn't resist as she tucked her hands under his arms and began dragging him backwards. He was heavy, but there wasn't far to go. It was only when his hips bumped

34

down off the porch that he seemed to realize what was happening.

'Whoa—' he said, stiffening, and Kate let him drop.

His head cracked on to the concrete path, but even as the '*Ow!*' was forced from him she was already running back inside. She banged the front door shut and leaned against it, panting. Her back and shoulders ached from the effort.

For a few seconds there was silence outside, then she heard him grunt and curse as he scraped to his feet.

'Fuck!' Another groan. 'Bitch!'

She heard him take a step towards the porch. 'If you're still there when I get upstairs, I'm calling the police!' she shouted. Pulling her bathrobe tight around her she hurried upstairs into the lounge.

Keeping to the side of the window, she edged forward until she could look down on to the path. Paul was standing by the gate, rubbing the back of his head and glaring into the porch. He glanced up at the window. Kate jerked back, but he gave no sign of having seen her. Finally, with a last black look, he turned and walked away.

Kate watched until she could no longer see him in the dusk. Then she sagged. Her legs felt weak, and it was all she could do to make it to a chair before they gave way. She shook as she wrapped the bathrobe tight across her chest and hugged herself.

The sudden trilling of the phone made her jump. *God! Now what?* There was no caller ID and she almost didn't pick up, fearful it might be Paul. But that was stupid; she wasn't going to let herself hide from him.

She snatched up the phone. 'Hello?'

A recorded voice intoned that her taxi was waiting outside. Kate rang off and rested her head against the wall. She almost called the taxi company to cancel: the urge to lock herself inside and crawl into bed was overwhelming.

But she wasn't going to do that either. Taking a deep breath, she hurried off to get dressed.

2

The little girl was losing the fight to stay awake. Her eyelids drooped, flicked open, then drooped again. This time they stayed shut. Kate waited until she was sure Emily was asleep before softly closing the book and standing up. Disturbed by the slight shift of the mattress, the little girl turned on her side and burrowed under the duvet until only a tuft of pale hair was visible.

Kate quietly slid the book on to the shelf. In the other bed Emily's brother, younger by almost two years, lay on his back, sturdy arms and legs thrown out with eighteen-month-old abandon. Angus had kicked off the quilt. Kate pulled it over him again. She turned down the dimmer switch on the wall until the light from the Mickey Mouse lamp faded to a dull glow.

The sound of the two children's breathing was a soft sibilance in the half-light. Kate had been absurdly flattered when they had both wanted her to take them to bed, Angus first, then his sister half an hour later. A wave of affection constricted her throat as she looked at the two of them sleeping. Gently, she closed the bedroom door and made her way downstairs.

The house was a decaying detached villa in Finchley, with high moulded ceilings, a mahogany-banistered staircase and a small walled garden that Lucy called 'the jungle'. The ceilings were flaking and the banister cracked, but it was better than the cramped and cold apartment where Lucy and Jack had lived before. The house had been left to them several years earlier by an aunt, and they still didn't seem to have unpacked properly. Toys, papers and clothes were scattered on chairs, on the floor and over the backs of radiators. It was the sort of house Kate wished she'd been brought up in. She stepped over a red tricycle lying on its side at the bottom of the stairs and squeezed round a pile of boxes stacked untidily against the wall. Jack ran his small publishing and print business from the converted garage, and the overspill from it cluttered the entire house.

Lucy was putting more wood into the log-burning stove as Kate went into the lounge. Shutting the stove door, she wiped her hands on a rag. Her eyes were a vivid, almost violet blue as she looked up at Kate.

'She get off OK?'

'Out like a light.'

'You should come more often. They're always on their best behaviour when you're here.'

Kate smiled and sat on the floor. The logs had smothered the fire, but flames were already flickering yellow behind the glass panel. The lounge was big and draughty, and Lucy and Jack kept a fire going on all but the hottest nights. Kate curled her legs under her and leaned back against the settee. In front of her, the coffee table was littered with the wreckage of a Chinese take-away, fried rice and noodles congealing in foil containers. A half-empty bottle of wine stood among them.

Lucy pushed a blonde curl out of her eyes and sat down on the floor near Kate. She picked out a cold prawn. 'I knew I should have cleared this lot away,' she said, chewing. 'I'll have put on half a stone by tomorrow.'

'You could always come to the gym with me.'

'No, thanks. If God had meant women to be slim he wouldn't have invented chocolate.' She popped another prawn into her mouth. 'Anyway, look what happened the last time I went to a gym. I met Jack.'

Kate poured them both more wine, then settled back against the old leather settee. She felt drowsy and comfortable. She had known Lucy for seven years, but it seemed much longer. Lucy had been a receptionist at the agency where Kate had been given her first PR job, and where Paul Sutherland had been marketing director. Her pneumatic figure and tendency towards tight clothes had turned men's heads, but two children and a sweet tooth had changed all that. If she minded the trade, though, she didn't show it. Sometimes Kate envied her. Often, in fact.

Lucy sucked her fingers. 'So you're adamant you're not going to the police about Paul?'

'I don't think there's much point. It'd only be his word against mine.' Kate reached for her wine glass. 'Besides, nothing really happened in the end.'

'It would have if you hadn't stopped him. And how do you know he won't try it again?'

'I'll be more careful. I don't think he will, though. He was just drunk and worked up about losing the pitch. I can't see even Paul being stupid enough to make a big thing of it.'

Lucy gave a laugh. 'I can.'

Kate accepted this without comment. Lucy had tried to warn her off Paul Sutherland from the start. She hadn't listened.

'So what happens now you've won the account?' Lucy asked. 'Are you going to back off and take things a little easier?'

'I wish. Now's when the hard work really starts.'

Lucy selected another prawn. 'So delegate. You're always saying how good Clive is.'

'He is, but I can't dump everything on him.'

'So you'll try and do it all yourself, until you have a—' Lucy broke off. 'Well, until you drop,' she finished.

The first flames licked over the wood as the fire began to burn in earnest. Kate watched them. 'I enjoy working,' she said.

'That doesn't mean you can't have a social life as well.'

'I've got one.'

Lucy snorted. 'Going to the gym's hardly what I'd call being a party animal.'

Kate rubbed her neck. Probing tendrils of another headache announced their presence. 'Don't go on about it.'

'I'm sorry, Kate, but I can't just sit back and watch you work yourself into a frazzle.' The firelight gave

Lucy's blonde hair a reddish tint. 'I know running a business isn't easy. God knows Jack puts enough hours into it. But you need some sort of existence outside work.'

Without warning, Kate's vision blurred. The fire dissolved into sparkling prisms. She turned away, blinking her eyes clear.

'Kate? What's wrong?'

'Nothing. I'm all right.'

Lucy tore off a piece of kitchen roll and handed it to her. 'No, you're not. You've been in an odd mood all night.' She waited until Kate had mopped her eyes. 'Is it what happened with Paul?'

'No, I'm just being a silly cow, that's all.'

Lucy looked at her.

'I don't *know* what's wrong,' Kate blurted. 'I should be ecstatic, but I just feel . . . I don't know how I feel.'

She stared at the stove, watching the flames curl over the logs. A thin trail of smoke streamed up from one. Kate looked away, unconsciously brushing at her sleeve.

'You need a holiday,' Lucy said, taking a drink of wine.

'I don't have time.'

'Then make time. I know starting your own agency was the best thing you could have done after the mess with Paul, I'm not disputing that. But it's not healthy to carry on burying yourself in it. If you were enjoying yourself I wouldn't mind, but you're obviously not.'

'I'm just feeling a bit low, that's all.'

'Oh, come on, Kate, that's bollocks and you know it.'

Lucy sighed and set down her glass on the coffee table. 'Look, I don't want to go on about it, but you can't let one bad experience sour you for life. It's time you put it behind you.'

'I have put it behind me.'

'No, you haven't. Before you started seeing Paul you used to go out all the time, but since then you've just cut yourself off from everybody.'

Kate shrugged. 'People lose touch.'

'Only if you let them. How many people did you bother to tell when you moved into your flat? I bet most of them don't even know where you live any more.' Lucy waited for her to deny it. Kate didn't. 'And you haven't so much as been out for a drink with another man since you split up with Paul, and that's been more than three years now.'

'I haven't met anyone I want to go out with.'

'You haven't tried. I've seen you when we're out together. You've got this aura around you that says, "Don't touch."'

'What do you want me to do? Fall flat on my back for every man I meet?'

'No, but you don't have to turn into a nun, either. Come on, be honest. Can you seriously tell me you don't miss sex?'

Kate avoided looking at her. 'I don't think about it much.'

'That's not a straight answer.'

'All right, then, no, I don't particularly miss it. OK?'

'Then there's something wrong with you.' Lucy began to take a drink, then lowered her glass as another argument occurred to her. 'I know some women are perfectly happy putting their career before everything, but I just don't think you're one of them. And, let's face it, you're not getting any younger.'

'Thanks.'

'Well, you're not. You're thirty-four next year. You might like to think you're Superwoman, but your biological clock's running the same as everyone else's. Don't you think it's about time you started thinking about having a family, and—'

'Oh, come *on*!' Kate's wine sloshed as she banged down the glass.

'Hear me out—'

'I don't have to, I know what you're going to say! I should get married, settle down, cook tea! Sorry, but I don't think so. You might be happy being a housewife, but it's not what I want!'

She was surprised herself by the heat in her voice. Lucy looked at her for a moment, then wrapped her arms around her legs and gazed at the fire. 'Perhaps not. But I'm not the one who's been in tears, am I?'

The flames popped and crackled in the silence.

'Sorry,' Kate said. 'I didn't mean that.'

'It's all right.' Lucy turned to her again. 'I meant what *I* said. And you can scream and shout all you like about not wanting a relationship, and not wanting to settle down. But I've seen how you are with Angus and Emily, so don't try to tell me you don't want children, because I won't believe you.'

Kate tried to produce a denial, but none came. Lucy nodded, as if this confirmed her point, but before she could say anything else they heard the front door being unlocked.

'Sounds like the meeting finished early,' Lucy said, cocking her head. She leaned forward quickly and put her hand on Kate's knee. 'All I'm saying is, ask yourself what you really want. And then do something about it.'

She fixed Kate with a firm look, then sat back as footsteps approached down the hallway. Kate reached for another piece of kitchen roll.

'Are my eyes red?'

Lucy stretched, twisting her hands from side to side above her head. 'No, and it wouldn't matter if they were,' she said, through a yawn. 'When Jack's had a couple of pints he wouldn't notice if you were starkers.'

The lounge door opened and a heavily built man bustled in. His wiry black hair was thicker on his forearms than it was on his head. He bent and kissed Lucy.

'All right, luv? Hi, Kate.'

Kate smiled at him. He examined the cold contents of the foil containers, absently rubbing his slight paunch, then sank down into the high-winged leather armchair behind Lucy. Lucy leaned back against his legs.

'Good meeting?'

'Not bad. Gavin's got a new collection of poetry he's thinking of putting out, and Sally's got an idea for a new distribution system . . .'

Kate stopped listening. Although being with Jack and Lucy was like putting on a comfortable pair of slippers, she knew she would leave soon. The thought of going back to the barrenness of her empty flat depressed her, but sometimes she couldn't help feeling like an outsider, a spare setting at an already complete table.

She stared into the stove as Lucy and Jack's voices lapped around her. A burning log made a snapping noise. The flames danced and quivered, always on the verge of shapes that she could never quite recognize.

3

Later, she was to wonder what would have happened if she hadn't seen the magazine. Redwood had called again, making yet more amendments to the campaign. Two weeks after winning the pitch, he was still calling her most days, and when he finally rang off Kate put down the phone with a feeling of weariness. She opened the Trust's file, stared at it for a moment, then tossed it down on her desk and sat back.

Sod it.

She went down to the basement kitchen, deciding to have tea instead of coffee for a change. The kettle was half full. Kate switched it on and dropped a teabag into a mug as she waited for it to boil. On the work surface nearby was a copy of a women's magazine. Idly, she picked it up. The glossy cover offered the usual mix of celebrity interviews and sex. One of the straplines declared, 'Men: Who Needs Them?' Underneath, in smaller letters, it added, 'Donor Insemination: The Shape of Things to Come?' Kate ran her eye over the other straplines. Then back. She flicked through the pages.

She began to read.

Behind her, the kettle spouted steam. Kate didn't look up. She stood with her hip resting against the work surface, motionless except for when she turned a page. Only her eyes moved, running over the words in a waking REM. At one point she flipped back to re-read a passage on a previous page. She lingered over it, then resumed where she had left off. She was turning to the next page when the door opened.

Kate jerked her head up. Josefina paused in the doorway. The Spanish girl had an empty coffee jug in her hand. She gave Kate a nervous smile.

'I didn't mean to frighten you.'

'No, I was . . . I was just making a cup of tea.' Flustered, Kate turned to the kettle and saw it had already switched itself off. She clicked it on again. The girl went to the sink. Kate saw her glance at the magazine and hurriedly closed it.

'Sorry, is this yours?'

Josefina brushed a heavy hank of hair from her eyes. 'It's all right. You can read it if you like.'

'No, I've finished with it, thanks.'

Kate put the magazine back on the work surface as Josefina began to fill the coffee jug from the tap. There was nothing knowing about the way the Spanish girl had smiled, Kate told herself. Why should there be? She'd only been reading a women's glossy, for God's sake. There was nothing wrong with that. So why was she blushing?

The kettle boiled. Kate busied herself pouring boiling water on to her teabag.

On her way home, she stopped off and bought a copy of the magazine from a newsstand.

Lucy was already at the café when Kate arrived. It was lunchtime and most of the tables were already full, but Lucy had managed to claim one on the pavement under the red awning. As Kate approached, she was flirting with a waiter, a pair of sunglasses pushed back on her head to hold her hair from her eyes. The waiter grinned as he went back inside.

Kate pulled back the white plastic chair from the table and sat down. It was warm from the sun.

'Not interrupting anything, am I?'

Lucy gave an easy shrug. 'Don't begrudge me my little pleasures. I've got to pick the kids up from the crèche in just over an hour.'

They opened the menus. Kate ordered a Greek salad without really looking. Lucy ordered moussaka, giving the waiter another smile as she thanked him. He took the menus with a flourish. She watched him walk away.

'Have you ever noticed how Greek men have lovely bums?' She turned back to Kate with a sigh. 'Anyway, this is a surprise. I thought I'd never see you now you've got the new account. How's it going?'

'Don't ask.'

Lucy didn't. She was more interested in the argument she and Jack were having over buying new equipment for his business. Kate fuelled her monologue with the occasional nod and smile, hearing none of it. Further down the street, a group of workmen were digging up the road. A traffic warden stopped by a car, noting its registration number. A few feet from him, a shabbily dressed man rummaged in a waste bin. Kate watched them without seeing. She looked back at Lucy and tried to pay attention. She found herself twirling and untwirling her napkin around her finger and made herself stop.

The waiter returned and set their food on the table. Kate picked at the oil-drenched salad and white cubes of feta without appetite. She realized Lucy was looking at her expectantly.

'Sorry?'

'I said, how's the salad? These aubergines are gorgeous! I tried this new recipe for moussaka from a magazine, but it didn't taste anything like this!'

The opportunity made Kate's heart race.

'I was reading a magazine article the other day.' Her tone was studiedly casual. 'About artificial insemination.'

'Oh, yes?' Lucy didn't so much as glance up.

'Yes, it's ... you know ... surprising how many women have it.'

Lucy was engrossed in a mouthful of moussaka. 'Jack's cousin did. Her husband was impotent. Some sort of hideous accident or something, so the only way they could have kids was with that.'

Kate forgot her nervousness. 'Did they use his sperm or a donor's?'

'Oh, Kate, *please*, not while I'm eating!' Lucy pulled a face. 'Anyway, I don't know all the details. They emigrated.' She bent over her food again, then stopped. She gave Kate a sharp look.

'How come you're so interested?'

Kate made a show of forking up more of her salad. 'I'm not. It's just . . . you know, an interesting subject.'

She was acutely aware that Lucy was still not eating. There was a silence. Kate kept her attention on her food. Then Lucy spoke.

'You're *not*!'

'Not what?'

'Thinking about having it!'

Kate tried an incredulous laugh. 'Me? Oh, come on!'

'You *are*, aren't you!'

'No! Of course not!' She tried to look Lucy in the eye, but couldn't. 'Not seriously. I was just, you know . . . Look, will you stop staring at me like that?'

'Sorry, but . . . well, it's a bit of a bombshell, you've got to admit.' Lucy set down her knife and fork, the moussaka forgotten. 'So what's brought this on? Not what I said the other night, surely?'

Kate was relieved the subject was finally broached. 'Partly. But when I thought about it, you were right. It *is* time I decided what I want.'

'Yes, but I didn't mean you'd got to rush into something straightaway.' Lucy was looking at her worriedly. 'Certainly not this.'

'I know, but when I saw that article, it just *gelled*.' She leaned forwards, warming to her argument. 'I mean, I *do* want children. I even considered it with Paul, God help me. I've not given it any real thought since then, because. . . Well, I just assumed it wasn't an option. But why shouldn't it be?'

'Bloody hell, you're serious, aren't you?'

Kate felt her enthusiasm waver. 'I've not actually decided anything. I just wanted to see what you thought.'

Lucy sat back. 'Lord, Kate, I don't know what to say. Don't get me wrong, I've nothing against artificial insemination. For a couple who can't have kids I suppose it's a godsend. But not for you.'

'Why not?'

'Do you really need to ask? Raising kids is hard enough when there's two of you, let alone for a single parent!'

'Plenty of women manage. And work as well. And at least I'm my own boss.'

'Think about the timing, then. You were chasing that big account for ages. How are they going to react if you spring maternity leave on them now?'

Kate noticed that the woman at the next table was sitting very still, her head cocked in their direction. She leaned closer to Lucy.

'I could work from home, and it wouldn't be for months yet anyway. Come on, Lucy, what happened to you telling me I needed a life outside work? You know, deciding what I want and then doing something about it?'

'Yes, but within *reason*! All right, if you want a baby I can understand that. But don't you think this is jumping the gun a bit? What's wrong with trying the normal way? You know, husband first, baby second?'

'I don't want a husband. Or a partner. I'm not going trap myself in a long-term relationship just so I can have a baby. There are enough dysfunctional families as it is.'

Kate glanced at the woman at the other table, who seemed to have edged her seat nearer. She lowered her voice. 'I'm not some naïve teenager, I'm used to looking after myself. I *like* being independent. If I can afford to do it, why shouldn't I?'

'Because . . .' Lucy shook her head, exasperated. 'I really don't know where to start. These clinics don't even tell you who the father is, do they?'

'No, but they're careful. They screen all the donors.'

'I should hope they do, but it still doesn't alter the fact that you wouldn't know who he was, would you?'

'Not if I went through the normal process, no. But there are introduction websites that put you in touch with prospective donors.'

Lucy stared at her, appalled. 'You mean like a dating service for sperm? You'd actually consider getting pregnant by a complete *stranger* who's been touting his wares online? For God's sake, Kate, you can't be serious!'

'I didn't say I was considering it,' Kate said, aware that wasn't entirely true. She had looked into it, but the introduction sites were unregulated and had varying standards when it came to vetting. Some prospective donors also seemed keen to offer 'natural insemination', which made her suspect their motives might not be completely altruistic. 'I was just, you know, pointing out that there are options.'

'Yes, you could meet a nice man, settle down and have kids the normal way, like everyone else.' Without warning, Lucy turned to the woman at the next table. 'Perhaps you could give us your opinion, since you seem so interested. How do you prefer your sperm, hot or cold?'

The woman reddened and quickly turned away. Lucy looked back at Kate with a sweet smile.

'What was I saying?'

Kate covered her eyes with her hand, trying not to laugh. 'You were telling me it's a bad idea.'

Lucy gave a shrug. 'Well, what else can I say? I can't believe you're even considering it. I'm sorry, but you asked what I thought, and that's it.'

'OK.'

Kate prodded at the salad with her fork, trying to hide her disappointment. Lucy sighed.

'Obviously that's not what you wanted to hear.'

'I just wanted your opinion, that's all.'

Lucy's eyes were very blue as she looked across the table. 'I don't know why. You're going to please yourself anyway.'

She looked down at her plate, torn between further censure and the cooling moussaka.

'If you're really set on the idea, then I don't suppose it can hurt to talk to someone. They'll probably tell you the same as me, but at least you'll have got it out of your system.' Lucy spread her hands. 'There. Is that what you wanted me to say?'

Kate grinned, but Lucy hadn't finished.

'I just hope you don't do something you'll regret, that's all.'

Without waiting for Kate to respond, she turned to where the waiter was wiping down another table. She beamed at him and held out her plate.

'You couldn't be a love and pop this back in the microwave for two minutes, could you?'

They walked to the tube station. The café was on a side road near Oxford Circus, a convenient midway point for both of them. Lucy was chatting about something, but Kate barely listened. She felt that even her fingertips were tingling with excitement. Now that she'd told Lucy it was as though a burden she'd been carrying around had been shucked off and left behind.

Lucy was still talking as they started down the steps to the Underground. Suddenly, she gripped Kate's arm.

'Oh, shit.'

Kate looked up. Her excitement curdled and died.

Paul Sutherland was walking up the steps towards them.

A second later he saw them, and it seemed to Kate that a flicker of unease crossed his face before his customary arrogance replaced it. She faltered, but Lucy forced her to keep moving.

'Come on. Too late for that.'

He stopped directly in front of them, blocking their path.

Kate ignored the irate looks from the other people who had to jostle past. Her mouth was dry.

'Hello, Paul,' Lucy said brightly. 'Assaulted anyone else lately?'

He gave her a cold look. 'You've put on weight.'

'That's what having two children does for you. What's your excuse? Still taking lunch from a bottle?'

His jaw muscles worked, but he didn't respond. He looked at Kate.

'You ruined my shirt and nearly cracked my head open. I hope you're satisfied.'

The impulse to apologize almost won through. She felt herself wavering, on the brink of reverting to a former self. Then her anger kicked in.

'What did you expect?'

'I didn't expect you to get hysterical, that's for sure.' His tone was scathing and familiar. 'You need to see a shrink.'

Kate struggled for a response, but Lucy spoke for her.

'One of you does, but it isn't her. And I think you'll find attempted rape's more a police matter anyway.'

Heads turned as people streamed past. Paul gave Lucy a murderous look. 'Stay out of this.'

Kate had regained control of herself. 'There's nothing for her to stay out of. You're not worth bothering with.'

She took another step down, so they were almost touching.

She stared at him.

'Are you going to let us past?'

There was a moment when none of them moved. Then he broke his gaze from hers and stepped to one side. Kate brushed past without giving him another glance. She held herself tensely as she walked, feeling him staring after her. Lucy followed a step or two behind. The sunlight was cut off as they entered the cool of the subway tunnel. Paul's shout reverberated after them.

'*Fucking bitch!*'

Kate carried on walking, her eyes fixed straight ahead. The shouts pursued her, bouncing off the hard walls.

'*Think you're so fucking clever, don't you? Well, ask your friend who she used to fuck. Go on, you smug bitch! Ask her!*'

The shouts became indistinct as they went further into the station. Kate was conscious of Lucy but didn't look at her. Neither spoke. She walked through the crowded foyer and stopped by an out-of-order ticket machine. A few feet away the turnstiles rattled and clacked as people pushed through. Lucy cleared her throat.

'Look, Kate . . .'

'Is it true?'

Lucy hesitated, then nodded. The rigidity that had supported Kate so far ebbed out of her.

'Why didn't you *tell* me?'

'Because it was before you started seeing him. I didn't even *know* you then. I hadn't even met Jack. It wasn't anything serious.'

'So why keep quiet about it?'

'What else could I do?' Lucy sounded agonized. 'I couldn't say anything once you'd started seeing him, could I? You'd have thought I was just being catty!'

'But why didn't you tell me afterwards?'

'What, in the state you were in when you split up? How could I?'

'Lucy, that was three years ago! Why haven't you said anything before now?'

Lucy shook her head helplessly. 'I always meant to,

56

honestly. But the longer I left it, the harder it got. I just
. . . well, I never seemed to get around to it. I'm really
sorry, Kate.'

Kate turned away. Coming on top of her earlier excitement, the revelation had left her drained. But, as the
initial shock wore off, she realized that if Lucy had con-
fessed to having slept with Paul it would have ended
their friendship. Even up to a year ago, perhaps less,
Kate knew she probably couldn't have coped with it. So
how could she blame Lucy for keeping quiet? More to
the point, if it had been before Kate even met him, what
business of hers was it anyway? Suddenly, it all seemed
too long ago, involving people she could barely
remember.

Lucy was watching her anxiously. Kate gave her a
tired smile.

'Don't look so grim. I'm not going to excommunicate
you.'

Lucy was still unconvinced. 'You're not cross?'

'No, I'm not cross.'

Lucy's face lightened. 'Oh, thank God for that! If that
bastard had gone and stirred things up after all this time,
I'd kill him!' Sudden doubt presented itself. 'He hasn't,
has he? You really mean it?'

'Of course I mean it.'

As she spoke, Kate wondered if that was true. There
was no jealousy or resentment, but Lucy's contempt for
Paul had always been a reassuring constant. Now it
seemed unreliable. Abruptly, Kate wanted to be alone.

'Look, you'd better go,' she said. 'You'll be late for
the kids.'

Lucy gave her a hug. 'I'll ring you.'

Kate watched her disappear into the crowd, then went through the turnstile and made her way to the Victoria line. She stood on the escalator, letting it carry her at its own speed instead of walking down as she usually did. *Lucy and Paul.* Even the words didn't seem right together.

A movement caught her eye. A bearded man was coming up the opposite escalator, carrying a baby in a papoose on his back. The baby was goggling across at the people on her side, and Kate smiled as it spotted her. She turned her head to watch it go past, and a sudden thought took the smile from her face.

She could have had a child by Paul.

The thought made her go cold. She reached the bottom of the escalator and stepped off. Around her, people were rushing for the platform where a train had pulled in, but Kate barely noticed. She walked slowly, lost in the narrowness of her escape. If, *if*, she decided to have a baby, she would make damn sure it had a better father than that, even if he was only a father *in absentia*. Faceless donor or not, before she committed herself she would want to be sure he wasn't another Paul. She'd made a bad mistake once.

This time she would be more careful.

4

When she was a little girl there had been an old cinema not far from her home. It had been run-down and struggling even then, on a downslide that would end with it becoming first a bingo hall, then a supermarket and finally a car park. But for Kate, who had never been to any other cinema, the chewing-gum-patterned carpet and threadbare seats didn't matter. They were part of the darkened atmosphere, along with the rustle of crisp bags and the cigarette smoke that meandered in the flickering beam of light overhead. The images on the screen were a window to another world, and once lost in that Technicolor glamour, the shabby theatre, school and even home itself became insubstantial as ghosts.

Her visits to the old cinema were rare, but all the more treasured because of that. When she found out that *The Little Mermaid* was being shown, it became her mission in life to see it. Her mother told her they would go to see it 'soon', a typically vague assurance that she was already coming to interpret as 'never', unless she pushed. Which she did, until finally her mother agreed to take her one Saturday morning.

First, though, there came the ritual of weekend shopping. Kate's mother had insisted that the best cuts of meat for her father's tea, and for Sunday lunch the next day (another ritual, equally sacred), would have gone by the time the film was over. So Kate had trailed around after her, agonizing over each minute spent in the butcher's and greengrocer's as her mother intently considered each item before she either bought it or moved on to another.

By the time they arrived at the cinema the feature had already started, and Kate's mother refused to pay for something they wouldn't see all of. The ticket clerk suggested coming back for the later showing, but her mother was already drifting out, the attempt made, duty done.

They had gone home, where her mother had continued with the business of fretting over her father's tea. Kate watched as she chopped vegetables and carefully cut off every scrap of fat from the meat, so that her husband wouldn't have to face that chore himself when he ate it. Kate had waited until her mother was completely engrossed, and then quietly set off for the bus stop.

The ticket clerk, a florid woman with badly dyed hair, had recognized her when she slid the money she had taken from her piggy bank through the hole in the glass screen. 'Let you come on your own, has she?' the woman asked, mouth tightening in disapproval.

Kate let her silence answer. The woman pushed her ticket through the slot.

'Don't deserve kids, some people,' Kate heard her mutter, as she went inside.

It was early evening when she arrived back home. Her parents were furious. Looking back, Kate supposed they must have been worried, but that didn't come through at the time. Only the anger. Her father had hit her and sent her to bed without anything to eat. Her mother, bewildered at her daughter's wilfulness, followed his example, as she always did. 'Your father's tea was ruined! Ruined! You selfish, *selfish* girl!' she had hissed before closing the bedroom door.

Kate cried herself to sleep, hungry and with her father's handprint livid on the skin of her leg.

But she had still seen the film.

As she had grown older, the incident had passed into family lore, diluted and joked about, but never forgotten. 'Just took herself off, without a word to anyone,' her mother would say at family gatherings. 'Typical Kate. Even then she was always a stubborn little thing. Determined to do what she wanted.'

And, accepting the polite laughter, Kate would look at her mother and still see the perplexity in her eyes behind the social smile.

She wondered what her parents would say if they had been alive to see what she was doing now. She told the taxi driver to stop as soon as she saw the petrol station she'd been given as a landmark. She knew it was irrational, but she didn't want him to know where she was going. The driver, a middle-aged man, spoke to her over his shoulder through the glass partition as she handed him the fare.

'Do you want a receipt?'

It was her suit, Kate thought, that and the leather

briefcase, marking her as a businesswoman. She had worn them as camouflage, she saw now, a pretence that her visit was official, not personal.

'No, thanks.' She wanted only to be away from the taxi, with its musty odour of fast-food and worn leather. She climbed out quickly, delaying over putting away her wallet and smoothing her skirt until the cab pulled away with a rattle of blue exhaust. The fumes trailed in the still air, dissipating slowly.

Squinting in the harsh sunlight, Kate looked around to get her bearings. The street was deserted. Nearby, a newsagent's shop stood with a curtain of multi-coloured plastic strips hanging in its open doorway. Further along was a garage, doors opened to reveal a shadowed interior. The tinny echo of a radio came from inside, but there was no other sign of life.

The clinic was on the other side of the road. It was set back slightly from the pavement, with spaces to park in front. Flat-roofed and built of brick, it was as unprepossessing as a warehouse.

Kate felt a flutter of nerves as she approached. A single step led to a glass-panelled door. On the wall next to it was a small white plastic sign. In plain black lettering it said *Assisted Fertility Unit*.

What am I doing? The question jumped out at her with sudden clarity. She looked around guiltily. But no one was watching. The street was still empty. The door creaked as Kate went inside.

It swung shut behind her with a squeal. She stood in a small foyer. The floor was tiled with yellow vinyl squares, scuffed and pock-marked but clean. The place had the bottled-up smell of any public building. A sign saying *Reception* pointed down a corridor. Kate hesitated a moment before following it.

The door to the office was slightly ajar. She knocked lightly on it and pushed it open. The two women in the room turned to look at her. One was middle-aged and sat behind a desk. The other was younger and stood holding a folder.

'I'm . . . I have an appointment,' Kate said. 'Kate Powell.'

The younger woman smiled and strode forward, her hand outstretched. Kate took it. 'I'm Maureen Skinner. We spoke on the phone.'

Her manner was relaxed and friendly and, with a sudden inversion, the building no longer seemed quite so dingy and alien. Kate smiled back, relieved.

The woman spoke to the older one. 'We'll be in the end interview room, Peggy. Would you like a cup of tea, Kate? Or there's water. The coffee machine's on the blink, I'm afraid.'

'Tea's fine,' Kate answered, realizing as she said it that she didn't really want anything. But the other woman was already walking out.

'We're just down here.'

Kate fell in step beside her. Their footsteps clicked on the tiled floor, slightly out of synch. The woman opened a door at the far end, holding it open for Kate to precede her. Inside, it was hot and airless. Several low plastic armchairs were set around a wooden coffee table. It looked like a teachers' staff room, Kate thought.

The woman went to the big window and began

wrestling to open it. 'I think we'll let some fresh air in before we start,' she said, straining against the catch. 'Sit down, make yourself comfortable.'

Feeling anything but, Kate chose the nearest chair. Air leaked out of the plastic cushion in a slow hiss as she settled into it.

The window came open with a jerk, and the woman brushed her hands.

'There. That's better.'

She sat down and gave Kate another smile. 'You found us without too much difficulty, then?'

'Yes, fine. I got a taxi from the tube station.'

'Probably wise.'

Kate smiled politely. She knew the small-talk was intended to put her at ease, but it was having the opposite effect. She felt her edginess returning.

The woman set her file on the low table between them. 'Are we the first clinic you've approached?'

'Yes.' Kate hoped her nerves didn't show.

'So you haven't had any counselling on donor insemination before?'

'Uh, no, no I haven't.'

'Fine, that's no problem. So how much do you know about DI? Or artificial insemination by donor, as it's sometimes called?'

'Only what I've read online.' Kate realized she was knotting her fingers. She shrugged. 'Just the basics.'

'That's good, but I'll still run through it all again, if that's OK? Now—'

There was a rap on the door. It opened immediately, and the older woman Kate had seen earlier came in, carrying a tray. There was a pause while she set it down and left. Kate fought the urge to fidget, answering yes to milk, no to sugar as the tea was poured and stirred. A cup and saucer was passed across. Kate took it and sipped, tasting nothing but heat and a faint sourness of milk.

The woman took a sip from her own cup before placing it on the table.

'To start with, I'm a counsellor, not a doctor, and this is just an introductory session. If you have any questions feel free to ask.'

Kate sat forward, her nervousness forgotten.

'Right, now, I gather you're single?' the counsellor continued.

'Is that a problem?' Kate set down the teacup without drinking.

'No, not at all. However, we are required by the HFEA – that's the Human Fertilisation and Embryology Authority, the regulatory body – to take into account the welfare of the child. So later I'd like to talk about how you see yourself dealing with issues like combining work with raising a child, and the pros and cons of telling your child how it was conceived. Is that all right?'

Kate said it was. The words 'your child' rang in her head, so that she had to concentrate on responding.

'The insemination procedure itself is quite straight-forward,' the counsellor went on. 'The donor sperm is washed and filtered, before being frozen. When we're ready to use it, we thaw it out and insert it into the womb through a catheter. It doesn't hurt, you don't need an anaesthetic, and there's no more risk of miscarriage than with a normal pregnancy. You don't even have to get undressed, except for your pants and tights. And you can carry on as normal afterwards, just as you would after ordinary intercourse.'

Kate's nervousness was forgotten now. 'How do you know when to do it?'

'Obviously, it has to coincide with your ovulation cycle, which you'll be responsible for timing yourself. We'll double-check ourselves when you come in for your treatment, to make sure the egg's about to be released. If it was, and we were satisfied everything was OK, we'd go ahead.'

'How many, uh, treatments does it usually take?'

'It varies. Some women become pregnant in the first cycle, but we can go up to six. Other clinics might do more, but we take the view that if it hasn't worked by then, it probably isn't going to. And at five hundred pounds per cycle it wouldn't be fair to carry on indefinitely.'

She gave Kate an apologetic look. 'I should point out that as a single woman it's unlikely you'll be eligible for treatment through the NHS. You are aware of that, aren't you?' Kate said she was. She hadn't expected any help anyway. 'In that case I'll move on to the donors themselves,' the counsellor said, and Kate felt some of her earlier nervousness return. 'To begin with, we screen every one for relevant medical and family history, and test them for HIV, hepatitis and other sexually transmitted diseases. After the sperm is frozen, it's quarantined and stored for a minimum of six months, and then the donor is tested again before it's used.'

Kate had been listening intently. 'And the donors are all anonymous?'

'If you mean as far as you would be concerned, then yes. But of course their identity's known to the clinic. And although donors have no legal rights or responsibility if you conceive, once the child reaches eighteen he or she is legally entitled to find out the donor's identity from the HFEA.'

'But there's no way I could find out who it was? If I wanted to, I mean,' Kate persisted.

'Absolutely none. We're forbidden by law to reveal who they are.'

'But what if there's a mistake, or something goes wrong?'

The counsellor was clearly used to such anxieties. 'If we had any doubts about a donor, we wouldn't use them. That's why we check with their GP and carry out all the tests beforehand. But we have to protect their interests as well. We can't disclose their identity any more than we can disclose yours. And I'm sure the last thing you'd want would be for some stranger to turn up and announce that he's the father of your child and wants visiting rights.'

Kate hesitated before asking the next question. 'How much would I know about the father?'

'It's better to think of them as the donor, not the father,' the counsellor corrected her, with a smile. 'We're allowed to divulge certain non-identifying information, such as their hair and eye colour, occupation and interests. But any more than that would risk infringing the donor's anonymity.'

'So who decides which donor to use? It isn't just a random selection, is it?'

'Oh, no! We use donors from the same ethnic group as the recipient, and we try to get as close a match as possible as far as body type and colouring. Even blood group, if we can. We can't guarantee a perfect match, but we do our best.'

Despite the reassurance, Kate felt her unease growing. 'Supposing I didn't want the same physical type as me? Can I specify what sort of donor I want?'

'Well, we try to co-operate with your preferences within reason, but there are limitations. For one thing we only have a limited donor panel to choose from, so if we have to change the donor during treatment it might not be possible to find exactly the same physical type again.'

'You mean you might use more than one donor?' That was something she hadn't realized.

'We'd try not to, but sometimes it's unavoidable. If, for example, we ran out of samples by the donor we'd been using.' The counsellor's face grew concerned. 'You look as though you have a problem with that.'

Kate couldn't hide her disappointment. 'It's just that . . . well, I know the donor has to remain anonymous, but I thought I'd have more say in who it was. I didn't realize I'd have to let someone else decide for me.'

'I'm afraid we can't let people pick and choose to that extent,' the counsellor said, sounding genuinely sympathetic. 'It isn't the same as a dating agency. There are strict guidelines we have to follow.'

Kate couldn't bring herself to look at the other woman. 'It still seems like I'd have to take an awful lot on trust, that's all.'

'We do vet the donors very carefully.'

'I know, it isn't that. I just can't imagine having a child by someone I know so little about.' She gave an embarrassed shrug. 'I'm sorry, I've wasted your time.'

'Not at all. That's what these sessions are for. It's a big decision, and you need to be sure before you make it.'

'I suppose it's the same at every clinic?' Kate asked, without much hope.

'More or less. You certainly wouldn't be able to find out more information about the donors, wherever you went. Unless you go abroad, perhaps. I dare say in some countries you can even choose the donor's IQ and shoe size. Not that I'm suggesting you do anything like that,' she added hurriedly.

Kate forced a smile. She'd already looked into having the procedure abroad. But even if she could afford the time and money to go overseas for treatment, the laws and safety standards varied from country to country. She prepared to leave. But before she could, the counsellor, who had been watching her worriedly, seemed to reach a decision.

'Of course,' she said carefully, 'some women don't bother with clinics at all.'

Her expression was guarded as she looked across at Kate.

'It isn't something I'd recommend. But it's not unheard of for some women who have difficulty obtaining the treatment at a licensed clinic, for whatever reason, to carry it out themselves. Assuming they have a co-operative male friend, obviously.' She paused to let that sink in. 'It really isn't all that difficult when you think about it. All you need is a paper cup and a plastic syringe.'

Kate's expression must have showed her surprise.

'I'm not suggesting anyone should try it, you understand,' the counsellor added quickly. 'It would mean using fresh sperm, so there wouldn't be any of the legal or medical safeguards there'd be at a clinic. I just thought I'd mention it as a matter of interest.'

'Yes, but I don't think . . .'

'No, no, of course. I probably shouldn't have said anything.'

She clearly wished she hadn't. There was a silence. The counsellor sighed.

'Well, perhaps you'd like to have another think about what you want to do,' she said.

Depression settled on Kate as she waited at the tube station. When the train arrived, she sat in a window seat and stared out into the blackness of the tunnel. Her reflection in the glass would wink out when the train came to the sudden brightness of a platform, only to return again when the platform was left behind. At one stop, a sullen-looking young woman got on with a fractious baby. Kate watched as she hissed a warning to the child, giving it a quick shake, which did nothing but make it cry harder. After that, the young woman ignored it, staring into space as if the squalling infant on her knee wasn't there.

Kate looked away.

She came out of King's Cross into the weak afternoon sun and made her way to the agency. The burned-out warehouse was still standing, although the lower-floor windows had been boarded up. Its blackened roof timbers stood out against the blue sky like steepled fingers, and the air still smelled of charred wood. Kate had almost grown used to it, but now she walked past quickly, like a child hurrying by a graveyard.

She threw herself into her work for the rest of the day, succeeding in holding back the disappointment for a little while, at least. But it was still there waiting for her. Her stomach sank when she heard the others preparing to go home, and knew it couldn't be avoided for much longer. She was still trying to, even so, when Clive came up to her office.

'We're going for a quick drink,' he said. 'Do you fancy coming?'

'Oh . . . thanks, but I think I'll skip it for tonight.'

Clive nodded but didn't leave. 'Look, don't mind me asking, but are you all right?'

'Fine. Why?'

'You just seem a bit preoccupied lately.'

The impulse to tell him almost won out. 'It's probably trying to guess what quibble Redwood's going to come up with next,' she said lightly. 'Thanks for asking, but I'm fine, really.'

He looked at her for a second or two, then accepted it. 'OK. See you tomorrow.'

Kate said goodnight. Clive went back downstairs, and a little while later the front door slammed. In its aftermath, the office sank into the hollow quiet of an empty building. She tried to continue working but found herself listening to the stillness until it seemed to be soaking into her. She cleared her desk and went home.

The sun was setting when Kate arrived at her flat. As she went down the path, she took her keys quietly from her bag, hoping to get in for once without being intercepted by Miss Willoughby. But as she reached out to unlock the front door, it swung open of its own accord.

Cautiously, Kate pushed it open the rest of the way. The door to her flat was still closed and unmarked, she saw with relief, and afterwards she would recall with guilt that her first concern had been a selfish one. Then she saw that the old lady's door was ajar.

'Miss Willoughby?' Warily, she stepped into the entrance hall and knocked on the half-open door. 'Hello?'

Silence greeted her. Kate gave the door a gentle nudge. The flat's hallway yawned in front of her. At the far end, a doorway led into the lounge. A noise was coming from it, a low murmuring, indistinct but constant.

'Miss Willoughby? Are you there?'

There was no answer. Kate stood uncertainly, then went into the old lady's flat. A fusty smell of boiled vegetables and camphor, a distillation of old age, closed around her. Kate slowly made her way down the hallway towards the lounge. She stopped just before she reached it, suddenly struck by the absurdity of what she was doing, wondering if she shouldn't simply run upstairs and call the police. But the silence of the place mocked that as cowardice. She stepped forward and pushed open the lounge door.

The noise she had heard came from the television, playing at low volume. Light from it flickered over the dark Edwardian furniture and over the potted plants that filled the room. Their profusion was so great that it took Kate a moment to see that the drawers on the old bureau were pulled out. The cupboard doors of a sideboard were also open, their contents strewn untidily on the floor.

'Miss Willoughby?'

There was a low moan. Kate turned and saw a pair of thin, stockinged legs sticking out from behind the drop-leaf table.

She hurried over to them.

The old lady was lying on her back. Her head was turned sideways, and her forehead and cheeks were smeared with blood. It looked like black oil in the dim room. One eye was swollen shut. The wig she always wore had slipped off, exposing a bony scalp covered with thin strands of white hair. She looked like a baby bird fallen from the nest.

The eye that wasn't swollen flickered open as Kate crouched beside her. She muttered something indistinct. 'Don't try to talk,' Kate told her, frightened that the effort would cause the ragged breathing to slow and stop. She quickly looked around, making sure there was no one behind her. There wasn't, but as the eye slid shut and the voice slurred into silence Kate's hands still shook as she took her phone from her bag.

5

The running machine whirred at a higher pitch as Kate stabbed her finger on the touchpad to increase its speed. The rubber belt of the treadmill whipped away from under her feet, almost throwing her off it. She picked up her pace, arms and legs pumping, chest heaving as she went into the final sprint.

Of all the equipment in the gym, Kate liked this the best. There was something faintly absurd about running as fast as you could without actually getting anywhere, like a hamster on a wheel. It was exercise reduced to its most basic, pointless form, yet she still found it satisfying. Its repetitive nature relaxed her, loosened the kinks in her mind.

In the early post-Paul days, she had tried different types of meditative techniques, from simple deep breathing to yoga. She had abandoned them all, finding the effort of sitting still too taxing. But pounding away the miles on the treadmill, Kate found she could pass whole chunks of time either thinking about nothing at all, or concentrating on a particular problem while her body exercised itself.

It didn't help now, though. There seemed too many strands, all plucking her in different directions at once. She had slept badly after finding the old lady the night before. The hospital had told her that morning that, as well as suffering from shock, Miss Willoughby had a broken hip, broken wrist and concussion. From what the police could gather, two youths, one white, one black, had knocked on the door claiming that one had been taken ill. Once inside, they had punched her and then ransacked every drawer in the flat. Probably looking for money for drugs, the police had said.

Kate hammered away on the treadmill, trying to burn off some of her anger. Her emotional landscape was clouded enough as it was after the visit to the clinic. She was still unable to reconcile herself to the idea of becoming pregnant by someone she knew virtually nothing about. She had tried telling herself that there was no option, that if she was serious about having a child she would be happy to abide by the clinic's rules, and the clinic's choice.

But she couldn't accept that, either.

The running machine beeped as the programmed time elapsed. She stabbed at the touchpad again, reducing the speed until she was running at a gentle jog. She continued for a few more minutes at that pace, then gradually slowed the treadmill to a stop and stepped off. Her breathing was deep and heavy, but not laboured. She went to the water cooler and drank two paper cupfuls before going into the changing room and stripping off her sweat-soaked gym clothes. The shower jets peppered her face as she held it up to the spray. She waited until it stung, then turned off the stream before putting on her swimming costume and going into the sauna.

The dry heat wrapped itself over her like a hot towel. The scorched air, spicy with the smell of baked pine, pricked the inside of her nose when she breathed. Another woman was sitting on the lowest of the three benches, sweat running off her. She offered Kate a smile as she closed the door and stepped up to the highest bench. Kate returned it and spread her towel on the hot slats before she sat down.

The heat bored into her. She settled back, gingerly letting her shoulders touch the hot wooden panelling. Almost immediately she could feel the water from the shower dry on her skin and be replaced with perspiration. Through the wall, she could feel the pulse of a distant generator. Other than that, the sauna was dark and silent, separate from the world outside. She closed her eyes and let herself drift.

'Best part of it, this, isn't it?'

Kate opened her eyes and gave the woman an acknowledging smile but said nothing. She wasn't in the mood for conversation. The woman, though, apparently was.

'Do you mind if I put some water on the stones?'

Kate opened her eyes again. 'No, go ahead.'

The woman rose from the bench and went to the wooden bucket by the brazier. She took the ladle from it and poured water on the hot grey rocks. Steam gushed from them with a hiss, and Kate felt a wave of heat hit her. The woman sat down again on the low bench. She was about Kate's age but heavily built, with large breasts and a loose, flabby stomach that stretched the fabric of her blue bathing costume.

'Two more minutes and I think I'm done,' the woman said amiably. She puffed out her cheeks and wiped a strand of damp hair from her forehead. 'You feel as if you've sweated about a stone off just from sitting here, don't you?'

'I wish,' Kate said. The woman glanced at her and cocked an eyebrow.

'You don't look as though you need to.' She patted her stomach. The flesh of it wobbled. 'It's when you get one of these that you've got to worry. I was expecting to snap back into shape after I'd given birth. Fat chance.'

'What did you have? A girl or boy?' Kate's disinclination to talk had vanished. She tried to keep her eyes on the woman's face, but the flaccid stomach held a morbid fascination for her.

'Both. Twins, six months old now. We'd got it all planned, we were going to wait until we were thirty and then just have one.' She chuckled. 'So much for planning. And to add insult to injury I've got this as a reminder.'

She nodded down at the folds of flesh. 'They call it an apron, would you believe? The doctors have told me I can have plastic surgery, but I thought I'd try and work it off first. I feel like telling everybody, "I'm not really fat! This isn't my fault!"' She laughed again. 'Well, I suppose it is. Serves me right for having kids in the first place. I just wish they'd warned me I could end up looking like this. I might have had second thoughts.'

'Do you think you would?' Kate felt a twinge of

unease, not so much from the idea of her own body changing as the thought of regret afterwards.

The woman wiped sweat from her forehead. 'No, not really. You know what you're getting into, don't you? But if I were you I'd make the most of a flat stomach while you've got it. It's never the same afterwards, I don't care what anyone says.'

She stopped and suddenly regarded Kate. 'Don't tell me you *have* got kids?'

Kate was glad her face was already flushed from the heat. 'No. Not yet.'

The woman laughed again. 'Thank goodness for that. I'd have thought life really was unfair!'

She stood up. Her stomach hung in front of her like a deflated beach ball.

'Well, that's enough for me. Bye.'

Kate smiled as the woman left the sauna. Cool air swirled briefly against her as the door was opened and shut, then the heat closed in again. She looked down at her own stomach, taut and unlined, and tried to imagine it flabby and loose.

She closed her eyes again and tried to relax, but the post-exercise mood was gone. When another woman entered the sauna, Kate went out to shower and dress.

The hospital was only two tube stops away from the gym. She went through the automatic doors into the clinical atmosphere of overheated air and disinfectant with a familiar sense of apprehension. First her father, then her mother had died in hospital. Her father had lingered in a coma for weeks after being knocked down, and after that her mother seemed to fade away. She had died less than a year later in the same intensive care unit, as her reluctant heart finally gave up. Since then, the long corridors and harshly lit waiting rooms of any hospital seemed to Kate like a separate world, a surprise cul-de-sac from normal life where death and bad news waited. As she went into the lift, it occurred to her that maternity hospitals were an exception. The thought cheered her, briefly, before the lift doors closed.

The ward was long, with a central aisle running between parallel rows of beds, like a barracks. Walking down it, Kate almost went past Miss Willoughby without recognizing her. One side of the old lady's face was a livid bruise, with stitches cutting across her forehead and cheek. The eye that had been swollen shut the night before was now the size and colour of a Victoria plum, startlingly vivid against the pale flesh and white wisps of hair. Her wig had been left behind when they had loaded her into the ambulance, and without it she looked shrunken and robbed of identity.

Kate stared at her from the bottom of the bed, shocked despite having told herself what to expect. The old lady was asleep, and Kate felt an urge to turn round and leave. But as she was wrestling with the temptation, Miss Willoughby stirred, and her single good eye slid open.

Kate forced herself to sound cheerful. 'Hello there!'

The old lady looked at her without recognition. Then a slow smile lit up her face. 'You shouldn't have bothered to come.'

Her voice was slow and drowsy with painkillers. She

made a feeble attempt to push herself up on her pillows, but it amounted to little.

Kate held out the bunch of flowers she had brought. 'I hope you like chrysanthemums.' As she said it she saw that the old lady couldn't take them with her wrist strapped up. 'I'll put them in water.'

There were several empty vases by a sink at the end of the ward. Kate arranged the flowers in one and took them back to Miss Willoughby's bed. A burst of laughter came from the bed opposite, where a group of visitors were clustered around an elderly woman. She was sitting propped up by pillows, surrounded with cards and flowers. Kate set down the vase on Miss Willoughby's bedside cabinet. There was nothing else on it except for a water jug and glass.

'So, how are you?' she asked, aware that the question was inane, but unable to think of anything else to say.

'Not too bad.' It was an effort for the old lady to keep her eye open. Her mouth worked as if she was thirsty. 'They've pinned my hip, so that's all right. My eye hurts a little, though.'

Kate looked at the swollen flesh of her face. It made the back of her legs creep. 'Can you remember what happened?'

A frown crossed the old lady's face. 'I can remember two young men coming to the door. Boys. They were very polite. One of them felt ill . . . He wanted a drink of water, so I let them in. I started to ask if they wanted tea, but . . . I think one of them must have pushed me . . .'

Kate couldn't bring herself to say anything. Miss

Willoughby moved her head slightly from side to side in a tired shake.

'I can't understand it . . . I used to teach, but it wasn't like this . . . I'd got nothing for them to steal. Why do this for a few pounds?'

'I didn't know you were a teacher,' Kate said quickly, seeing her growing upset. The old woman's frown faded as older memories replaced the more recent one.

'I taught for nearly forty years. At the same school. Girls.'

Her eye slipped shut, and Kate thought she'd fallen asleep. But a moment later she spoke again. 'You wonder where it goes to, the time.'

She dozed for a while then. Another burst of laughter came from the group opposite. Kate looked over at the sprawl of generations, from the elderly woman in the bed to a toddler a girl was helping to balance on the foot of it. A middle-aged woman saw Kate looking over and smiled. Kate smiled back and looked away.

She quietly pushed back her chair and stood up, but Miss Willoughby's eye twitched open again.

'I'd better get off,' Kate said, feeling as if she had been caught out. But the old lady only nodded.

'Thank you for coming.' Her voice was more drowsy than ever. 'Lovely to see you.'

Kate felt a prick of conscience. 'I'll come again. Is there anything you'd like me to bring? Or anyone you want me to phone? To tell them where you are?'

'No. No one, thank you.' A worried expression crossed her face. 'My plants, though . . . They're due for watering . . .'

'Don't worry. I'll look after them.'

The old lady looked relieved. 'I think the key's in there . . .' Her unbandaged hand jerked towards the cabinet. Kate opened it and found a key ring on top of Miss Willoughby's clothes.

'I'll come again soon,' she said, but the old lady gave no sign of having heard. Kate made her way out. At the entrance to the ward she looked back. The visitors surrounding the other bed were also getting ready to leave, slipping on coats in a torrent of goodnights. The elderly woman kissed them all in turn. A few feet away, Miss Willoughby lay alone. The solitary vase of chrysanthemums on the bare cabinet looked as stark as an exclamation mark.

Kate went down the corridor to the lifts.

6

As soon as she saw Lucy, Kate could tell that something was wrong. They had arranged to meet at lunchtime in the park, where they could have a sandwich from the snack bar while Angus played. But as she approached the bench where Lucy sat, she could see that her face was flushed behind her sunglasses, her blonde hair even more unkempt than usual. Emily was at nursery school, and Angus sat alone on the grass in front of his mother, bleary-eyed and snuffling in the aftermath of recent tears as he half-heartedly played with a toy fire engine.

The child looked at Kate through wet lashes, unsmilingly, as she greeted him and sat beside Lucy on the bench. She had been almost bursting with her own news, but now she pushed it forcibly into the background.

'What's been going on?' she asked.

Lucy gave a terse shake of her head. Through the dark screen of the sunglasses, her eyes were all but obscured. 'Don't ask. He's feeling sorry for himself because he's had a smack.'

Kate looked at Lucy in surprise. Her reprimands were

usually no more than stern words, and even they were rare.

'What did he do?' she asked. 'Murder somebody?'

It was meant to lighten the situation, but Lucy's mouth tightened as she glared at her son. 'Practically. We were by the pond and this little girl came up to him, just wanting to play, so he hit her on the head with his fire engine.'

Kate's mouth twitched, but it was obvious that Lucy wasn't in a laughing mood. 'He didn't hurt her, did he?'

'Of course he hurt her!' Lucy leaned towards him, raising her voice. 'You made her head bleed, didn't you? You bad boy!'

Angus began to cry again, covering his eyes with pudgy hands.

'Oh, Lucy . . .' Kate said.

'Don't feel sorry for him! Bullies don't deserve it!' The last was addressed to her son again. Still sobbing, he clambered to his feet and tottered towards them, arms outstretched. 'No, I don't want you,' Lucy said, as he approached her. 'I don't have anything to do with bullies.'

With a heartbroken wail, the little boy turned and put his arms round Kate's legs. She could feel him quivering with the force of his sobs and, knowing Lucy wouldn't like it but unable to help herself, she reached down and picked him up. His small body was heavy and solid, radiating heat. He settled against her, burying his face against her neck. It felt hot and wet.

'Come on, Lucy,' she said, over his head. 'Don't you think you're going a bit over the top?'

Lucy didn't say anything for a moment, then some of the tension seemed to ebb from her. 'OK. Give him here.'

Sensing his mother's change in mood, Angus turned to her, holding out his arms. Lucy heaved him over from Kate and set him on her knee. Kate felt a momentary sense of loss as the child was taken from her. She watched the little boy snuggle against his mother.

'Are you sorry now?' Lucy asked, but the bite had left her voice. 'You're not going to be a bully again, are you?' Angus shook his head, hiccuping as his sobs began to subside. Lucy smoothed his damp hair off his forehead and gave Kate a rueful smile.

'You've got snot on your shoulder.'

Kate wiped it off with a tissue. She could still feel the weight of the child's body against her, like ghost pains after an amputation.

'So what's really the matter?' she asked.

Light sparked off Lucy's sunglasses, hiding her eyes. 'One of Jack's clients has just gone bust. Owing us twenty thousand.' She broke off, looking out over the park. 'We can't afford to lose that sort of money. And Jack's just upgraded all his business equipment. He spent a fortune on a new scanner and printer . . .' She gave a shake of her head, still not looking at Kate. 'I don't know what we're going to do. We might have to sell the house.'

'Oh, Lucy, no!'

Lucy shrugged. 'It might not come to that. Jack's gone to see the bank today. But if they turn sludgy . . .' She didn't bother to finish.

Kate quickly ran through her own financial situation. 'I might be able to lend you something. Not twenty thousand, but it might help tide you over.' She knew how much Lucy and Jack loved their home. If they had to sell, they would never have anywhere like it again.

Lucy smiled bleakly. 'Thanks, Kate. I appreciate it, but we might end up having to sell the house anyway. It's lovely but it's just too big and old. We can barely afford to heat the place, let alone repair it. Jack's hoping all this new investment will pay off, but if it doesn't . . . Well, let's see what the bank says.'

'Lucy, I'm so sorry, I didn't realize . . .'

'No reason why you should. But you can imagine I wasn't in the best of moods to start with. And when this little monster . . .' she gave Angus a squeeze, '. . . turned into Hannibal Lecter, it just capped things off nicely.'

She gave a grin. 'Anyway, so much for my traumas. How's your neighbour?'

'About the same.' Kate had visited Miss Willoughby again, but the old lady didn't seem to have improved.

'Have the police caught the sods who did it?'

'Not yet. She hasn't been able to give very good descriptions, so unless they catch them doing something else it isn't very hopeful.'

Lucy shook her head. 'God, doesn't it make you seethe, though? They want birching! An old woman in her eighties, and on her own, too! What a way to end up.'

Kate was silent. She thought about the old lady's flat, bare of family mementoes. The only photographs on display were formal framed ones of a school, fading pictures of Miss Willoughby with other people's children, all long since grown up. She wondered if any of them ever remembered their old teacher.

'I've found a clinic,' she said.

Lucy looked startled at the change of tack. 'What?'

'I've found a clinic. To carry out the donor insemination.'

'I thought you'd given up on that idea?'

'No. I just didn't like the thought of an anonymous donor. But some clinics will let you use a known donor instead. Someone that you've picked yourself.'

'Please tell me you're not still thinking about using somebody you've found on a website?'

'No, of course not. But if it could be someone I know and trust, then that would be different, wouldn't it?'

Lucy huffed out an irritated breath. 'Like who?'

'I don't know yet. But at least this way it'll be my choice.'

'I thought the whole idea was that you didn't want the father involved?'

'I still don't, but that doesn't mean I don't care who he is.'

'Yes, but the point is he'll know who you are as well, won't he? At least with an anonymous donor you don't have to worry about what he's going to do afterwards. Supposing he changes his mind and decides it's his baby as much as yours? You're leaving yourself open to all *sorts* of problems!'

'Not if I'm careful who I choose. And he'll only have the same standing as an ordinary donor. He won't be recognized as the legal father, so he won't have any

88

rights to custody or anything. I'll just have to make sure that's clear from the start.'

Lucy bit off whatever she had been going to say. 'So have you actually found a clinic that'll do it?'

'There's one in Birmingham—'

'Birmingham!'

'I know it's a long way, but they seem really good.' That wasn't the only reason. There were other, nearer clinics she could have gone to, but for some reason Kate felt drawn to try outside London. Maybe it was just the idea of going somewhere different, a symbolic journey to start a new life. Or maybe she was just tired of London. Either way, the clinic in Birmingham had appealed. And when it came down to it, it wouldn't take much longer to reach on the train than trekking across London on the tube.

Lucy shook her head but only asked, 'So what do you do now?'

'I've made an appointment to see the counsellor. I suppose I'll take it from there.'

Angus had begun to fidget. Lucy slid him off her knee. Sniffling, he tottered back to his fire engine. 'Don't you think this is all getting a bit out of hand?'

'Why? You said yourself there was no harm in talking to somebody about it.'

'Yes, but you've already done that.' Lucy watched Angus sit down heavily on the grass and pick up the red plastic toy. 'This isn't just talking any more, is it? You're acting like you're planning to actually go ahead.'

'You mean you thought I wasn't serious.' Kate heard the acerbic note creep into her voice.

'No, but . . .' Lucy stopped.

'What?'

'It doesn't matter.'

'Yes, it does. What?'

Lucy sighed, as though she found the entire subject tiresome. 'Well, I just know what you're like. If you get your mind set on anything, you're like a dog with a bone. You won't let go, and I can see this turning into something like that. Another "project" you've got to see through. And I think you're making a big mistake.'

Kate felt blood rush to her face. 'And that's all it is, is it? Another project?'

Lucy wore the expression of someone who wanted to talk about something else but wasn't prepared to let go of their point. 'No, I'm not saying that's *all* it is, but—'

'Yes, you are!' Kate could feel her temper slipping away. 'You act like this is just some sort of *whim* you can talk me out of!'

A flush had begun to creep up Lucy's neck to her cheeks, which were still red from earlier. 'Look, Kate, it's your life. If you're serious about wanting a baby like this, then I'm not stopping you. But I still think you're digging a hole for yourself and you're not going to get me to change my mind, so you might as well stop whingeing on about it.'

The words hung in the air between them. The silence grew, broken by distant laughter in the park and the sound of Angus pulling the fire engine's ladder up, then down.

'I'd better go,' Kate said.

Lucy gave a terse nod. Neither of them mentioned the

lunch they were supposed to be having. Kate walked away without looking back.

Her anger barely diminished during the tube ride back to the agency. Even there the conversation still left her raw enough to snap at Caroline for being slow to post details of a new account on social media. She went upstairs to her office. It was stuffy and close, so she opened a window and turned on the fan before sitting down to work.

The breeze from the fan stroked her face as she called up the Kingsmere Trust file. But the concentration wouldn't come. She found herself either staring out of the window or doodling on her notepad while the cursor blinked on the screen, waiting. When the phone rang, she answered it irritatedly.

It was Lucy. 'Sorry,' she said. 'I shouldn't have had a go at you.'

Kate's sense of umbrage lingered a moment longer, then collapsed. 'It's OK. I was a bit touchy myself.'

'Fancy coming round for dinner some time this week? We can have a proper talk then. And I promise I won't let Jack anywhere near the kitchen.'

Smiling, Kate accepted, glad the near-argument had been patched up before it could begin to fester. But Lucy's words still stayed with her, adding to her own sense of doubt.

Am I doing the right thing?

There was a commotion from downstairs. Kate hoped a drunk hadn't wandered in. It happened sometimes. She pushed herself back from her desk, and as she did so the raised voices were drowned by sudden thuds and bangs. There was a scream, and then Kate was out of her office and running downstairs.

The door at the bottom of the stairs opened before she reached it, and Caroline ran out. From behind her it sounded as though the office was being wrecked.

'*They're fighting! They're fighting!*' Caroline yelled, wide-eyed. Kate pushed past her. Josefina was on the other side of the office, white-faced. A desk was tipped on its side, a computer monitor lying beside it. Chairs were scattered, and in the middle of the room two figures wrestled. One was Clive. The other was Paul.

'Stop it!' she shouted. They took no notice. Clive flicked her a quick glance and then grunted as they slammed into a filing cabinet. It rocked, almost falling. Kate ran to where the fire extinguishers were clipped to the wall. There were two, one with CO_2 for electrical fires and a bigger one containing water. There was a crash from behind her as she grabbed it. The two men had fallen on to a second desk, still clutching each other. Hugging the extinguisher under one arm, she pointed the nozzle at them and set it going. A jet of water shot out, and Kate moved nearer, directing it into their faces. They spluttered, shielding their eyes, but Kate kept it on them until they broke apart.

'Get away from him, Clive!' she ordered, still keeping the spray on them. Clive hesitated. 'I said get away! Now!'

Reluctantly, Clive moved back. Kate struggled to turn the extinguisher off. The water finally died to a dribble, then stopped. She glared at where Paul and Clive stood, both panting, water plastering their shirts to their chests and dripping off their faces. Around them, the office was in turmoil. The monitor appeared in one piece but one of the chairs was broken and the overturned desk had lost a leg. Kate turned on Paul.

'What the *bloody* hell do you think you're doing?' She was shaking, more from anger than anything else.

Paul wiped water from his face. One cheek was swollen.

He pointed at Clive sullenly. 'I came to see you, and this prick wouldn't let me!'

'He came in drunk and tried to barge upstairs,' Clive said, glaring at him. Paul started forwards again, and before they could restart the fight Kate moved between them.

'Get over there, Clive. Go on.'

Still glowering at the other man, Clive moved across to the other side of the office, where Josefina and Caroline, who had ventured back in, huddled. Kate confronted Paul. 'Well, I'm here! What do you want?'

He seemed deflated by her aggression. It took him a moment to pump up his anger enough to answer. 'I came to give you some good news! I've been fired! Satisfied now, are you?'

Kate felt a pang of regret. And guilt, she admitted. She stamped down on both. 'I'm sorry you've lost your job, Paul. But it's nothing to do with me.'

He gave a bitter laugh. 'Yeah, I bet you're heartbroken, you bitch!'

Clive started forward. She shot him a look, stopping him, and turned back to face Paul. 'Grow up, Paul. You got yourself fired because you're a self-pitying drunk, so if you want to blame someone, blame yourself. Now get out of my office before I call the police.'

Paul blinked. He glanced around and for the first time seemed to notice that other people were watching. He looked bewildered, then he drew himself up and tried to sneer.

'You think I'm finished? You wait. You just fucking wait.'

He went out, slamming the door. It bounced back on its hinges and swung open again. Kate watched, half expecting him to reappear, but he didn't. She could feel herself beginning to tremble as reaction set in. She looked around the wreckage of the office and felt a lump form in her throat.

'I'm sorry, Kate. It all got a bit out of hand.'

Clive looked shame-faced. He was still soaking wet. Kate saw that his lip was bleeding.

'Are you OK?' she asked.

He touched his hand to his mouth and gave a weak grin. 'I think so. Been a long time since I've been in a scrap.'

'It wasn't Clive's fault,' Caroline said, coming forward. 'He just tried to stop him when he started going upstairs. Clive didn't start it.'

Kate nodded and managed to give Clive a smile. 'No, I know. But in future—'

The window behind her shattered. She ducked as broken glass struck the back of her head and shoulders, and felt something flying past. She looked up in time to see Clive race to the door and tear it open.

'No, Clive! *Clive!*' she shouted. He stopped, poised on the doorstep. 'Let him go.'

Clive hesitated, then closed the door. Glass crunched under his feet. Kate looked at the window. The blind was hanging half off. Where the name of the company had been stencilled on the glass, now there was only a jagged hole.

There was a moan. Kate turned around and saw Josefina clutching her arm, her face screwed up in pain. Caroline was supporting her, looking if anything even more stricken. 'She got hit by that,' she said, nodding at a half house brick on the floor.

Kate went over. The Spanish girl slowly removed her hand to reveal a bloody gash on her forearm. Josefina sucked in air with a hiss and sat down.

'It only just missed your head,' Clive told Kate.

The back of her neck prickled as she looked at the sharp-cornered house brick, then she pushed the thought aside.

'Get the first aid box, will you?' she told him. 'I'll phone the police.'

Kate cleared up the wreckage of the office by herself after the police had taken their statements and left. Clive had gone to the hospital with Josefina, and she had sent Caroline home early. The girl was too shaken to be of any use, and Kate didn't really want help anyway. Setting the office to rights was a sort of penance for letting her private life spill over into business.

It took longer than she'd expected, and by the time she arrived at her flat that evening she felt exhausted. She poured herself a glass of wine and put some pasta on to boil, before remembering that she'd told Miss Willoughby she would visit.

95

Kate looked at her watch. There wasn't time to make it to the hospital before visiting time ended. Feeling relief tinged with guilt, she phoned the ward.

'I was supposed to be visiting Miss Willoughby tonight,' Kate told the nurse. 'Can you give her my apologies and tell her I'll see her tomorrow instead?'

There was a hesitation. 'Are you a relative?'

'No, just her neighbour. But I've been visiting her.' She knew from the nurse's tone but still asked, 'Is everything all right?'

'I'm afraid Miss Willoughby died last night.'

Kate felt no real surprise, only a tired sadness. 'What was it?'

'Cardiac arrest. It was very quick. There's always a risk at that age, and after the sort of shock she'd had. Actually, I'm glad you've called,' the nurse went on, bad news delivered. 'She put down her solicitor as next of kin, but we're not sure what to do with her personal effects. Do you know if she had any relatives or friends?'

'No,' Kate said. 'No, she didn't have anybody.'

7

It was late afternoon when the train arrived back at Euston. Kate stepped down from the carriage and made her way with the few other travellers towards the exit. Their footsteps echoed in a complicated cross-rhythm. The platform was strangely deserted on the hot Saturday. With the sunlight suffusing through the high windows, it assumed a hushed, almost dream-like quality.

She caught a taxi outside the station. It was an extravagance when the tube was almost as convenient, but she didn't care. She gave the driver Lucy and Jack's address and sat back, feeling her body hum with barely suppressed exuberance.

The taxi dropped her outside the house. She struggled with the gate, which was almost as dysfunctional as hers, and went up the path. After a moment Lucy answered the door, wiping her hands on a towel.

'So how was Birmingham?' she asked, standing back to let Kate inside.

'Oh . . . OK.'

Lucy cocked an eyebrow. 'Judging by the look on your face it went better than OK.' She closed the door.

'Go straight through. We're out back. I'll be with you in a minute.'

She went upstairs. As Kate set off down the hallway, Lucy leaned over the banister that fronted the first-floor landing. 'And keep an eye on what Jack's up to with the barbecue, will you? He pretends he knows what he's doing, but he hasn't a clue.'

The warped French windows in the lounge were thrown open. Beyond them, the garden was overgrown and unkempt. Someone had made a token effort to cut the grass, trimming a shaved square in the centre of the ankle-deep lawn. Over one corner of the high, crumbling brick wall that screened the house from its neighbours hung the heavy branches of a laburnum.

The children ran up to Kate as soon as she went out. Emily, older and more shy, presented her face for a kiss, but Angus, still unsteady on his feet, demanded to be picked up. His mouth was orange from the ice-lolly he clutched in one fist.

Jack was standing by a home-built barbecue, made from bricks. Smoke crept up from the grey-black lumps of charcoal, jerking back and forth as he fanned it vigorously with a piece of wood. He wore a grubby white T-shirt, and his hairy legs stuck out from beneath a pair of knee-length shorts. He grinned at her, red-faced and sweating.

'How you doing, Kate? Grab a beer. Or there's wine in the kitchen, if you want it.'

'Beer's fine, thanks.' Setting Angus down, she went to the plastic cooler beside the barbecue and took out a chilled bottle. She opened it and drank. She hadn't

98

realized how thirsty she was until she tasted the cold liquid.

'Look at you, dressed up to the nines and swigging beer from a bottle,' Lucy said, as she came through the French windows. 'Oh, God, you've let Angus near you. There's orange lolly all over your skirt.'

Kate glanced down at the stains on the pale fabric. There was a smear on her sleeveless white top, too. She didn't care. 'It doesn't matter.'

Lucy regarded her. 'My, it must have gone well!' She led Kate over to a table and plastic chairs, clustered in the shade of the overhanging laburnum. Emily went with them.

'Go and help Daddy, Emily, there's a good girl,' Lucy told her.

'Angus can help Daddy,' the little girl said, climbing on a chair next to Kate.

'Angus'll get in the way. Go on, you'll have all evening to pester Kate, but Mummy just wants to talk to her now.'

With a moue of disappointment, Emily slid off the chair and trudged over to the barbecue.

'I don't mind her staying,' Kate said.

'No, but I do. I've not told her the facts of life yet, and I don't want her suddenly asking what "insemination" means in the middle of Tesco's.' Lucy settled back in her chair. 'So. How did you get on?'

Kate tried to sound blasé. 'Fine. They gave me a physical and did some blood tests. I'll need to go back for an ultrasound scan to make sure my tubes aren't blocked or anything. But everything looks OK so far, so assuming they don't find any problems there's no reason why I can't go ahead.'

'And they're willing to use whoever you pick for the donor?'

'They say so, yes.'

Lucy's face showed what she thought of that. 'So they'll basically impregnate anybody who pays them.'

'Of course not.' Kate tried to contain her irritation. 'Particularly not anyone single, like me. You have to satisfy them that you're capable of bringing up a child on your own. Emotionally as well as financially. And they wanted to know how I'd cope with working and being a mother.'

The word 'mother' sent a thrill through her. It seemed to take on a whole new context. She cleared her throat. 'I told her – the counsellor – that for a lot of the time I could work from home or even take the baby to the office with me. Then, later, I'd have to think about finding a nursery.'

Lucy gave a snort. 'You haven't even had the poor mite and you're already farming it out.'

'I'm being realistic. You'd be the first to criticize me if I wasn't. Anyway, the counsellor was satisfied, and they take the child's welfare pretty seriously.'

'So that's it, then? You're going ahead?'

Kate looked away from Lucy's interrogative stare, watching Emily and Angus as they played near their father. 'I don't know. I haven't made up my mind.'

'Are you sure?'

She tried to sidestep the question. 'It's no good deciding anything until I get the results of the tests.'

She could feel Lucy watching her. After a moment Lucy sighed. 'What's this place like, anyway?'

Kate took a colour brochure from her bag and handed it across the table. Lucy studied the photograph of the tree-shrouded building on the cover.

'"*The Wynguard Clinic*,"' she read. 'Well, that's certainly not NHS, is it?'

'No, it's private.' Kate told herself there was no reason to feel defensive. 'They carry out all sorts of fertility treatments. And they've got a fully equipped maternity unit.'

Air-conditioned and carpeted, it had been a far cry from the first clinic she had visited. Lucy's mouth turned down slightly at the corners as she flicked through the brochure. 'So how much is this going to cost you?'

Kate noticed that Lucy spoke as if the decision was already made. She didn't correct her. 'It's more expensive than the other place.'

'How much more?'

Kate felt her face going red. 'It's . . . er, eight hundred pounds. A cycle.'

Lucy's head came up from the brochure. 'Eight hundred quid? Each time you have it done?'

Kate nodded, uncomfortably aware of Lucy and Jack's financial problems. Even though she told herself she'd offered to help them out, she felt guilty admitting to spending that sort of money on herself.

'It isn't that bad, really. You know, considering how few places actually do it. They give you two inseminations per cycle. And they'll continue the treatment for up to twelve cycles instead of six.'

101

'I should think they bloody will at eight hundred quid a shot!' Lucy stared at her, incredulous. 'Bloody hell, that's ridiculous! I mean, it could end up costing you, what – nine, nearly ten grand! And there's no guarantee you'll even *get* pregnant, is there?'

'There's a good chance. And it might work first time.'

'And it might not!' Lucy put down the brochure. 'Look, if you're this serious about having a baby, why don't you just find somebody and . . .' she glanced over to where Angus and Emily were playing, and lowered her voice, '. . . and *sleep* with them, for God's sake? There's just as much chance of getting pregnant, and even if you don't, at least you'll have *enjoyed* yourself! This is just . . .' She threw up her hands, speechless.

The last vestige of Kate's good mood disappeared. 'So what do you want me to do? Trawl through singles bars and ask anyone who takes my fancy back for a quickie?'

'No, of course I don't!' Lucy's mouth quirked upwards. 'It doesn't have to be quick.'

Despite herself Kate laughed. But she was still annoyed. 'Well, that's what it amounts to, isn't it? I mean, to start off with you say that you disapprove of me having a baby, full stop. Now it's OK for me to get pregnant, provided it doesn't cost me anything, even if I have to turn into Supertart to do it!'

Lucy's lips were clamped in a tight line. 'It's your money, Kate, you can do what you like with it. But millions of other women manage to get pregnant without having to pay ten thousand quid for the privilege, and I can't see why you have to be any different.'

There was a shriek of laughter from nearby. They looked round as Angus tottered towards them in an unstable run, hands held up in the air, orange-stained face split in a wide grin. Emily was close behind, laughing, and as she caught up with him Angus tumbled and thumped down on the grass.

Lucy went to pick him up. 'Oh, now you haven't hurt yourself,' she said, as his face puckered uncertainly. She rubbed the grass stain on his knee. 'There, is that better?' Angus still didn't seem too sure, but Lucy plonked him back on the lawn. Emily hung back, watching her apprehensively.

'I thought I told you that Mummy and Kate wanted to talk?'

'Yes, but Angus started running over, and I was only—'

'You were only chasing him. Now go over and help Daddy, like I said. We won't be long.'

'But, Mummy!'

'No buts. Go on.'

Sulking, Emily turned and walked away. Angus ran after her, his fall already forgotten.

Lucy came back to the table and sat down. The interruption had taken the heat out of the argument, but Kate waited until the children were out of earshot before she spoke.

'Look, Lucy, I know you don't approve. But what's the alternative? I don't want casual sex, I don't want any complications. I just want a baby. This way I can have control over who the father is *and* have the legal and medical protection of using a clinic. You don't get that on a one-night stand, do you?'

Lucy looked unconvinced. 'I know, but it just seems so . . . *impersonal*.'

Kate nodded emphatically. 'That's what I want.'

'But what about when the baby gets older? What will you tell it?'

Kate had asked herself the same question. She attempted an insouciance she didn't feel. 'The truth. It's nothing to be ashamed of.'

'And what if he or she wants to know who the father is? They can find out now when they're eighteen, can't they?'

'Then that'll be their decision.' She meant it: despite what Lucy might think, she wasn't rushing into this blindly. Lately she'd thought of little else. 'Come on, Lucy. This is what I want. Be pleased for me.'

Scepticism remained on Lucy's face. She looked at Kate for a moment longer, then relented.

'I am. Ignore me.' She gave a wry grin. 'Anyway, I thought you hadn't decided anything yet?'

Kate smiled but said nothing. Lucy stood up.

'Come on. Let's go and stop Jack from burning everything.'

They left the shade of the laburnum and went over to the barbecue. Jack had given up fanning the charcoal and was regarding the tray of sausages and marinated meats with a dubious expression, a spatula in his hand. They were still pink and raw.

'Is it hot enough?' Lucy asked, as they came up behind him.

'It should be. I've spent long enough fanning the bloody thing.' His sparse dark hair was plastered to his forehead.

'Why don't you put some of that fluid stuff on?'

He gave Lucy an exasperated look. 'I have.'

'Well, I should put some more on, if I were you. It'll be dark at this rate.'

He held out the spatula to her. 'Do you want to do this?'

Lucy threw up her hands. 'No, thanks, I cook every day. Having a barbecue was your idea. And don't let Angus get too near, he'll burn himself.'

Jack sighed and steered his son away from the bricks.

'I hear you've got refinancing from the bank,' Kate said, hoping to divert a family squabble. 'Congratulations.'

He smiled. 'Yeah. I was sweating there for a while. Twenty grand down on top of investing in new equipment, things were starting to look a bit grim.' He stopped, suddenly self-conscious. 'Thanks for offering to help out, though. Lucy told me.'

'I'm glad it didn't come to that.'

'Probably as well it didn't,' Lucy cut in. 'Kate might need refinancing herself now, Jack.'

He looked at Kate, surprised. 'I thought the agency was doing well?'

'I don't *mean* the agency,' Lucy said, giving him a look.

'No? Oh, right!' His face lightened. 'So you're going ahead with it, then?'

Annoyed at the way Lucy had introduced the subject, Kate just nodded. Jack grinned at her.

'Good for you.'

'You don't know how much it's going to cost,' Lucy said pointedly.

'So what, if it's what she wants?' He winked at Kate. 'It's your life. You go for it.'

He turned back to the barbecue, rubbing his hands together. 'Right, let's sort this out.'

He picked up the plastic bottle of barbecue lighter fluid and, holding it at arm's length, squirted it liberally on the charcoal. Nothing happened. He took a box of matches from his pocket and struck one.

'Stand back.'

There was a *whuff* as a sheet of pale flame shot into the air. They flinched from the sudden heat. Jack made darting grabs for the wire tray as the fire engulfed it, but after a moment he gave up, blowing on his burned fingers.

'Do you think you put enough on?' Lucy asked, and they began to laugh as the air above the barbecue shimmered, and the meat started to blacken and curl in the flames.

They ate green salad and takeaway pizza at the table under the laburnum tree. The remains of the barbecue, charred and foul with the taste of the fluid, lay untouched above the still-hot embers.

Angus had become tired and fractious and had gone to bed in tears, while Emily sat on Kate's knee, almost asleep herself. The sun had gone down, but the evening was still warm. Several beer bottles and a bottle of wine sat on the table by the plates. Kate moved slightly, easing Emily to a more comfortable position. The little girl stirred and yawned hugely.

'Time for bed, young lady,' Lucy said. Emily gave a half-hearted moan of protest. Lucy ignored it. 'Kiss Kate goodnight. Daddy'll take you.'

'I want Kate to take me.'

'No, Kate's going to stay with Mummy.' Lucy motioned with her head at Jack. He took the hint and stood up with a crack of knee joints. Rubbing her eyes, Emily allowed him to pick her up. Her breath was sweet with cherryade when Kate kissed her.

Lucy waited until they had gone inside. 'So have you thought about who you want to be the donor?' she asked, out of the blue. 'Assuming you decide to go ahead, obviously.'

It was a question that Kate had been avoiding. 'No, not yet.'

'Any ideas?'

'Not really.'

Lucy pushed her glass around on the table with her finger. 'You must have thought about it.'

Kate had started nudging her own glass around, smearing the wet rings on the table top. She took her hand away. 'I haven't got that far yet. I've been too busy trying to find out if I could have it done to worry about anything else.'

'Surely you've got some idea, though?'

'Lucy, I don't *know*, all right? Why are you going on about it?'

Lucy was watching her with a strange expression. 'Not Jack.'

'What?'

'Not Jack. I don't want you asking Jack.'

Kate stared at her. 'Lucy, I . . . No, of course not! I'd never even considered it.'

But as she said it, she knew she had. She liked Jack and, more importantly, trusted him, and the thought of using him as the donor must have been loitering at the back of her mind. It was enough to redden her face now. Both she and Lucy looked away from each other at the same time.

'I'm sorry, but I'd got to say it,' Lucy said.

'It's OK.'

'I know it's selfish, but I just couldn't handle that.'

'It's all right, really.'

A silence built between them. Lucy cleared her throat.

'So are you going to make a list of possible candidates?'

'I suppose so, yes.'

'Who—' Lucy began, then stopped when she remembered they had already gone over that. 'I mean, do you think you'll have any trouble finding someone?'

Kate was as keen as Lucy to leave the brief awkwardness behind. 'I don't know.' She felt obliged to add more. 'I suppose when it boils down to it I don't know that many men. Not well enough to ask anyway.'

'What about Clive? I'd have thought he was an obvious choice.'

Kate had begun sliding her glass around on the table again. She put her hand in her lap. 'He would be, but I don't think it'd be a good idea.'

'Because the baby would be mixed-race, you mean? I wouldn't have thought that would bother you.'

There was a faintly arch note in Lucy's voice. Kate ignored it. 'It wouldn't, but having to work with Clive again afterwards would. And if I asked him and he said no, that'd be almost as bad.'

'Isn't there anyone at the gym?'

'No one I'd want to ask.'

Lucy sighed, though whether in sympathy or exasperation it was difficult to tell. 'Looks like you've got a problem, then, doesn't it?'

'What problem?' Jack asked, coming up to the table.

Neither of them had heard him approach.

'Kate can't think of a donor,' Lucy said, and Kate tensed, waiting for him to make some joke about himself.

'Big decision.' He sat down and poured himself a glass of wine. 'Who've you got it narrowed down to?'

'Nobody yet,' Kate admitted.

'Spoiled for choice?'

'Hardly. The only people I can think of, I either wouldn't want to ask or I can't because it'd cause too many complications.'

She had meant Clive but realized as she spoke that this last point applied equally to Jack. Lucy gave her a sharp look. 'Which really makes a mockery of the idea of a known donor, doesn't it?' Lucy said, with a slight edge. Kate tried not to react.

'Not really. Just because I don't think it's a good idea to ask someone who'd see me – and the baby – regularly, it doesn't mean I'm going to settle for someone I've never even met.'

Lucy gave a snort. 'Well, if you don't want anyone you don't know, and you won't ask anyone you *do* know, there's not a great deal left, is there?'

Kate was about to respond when Jack spoke.

'Why don't you advertise?'

'Oh, don't be stupid,' Lucy snapped.

'I'm not being stupid,' he said equably.

'Well, where's she going to advertise? The post-office window?'

Jack gave Lucy an irritated glance before turning to Kate. 'Have you thought about the personal columns?'

'Oh, come on!' Lucy exclaimed. 'You can't advertise for a sperm donor in a newspaper!'

'Why can't you?'

'Because you *can't*!'

Jack ignored her. 'You can word the ad to specify the sort of bloke you want,' he said to Kate. 'You know, intelligent, professional, good looking. Own teeth. Whatever.'

'For God's sake, Jack!' Lucy protested. 'I can't believe you're suggesting this!'

'Why not?' Kate thought he was enjoying his wife's outrage. 'It's only like advertising for a job.'

'It's completely different! For a start you don't have to masturbate at a job interview. I've never heard anything so ridiculous in my life! You could get anyone answering! You might as well just meet someone selling sperm from one of those dodgy websites!'

'What websites?' Jack asked.

'Never mind,' Kate told him before answering Lucy. 'It wouldn't be the same at all. The people I'd be aiming for wouldn't be actively offering their services, for one thing. And I could be selective about where I place the ad. Target specific groups.'

'Exactly,' Jack said. 'You could place it somewhere like the *Guardian* or *Independent*, rather than a tits-'n'-bum tabloid. You'd get a better class of wanker from them.'

'Jack, this isn't funny!' Lucy snapped, but Kate didn't mind. Jack's jokes aside, she felt genuinely fired up by the idea.

'I was thinking more about professional magazines and websites,' she said. 'Something that won't be seen by a casual browser. Go for professions that'll be more responsible, like teachers or lawyers.'

Jack pulled a face. 'I don't know about lawyers . . .'

Kate laughed. 'Doctors then. I could advertise in medical journals. I can't see anyone working in medicine being easily shocked. And they'd be more likely to take it seriously.'

'Just listen to yourself!' Lucy looked horrified. 'You're not really considering it?'

'Well,' Kate said, 'it's worth thinking about.'

She batted at a moth that had blundered into her face. It fluttered off into the growing darkness, towards the still-glowing barbecue.

8

Kate received her first reply on the same day that Paul Sutherland's case was heard at the magistrates' court.

There was a delay on the Underground line, and she was late reaching the court building. A light drizzle was falling when she arrived. Too fine to merit an umbrella, it salted her hair with fine beads of water, misting on her cheeks like sweat in the windless morning. A middle-aged man and woman stood outside on the steps. She was crying, leaning against the man's chest. He stood with one arm around her, staring at nothing over the top of her head. Kate hurried past and went inside.

The case had already been called when she found Josefina and Clive waiting in the corridor outside the courtroom. Only Caroline hadn't been called as a witness, and Kate hoped that the girl would cope at the office by herself. She sat next to Clive on the padded bench, torn between begrudging the wasted time and dreading the moment when she would have to go in and testify.

Predictably, Paul had pleaded not guilty. As well as assault and criminal damage, he'd been charged with

Actual Bodily Harm. The wound on Josefina's arm turned out to be less serious than it first appeared, but there was still a possibility that he'd be given a custodial sentence. Kate had mixed feelings about that; in spite of everything she wasn't sure she wanted to see Paul go to prison.

She had been resigned to a lengthy wait, but after only ten minutes a clerk emerged from the courtroom and approached them.

'Josefina Mojon, Kate Powell and Clive Westbrooke?'

Kate felt her stomach knot as they gave obedient nods. The man was thin, in a crumpled suit and mismatching tie. He gave a flickering smile that quickly switched off.

'I'm sorry, but I'm afraid we won't be needing you after all,' he said. 'Mr Sutherland decided to change his plea to guilty at the last minute.'

Paul had been given a suspended three-month sentence and ordered to pay damages and compensation, the clerk told them. He gave details of how the payments would be made and then left. They remained where they were, trying to adjust to the anticlimax. Clive spoke first.

'Well, the bastard managed to make us all waste a morning. I'm sure he'll be happy about that.'

Kate didn't bother to dispute it. 'I suppose we might as well go,' she said. They stood up, but then the courtroom door opened and Paul Sutherland came out.

He glared at them. His face was sullen and accusing, the flesh under his eyes swollen. Kate tensed, waiting for him to say or do something. But he just stared at her before turning on his heel and walking away.

She let out her breath, slowly.

'Not the type to forgive and forget, is he?' Clive said.

'No,' she agreed.

They flagged down a taxi outside the court, but neither Josefina nor Clive made any comment when Kate didn't get in. She felt like a truant when she told them she'd see them back at the office, then walked to the nearest Underground. The Royal Mail delivery office was only a short tube ride away, and Kate emerged from the station with the now customary sense of anticipation. The feeling wasn't as intense as it had been the first few times she had checked, but it still made her quicken her step as she drew near.

She went to the counter and handed her authority card to the unsmiling woman, who took it without speaking and disappeared through a doorway.

Kate tried not to build up her hopes as she waited. The advert had been running for two weeks now. She had spent hours agonizing over its wording before finally settling for a simple, bare statement of fact.

'*Professional woman seeks donor for artificial insemination.*' Kate had placed it in a variety of medical journals and on websites, from psychiatric to gynaecological. Some had flatly refused to run the ad, and she had felt a hot flush of embarrassment at each rejection. But most had accepted it without comment, and Kate had begun calling into the delivery office regularly to check for replies. So far, though, her PO box had remained mockingly empty.

The woman seemed to be gone a long time. When she came back, the white rectangle of the envelope was bright against the blue of her uniform.

Suddenly clumsy, Kate signed for it with a scribbled signature that only faintly resembled her own. Part of her noted that the envelope was thin and floppy, the handwriting untidy, but her excitement overwhelmed the awareness. She resisted the urge to open it until she was outside the delivery office, and then she stopped and tore open the flap.

There was no letter. Her first impression was that the envelope was empty, but then she saw something crumpled in the bottom. She realized what it was just in time to stop herself from pulling it out.

Bile rose in her throat, from humiliation as much as disgust as she snapped the envelope shut on the used condom. Her eyes stung as she threw it in a nearby bin, before cleaning her hands thoroughly on a wipe.

Feeling pervasively soiled, she walked back towards the tube station.

The summer passed its midway point. Lucy and Jack took the children camping to Devon. They were worried about leaving the house untenanted, so Kate offered to stay there while they were away. She'd never been wholly at ease in her own flat after Paul had barged his way in, and since Miss Willoughby's solicitors had put the old lady's up for sale she had felt even less so. Kate still wasn't comfortable with the thought of living above the empty rooms. Two weeks in Lucy and Jack's rambling house felt like a holiday.

'You should go on a proper one yourself,' Lucy had commented, when Kate had said as much.

'Perhaps later,' Kate had replied, and both of them knew she had no intention of going away.

The house seemed odd, much bigger and less friendly now that she was alone in it. Lying in bed in the spare room on the first night, she had listened uneasily to the unfamiliar creaks and noises until at some point she had fallen asleep. After that she had grown accustomed to the solitude, until it no longer bothered her. Echoes of the family still filled the house, scattered toys and books and clothes, so that it didn't seem empty so much as paused, a *Mary Celeste* waiting for voices and life to resume. Sometimes Kate felt like a ghost moving through it, living there but leaving no trace of herself. It was a gentle, lulling feeling.

Going there at night became a pleasure, so that she resented having to call at home to feed Dougal and check the post. The evenings were hot and muggy, and she would prepare a salad and eat it outside in the garden. Afterwards she would either just sit, or read until it became too dark to see. Then she would go inside and listen to Jack's jazz and blues collection on the over-stuffed sofa as Billie Holiday bared her heart and the moths bumped and whirred against the lampshade.

It was so long since Kate had felt relaxed that it was an unfamiliar sensation. Only the question of finding a donor still chivvied away at her, but as the weeks passed with no further response to her advert, she had begun to

116

accept that there was unlikely to be one. She was already considering her next step when the letter arrived.

She had not checked the box in over a week, and it was with a sense of obligation rather than hope that she called in at the delivery office one lunchtime. When the woman returned with an envelope, Kate felt flustered as she signed for it and took it outside. The memory of the condom made her handle it cautiously, and she superstitiously moved to another spot to open it.

This time there was a letter inside, neatly handwritten in blue ink on good-quality paper. There was an Acton address with a landline and mobile number. Kate saw by the date that it had been posted over a week ago. It had been waiting for her to collect it all the time she had been lotus-eating at Lucy's.

The letter began without preamble. 'I'm writing in response to your advertisement in *Psychology News* for a donor for artificial insemination. I'm a thirty-eight-year-old clinical psychologist, single with no children. If you would like to discuss this or meet up, please call me after 6pm.' It was signed 'Alex Turner'.

Kate had begun walking without having any idea of where she was going. She stopped, looking around. The sunlit street suddenly seemed unfamiliar. Its brightness dazzled her, and for an instant she felt dizzy. Then the sensation had passed. Folding the letter back into the envelope, she set off for the tube station.

She sat in the garden again that evening, but now its peace had been shattered. Her meal had consisted of a mug of tea, which sat cooling and untouched on the table in front of her. Next to it was the letter. She picked it up and re-read it from time to time, as though she might be able to glean something else from the small, careful handwriting.

The thought of meeting the man who had written it terrified her. This was what she had wanted, but now it had actually happened even the thought of telephoning him seemed daunting. She'd Googled 'Dr Alex Turner, Clinical Psychologist, London' and found someone by that name worked at a place called the Ferndale Centre, an NHS clinic in Ealing. But she hadn't learned much more than that. She hadn't been able to find him listed at the Acton address he'd given, or even see what he looked like. There were no photographs of him online, or rather there were too many – an image search turned up dozens of different Alex Turners, with no way of knowing which he might be. He didn't have a website, and she couldn't find him on Facebook or Twitter, or even LinkedIn. That seemed strange, and she found herself remembering Lucy's warning: *You could get anyone answering*. Maybe Lucy was right – for all Kate knew he could be a conman, or some kind of opportunist predator.

Except . . . he hadn't stumbled across her advert in some tabloid or introduction website. He'd seen it in a reputable professional journal, one of several medical periodicals she'd carefully selected. And at least she'd established that there really was a clinical psychologist called Dr Alex Turner. Who worked in Ealing, which wasn't too far from Acton where the letter said he lived. Even his absence from Facebook wasn't necessarily

118

damning. Although she used social media sites all the time for the agency, Kate was uncomfortably aware that she didn't actually have any accounts herself. If asked why, she could convincingly claim that there was no need, that she preferred to use the agency's rather than have duplicate accounts. But the real reason was more embarrassing. The truth was that, except for anything work-related, she had virtually no social life to talk about, which would quickly become obvious if she signed up to Facebook and Twitter herself. That would hardly reflect well on the head of an up-and-coming PR company.

So she could hardly be too suspicious of anyone else when she was guilty of the same thing herself. Besides, as a clinical psychologist Alex Turner probably came into contact with all sorts of disturbed individuals. It wasn't unreasonable to think that he didn't want any of his patients stalking him, either online or in person. Or for someone in his line of work to have an ex-directory phone number.

Kate looked at the letter again, trying to gauge a person behind the formal words. A piece of bark from the laburnum tree lay on the white plastic of the table. She nudged it absently with her finger, and the shape resolved itself into the dry husk of a dead moth. Grimacing, she brushed it off the table and then abruptly picked up her phone. She stabbed out the first three digits before cancelling and putting it down.

'Come on, get a grip,' she murmured. She wished Lucy were there so she could talk it out, and immediately felt a surge of anger with herself.

She picked up the phone again and quickly tapped in the number. The handset felt clammy in her hand, and there was a tightness in her chest as she heard it begin to ring.

'Hello?'

It was a man's voice that answered. Kate found she had no idea what to say. She quickly checked the letter for his name.

'Can I speak to . . . to Alex Turner, please?'

There was a pause. 'This is Alex Turner.'

Kate swallowed. 'My name's Kate Powell.' Belatedly, she remembered she hadn't intended to give her name. 'You answered my advertisement. For a . . . a donor.' She closed her eyes, squirming.

'Oh . . . Yes.'

'I was wondering – that is, I suppose we ought to meet up.'

Another pause. 'OK.'

Kate tried not to be discouraged by his lack of enthusiasm. 'So, when's convenient?'

'Whenever.'

Kate wished she had never phoned. 'Well . . . er, how about . . .' She blanked. 'Tomorrow lunchtime?' she gabbled, and immediately regretted it. *Too soon, too soon!* She willed him to say no.

'Yes, tomorrow's fine.'

'Oh. OK . . .' Her memory failed to come up with an obvious place to meet. 'Do you know Chez Michel?'

It was the first name that occurred to her, and Kate winced. The restaurant was French, pretentious and expensive. She had never liked it, but she was too embarrassed now to change her mind. She heard him hesitate.

'No. Sorry.'

'It's just off Soho Square,' she told him, and gave directions. 'How about one o'clock?'

'Fine.'

She waited, but there was no more. 'OK, then. I'll see you tomorrow.'

She ended the call and put her phone down. It was only then she realized she should have blocked her number before she'd called him. But it hardly seemed important now: she was meeting him tomorrow anyway. A prospective donor, the possible father of her child. She looked around the darkening garden. The need to talk, to tell someone, was like a suppressed shout. But she was on her own.

She phoned the restaurant to make the reservation.

9

The restaurant was full. Conversation bubbled along, snatches of laughter occasionally surfacing through it. Waiters swirled around the tables like eddies in a stream, trays balanced, pads held at the ready.

Kate flinched as a loud hiss and billow of flame showed through the open hatch into the kitchen. She looked again at her watch. It was five to one. She had been there since a quarter to, long enough to feel as though she'd been waiting a lifetime.

She stiffened as the door from the street opened. A man walked in, dark hair swept back, wearing a bow tie and camel-coloured waistcoat despite the hot day. He spoke to the girl behind the reception desk, who scanned the book in front of her before answering. The man looked imperiously around the room, and his gaze stopped on Kate. Just as she was about to give a tentative smile, he turned away. The girl escorted him to another table, where two men greeted him.

Kate felt a small wash of relief.

She had spent the night before trying to reassure herself. It was no different from a business lunch, really. If they reached an agreement, fine. If not, then what had she lost? It wasn't as though she was committing herself. He didn't know where she lived, and if she didn't like the look of him she didn't have to take it any further. After two of Jack's brandies, she had been almost convinced.

But when she had woken that morning, the doubts had descended again. By the time she reached the agency they had developed almost to full-blown panic. She had gone to her office and done deep-breathing exercises, trying to clear her mind until she was calm.

When her nerves had steadied – or at least steadied enough so she could function – she went online and found the number of the Ferndale Centre in Ealing. Phoning it, she asked the receptionist if she could speak to Dr Alex Turner. She'd been prepared for confusion, half expecting to be told there was no one there by that name. Instead the woman simply asked who was calling.

'Ka . . . Caitlin Smith,' she said, caught out.

'One moment, I'll put you through.'

Kate had quickly hung up before she could be connected. Her heart was racing, but at least she'd established that Dr Alex Turner actually existed.

Now, though, both the doubts and the panic had returned. She could feel them pressing against her as she sat at the table, waiting. They surged up as the restaurant door opened again, but this time it was a young couple who entered.

Feeling a mix of disappointment and relief, Kate turned away and stared out of the window. The street outside was bright and sunny beyond the low awning.

The sound of it was lost against the restaurant's busy hubbub, so that it was like looking at a silent film.

She looked up as a waitress approached. Behind her was the man who had just arrived. Kate looked beyond him and saw that the woman he had come in with was kissing someone at the far side of the room. Not a couple, she realized. She tried to gather herself as the waitress moved off, leaving the man standing uncertainly by her table.

'Kate Powell?' he said hesitantly. 'I'm Alex Turner.'

Kate half rose to her feet, feeling the blood rush to her face. 'Oh, I'm sorry, I thought . . . I saw you come in with someone, so I assumed . . .'

He looked confused for a moment. 'Oh! No, we just arrived at the same time.'

They were both standing, facing each other across the table. 'Please,' Kate said. 'Sit down.'

She tried to gather her wits as they arranged themselves. He didn't look at all how she had imagined. From his voice, she'd pictured someone altogether more like the man she'd seen earlier, all bow tie and arrogance. But he didn't give that impression at all. He looked reassuringly normal: slim, with youthful, clean-cut features that belied his thirty-eight years. He wore new-looking jeans and a navy-blue shirt with rolled sleeves that made Kate feel overdressed. His dark hair was the sort that would always resist a comb, and a blue shading of stubble was already shadowing the line of his jaw. He was attractive, good looking even, although without any of the swagger that often went with it. At least, none that was evident now. Although he was trying to hide it there was an awkwardness about him, and as he sat down Kate realized he was just as ill at ease as she was.

The knowledge gave her confidence.

She smiled. 'You managed to find it all right, then?'

'Yes, no problem.'

He returned her smile but his tension was palpable. Under the open neck of his shirt Kate could see the glint of a fine silver chain. His hand went to touch it but then he seemed to realize and stopped himself. Seeing his discomfort made Kate's own anxiety diminish even further. Bizarrely, she found herself wanting to put him at ease. 'It's a bit of a funny situation, isn't it?' she said, voicing her thoughts. 'Meeting for something like this?'

'Yes.' He cleared his throat. 'Yes, I suppose it is.' He looked around the restaurant again, as though he was unable to maintain eye contact with her for more than a few seconds. She thought about how he'd sounded on the phone the previous evening. He hadn't been arrogant after all. Just nervous.

'So, you saw the ad in *The Psychologist*, was it?'

'No, it was *Psychology News*. By accident, really.' He gave a self-conscious shrug. 'The, uh, the clinic where I work still gets the print edition, but I didn't get around to reading it till weeks after it came out. Otherwise I'd have contacted you sooner.'

There was a faint stumble in his speech, not so much a stammer as a syncopation on certain words. C-contacted. Kate took it as a further sign of nerves and felt bad for the small trap she'd laid with the magazine title. But not bad enough to stop vetting him. The waitress returned and handed them each a tall menu. 'Would you like something to drink?' she asked.

'Mineral water for me, please,' Kate said. 'What about you, Mr Turner?'

'Oh . . . I'll have the same, thanks.' He waited until the waitress had left before adding, 'And, er, please call me Alex.'

Kate gave a non-committal smile. 'You said you're a clinical psychologist? Whereabouts do you work?'

'In Ealing. Part of an NHS unit. I've been there for nearly six years now.'

She pretended to study the menu, hoping her duplicity wasn't showing on her face. She'd make a poor spy, she told herself. 'I'm afraid I don't know much about clinical psychology. Is it interesting work?'

'It can be. Mostly it's just routine. Though not for the patients.' He frowned at the French script in the menu. 'How about you?'

'I've got my own PR agency.' She just stopped herself from saying whereabouts it was. *Careful. Don't give anything away about yourself.*

He seemed impressed. 'Really? Is it doing well?'

'At the moment.' She smiled, drawing unexpected satisfaction from the simple statement. He smiled back, and for a moment their reserve was gone.

The waitress returned with the drinks, and the contact was broken. Kate ordered a salad. Alex, after a pause, chose a plain omelette.

'So,' Kate said into the silence left by the waitress's departure. 'I suppose I'd better ask you to tell me a little bit about yourself.'

He nodded. 'OK.' *O-okay.* 'I went to university in

Edinburgh, came away with a degree and Masters in psychology, then took a Doctorate in clinical psychology at Hull. I worked in a secure unit in Brixton before moving to the clinic in Ealing. Er, what else . . . ? I'm single, I don't smoke or do drugs. Obviously, I'm fully DBS checked—'

'DBS?'

'Sorry, it used to be the CRB – Criminal Records Bureau. You know, because of my work?'

'Right, of course.' That was good to know, but she was annoyed it hadn't occurred to her. 'What about your family?' Alex had picked up his fork, holding one end loosely in his fingers, slowly turning it. His fingers were slender, Kate noticed. 'My mother and father are both retired. They live in Cornwall now.'

'Have you any brothers or sisters?'

'Two brothers, both older than me. One's in Australia, and one's in Canada. We're pretty scattered, I suppose. How about you?'

Kate smoothed her napkin on her lap. 'No. I've no family. My parents are dead.'

Alex looked unsettled again. 'I'm sorry.'

'It's OK.' She turned the conversation back to him. 'So what made you want to be a psychologist?'

'Oh . . . I'm not sure, really.' He put down his fork, considering. 'It was just something that's always interested me, I suppose. I'm a better listener than a talker, which helps.' He gave a shy grin. 'And I read the *Foundation Trilogy* when I was a kid, so perhaps that had something to do with it. Have you heard of Isaac Asimov? The classic science fiction writer?'

'Er . . . the name's familiar.'

'It doesn't matter.' He seemed embarrassed but continued. 'I used to read a lot of science fiction when I was a kid, and . . . well, he wrote this series about a society built by really advanced psychologists. You know, sort of "super-psychologists", who've developed the science so far that spoken language has become redundant. It sounds silly now, but at the time it made a big impact on me. They don't even have to speak to communicate or know what someone means. God, I thought that was great! You know, being able to understand people like that. Understand why they do things. And understand themselves, as well. It just seemed . . . Well, like I say, it sounds silly now.'

He broke off, embarrassed, as the waitress returned with their food.

'Go on, you were saying?' Kate asked, when the girl had gone. She noticed that he waited for her to begin eating before he started himself, which struck her as quaint. Nice.

'Oh, nothing. That was all, really.'

His reserve was back. Kate smiled, wanting him to relax again. 'And are you a "super-psychologist"?'

He gave an embarrassed smile, rubbing the back of his neck. 'No, I don't—'

There was another loud hiss and burst of flame from the kitchen hatch. Alex jerked, and the piece of omelette he had just picked up on his fork flipped off and landed neatly in his water glass.

'Oh, God! Sorry!'

His expression was so mortified that the laugh escaped

Kate before she could stop it. He glanced at her, then grinned. He had a nice smile, she thought.

'It was too hot, anyway.' Blushing, he fished the omelette out of the glass and set it on the edge of his plate. 'So how did you get into PR?'

The blush was fading from his face now. It made him look very young, Kate thought.

'Oh, I just drifted into it, I suppose,' she said. 'I'd done a couple of years of an English degree, but then my parents died quite close to each other, and I dropped out. I wasn't sure what I wanted to do after that, so I worked at a few places and then got a job at a PR company.'

'How long have you had your own agency?'

'Two years now.'

'And what sort of work do you actually do?'

He was looking at her with genuine interest. His manner had changed, becoming more confident now that he was asking her questions. There was no trace of the earlier hesitancy in his speech.

'Do you mean, who do I work for? Or what does it involve?'

'Both, really. It isn't something I know much about,' he admitted.

'Well, we handle all sorts of accounts, anything from independent record labels to publishers who want to get somebody reviewed in newspapers or interviewed on TV and radio. Or it can be somebody who's got a particular product that they are looking to launch. The biggest account we've got is a charitable trust who've asked us to raise their profile as subtly as possible, but most of our clients want as much publicity as they can get.'

'So how do you go about it?'

'It varies from client to client, but basically it's about engaging people's attention. That can be with anything from a press release to a poster campaign, depending on the client's target audience and budget. And obviously social media's hugely important. We'll use sites like Facebook, Twitter, Instagram to raise public awareness of a brand, get bloggers talking about it. Generally try and generate an online buzz.'

She paused, reproaching herself for letting down her guard. She wasn't here to talk about herself. Pretending interest in her salad, she tried for a casual tone.

'How about you? Are you a Twitter addict?'

'Me? No, I don't much bother with that sort of thing.'

'What, not even a website? Or LinkedIn?' she asked, already knowing the answer.

'I can't see the point. Maybe if I was in private practice.' He gave her a quick look. 'Don't get me wrong, I've nothing against networking. But in my line of work it's not a good idea to broadcast your personal life online. Some of my patients are . . . Well, let's say it's better to keep a low profile.'

Kate was surprised by how relieved she felt. Given his job, of course he wouldn't want to risk making his private life public. Who would? Her smile became more genuine. 'Is that the "super-psychologist" in you talking?'

He grinned, briefly making eye contact before dropping his gaze. 'No, just the realist. And now you're laughing at me.'

'Only a little.' She found herself grinning back before remembering that this wasn't a social lunch. 'To get back to your background, do you have any family history of illness? Diabetes, anything like that?'

'Uh, no, not that I know of. My grandmother had arthritis but not till she was in her seventies.'

Kate nodded, trying to be business-like. Assuming she went ahead, the clinic should look into his medical history, but it didn't hurt to be sure. She tried to think what to ask next, but all the carefully prepared questions suddenly eluded her. God, why hadn't she just written a list? Then, as the silence stretched on, the most important one presented itself.

'Why do you want to be a donor?'

He appeared taken aback. 'Well, I don't know. It seemed like a good thing to do. It doesn't hurt me, and if I can help somebody, then . . . you know, why not?'

'Have you donated sperm before?' Kate refused to let herself be fazed by saying 'sperm' to a complete stranger. 'Or given blood?'

'N-no, no, I haven't.' The syncopation was back.

'Then what made you decide to now?'

'Uh, well . . .' A flush had crept into his face. 'It, er, it wasn't something I'd even thought about before I saw your advert, really. But I suppose I like the idea of, well, fatherhood without the ties.'

'You could have the same thing by going straight to a sperm bank.'

He seemed flustered. 'I know, but . . . Well, it might sound stupid but that's all a bit too anonymous.' His face was very red now. 'I wouldn't like the thought of letting just anyone have my . . . my child, if you know what I mean.'

It had never occurred to Kate that a man might feel the same way she did. 'You do know that you wouldn't have any of a father's rights, don't you? You'd still only be the donor. Assuming I decide to go ahead, the child wouldn't legally be yours and there wouldn't be any contact between us afterwards. None at all.'

'No, I realize that.'

'In fact you'd be getting the worst of both worlds,' she went on, almost wanting to be cruel. 'Regardless of whether I tell them or not, when they're eighteen they'll be able to find out who you are. So even though you won't have any rights or contact, he or she might turn up on your doorstep years from now. You could have a family of your own by then.'

'Yes, I . . . I understand all that.'

'And it'll mean a lot of inconvenience. The clinic's in Birmingham, and you'll have to make a lot of trips. They need quite a few . . . samples.'

He nodded acceptance.

'I'll pay expenses,' Kate went on briskly, shutting out the thought of what she was discussing. 'For your time as well as travel. I'll pay you either a flat fee or a daily one each time you go.'

Alex shook his head emphatically. 'I don't want paying.'

'I wouldn't expect you to do it for nothing.'

'I'd be doing it because I want to.'

Kate decided not to argue. She still hadn't decided anything yet, so there was no point. 'You'll have to be screened for things like HIV and hepatitis. And they won't go ahead with the . . . the treatment for at least six months, until they're certain everything's clear.'

He looked startled.

'Is that a problem?' Kate asked.

'Oh, no, it's just . . . I didn't expect it to take so long, that's all.'

'They do the same tests on every donor. It isn't any reflection on you personally.'

'No, no, it's OK, really. I just didn't realize. But it's no problem.'

Kate tried to think of what else she had to say. Nothing came to mind. 'Is there anything you'd like to ask?'

Alex minutely repositioned his knife and fork on his plate. Except for the piece he had dropped into the glass, his omelette was still untouched.

'Are you married?'

Kate stared at him levelly. 'Why?'

He was disconcerted by her reaction. 'Sorry, I – I know it's none of my business. I just wondered if you were doing this because you were single and wanted to, or whether you were married and your husband was . . . was . . .' he gestured with his knife, stepping around the reference to sterility, '. . . wasn't able to have children,' he finished. 'Your advert didn't say one way or the other.'

Her face had become hot. 'Does it matter?'

'No, of course not. I'm sorry, I didn't mean to pry.'

133

He was so obviously reluctant to offend that Kate relented. 'No, I'm not married. I'm doing this because I want to.'

'Good. I mean, you know, good for you.'

Kate studied him for a few seconds. He picked up his knife and fork and half-heartedly began to cut up the omelette. 'Why are you so nervous?'

She had asked the question without intending to. He shot her a quick look.

'I'm not nervous. Not really,' he amended, as though realizing there was no use denying it. 'I've just, you know, never done anything like this before.'

He looked so chagrined that Kate couldn't keep from smiling. 'It isn't something I've made a habit of, either.'

He glanced up at her, then smiled himself. 'No, I suppose it isn't,' he acknowledged. His smile faded. 'I expect you'll have interviewed quite a few other people, though. I mean, I know I won't be the only one and . . . Well, it's a bit nerve-racking, that's all.'

Kate didn't correct him. He had gone back to playing with his omelette. His face was serious again.

'Is this so important to you?' she asked.

He didn't speak for a moment. Kate got the impression he was wrestling with the answer. Then he looked across at her. His eyes were a darker blue than Lucy's.

'Yes,' he said, simply.

'Why?'

He looked down at his plate. 'I want children. I'm just not . . . I'm not the marrying kind. I'm not gay, in case you're wondering. I just can't see myself settling down and having a normal family or . . .' His voice tailed off, as though he had changed his mind about what he was going to say. 'This seems like the next best thing.'

'Even though you'll never see the baby? Not even know if it's a boy or a girl?' Kate felt brutal, but she had to be sure he understood.

All at once his face looked immeasurably sad. He stared at the unlit candle in the centre of the table, but Kate doubted he saw it.

'I'll know it's there, though.' He came to himself with a little start. 'If you decide to choose me as the donor, that is. I don't want you to think I'm taking anything for granted.'

Now Kate looked away. 'I've been keeping you from your lunch,' she said, going back to her salad.

She asked him for his card as they left the restaurant. 'I'll call you next week and let you know what I've decided,' she told him, feeling both cowardly and pompous.

'Of course, whatever you think.'

He searched through his wallet. It was well worn and over-stuffed with receipts and credit cards. Kate was able to read the upside-down name on the topmost one: *Dr Alex Turner*.

'Sorry, there's one in here somewhere. Ah, here we go.' He gave her a simple white business card. 'It only has my work number on it, but I'd rather you didn't call me at the clinic. I'm often with a patient, and . . . well, to be honest, I don't really want anyone to know about this.'

He sounded apologetic. Kate nodded. 'I understand.'

She pretended to scrutinize the card rather than look at him, conscious that she'd already phoned the clinic to make sure he worked there. But she doubted the receptionist would have bothered to mention 'Caitlin Smith'.

'If you want to get hold of me it's best to use my mobile or try me at home,' he went on, sounding relieved. 'Evenings are best. I generally have my phone switched off at work, for obvious reasons. Most Saturdays too – I do an out-of-hours clinic then. But I check for messages and texts regularly, so you can always contact me that way. Do you still have my numbers? I can write them on the card?'

'No, that's OK. They're on your letter.'

'Right. Sorry, I'm gabbling a bit.' He grinned, abashed. Kate smiled back. 'It's just that I've moved house recently, and I'm ex-directory. So if you lose them you might find it hard getting hold of me.'

She tried not to react to the information. *See? Ex-directory. Just like you thought.* The fears of the previous night seemed ridiculous now. 'I won't lose them.'

'Great.' He squinted off down the bright street. 'And . . . you will get in touch? Either way, I mean? I'll respect whatever you decide, I'd just . . . I'd like to know.'

He seemed so earnest she had to resist the urge to reassure him. 'Next week,' she said, and couldn't keep from adding, 'I promise.' They shook hands, both a little awkward. Kate felt the heat and pressure from his even after she was no longer holding it. She watched him walk down the street, a slim figure, already lost in thought, hands shoved casually in his pockets.

Catching sight of herself in the restaurant window as she turned away, she saw she had a smile on her face.

Back at the office Kate couldn't switch her mind on to her work. She kept replaying the meeting she'd just had, going over and over it again. Alex – no, make that Alex Turner, he wasn't a new friend – wasn't at all what she'd expected. Not that she'd known what to expect. Somebody who looked older and was more formal, perhaps. An authority figure. Not the laid-back, casually dressed man who'd arrived. Well, perhaps not quite laid-back, she thought, recalling his nervousness. But certainly approachable. Likeable, even.

And good looking, let's not forget that.

She chided herself that that was irrelevant, before allowing that it was OK to be pleased. This was the prospective father of her child, she thought, with a thrilled, disbelieving tingle. Why shouldn't she want him to be attractive? Good genes were important, that was the whole point of what she was doing. Wasn't it?

She studied the business card on her desk. Dr Alex Turner, Clinical Psychologist (Chartered) BSc, MSc, DClinPsy. The clinic's phone number and address were the same as those she'd found online. She tapped the card thoughtfully, then put it aside and went on to the British Psychological Society's website. When she entered his name in a search facility, it came up with the address of the Ferndale Centre in Ealing. *OK, you've already confirmed that. Find something else.* But there wasn't much to find, at least nothing that meant anything to her. There was a link to a site that gave a list of articles he'd had published in psychological journals, and she was impressed to see how many there were. It was subscription only, so she could only access the abstracts – a sort of brief synopsis – rather than the entire articles, but that was enough. The title of the first was 'The Role of Upbringing and Environment in the Forming of Obsessional Behaviour'. Catchy, thought Kate with a smile as she read on.

Obsessional behaviour is frequently attributable to a specific event or events in an individual's background. Frequently, memory of these has been suppressed, so that the root of the obsession is obscured. This paper suggests that the success of therapy for such obsessions may be substantially increased when these seminal events are recognized. Six patients were helped to recall these using hypnosis, with positive results.

There was nothing of interest there, so Kate moved on to the next record. This article had been published by an American journal, she saw, impressed. The title was 'Blood Ties: Impulse-control disorders as an inherited trait?' It meant little to her, and the abstract wasn't much help, either.

Identical twins, separated at birth and given contrasting upbringings, were convicted of theft within twelve months of each other. This study considers the possibility of an inherited tendency towards impulse-control disorders, and suggests this as a subject of further research.

Her attention wandered before she got to the end. She went to the next abstract, this one about pyromania, then sat back without reading it. Enough was enough: Alex Turner was clearly who and what he said he was.

Which left her with a decision to make.

She jumped at a knock on the door. Clive walked in, leafing through a file.

'Sorry to bother you, but I've just been talking to Bryony at Winter Music. She wants to discuss a launch for a new jazz compilation they've got coming out.' He paused, looking at her. 'Everything OK?'

'Yes, fine.'

She could feel her face burning as if she'd been caught doing something wrong. Even though he couldn't see her computer screen from where he stood, she had to resist the urge to close it down.

Clive was still giving her a quizzical look. 'You sure?'

'Yes, I'm just . . . miles away. So, Winter Music?'

She made herself pay attention as Clive spoke, but as he turned to go he hesitated. He regarded her with a puzzled grin.

'Are you absolutely sure you're OK? Has something happened?'

'No, nothing at all. Really,' she insisted.

But she knew the broad smile on her face gave her away.

* * *

Lucy and Jack returned that weekend. Kate waited through tales of collapsing guy-ropes, sunburn and ice-cream indigestion, before Lucy wound down.

'Are you going to be free one night next week?' Kate asked.

Lucy was slumped in an armchair. 'I think you'd have to drag me out of the house after the last fortnight. Why?'

Kate couldn't keep it in any longer. 'There's someone I'd like you to meet.'

10

'This is Alex.'

The four of them stood in Lucy and Jack's living room, stiff smiles on all their faces. The planned barbecue had been rained off. Instead, the big table at the back of the room was now draped with a heavy white table-cloth, and set with Jack's aunt's best cutlery and glasses. Two heavy silver-plated candlesticks stood in the middle, the beeswax candles in them slightly askew.

Lucy gave Alex a bright smile. 'Pleased to meet you.' Kate thought that she was going to step forward and kiss him, but she didn't.

Jack stuck out his hand and gave Alex's a firm shake. 'How you doing?'

There was an awkward lull while everyone waited for someone to speak and no one did.

'Well, isn't this just typical English weather?' Lucy declared. 'If there's one certain way of getting it to rain, it's for us to decide to have a barbecue!'

They laughed, a little more heartily than was strictly necessary. Before the silence could descend again, Jack rubbed his hands together.

'Right, who's for a drink? Kate?'

'Red wine, please.' She reminded herself to drink slowly. She hadn't been able to eat anything all day.

'Alex?' Jack said. 'Beer, wine. Something stronger, if you'd like it?'

Alex looked momentarily lost. 'Er . . . beer, if you've got one.'

Jack's face split into a grin. 'You can have Budweiser, Boddy's or Old Speckled Hen.'

'You can show him your beer collection later,' Lucy said, disguising the sharpness behind a smile. 'I'm sure Alex isn't bothered.'

Jack's smile was just as cosmetic. 'Well, let's let him decide, shall we?'

Kate knew Lucy and Jack well enough to gather that they had been arguing. She had felt anxious enough before she arrived, and the tension between them didn't make her feel any better. She suddenly felt certain that the night was going to be awful.

'I'll have a Bud, please,' Alex said. Jack gave Lucy a triumphant glance, clearly taking the nickname as proof of a kindred spirit. He went through into the kitchen.

'I'll have white wine, since you've asked,' Lucy called after him sweetly. She smiled back at Kate and Alex. 'You might as well sit down.'

They went to the sofa and chairs set around the unlit wood burner. As she passed Kate, Lucy lowered her voice. 'New dress?'

Kate nodded. It was plain white, sleeveless and ended well above her knee. Lucy raised an eyebrow at her but made no further comment as she settled into one of the armchairs. After hesitating by its twin, Kate sat on the sofa with Alex, though at the other end. She was conscious of her dress riding up over her thighs. It was shorter than she was used to.

Lucy gave him a hostess's smile. 'Kate tells me you're a clinical psychologist?'

Alex nodded. 'Er, yes, that's right.'

'You'll have to forgive my ignorance, but I'm not sure what that is. I mean, I know what a psychologist is, but I'm not sure about the clinical bit.'

He cleared his throat. 'Well, it, er, it basically means I work with patients rather than on the, uh, theoretical or research side.'

He sat with his legs crossed and one arm thrown casually over the arm of the sofa, but Kate sensed the same rigidity in him she had noticed in the restaurant. He seemed to be holding himself in the relaxed posture by an effort of will.

'So you treat schizophrenics and people like that, instead of getting rats to run round mazes?' Lucy persisted.

'Ah, no, I wouldn't treat anyone for schizophrenia. That's more a psychiatric condition, really.'

'What's the difference?'

'The difference?' Alex looked discomfited at being quizzed. Kate wished Lucy would change the subject. 'Well, psychiatry deals with, er, with mental illness. Psychology, – c-clinical psychology – is more concerned with behavioural problems.'

The faint catch was back in his voice, an almost imperceptible stumble over his consonants. Kate wondered if Lucy could tell how nervous he was. She was beginning to regret the enthusiasm that had led her to take him there. It hadn't been her intention to put him on display, but that was how it must seem.

'What made you choose it? The clinical thing, I mean?'

Kate wondered if she had sounded as inane when she'd first met him. She waited for Alex to tell Lucy about the 'super-psychologists'.

'Oh, no particular reason. It was just something I liked the sound of.'

He didn't look at her, but Kate was suddenly sure that Alex knew she was conscious of the omission. And, for some reason, she was glad he hadn't told Lucy.

'What sort of—' Lucy began, but Kate never knew what her next question would have been. She broke off as a small figure came into the room. Dressed in a pale-yellow nightgown, Emily hung back at the edge of the circle formed by the sofa and chairs. She had a shy smile on her face as she looked up coyly at Alex from under her hair.

'And what are you doing out of bed, young lady?' Lucy asked, affecting sternness.

Emily twirled back and forth on her toes, not taking her eyes from Alex. 'Couldn't sleep.'

'And I don't suppose that's because you wanted to see who was here, is it?'

Emily smiled but said nothing. Lucy sighed and turned to Alex. 'I don't suppose you know anything about child psychology, do you? Like what to do with nosy children?'

He gave an uncertain grin. 'No, sorry.'

As if Emily had been waiting for him to speak, she edged closer. 'Are you Kate's boyfriend?'

'Time for bed, I think,' Lucy said, coming out of her chair and swooping her up so quickly that they were halfway down the hallway before the little girl's objections sounded.

As the noises of protest receded Kate forced herself to smile at Alex. Separated by the width of a cushion and mutual embarrassment, they waited for Jack to return with the drinks.

Lucy had cooked roast chicken, rubbed with lemon and garlic and served with green beans and minted new potatoes from their garden. When she put her mind to it, she was a good cook, but she had obviously lost interest by the time it came to preparing a dessert. The chocolate gateau she produced was mainly synthetic cream and additives, and misshapen on one side where it had been squashed in the shopping bag. But by that time the drinks had relaxed them enough so they could laugh about it.

Kate felt light-headed, from relief as much as the wine she'd vowed not to drink. The initial awkwardness had slipped away unnoticed during the meal. Alex had unwound and seemed to hit it off with Lucy and Jack, who had either shelved or resolved whatever had been bothering them. Lucy had begun to flirt mildly with him, a sure sign of approval, and he and Jack had found common ground in books.

Lucy caught her eye as Jack began to tell Alex about his business.

'Give me a hand with the dishes?'

Suddenly nervous, Kate helped her collect the dirty plates and followed her into the kitchen. Lucy closed the door behind them and turned to face her.

'Tell me you're not still planning to go through with it.'

Kate had known Lucy was about to give her verdict, but this wasn't what she expected. 'Why? Don't you like him?'

'Of course I like him! He's a bit shyer than I'd have expected, but apart from that I think he's lovely.'

'What's wrong, then?'

'Nothing's *wrong*. Except that you've been lucky enough to meet a really nice bloke, never mind how, and if you're still even *considering* going ahead with that artificial rubbish, then you want your head looking at!'

Kate felt the tension drain out of her. 'I thought you were going to say you didn't approve of him.'

'The only thing I don't approve of is if you still plan to go ahead with this stupid idea of yours. You've really fallen on your feet. Again. I just hope you make the most of it.'

'Lucy, I'm looking for a donor. That's all.'

'Oh, yes?' Lucy arched her eyebrows. 'I suppose you're going to tell me you don't fancy him, either?'

'I don't. I'm glad he's turned out to be a nice bloke and I don't deny I like him, but it doesn't go any further than that.'

Lucy looked pointedly at Kate's dress. 'And I suppose that outfit's just coincidence, then?'

Kate blushed. 'I decided to buy myself something new, that's all.'

'Which just happens to show off your legs and boobs. Come on, I'm not stupid. You didn't put that on for my benefit. Or Jack's.'

Something in her tone alerted Kate. Remembering the tension between Lucy and Jack when she'd first arrived, she asked, 'Is everything OK? Between you and Jack, I mean. I'm not prying,' she added hurriedly, seeing Lucy's suddenly closed expression, 'but you seemed at bit . . . edgy with each other earlier.'

Kate thought she wasn't going to answer, but then Lucy turned away.

'We had a bit of an argument, that's all.' She paused. 'About you, actually.'

'Me?'

Two patches of colour had entered Lucy's cheeks. She looked at Kate with something like defiance.

'Jack seems to think I'm being too hard on you. He says I should be more supportive. I told him I was only saying what I thought was for your own good and that I wished he'd be half as bloody supportive towards me.' Her mouth tightened. 'But then I wouldn't look as good in a white mini dress, would I?'

Abruptly, she squeezed her eyes shut.

'Oh, Christ, I didn't mean that. I'm sorry.'

Kate said nothing. She became aware of a tap dripping, rhythmically, into the silence.

Lucy's forehead was creased in anguish. 'Ignore me, I'm just in a bitchy mood, that's all. It wasn't only about you, anyway. Jack and I have been going through a bad

147

patch lately, the kids have been brats. And to top it off I'm having an absolute bugger of a period – my stomach's swollen like a balloon, I feel yukky, and then you come walking in looking like Audrey bloody Hepburn. And instead of some geeky pervert, the only bloke who replies to your advert turns out to be a bloody catch!' She gave a weak smile. 'Sometimes, you know, things just get on top of you.'

Kate felt as though she'd inadvertently opened a door that should have stayed locked. 'Do you want us to leave?'

'No, of course I don't! Oh, look, please don't take any notice of me. I'm just in a bad mood and feeling sorry for myself.'

The tap made a metallic *plink* as each drip hit the sink. Lucy reached out and tightened it. The drips slowed but didn't stop. She watched it, her arms folded around herself. 'You'd better go back and rescue Alex,' she said. 'Jack'll have bored him witless about work by now. I'll be through when I've made the coffee.'

Kate opened the door.

'Kate?'

She looked back. Lucy gave a small shrug.

'Sorry.'

Kate went out, letting the door close behind her. The glimpse of Lucy's bitterness had been as unexpected as a mouthful of rot from a wholesome apple. She stood for a while in the dark of the hallway. From behind her in the kitchen came the muted click of a cupboard being opened, the chink of crockery. Ahead of her a spill of light fell through the partly open lounge door. There was no sound of conversation. Kate went in.

Alex didn't look up when she entered. He was alone at the table, his face full of shadows in the candlelight. His expression was lost and faraway as he regarded the small wisp of fire swaying from the candle nearest him. Kate hung back as he passed his finger through the yellow tip, halted, then steadily passed it back. The flame fluttered with each passage, leaning towards his finger as though trying to catch it.

Kate moved towards the table. 'Doesn't that hurt?' Alex's eyes were wide and startled as his head came up. 'What?'

'Running your finger through the flame like that. Doesn't it hurt?'

He stared at his finger and the candle as though he had only just noticed them. 'Uh, no, not really.'

Kate sat down. 'It must burn, though, surely?'

He looked back into the flame. 'Only if you let it.' He smiled at her. 'Try it.'

Kate laughed and shook her head. 'No, thanks.'

'It doesn't hurt. Not if you're fast enough and don't go too close to the wick.'

She gave him a sceptical look.

'Honest. It won't burn if you do it right.'

They were staring at each other over the candle. Tentatively, Kate held out her finger until it was only a few inches away from the flame.

'No,' she said with a laugh, snatching it back.

'Come on. Trust me.'

She looked at him and extended her finger again. A

slim line of smoke rose from the flame. She could feel the heat against her skin. Her finger quivered.

From the hallway came the sound of Jack returning from the bathroom. Kate quickly drew back her hand, feeling both relieved and cowardly.

'I'll take your word for it.'

They shared a taxi home. Alex insisted on dropping off Kate first, assuring her that it was quicker that way. After a second's hesitation, she accepted. She hadn't planned on letting him know her address but, since he'd just been to Lucy and Jack's, that seemed petty and pointless. They sat next to each other on the back seat. To begin with, they talked easily enough. Alex seemed almost garrulous when she asked him about where he lived, explaining how he was in temporary accommodation after being caught up in a chain of house buyers. After exchanging contracts with the couple who were buying his flat, the people whose house he was supposed to be buying had withdrawn theirs from the market.

'I'd got three days to find somewhere else before the new owners moved into mine,' he told her. 'So now most of my stuff's in storage, and I'm stuck renting a studio flat until I can find somewhere else.'

'Have you seen anywhere yet?'

'Uh, no, not really. I don't have much time to look. You know how it is.' His self-consciousness had returned.

They lapsed into silence. Their isolation in the dark intimacy of the cab began to impose an awkwardness on them both. In the confined space, Kate could make out the clean, alcohol tang of Alex's aftershave. Paul had always drenched himself in the stuff, as though the reek of it declared his masculinity. Alex's was more subtle. She liked it.

The taxi lurched round a bend, throwing her against him. Kate reached out to steady herself, and put her hand on his thigh. She jerked it away and straightened, stammering an apology. Her face was hot as she stared fixedly out of the window. Beside her, she sensed that Alex was equally tense. The air between them seemed charged with awareness, so that the slightest movement was magnified.

She slid down the window, letting the breeze freshen her face, and breathed deeply. *Too much wine.* 'Is it too windy for you?' she asked Alex.

'No, it's fine.'

There had been no mention of the reason they were together. Alex hadn't pushed her for a decision, for which she was glad. They might almost have been out on a date, in fact. Kate quickly put that notion out of her head.

'I hope tonight hasn't been too much of an ordeal,' she said.

'Not at all. I've enjoyed it.'

She nearly said, *So have I*, but stopped herself. She glanced at the taxi driver. He probably couldn't hear through the glass partition, but she lowered her voice anyway.

'I don't want you to feel you've been on trial, or anything.'

'It's OK, really.' He smiled. 'I liked them. They're a nice family.'

They were approaching Kate's road. 'The next corner, please,' she told the driver. She turned back to Alex, lowering her voice again. 'Look, I appreciate how patient you've been, and I don't want to mess you about, but . . . Well, will it be all right if I let you know in a few days? About what I decide?'

He nodded quickly. 'Yes, no problem.'

'It's just a big decision to have to make. I don't want to rush into anything.'

'No, of course. It's OK, I understand.'

The taxi grated to a halt. Kate reached into her bag and handed the driver a note to cover the fare, against Alex's protests. She put her hand on the door handle.

'Well. Goodnight, then.'

'Goodnight.'

There was a moment when neither of them moved, then Kate pressed down the handle and climbed out.

'I'll be in touch by the end of the week,' she told Alex, through the open window.

She phoned him the next evening.

It was a doctor they saw, not the counsellor Kate had met on her first visit to the clinic. The three of them sat in her office around a low ball-and-claw-footed table in comfortable leather chairs. Beside them, unused for the moment, was an antique cherrywood desk, dark and rich with the scent of beeswax. Sunlight striped the carpet through the horizontal bars of the blinds. The window itself was closed, but air conditioning made the office pleasantly cool. The entire hospital seemed to exist in an environment completely separate from the outside world.

'The thing you have to remember, and I really can't stress this enough, is that legally "donor" and "father" are two different entities,' the doctor was saying to Alex. Dr Janson was an attractive woman in her forties, with carefully styled blonde hair and clothes that reflected the hospital's charges. She had told them that scheduling problems had meant she would see them instead of another counsellor, but Kate wondered if it wasn't more because she wanted to handle an unusual case herself.

'It doesn't matter whether the donor is anonymous or, as in this instance, known to the patient,' she continued. 'If you donate through an HFEA registered clinic, then your responsibility begins and ends with the donation of the sperm. It's very important that you understand that.'

Alex nodded. He was leaning forward in his chair, listening to what the doctor said with an intent, almost anxious expression. He had been silent for most of the journey from Euston, but then Kate hadn't felt like talking either.

Satisfied that the point had been made, Dr Janson continued. 'Before we go any further, I should say that we're obliged to offer counselling before you give your consent for your sperm to be stored and used. Not everyone feels they need it, but it's there if you do. It's important you fully understand the implications of becoming a donor.'

She waited, a polite smile on her subtly made-up face.

Alex glanced uncertainly at Kate.

'Er . . . I don't think that's . . . I mean, no, it's OK, thanks.'

The doctor inclined her head. 'As you wish. Just so long as you're aware that the offer has been made.' She took out a gold-plated fountain pen and unscrewed its cap. 'Now, I'll have to ask you a few questions about your general health and medical background.'

Kate let their voices wash over her as the doctor read out questions and Alex answered. Through the window she could see a small ornamental pond. A miniature willow hung its branches forlornly over the water's surface. Beyond it, the grounds were set out like a park, a tame landscape of trees and shrubs. *This is what I'm paying for*. The thought was obscurely disturbing.

She turned away from the window as the doctor handed Alex a sheet of paper.

'We need your consent to contact your GP, in case we have to find out more about your medical history, so if you could just fill in this form, please.'

Alex took the form. 'I, uh, I don't have a pen.'

Dr Janson handed him her gold fountain pen. He began to write, then stopped.

'Sorry, I don't, er, I don't know the surgery's address.' His face had gone red. The doctor smiled reassuringly. 'Don't worry about it. Just put your GP's name and then sign it. You can give us the address next time you come. Provided there's no problem with the blood tests it's usually just a formality, especially since you're a known donor. Known to the patient, I mean, as opposed to an anonymous donor.'

Alex wrote quickly and passed back the sheet. The doctor put it to one side and handed him another.

'This is a consent form for us to store and use your sperm. Read it carefully before you sign it, and please ask if you have any questions.'

She handed Kate another sheet of paper. 'And while he's doing that, you might as well be filling in your consent form for the treatment.'

It was surprisingly straightforward. Kate filled it in and signed it. She gave it back to the doctor.

Alex looked up from his own form, frowning. 'It says here about giving my consent for my, er, my sperm to be used after my death.' He stumbled a little over *consent*.

'That's so we can carry on using your samples in case anything happens to you before the treatment is concluded,' the doctor answered smoothly. 'You don't have to give it, and we hope it won't be necessary. But if it was, without your consent we wouldn't be able to continue. It's best to be covered, just in case.'

Alex still looked uncomfortable. 'What happens to any . . . any samples that are left over? Afterwards, I mean?'

'That's entirely up to you.' She smiled. 'Obviously, the clinic is grateful for any donations. So if you've no objection we'd like to keep them frozen as part of our donor panel.'

'So they can be used for someone else?'

'Or for research, yes.'

Alex shook his head. 'No. No, I don't want that.'

The doctor's smile never slipped. 'That's your prerogative, of course. You can stipulate on the form that you only want them to be used for treating a specific person.'

Alex gave a short nod and began to write. The office was silent, except for the scratching of the pen nib. He rested on the low, glass-topped table. Incongruous in the centre of it was a modern, fluid-filled ornament, like a rectangular spirit-level. Inside it, pink globules drifted sinuously in a viscous-looking red liquid. When enough had gathered at one end, it slowly tilted, forcing them to float up to the other. It looked vaguely obscene. Kate wondered which reflected Dr Janson's taste – the antique furniture or the disturbing ornament.

Alex finished writing. He straightened and considered the form for one last time before passing it across to the doctor. She put it with Kate's.

'Right,' she said, smiling with easy confidence. 'The next step is for you to give us a sample, so we can check that you aren't azoospermic. That means you either have a very low sperm count or no sperm at all,' she explained, when Alex looked doubtful. 'It's a routine test, but we obviously have to make it. You can book an appointment with the receptionist on the way out.' She tilted her head. 'Unless you want to make a start straight away?'

'Now, you mean?' Alex looked horrified.

'The sooner you start the better, really. And there's no

point in making any more journeys than you have to, is there?'

The doctor's expression was bland, but Kate wondered if she wasn't taking a subtle revenge for Alex's insistence over the consent form.

'If you'd rather leave it till next time it's OK,' Kate said, seeing him flounder.

'Uh, yes, I – I think I would.' His face had gone crimson.

Dr Janson smiled.

Kate telephoned for a taxi to take them back to the station. The gravel drive crunched under their feet as they went out to the main gate to wait for it. After the clinic's air-conditioned chill, the sun's heat was smothering. Kate could feel the hot prickle of sweat breaking out. They walked in silence to the shade of the horse chestnut that overhung the stone-pillared gateway. The spiky yellow nuggets of conker shells were already visible among the splayed leathery leaves.

'You OK?' Kate asked.

Alex nodded, without looking at her. 'Fine.'

They fell silent again. Patches of bright sunlight dappled through the leaves, like hot coins where they fell on Kate's bare arms.

'You don't mind, do you?' Alex asked suddenly. 'I just wasn't expecting to have to . . . you know, to start today.'

'It's all right, I wasn't expecting you to either. Just come whenever it's convenient.'

She realized the double entendre as soon as she had

spoken, and went on quickly to cover her embarrassment. 'I mean, I know you'll have to fit the trips in with work and everything. I don't want you to go to any more trouble than you have to.'

'It won't be a problem.'

The drone of a car engine became audible. A taxi was pulling up the hill towards the clinic. They moved out from beneath the tree as it approached, but it went past without stopping. The sound of its engine trailed away in the heat. They stood for a second or two on the pavement edge, staring after it, then went back to the tree's shade.

'What do your parents think about this? About what you're doing?' Kate asked.

'My parents?' Alex seemed startled. 'Oh, I haven't told them.'

'Are you going to?'

'No, I don't think so.'

'Wouldn't they approve?'

He looked up through the leaves, squinting into the light. 'No.' Then, as if he felt this wasn't enough, he added, 'They aren't prudish, I don't mean that, and they've always been really supportive. But something like this is . . . Well, you know.'

'So you aren't going to tell anyone?'

He was silent for a moment. 'I'd tell my grandmother, if she was still alive. She'd be pleased. No one else, though.'

Kate saw a small piece of twig caught in his hair. She almost reached out and removed it before she stopped herself. 'Were you very close?'

Alex nodded absently. Then he looked at her, concerned. 'Not that I'm not close to my parents as well. I don't want to give that impression. It's just that my grandmother was . . .' He was self-conscious now. 'Well, she was special.'

Another taxi was approaching the clinic. This time they watched until it indicated and pulled to a stop.

'I think this one's ours,' said Kate.

They were quiet for most of the journey back to London.

Alex sat opposite her, staring out of the window, swaying slightly with the movement of the train. His eyes were sleepy, half-lidded against the sunlight angling into his face through the glass. He looked vulnerable, Kate thought, much younger than the thirty-eight she knew him to be.

A sudden lurch roused him. He turned and caught her staring before she could look away. She smiled.

'There's a piece of twig stuck in your hair,' she said.

He looked bewildered. She pointed. 'You've got a twig caught in your hair.'

'Oh. Right.' He pulled it out. 'Thanks.'

He looked around for somewhere to put it. She could see him considering the seat, the table and the floor before he dropped it in his pocket.

'No bin,' he explained, with an embarrassed smile.

Kate hid her amusement by searching in her bag. She pulled out a white envelope and passed it across to him. 'There's a cheque in there for your expenses,' she said. 'I've based it on train fares for fifteen visits to start with, plus taxis to and from both stations.'

Alex held the envelope without opening it.

'If you want to work out how much you think I'll owe you for your time, I'll be happy to pay that in advance as well,' she offered, seeing his expression.

'No! I didn't mean . . .' He hurriedly put the envelope down on the table. 'I told you, I don't want paying for this.'

'I don't expect you to do it for nothing.'

He shook his head. 'I can't take money from you.'

'In that case we'd better forget the whole thing.' She had meant it lightly, but Alex looked as though she had slapped him. 'It's only your travel expenses,' she said, smiling to show she hadn't been serious. 'We can discuss a fee later, if you like. But I can't let you be out of pocket.'

She pushed the envelope across the table towards him. 'Now, please, no arguments. I insist.'

He was clearly unhappy, but after a second he picked it up. 'OK. If you're sure.' He put the envelope in his pocket, still unopened.

Kate glanced out of the window. 'We'll be at Euston in a few minutes.' She cleared her throat. 'Look, I don't quite know what to say, but . . . well, I really am grateful for what you're doing. Thank you.'

Alex kept his head averted. 'I'm glad to do it.'

Kate hid her embarrassment behind a no-nonsense tone. 'All the same, I really appreciate it. And I'll find out from the clinic how many extra visits you have to make and send you a cheque.'

He looked up sharply. 'Aren't we . . . I mean, won't I see you again?'

'I don't think there's any point.' She was unprepared for how blunt that sounded. 'If there are any problems, or anything you want to ask, you can always ring me. You've got my number. But I don't expect there will be. And the clinic'll keep me notified with how things are going.'

'Oh . . . yes, I suppose . . . yes, you're right.'

They didn't speak again for the rest of the journey. When the train pulled into the shadow of the station, they avoided looking at each other as they left their seats and filed out of the carriage with the rest of the passengers. The platform was hot and airless. Kate turned and held out her hand.

'Well. Thanks again.'

Alex took it. His palm was hot and dry, and she remembered the other occasion on which she had shaken it, outside the restaurant the first time she had met him. She pushed the memory to one side.

His blue eyes were troubled as he looked at her. He seemed about to say something, but then he dropped his gaze.

'Bye.'

Kate let go of his hand with a last polite smile and set off down the platform. She wished she had waited until they had reached the concourse to say goodbye, because now they both had to walk in the same direction anyway. But there was no sound of his footsteps following hers. She told herself it was the claustrophobia of the busy platform and the diesel fumes that suddenly seemed depressing, and determinedly walked faster.

She heard someone running only a second before the shout.

'Kate!'

She turned around. Alex slowed as he reached her, and the urgency on his face gave way to confusion.

'Look, I was just wondering . . .' he began, breathlessly, 'I mean, if not, it's OK, but . . .' He seemed to gather himself. 'Well, I – I just wondered if you wanted to go for a – a drink some time?'

Kate didn't even need to think of reasons why she shouldn't. It was far better to make a clean break now, rather than invite complications later. There was no point delaying it.

Alex stood in front of her, nervously waiting for her answer. She smiled.

'I'd like that.'

11

The summer burned itself out. The days were bleached by a sun that scorched grass and cracked the earth, while the nights hung unmoving in a breezeless haze. Newspapers ran features on global warming and droughts, and garden hoses were sneaked out after dark to sprinkle desiccated lawns and plants away from the eyes of watchful neighbours.

Everything seemed to be going smoothly. While they waited for the six-month quarantine to pass, the preliminary results of Alex's first sample and blood tests came back clear. He began making his own weekly trips to Birmingham. Kate didn't accompany him on those and he still hadn't cashed the cheque for expenses, she saw when she checked her bank account.

'I said I'd take it, I didn't say anything about cashing it,' he told her with a grin, when she confronted him. She argued, but this time he was insistent. 'We can sort it out later,' was as far as he would commit himself.

He rarely alluded to the visits, and Kate didn't press for details. She knew he was sensitive about them and didn't want to risk embarrassing him. She had spoken to

Dr Janson after Alex's first session at the clinic. It had not gone well. 'Non-productive' was the term Dr Janson used.

'Nothing to worry about,' she had told Kate. 'It happens to quite a lot of men. They find the whole idea of masturbating to order a bit off-putting at first. Especially in a hospital cubicle.'

Kate had decided against asking Alex about it, realizing that was probably the last thing he needed. He made no mention of what had happened but cried off from meeting her as they'd arranged, claiming he had too much work. He sounded tired and depressed, and the faint stammer, which had become hardly noticeable, was more pronounced than ever.

Her relief when the clinic told her there had been no problems with his next sample was as much for his sake as for her own.

They continued to see each other. They would meet in some pub or wine bar, generally one with a garden, where they could sit outside in whatever cool there was. One night Alex convinced her to go to an art house cinema in Camden, where they sat in sweltering discomfort and watched a retrospective of *The Wicker Man*. Afterwards, Kate joked that in the final conflagration scene Edward Woodward had probably been cooler than the audience. They spent the rest of the evening good-naturedly arguing the point in a Chinese restaurant.

She didn't admit to herself how much she looked forward to seeing him. When she thought about it at all, she rationalized that it was only natural to want to know him better, so that she could one day tell her child (and the thought of her *child* still gave her a little dip of vertigo) what sort of person his or her father was. There was nothing wrong in that, she told herself.

But she didn't think about it too often.

Only once was there a slightly discordant moment, and at the time Kate thought little of it. She had met Alex for a drink, and as they found a table in the pub's beer garden she noticed a smear of black on the back of his jeans.

'Have you got decorators in at work?' she asked.

'No, why?'

'It looks like you've got paint on yourself. No, hang on, I think it's ink.' She laughed. 'Don't tell me they've got you changing the printer cartridges at the clinic?'

'What? No, of course not.'

His face had drained of colour. 'It's all right, I have to do ours as well half the time,' she said, surprised. 'Caroline still can't get the hang of it.'

'I don't . . . I m-must have just leaned on something.' His stammer was noticeable again.

'Are you OK?'

'Yeah, of course.'

He gave a quick smile, and Kate let it drop. She wished she'd not said anything, even though she couldn't see why something so innocuous had embarrassed him. But the brief awkwardness was soon forgotten.

She never saw him wear those jeans again.

They saw quite a lot of Lucy and Jack. Alex enjoyed playing with the children, and he and Jack would preside over barbecues in the back garden with varying degrees of success. Lucy was pleased but exasperated by Kate's relationship with him, even though Kate insisted she didn't have one.

'You don't have to justify seeing him to me,' Lucy said once, when Kate grew defensive. 'I think it's great. I just can't understand why, since you obviously like the bloke, you're still intent on using the poor bugger as a donor. I mean, what's wrong with having it draught, like everybody else?'

'Lucy!'

'Well, I'm sorry, but it seems odd to me. I mean, have you slept together yet?'

Kate's face grew hot. 'That's none of your business!'

'So you haven't,' Lucy said blithely. 'Why? What's wrong with him? He's not gay or anything, is he?'

'No.'

'So why don't you sleep with him, then?'

'Because we're just friends!'

It sounded trite, even to her, but she doggedly refused to admit there was anything more than friendship between them. The ground rules of their relationship had been set at the beginning, by her, and since Alex seemed content to abide by them, Kate didn't let herself so much as consider an alternative.

One hot and restless Sunday, though, Kate broke with routine and phoned him to suggest they go for a picnic. She was mildly surprised to feel nervous in case he said no, but he didn't. They caught a train to Cambridge, where they bought a bottle of wine and baguettes filled with cheese and salad, and queued on the steps of the river for a punt. They took turns

166

in poling the unwieldy flat-bottomed boat upstream, laughing at each other's clumsiness, until they reached a relatively quiet spot in which to picnic. Kate almost overbalanced climbing on to the bank, and when Alex grabbed her arm to steady her the sudden contact embarrassed them both. She busied herself unwrapping the sandwiches, while Alex opened the wine and poured it into paper cups.

He'd taken out his phone and unobtrusively snapped a photograph of Kate before she knew what he was doing.

'Right, in that case I'm going to take one of you,' she said, and, over his protests, took one of him on her own phone. She caught him in the frame, grinning and flushed from the sun, looking absurdly boyish in his white T-shirt and faded jeans. The fine silver chain he wore around his neck gleamed in the sunlight. Kate had been meaning for some time to ask what he wore on it. She was about to now, but before she could phrase the question a middle-aged Japanese man detached himself from a family group and came over.

Smiling, he pointed to himself, then to Kate and Alex, and mimed taking a photograph.

The man nodded, still smiling, as Alex uneasily relinquished his phone. A little awkwardly, Kate moved closer to him. She felt her bare arm brush Alex's. They both grinned self-consciously as the photograph was taken.

'Thank you,' Kate said, as the man went back to his family. She and Alex both put away their phones and didn't take them out again for the rest of the picnic.

It clouded over as they took the punt back. The first fat drops of rain began to spatter on the steps leading up from the small wooden quay. They took cover in a nearby café as the drops became a downpour, and other people ran inside for shelter. They managed to find a table overlooking the river before the café became too full, and watched as the water's smooth surface splintered into fragments. A flash of light lit the copper-coloured sky, followed by a crack of thunder a few seconds later.

'Don't suppose you've got an umbrella handy, have you?' Kate asked Alex, and for some reason that struck them both as funny. They laughed helplessly as the other customers gave them curious glances and the storm clamoured overhead.

Afterwards, Kate was always to think of that as the end of summer. The sun returned in the wake of the rain but now with that subtle change in light that comes when the season has peaked. The mornings became fresher, and the evenings were shattered by more storms that spiced the air with ozone and the mustiness of rain on hot pavements. In the space of a week it was autumn.

The trees began shedding leaves, stirred by breezes that carried a chill hint of winter. Nights grew darker, afternoons dusky and seasoned with smoke. On bonfire night, Kate and Alex arranged to go to a firework display with Lucy, Jack and the children. But the day before, Lucy phoned to say that both Emily and Angus had been stricken with chickenpox.

Alex sounded disappointed when she told him.

'There's no reason why we can't still go,' she said. 'Is there?'

They met in a pub near the park where the display was being held. Kate laughed when Alex presented her with a packet of sparklers.

'God, I've not held one of these since I was a kid.'

He smiled, pleased with her reaction. 'That's the point of bonfire night. We can pretend we're kids again without anyone thinking we need locking up.'

They left the pub and made their way through the park towards the fire. The night was hazy with woodsmoke and sulphur. Exploding rockets peppered the sky with sounds like tearing cloth. As they drew nearer, the pungent smells of the hot dog and burger stalls threw their weight into the atmospheric stew.

They made their way through the crowd towards the bonfire. It towered behind a cordon of ropes, throwing a stream of sparks into the sky. A lifelike Guy was slumped in a chair balanced at the top, smouldering but not yet alight. One gloved hand, buffeted by the heat, moved disturbingly up and down, as though trying to beat back the flames.

Kate grimaced. 'It's a bit gruesome when you think about it, isn't it?' she said. 'Pretending to burn someone. Even if he did try to blow up Parliament. Not much reason to call it a "good" fire, is it?'

Alex was watching the Guy. It seemed to take a second for what she said to register. He looked at her with a quizzical expression.

'Bonfire,' she explained, feeling stupid. 'At school

they said it meant "good fire". You know, as in *bon*, French for "good".'

A smile touched his face. 'That isn't where it gets its name from. It's derived from "bone fire". Because they used to burn bones.'

Kate gave a horrified laugh. 'God, it gets worse! I thought it was bad enough celebrating someone being executed!'

Alex shook his head, turning back to the flames. 'That came later. To start with it was a Celtic fire festival called Samhain, when people built fires to mark the beginning of winter. It wasn't even on November the fifth, it was on the first. But after the Gunpowder Plot people were encouraged to burn effigies of Guy Fawkes on the fires, and the whole idea was hijacked.'

'You sound like you don't approve.'

He didn't answer at first. His face was jaundiced with reflected flame.

'It was something pure to start with,' he said. 'People celebrating fire as a counter to winter. Then it was turned into a political sham, a warning from the government to any other malcontents. Fawkes was a scapegoat. He was just a mercenary, an explosives expert hired to handle the gunpowder. Robert Catesby was the real leader, but no one hears about him. He was killed when they arrested the actual plotters, so they played up Fawkes's role instead. And the real reason for lighting the bonfires became lost.'

He stopped, giving her an apologetic grin. 'Sorry. Lecture over.'

'You sound like you've read a lot about it,' Kate

said. It was rare to hear him speak at such length.

Alex seemed about to say something else when a detonation above them lit the sky with a stuttering crack. Kate looked up and felt the pressure of the rocket's percussion on her face as the display began.

They were forced closer together as people pushed forward for a better view. Kate was conscious of him standing slightly behind and to one side as the fire-bursts boomed and flowered overhead. She swayed back, involuntarily, but in the moment before her shoulders brushed against him, a sudden waft of hot smoke stung her eyes. She turned away, blinking, and as she wiped them there was a commotion on the opposite side of the fire.

Through streaming eyes she saw a man duck under the rope cordon. A steward made a grab for him, but the man jinked around his outstretched hands like a rugby forward. He ran straight at the blazing stack of wood, and as Kate watched, still not believing what he was going to do, the man launched himself into it.

The steward's cry was drowned in the bang of another explosion overhead. He dodged back, throwing up his arm to shield himself as the bonfire collapsed in a frenzy of sparks. Behind him, the horrified, pale faces of the people standing by the ropes began to turn away, like lights blinking out. She heard screams above the clatter of the fireworks, but most of the crowd were unaware of what had happened. An *ahh* went up at another extravagant rocket-burst as stewards ran towards the fire.

Kate quickly turned away, clutching hold of Alex's arm.

'Let's go.'

Now more people were turning to look. A low murmur, almost a moan, went up from the crowd at some further movement from around the bonfire.

'Alex . . .'

He was still staring at the cluster of stewards. She tugged at him. He didn't move.

'Come on, Alex.'

His face was blank with shock as he let her lead him away. They pushed against the flow of a crowd that was now moving towards the fire to see what had happened. She almost lost her grip on Alex's arm, but then the crush thinned and they could move freely.

Kate gagged at the smell of cooked meat as they passed the hot dog and burger stalls. She held her breath until they had left them behind, and glanced at Alex. His eyes were unfocused. He walked loosely, as though he were concussed.

'Are you all right?'

Kate had to repeat the question before he responded. For a moment he looked at her without recognition, then he nodded.

'Yes, sorry, I . . .' His voice tailed off. In the distance they could hear sirens now, growing closer.

'Do you want to go for a drink?' Kate asked. They had reached the park exit. In the light from the street lamps she could see how pale his face was.

'No . . . no, I think I . . . I'd just like to go home.'

Kate flagged down a taxi. They rode in silence. Alex

seemed to have withdrawn into himself. He sat in a corner of the cab, staring out of the window. Lights from the street played over his face.

'Why would someone do that?' Kate said, unable to keep quiet any longer. She felt herself shaking as she spoke. For an awful moment, as the man had run for the flames, she'd thought it was some sort of terrorist attack. She'd been scared as well as shocked, and now reaction was setting in. 'Even if he wanted to kill himself, why pick such a – a *horrible* way?'

'Perhaps it didn't seem horrible to him.'

Alex spoke without turning from the window. His face was in shadow. Kate couldn't see his expression.

'But why do it like that? In front of all those people?'

She felt rather than saw him stir.

'It was a way of getting attention. Showing everyone he was there. Perhaps he wanted to hit out at them. Or at someone in particular. Like saying, "Look what I'm doing, this is your fault. You made me do this."' He was silent for a moment. 'Or perhaps he wanted to punish himself.'

Kate tried to shut out the memory of the steward's face, paralysed with horror and disbelief as he was forced to watch. She knew that no matter how bad her nightmares might be, his would be worse.

'It seems . . . I don't know. Selfish, somehow.'

'Selfish?' Alex had turned to look at her.

'Doing something like that in front of so many complete strangers. Not caring what it would do to them afterwards.'

'Would they have cared about him if he hadn't done it?'

'No, probably not, but—'

'So why should he care about them?'

The bitterness in his tone was like a rebuke. She didn't answer.

Alex sighed. 'I'm sorry.'

'It's all right.'

'No, I . . .' He gestured helplessly. 'It just got to me a bit, that's all.'

Kate was already regretting what she'd said. Alex rarely talked about his work, but she should have realized how this might have affected him.

Tentatively, she asked, 'Have you known someone like that?'

'No,' he said, looking back out of the window.

Lucy and Jack asked Kate over for Christmas Day, as they usually did.

'Ask Alex, too,' Lucy added. 'Unless you've both got other plans?'

Kate tried not to sound too evasive. 'I haven't. I'm not sure what Alex is doing, though.'

'Is he thinking about going to his parents'?'

'He might be, I don't know.'

'You don't *know*? Haven't you asked him?'

'Uh . . . No, not yet.'

'Not yet? Don't you think you're leaving it a bit late?'

Kate wouldn't meet Lucy's eye. 'I just haven't got round to it. Anyway, I expect he's already got his own plans.'

'And I expect he's thinking exactly the same about you. God, you're as bad as each other!' Lucy picked up her phone, looking exasperated. 'All right, what's his number? If you're not going to ask him, I will!'

'Don't you dare!'

Lucy smiled, the phone held ready.

Kate threw up her hands. 'All right, I'll ask him.'

'Now?' Lucy offered her the handset.

'Tomorrow,' Kate said firmly.

She told herself it was ridiculous to feel nervous, but that didn't make her feel any less so as she waited to broach the subject the next night. The theatre bar they were in was festooned with gaudy green and red baubles and tinsel. Christmas was inescapable, no matter how much you tried.

'Are you going to Cornwall for Christmas?' Kate asked finally, giving up any attempt at subtlety.

'Cornwall?'

'To your parents.'

'Oh! Oh . . . yes, I expect so.' He gave an unenthusiastic smile. 'Have to carve the turkey and listen to the Queen's Speech and everything.' He paused. 'What about you?'

Kate tried to sound unconcerned. 'Lucy and Jack have invited me over. They wondered if you wanted to go as well, if you hadn't already got something lined up. But I said you probably would have.'

'For Christmas Day?' He sounded surprised.

'Yes, but it's all right. We thought you'd be spending it with your family.'

The chime sounded for the start of the next act. 'We'd

better go back in,' Kate said, and blamed the flatness she felt on the poorness of the play.

It was two days later when Alex phoned.

'Looks like I've been ditched at Christmas,' he told her. 'My mother rang last night and asked if I minded if they went away instead. A last-minute offer from friends in Spain.'

Kate kept her voice neutral. 'So what will you do now?'

'Oh, I don't know. Probably just spend a quiet one on my own.'

Kate could almost hear Lucy's prompting, *Oh, for God's sake, just ask him!*

'You can still come over to Lucy and Jack's,' she said, trying to sound casual. 'I know they'd be pleased to see you.'

Christmas morning was bright with a crisp winter sun that struggled to melt the white frost garnishing the pavements. The big house smelled of roasting turkey and mulled wine. Nat King Cole vied for precedence with the TV as Jack took their coats. Alex had taken a carrier bag full of presents, and Emily and Angus delightedly shredded the garish paper from theirs, carried away more by the orgy of opening rather than the gifts themselves, which were an expensive but unimaginative doll and a toy car that Angus was too young to appreciate.

There was a bottle of whisky for Jack, Chanel perfume for Lucy. Her eyes widened when she saw it.

'Oh, my God, now that's what I call a present!'

She kissed Alex on the mouth. Kate felt a quick jab of

something that could almost have been jealousy, and then Alex came over to her.

'Happy Christmas.'

Almost shyly, he handed her a small parcel, and she suddenly wished she had bought him more than the bottle of Irish whiskey.

She took the parcel from him and unwrapped it, aware of the others watching her. Inside was a long box. Kate opened it and took out the plain gold chain and locket.

'I didn't know what size socks you took,' Alex said. The quip sounded rehearsed.

'It's beautiful,' Kate said. 'Thank you.'

She stepped forward and kissed him. The kiss was no longer than the one Lucy had given him moments before, but it was their first, and Kate felt acutely aware that Lucy and Jack were watching. When they moved apart she made a show of fastening the chain around her neck to hide her confusion.

Even though the treatments hadn't yet started, Kate had all but cut out alcohol completely. But it was Christmas Day, so she had a small glass of cava with lunch and then a cup of Jack's mulled wine during the afternoon. By early evening she felt pleasantly light-headed, and the pressure of anticipation that had been building in her all day finally found a focus.

She and Alex were in the kitchen, washing the stack of congealed dishes. She handed him a wet glass to dry, and as their hands touched, the thought came without warning.

Tonight.

Flustered, Kate turned away, briskly scrubbing at a greasy plate. She pushed all thought of the decision to one side, but the awareness remained for the rest of the evening: a faint breathlessness, a tensing in her lower stomach. And then she and Alex were saying goodnight to Lucy and Jack and climbing into the taxi, and all at once it confronted her with the suddenness of a slamming door.

Alex seemed to sense her tension. The atmosphere in the cab became strained. Familiar landmarks went past the windows like a countdown, and then the taxi was pulling into Kate's road. It stopped outside her flat.

Her heart thudded. The words felt clumsy in her mouth. 'Would you like to come in?'

She saw understanding dawn on his face. He looked away quickly.

'I'd, er . . . I'd better not. It's late.'

The rejection was so unexpected she felt nothing.

'Oh. OK,' she heard herself say, and then she was climbing out of the cab. The cold night air didn't penetrate any deeper than her skin. 'Goodnight, then.'

Alex didn't look at her. 'Goodnight.'

The taxi pulled away, leaving behind a fading blueness of exhaust. The street was deserted. Kate walked up her path. Her keys were in her hand, although she had no memory of taking them out. She reached up to unlock the front door, and then it hit her.

She squeezed her eyes tight, hand still outstretched towards the lock. For a long moment she stood, rigid, unable to make herself move. There was a miaow at her

178

feet. She looked down as Dougal twined himself around her ankles. The cat stared up at her, wide-eyed and indifferent.

'Happy Christmas, Dougal,' she said, and let them both into the empty flat.

12

The letter from the clinic arrived on a cold morning when the rain lashed against the windows and daylight was a sepia non-event. Kate knew what it would be, but that didn't make her any less nervous as she slit open the envelope, crested with the hospital's logo, and took out the letter.

The six-month quarantine was over, and Alex's latest blood tests were clear. The clinic wanted her to contact them to make arrangements for her first treatment.

Kate set down the letter on the breakfast bar. She didn't realize she was staring into space until the toast popped up, making her jump. Ignoring it, she went to her bag in the hallway and took out her diary. She had been keeping a temperature chart and testing her urine every day to time her menstrual cycle. It was so regular that she didn't really need to check when she was next due to ovulate, but she did so all the same.

It was just over two weeks.

Kate went back into the kitchen and absently scraped olive oil spread on to the toast. It had gone cold, and the first bite clogged in her mouth. She washed it down with tea and dropped the rest of her breakfast into the bin.

Although she wasn't supposed to make her appointment for the first treatment until her period had actually started, she couldn't wait. She called the clinic as soon as she arrived at work. The receptionist, polite, with only the barest trace of Birmingham in her voice, booked her in for a little over a fortnight's time and told Kate to telephone the day before to confirm. It was curiously undramatic, almost like making a dental appointment. The excitement was there, a taut anticipation, like sitting in a plane as it gathered speed to take off. But the knowledge of what she had to do first overlay any pleasure she felt.

She had continued to see Alex after Christmas, accepting the apology he had made on Boxing Day, a stammered account of over-indulgence and indigestion. She had even managed to convince herself that she had narrowly avoided a stupid mistake. But she had deliberately begun to tail off the number of times they met, preparing herself for the moment she now faced.

It didn't make it any easier.

Kate didn't phone him until that evening, feeling a sneaking relief that he had asked her not to ring him at work. His phone rang on, monotonously, and she was about to hang up when he answered.

'Yes?'

He sounded breathless, as though he'd been running.

'It's Kate, Alex.'

'Oh, hi! I wasn't expecting you to call tonight.'

She steeled herself against the pleasure in his voice. 'I've heard from the clinic. Your final blood tests are OK.'

'That's great! I knew they would be, but . . . well, you know.' He laughed, happy. 'So you can go ahead now?'

'Yes. The thing is . . .' She shut her eyes. 'I don't think we should see each other any more.'

There was a pause. 'Oh.'

'It isn't anything personal. But we always knew this was going to happen some time, and – and I think now's the time to do it. It's only going to complicate things if we don't, and I don't think that'll do either of us any good. Or the baby.'

The words sounded false.

'It's for the best . . . You can see that, can't you?' It was almost a plea.

'Uh . . . yeah, yes, I . . .' She heard him clear his throat. 'Yes, I suppose you're right.'

'I don't want you to think I'm not grateful for what you've done,' she said, knowing she was only making things worse but unable to stop. 'I'll send you a cheque for the rest of the money I owe you, and—'

'No!'

Kate stopped, surprised by the heat in his voice.

'No,' he went on, more calmly. 'I told you I didn't want paying.'

The conversation was over, but Kate couldn't bring herself to end it. She said the one thing she had determined not to say.

'I'm sorry.'

'Yeah.'

Kate kept the phone to her ear, waiting for him to say something else or break the connection. But the line remained silent.

She hung up.

Her dinner lay untouched on the coffee table. The music had finished playing, but she didn't get up to play anything else. She sat on the settee, her legs curled under her, idly stroking Dougal who was slumped asleep on her lap.

She told herself she had no reason to feel miserable. The whole point of what she was doing was because she didn't *want* a relationship. Alex had known from the start what the situation was. This would be *her* pregnancy, *her* baby. It would be cruel to let their relationship – or non-relationship, she thought, remembering Christmas – go on any longer.

With a sigh she slid Dougal on to a cushion and stood up. She picked up the plate of cold pasta and took it into the kitchen. As she was scraping it into the bin, the phone rang.

Expecting it to be Lucy, she went to answer it. 'Hello?'

'It's me. Alex.'

The sound of his voice brought a rush of mixed emotions.

He went on before she had time to sort them, not giving her a chance to speak.

'Look, I've been thinking. You're right, we should stop seeing each other, but, well, the thing is, I thought it would be nice to meet one last time. Perhaps after you've been to the clinic or something. You know, for a sort of farewell good-luck dinner.'

The words had come out in a rush. Now he stopped. When he spoke again it was more haltingly.

'It seems a shame to – to just end it like this. Without, well, without saying goodbye properly.'

His voice held a note of hope. Kate found her mood had lightened.

'Yes,' she said, smiling. 'I suppose it does.'

The horse chestnut tree by the clinic's gate was bare and black. Kate passed under it and walked up the drive. The gravel, dry and bleached the last time she had been, was dark and shiny with rain. Although it was only mid-afternoon, the day was reduced to a foggy twilight. Wind tugged at her hair and chapped her cheeks, and then the automatic doors slid open to let her pass into the warmth and light of the clinic.

The smiling receptionist took her name and asked her to take a seat. Kate sat by the window. Outside, the February bleakness blustered silently behind the double glazing. She unfastened her coat, already feeling the central heating dispel the chill.

After a few minutes a young nurse, smart in a tailored pale-grey and white uniform, appeared and led her over to a lift. Kate had only been on the clinic's ground floor before, but the first floor seemed little different. Their feet were silent on the wide, carpeted corridor. Lush plants in ornate pots provided a green contrast to the dead vegetation outside. Soft, piped classical music drifted from hidden speakers.

'The residential area's down there,' the nurse said, as they passed another corridor. Concealed lighting cast a gentle glow along the double row of wooden doors. It could have been a hotel.

'The rooms are all private, obviously,' the nurse added. 'There's a six-month waiting list for them, but I don't suppose you'll have got as far as thinking about the birth yet.'

Kate smiled dutifully. 'I'll get this bit over first.'

A woman in a crisp white maternity smock came towards them, the only other patient Kate had seen so far. Her stomach bulged, taut as a drum against the smock, but she was beautifully made up. She nodded in return to the nurse's hello and her glance took in Kate's damp hair, clothes and left hand. Her smile was perfunctory.

The nurse opened a door and stood back to let Kate enter. The room was windowless and small, but not claustrophobically so. A chair stood at one side, and a small rail at the far end held a row of coat-hangers. A dressing mirror was fastened to a partly open door, beyond which she could glimpse a sink and lavatory. Another door, closed, was opposite the chair.

'You'll find a gown and paper slippers for you to change into. There's no rush. Just press the buzzer when you're ready,' the nurse told her, indicating a button by the light switch, 'and someone will come in for you. OK?'

Kate said it was. She waited until the nurse had left with a final smile, then looked around. A single white gown was hanging on the rail. She went over and

185

touched it. It was made from soft paper, pliable as fabric. She remembered how the counsellor at the other clinic had told her that there would be no need to take off her clothes. The Wynguard Clinic clearly took a different view.

She sat on the edge of the chair. Her dislike of hospitals made her shiver. Turning, she caught sight of herself in the mirror, nervously perched with her thighs pressed together, her hands clamped between them. She stood up and began to undress.

Kate didn't hear any buzzer when she pressed the button, but one must have sounded because almost immediately the inner door was opened. The same nurse smiled at her.

'We just need to do a blood test to make sure you're ovulating,' the nurse said.

Kate looked straight ahead as the nurse took a blood sample. She had checked her temperature and urine herself that morning, and was as sure as she could be that she'd got the timing right. Even so, she was still anxious to have it confirmed.

The nurse put a sticking plaster on her arm and stepped away. 'OK, Dr Janson will be along in a few minutes.' She went out. The piped classical music drifted on in the background without relieving the loneliness of the empty white room. Kate swung her legs off the couch. The paper sheet covering it slid around slightly on the underlying vinyl. She looked down at her feet as they dangled above the ground, ridiculous in the elasti-cated paper slippers. She wondered if she would have had to wear them at a less expensive clinic.

The door opened and Dr Janson walked in. The nurse followed her. Dr Janson's hair was pinned up in a thick French pleat, and she somehow managed to look immaculate even in a white lab coat.

'Hello,' she greeted Kate brightly. 'Everything all right?'

'I think so, yes.'

'Good. Well, you'll be glad to know that the timing's fine. You've started ovulating, so we can go ahead with the first treatment as planned.'

Dr Janson smiled. She was wearing a pair of gold-rimmed glasses. She looked like a model from an optician's catalogue, Kate thought.

'Nervous?' the doctor asked. Kate nodded. 'There's no need to be. It isn't much different to having a smear. It won't take long, so just lie back on the couch and try to relax.'

That was easier said than done, but Kate did her best. She stared resolutely at the white ceiling, trying not to think as she heard the snap of surgical gloves.

'Can you raise your legs a little more, please? That's it.'

She made herself concentrate on the music. It was familiar. She tried to place it, tensing as she felt the cold touch of a speculum.

'OK, I'm going to introduce the catheter now. You'll be able to feel it but it won't hurt, so just lie nice and still.'

There was no real discomfort, but Kate's hands were still clenched and white. Vivaldi, she thought, staring at a hairline crack in the otherwise pristine ceiling. The

Four Seasons. *Le Quattro Stagioni.* But which movement, Spring or Winter?

At the end of the couch, Dr Janson straightened. 'Right. All done.'

Kate lifted her head to see the nurse gathering together the equipment in a stainless steel tray. Dr Janson smiled down at her.

'How do you feel? OK? Just lie still for a few minutes, then you can get dressed.'

'So I can carry on as normal?'

'Completely as normal. I'll see you tomorrow for the second insemination, and then that's it for this cycle. It's just a matter now of keeping your fingers crossed and waiting to see if you have your period. If you do, then we'll try again next month.' She gave Kate another smile. 'The nurse will bring you a cup of tea or coffee, so just relax for a few minutes. There's no rush.'

She left. The nurse asked Kate what she wanted to drink and then left also, carrying the tray containing the instruments and the doctor's latex gloves, crumpled on the gleaming metal like a beached jellyfish.

Kate lay back on the couch.

I've done it!

The thought was a silent, exultant cry. She was committed now. Even if she didn't become pregnant this cycle, there was always the next. Or the one after that. She had finally made the leap. Now it was simply a matter of continuing.

The nurse returned, carrying a china cup and saucer and a plate of biscuits.

'Another five minutes and you can get dressed,' she said.

Kate pushed herself upright as the woman set the tea and biscuits on the table at the bottom of the couch. She turned to go but then bent and picked up something from the floor.

'Is this yours?'

She held out the gold chain and locket Alex had bought Kate for Christmas. Kate's hand went to her throat.

'I must have caught it when I was getting changed. Thanks.'

Though the chain was light, Kate felt a heaviness at its cold touch as she fastened it back around her neck.

Subdued music, played on unfamiliar stringed instruments, was playing in the Japanese restaurant. The dining room was dark, but each table was lit by two fat candles so that walking down the aisles between them was like being in a temple. The air smelled of lemon and griddled seafood.

Alex was already at the table when Kate arrived. She had thought it best if they made their separate ways there, rather than share a taxi as they had in the past. The candlelight gave his face a melancholy cast as he stared into it, reminding Kate with a pang of the first night they had gone to Lucy and Jack's. Then he looked up and saw her, and she pushed the memory away.

'Sorry I'm late,' she said, as the white-shirted waiter pulled back her chair. 'The taxi didn't turn up, so I had to order another.'

'That's OK.' Alex smiled at her. 'You look . . . ah, you look great.'

Her hair was up in a chignon, and she wore a plain black long-sleeved dress. The locket hung around her bare neck. 'Thank you.'

They fell silent.

'So—' they began at the same time, and stopped.

'Sorry. You first,' Kate said.

'I was just going to ask how it went.' He lowered his voice slightly. 'You know, at the, er, at the clinic.'

She had finished her second insemination the day before. 'Oh, OK. I've just got to wait and see what happens now.'

'Well. I hope . . .' Alex struggled. 'Well, you know.'

She nodded. 'Thanks.'

The bubble of tension around them seemed to tighten, choking any chance of conversation. Kate looked at the other tables, islands of intimacy with their burning candles. The conversations were low but animated, a murmuring counterpoint to the tinkle of glasses. No one seemed miserable. She drew a deep breath.

'Perhaps this wasn't such a good idea.'

He looked hurt. 'Why?'

'It just might have been better to leave it as it was.' She shrugged. 'This is only dragging things out, isn't it?'

Alex nudged the warm wax pooled at the base of the candle with his finger. He didn't look at her. 'Do you want to go?'

'No,' she said, after a moment.

The waiter returned. Giving a short bow, he handed them each a menu.

'They serve sake. I'm sticking with water but why don't you have a flask?' Kate asked brightly.

Alex shrugged. 'OK.' He sounded apathetic.

They ordered but lapsed into silence again once the waiter had gone. There was a disturbance on the other side of the restaurant, where the head waiter, distinguished by a black shirt instead of a white one, was having a controlled but heated debate with the occupants of a table hidden by a bamboo screen. Finally, with a terse nod, he strode towards the kitchen. The distraction over, Kate tried to think of something to say.

'So how's work?' she asked.

'Oh . . . OK, thanks.'

She cast around for another conversational gambit, but they all evaded her. The waiter arrived with a truncated flask of sake and a bottle of mineral water. He filled their glasses and withdrew.

'Well. Cheers,' Kate said, raising hers. The bubbles from the water tickled her tongue. She noticed that Alex hadn't drunk from his glass.

'Look, Kate . . .' he began slowly, and she stiffened at the seriousness of his tone. 'I just wanted to say . . . I'm glad . . . uh, glad it was me.'

He broke off, his voice husky, and looked away quickly.

Kate felt her eyes sting, but she was saved from having to respond by the return of the waiter. He put a metal warming tray in the centre of their table and lit the four alcohol lamps inside with a taper he first held in a candle flame. Another waiter appeared and set out a series of small steaming bowls on top of the tray. They bowed again and left.

'Smells delicious,' Kate said. Her appetite had vanished.

Avoiding each other's eyes, they served themselves the subtly scented meat and vegetables. They both reached at the same time for a bowl of rice. Kate smiled and motioned for Alex to take it first, and as she did so there was another commotion from the other side of the restaurant.

The head waiter was standing beside the screened table again. This time he was shaking his head emphatically, talking in a low but firm tone against the more strident voice that was raised against him. Kate couldn't make out what either was saying, but the hidden speaker grew louder and more angry, and there was just time to register that the man's voice was familiar when there was the scrape of chairs being pushed back.

The screen shook as the couple who had been sitting behind it stood up. The girl was heavily made up, large-breasted and drunk. The man with her had his back to Kate but then he turned, and she felt a shock of recognition.

She dropped her gaze and stared down at her plate.

'Kate? What's the matter?' Alex asked. She shook her head without looking up. The exit was behind her, she realized. The couple would have to go right past.

'Are you OK?'

She nodded. Now she could hear them approaching, his heavier footsteps chased by the staccato tap of the girl's heels. She lifted her chopsticks, made a show of interest in the food.

The footsteps stopped by their table.

'Well, fancy seeing you here.'

She looked up. Paul had halted by the table. He had a lopsided smirk on his face as he stared down at her. The girl stood behind him, looking on with blowsy confusion.

'Hello, Paul.'

Even in the candlelight, she could see how flushed he was. His face was bloated and puffy. He looked from her to Alex.

'Aren't you going to introduce us?'

She felt surprisingly calm. 'Alex, this is Paul.'

Alex gave him an uncertain smile. Paul's grin was unpleasant.

'You haven't introduced us to your friend,' Kate said.

'Sorry, no, I haven't, have I? Forgetting my manners.' Paul motioned with his head at the girl, who was swaying with the effort of standing still. 'This is Kim. Kim, meet Kate. Kate's an "old friend" of mine. This is Alex, her "new friend". So what do you do, Alex?'

Alex glanced hesitantly at Kate. 'I'm, uh, I'm a psychologist.'

'A psychologist!' Paul's voice was growing louder. Kate was aware of heads turning in their direction. 'Don't tell me you're finally seeing a shrink, Kate? Or is this just a social thing? One way of getting treatment without paying for it, I suppose.'

More people were turning to look now. Kate felt a

cold detachment. 'You were on your way out. Don't let us keep you.'

'Yeah, I'm on my way out, all right.' His smile was a thin mask. 'Freud here doesn't know what he's letting himself in for, does he? You watch your back, mate,' he said to Alex, without taking his eyes from Kate. 'Little Katie here's always mixing business with pleasure. Until she's got what she wants out of you, and then boom! You're out!'

Alex's face was pale except for patches of colour on his cheeks. 'I think you'd better g-go.'

He said it quietly, and the syncopation was barely audible, but Paul picked up on it.

'You thu-think I'd buh-buh-better guh-go? Why, so you can psychoanalyse her with your dick?'

The surrounding tables had fallen quiet. Kate saw the head waiter coming towards them. Alex clenched his fists on the table.

'Ignore him,' she said, but now both men were focused on each other. Alex seemed to be almost quivering.

'G-get out!'

Paul leaned towards him. 'Fuh-fuh-fuck off.'

'Alex, no!' Kate said, reaching across to restrain him as he began to stand. He glanced at her, and while he was still half in, half out of his seat, Paul hit him.

The punch caught him on the cheek and knocked him sprawling over the table. It tipped up, toppling Alex off in a cascade of candles, food and breaking crockery. The noise was appalling as dishes, trays and glasses crashed to the floor. In the hush that followed, a plate spun lazily, spiralling to a gradual standstill. For a moment

194

everything was still, then Kate was out of her seat and kneeling beside Alex as white-shirted waiters were converging on them from everywhere.

Alex let her help him sit up. His mouth was bleeding. Broken plates crunched underneath him.

'Are you all right?' she asked. Dumbly he put his hand to his mouth. He blinked, staring at the blood on his fingers, and then glared up at Paul. Kate felt him tense.

'Don't, Alex! Please!'

She kept tight hold of his shoulders. Some of the tension went out of them, and then other hands were helping him to his feet.

Paul was surrounded by waiters. He looked surprised by what he'd done as he allowed himself to be hustled towards the exit. The girl, who hadn't spoken throughout, tottered along behind on her high heels. Kate saw Alex staring after him with a look in his eyes she hadn't seen before. Then Paul was roughly pushed out of the room, and the doors closed and shut him from view.

One waiter brushed the worst of the debris from Alex's clothes while another neatly stamped out the small puddles of blue flame that had spilled from the alcohol lamps. The table was swiftly righted and Kate and Alex were politely ushered along the aisles to the door as waiters set about removing the mess. Some people stared openly at them as they passed, others ostentatiously kept their eyes averted.

There was no sign of Paul or the girl in the foyer. The head waiter solicitously sat Alex in a chair and had hot towels brought to wipe him down. Alex held a napkin to his mouth, saying nothing. A taxi was ordered, and the head waiter smilingly refused Kate's offer to pay for the meal and damage. He was polite but clearly wanted them to leave. Kate glanced back into the dining room as the door swung open. Their table was already fully set and covered with a fresh white cloth, candles glowing sedately as though nothing had happened.

She tried to persuade Alex to let the taxi go straight to his home, but he refused.

'I'd rather take you home first,' he said. His voice was thickened slightly by the swelling on the side of his mouth where Paul had hit him. Something in his tone told Kate not to press.

Neither of them spoke again during the journey. Alex sat bunched in the corner, staring out of the window. Occasionally he dabbed at his mouth with the blood-stained napkin the head waiter had insisted he take. Kate sat at the other end. There could have been a glass wall between them.

The taxi pulled up outside her flat. Alex continued to stare through the window as she opened the door.

'I'm sorry,' she said. He nodded, still unable to look at her. Abruptly, she turned to the taxi driver.

'We'll both get out here, thanks.'

Alex looked startled. 'No, I'll go home—'

'No, you won't. The least I can do is let you get properly cleaned up.'

'No, really—' he began, but she was already on the pavement, the taxi door standing open as she paid the driver. After a moment Alex got out.

He waited behind her, silent, as she unlocked her flat and led him up the stairs.

'The bathroom's through there. If you want to change, I've got a T-shirt that'll probably fit you.'

Leaving him, she went into the kitchen and set the coffee percolator on to boil. Then, rummaging in a drawer until she found a baggy T-shirt, she went to the bathroom and knocked on the door. Alex opened it a crack. He had taken off his shirt and through the gap in the doorway she could see how white his skin was. The silver chain lay pale around his neck.

'Can't promise much for the style,' she said, passing him the T-shirt. He smiled, a little nervously, as he took it.

Kate went back to the kitchen. The coffee hadn't started to bubble. She set out two cups. Then, taking a tumbler from a cupboard, she went into the lounge and poured a large brandy into it.

There was a noise from the passage. Kate turned as Alex came in, pausing uncertainly in the doorway. It was strange seeing him in her lounge, wearing her T-shirt. She held out the tumbler.

'I thought you could do with this. Coffee's on its way.'

He accepted the glass with mumbled thanks. Kate sat in one of the armchairs. Alex went to the other. He took a sip of brandy and winced. Gingerly he touched his mouth again.

'How is it?' she asked.

'OK.'

She looked down at her hands. 'I'm so sorry about what happened tonight. You got dragged into a situation that wasn't your problem.'

'There's no need to explain.'

'Yes, there is. I owe you that much.' More than that, she realized she wanted to tell him. 'I used to be in a relationship with Paul. We worked at the same agency, until things got . . . complicated.'

Alex frowned into his glass. 'Complicated how?'

'Paul was the agency's marketing director. Believe it or not, he can be very charming when he wants to be. I was the new girl, and I suppose I was flattered when he took an interest. And gullible, because it turned out he took an interest in half the other girls at the agency. As well as anybody else who took his fancy.'

Kate paused, her mouth dry. She could feel Alex watching her and forced herself to continue.

'I didn't realize what was going on until after I'd moved in with him. I thought that meant some sort of commitment, but for Paul it was just a convenient arrangement. He'd stay out all night, or come home reeking of perfume. Whenever I'd confront him he'd deny it, and like a fool I'd believe him. I *wanted* to believe him. And then . . .'

'What?' Alex said, when she stopped.

'This is . . . it's difficult for me to talk about it.' She gave a nervous smile. 'I haven't told anyone else, only Lucy.'

'You don't have to tell me.'

Kate looked at him, but there was no doubt in the blue eyes. She took a deep breath before going on.

'Paul . . . He gave me an STD. Chlamydia, nothing horrendous, it was easily treated with antibiotics. But that was the last straw. Even though he was the only person I could have got it from, he denied it. Said he must have caught it from me, that I'd been unfaithful. We both knew that wasn't true, but that's what Paul does. He doesn't do blame, at least not for himself.'

She realized she was plucking at the chair arm and clasped her hands on her lap.

'To cut a long story short, we had a blazing row and he threw me out. We were living at his house, so there wasn't much I could do. I didn't have anywhere else to go, so I phoned Lucy. She and Jack had only just had Emily, but they let me stay with them until I found somewhere. It was . . . a really bad time. I felt so ashamed and bloody *stupid*. I couldn't go back to my job, not with Paul there, so . . . Well, I suppose I had a sort of breakdown. I cut myself off from all my friends, except Lucy. I was a mess.'

Alex was sitting forward, listening intently. 'You got through it, though.'

'That was down to Lucy and Jack again. Lucy fixed me up with some freelance PR work with someone Jack knew. One thing led to another, and gradually I started building up a client list and started my own agency.' She smiled awkwardly. 'Instant work therapy.'

It hadn't been anything like so straightforward at the time, but she didn't want to dwell on it. Telling Alex had been hard, but she was glad she had. It felt good to get it out in the open, like setting down a burden she'd forgotten she was carrying.

Alex looked down at his own hands. 'What about Paul?'

'I'm not with you.'

'I got the impression there was something else going on between you. Some sort of grudge.'

You could say that. Kate told him about winning the Kingsmere Trust account and how Paul had reacted afterward. 'That's what you ended up in the middle of tonight,' she finished. 'I'm really sorry.'

Alex said nothing. His face was unreadable, but there was a stillness about him Kate found unnerving. She was beginning to wonder if telling him had been a mistake when a smell she'd been peripherally aware of finally registered.

'God, the coffee!'

She leaped from her chair and ran to the kitchen. The odour of burned coffee became much stronger. The espresso percolator was blackened around its base. It was hissing threateningly as Kate turned off the gas. She picked it up by the black plastic handle and hastily set it down again, shaking her hand.

'Damn!'

Heat radiated from the metal as Kate used a cloth to pick it up this time. She turned a tap on and tentatively held the percolator under the stream of water. The sudden burst of steam almost made her drop it.

'I'd just leave it to cool. You'll crack the metal doing it that way.'

She hadn't heard Alex come in. Kate poured a little coffee into one of the cups, and wrinkled her nose at the sharp odour. She set the percolator back on the cooker.

'Looks like coffee's off. I've got instant, though. Or tea?'

'It's OK. I ought to phone for a taxi, really.'

His edginess was contagious. 'Whatever you like.' Turning away, she went to pour the coffee down the sink and, without thinking, touched the hot metal of the percolator. With a cry she snatched her hand away and boiling coffee splashed out as the percolator fell over. Kate jumped back but the scalding liquid spattered her bare wrists, and then Alex was beside her, steering her to the sink.

'Here.' He was spinning the cold tap on full. 'Put them under.'

She recoiled from the cold water, but he kept both her arms in the stream, turning them so that the water gushed over her hand and wrists. Red patches had already formed where the coffee had landed, and Alex kept them under the tap until her entire forearms started to ache from the cold.

'I think that'll do it,' she said.

Alex shook his head, still holding them in the icy water. 'Not yet. If you keep them in long enough it'll stop them from blistering.' She glanced at him. He stood pressed against her, his hands gripping her arms at the elbow, face intent. At last he turned off the tap.

'Is there a clean towel?'

'In that drawer.' Kate motioned with her head. Alex took one out and gently dabbed her arms dry. The livid patches were not as angry as they had been and no longer hurt. Her arms felt numb from elbow to fingertips.

'Have you got any aloe vera?'

'No, but there's some antiseptic cream.'

Alex gave a terse shake of his head. 'How about petroleum jelly?'

'There's some in the bathroom.'

'What about painkillers? Paracetemol, something like that?'

'It doesn't hurt.'

'It will, once the numbness has worn off.'

'It's OK, really.' Her arms were beginning to tingle, but now she'd started treatment at the clinic, she didn't want to take anything she didn't have to.

Alex fetched the petroleum jelly and smoothed it on to one burned hand and wrist. She watched him, touched and amused.

'I thought you were a psychologist, not a burns specialist.'

He kept his eyes on what he was doing. 'You'd be surprised what you pick up.'

He gently smeared gel on to her other arm. His fingers were light on the tender skin. 'There. That should take the worst of the sting from it.'

He was standing close in front of her.

'Thank you,' she said, and without planning it leaned forward and kissed him.

He stiffened. Kate could feel his sudden tension and for a second thought he was going to pull away. Then, hesitantly, he relaxed.

The contact between them was only slight, little more than a brushing of lips, and Kate dimly wondered what she was doing. She closed her eyes. She could taste the brandy on his mouth, feel the slight hardness where his lip was swollen. She touched it with the tip of her tongue.

His breath feathered against her skin. She kissed him again. Moving closer, she brought her arms up around his neck. His went tentatively around her. She kissed him more deeply, feeling him begin to respond. His arms tightened around her. She dug her fingers into his hair, forgetting the pain of the burns. He pressed himself against her and she drew away, leading him towards the hallway.

Alex seemed almost drugged as they went into the bedroom. It was dark, with only the light from the kitchen spilling through the open door. She kissed him again, stroking his back. When she slid a hand inside his T-shirt she felt him give a small quiver. She took hold of one of his hands and moved it to her breast. He cupped it lightly, and she felt a quiver spread through him. He was trembling as she undid his belt, then the top button of his trousers. She could feel him suck in a breath as the backs of her hands touched his bare flesh. He gave a low moan and clutched her more tightly, fumbling at her dress. She reached behind to help, stepping out of it as the dress tumbled slowly to her ankles.

He stared at her, breathing heavily, and then they were kissing. She dragged off his T-shirt, scarcely aware of it ripping as it came over his head and shoulders. His skin was hot against hers. He groped behind her, fumbling at the catch of her bra. She unfastened it for him and tugged his trousers over his hips. He wasn't fully erect, so she took hold of him, squeezing lightly. He gave a low gasp. Kate pushed down her own pants and stepped towards the bed, pulling him on top of her. She snaked her legs around him, and suddenly he was thrusting at her, head arching back as he gave an inarticulate cry. He hung above her for a moment, and then the tension went out of him. Kate stroked the back of his neck as he buried his face against her, trying to adjust to the abruptness of it being over.

After a while she felt him stir. He pushed himself off her and lay on his back.

'Sorry.'

Kate could barely see him in the darkness. 'What for?'

'You know. Being so quick.'

'It doesn't matter.' She meant it. Her initial disappointment had ebbed now.

'I'm not . . . I'm not very experienced.' The confession was blurted out.

Kate hid her surprise. She rolled on to her side, so that her body was touching his.

'That's nothing to be ashamed of.'

She put her hand on his chest. She could feel his heart beating under it. The chain he wore around his neck felt cold as she stroked her fingers through the hairs.

'Sorry,' he said again, and Kate lightly tapped him.

'Stop it. There's no need to apologize.'

Turning, she reached for the bedside table and switched on the lamp. Blinking in the sudden light, she looked back at Alex. His eyes were wet, she saw with alarm.

'Hey, come on!' She moved so she was lying half on top of him, propping herself up on her elbows. Her breasts brushed against him. She smiled. 'It wasn't *that* bad, was it?'

He smiled back but didn't meet her eyes. 'No. It's just that . . . I'm not very good at this sort of thing.'

'You seemed OK to me.'

He gave her a quick look and, with sudden intuition, Kate understood much of his past nervousness. The tenderness she felt for him closed up her throat.

'What's this?' she said, deliberately changing the subject. She fingered the disc hanging on the chain around his neck.

'It's just a St Christopher.'

Kate casually slid one of her legs over him as she examined it. The medal was about two centimetres in diameter, and the design of the man carrying the child across the water was crude and stylized, not at all obvious at first glance.

'It looks old,' she said, lifting it from his chest. It was thick and heavy.

'Yeah, I suppose it is.' He looked down at it. 'It was my grandmother's.'

'Did she leave it to you?'

Alex paused before answering. 'No, she gave it to me before she died. She said it'd bring me good luck.'

Kate laid it back on his chest. 'And has it?' She moved her leg gently up and down.

'I, uh, well, yes, I suppose it has.'

He was smiling now. Kate could feel him beginning to harden again under her thigh. The St Christopher was a cold disc between her breasts as she slid on top of him. 'It's a good job you said that.'

13

At times during the next two weeks Kate would feel an almost superstitious distrust of being so happy. It would come over her without warning, a pessimistic conviction that this couldn't last, that there would be a price to pay. Then the feeling would pass, a brief cloud over the sun, and she would be caught up again in the pleasure of the present.

The sex had quickly improved. Alex was an enthusiastic if not experienced lover, and they coupled like teenagers until both of them were sore and aching. They didn't go out often. Kate would hurry home at night and start preparing dinner. Alex would go to her flat straight from work and they would cook the meal together in an intimate awareness of the other's presence. Sometimes they would prolong the anticipation until afterwards, but often their clothes would be scattered over the floor, and they would make love while the pots bubbled unnoticed on the cooker.

There were times, though, when Alex would fall into a quiet mood, lost in some internal world. Kate liked watching him then, seeing his face take on an unguarded, almost melancholy cast. But while she enjoyed being able to study him in those moments, there was also a sense of exclusion. Once he looked up, without warning, and caught her watching him. For an instant his face seemed blank of recognition, and in a weightless second of panic Kate felt a sudden conviction that she didn't know him, that this was some stranger.

Then he blinked and smiled, and was Alex again. 'What?' he said.

Kate went over and hugged him. 'You were miles away. What were you thinking about?'

'Nothing much. Just miles away, like you said.'

The moment had passed, but not without leaving a faint trace of disquiet. To dispel it, Kate asked something she had been meaning to for days.

'Why don't we go to your flat sometime?'

Alex hesitated. 'Why?'

'Because I'd like to see where you live. You know, see if you're messy or tidy. What sort of books you've got.'

'I can tell you.'

'It isn't the same. What's the matter, are you hiding something there?'

It was meant as a joke, but Alex didn't laugh. 'No, of course not.'

She felt a rekindling of unease. 'Why not, then?' she asked, serious now.

'It's just . . .' He was frowning, not looking at her. Then he sighed. 'Well, it's a bit of a dump, that's all. I haven't bothered doing anything to it, because I wasn't planning on staying there very long. I'd be embarrassed for you to see it.'

The stirrings of alarm that Kate had begun to feel receded. 'There's no need to be. I wouldn't mind.'

'No, but I would.' He smiled. 'If you want to go there, we can. But give me a few days to tidy up first, OK?'

She grinned. 'OK.' Relieved, she put it from her mind. She wasn't in any hurry.

Besides, she enjoyed being in her flat with Alex. The first weekend there they had spent almost entirely in bed. They had ventured into the kitchen occasionally to prepare a snack, and once they had taken the quilt into the lounge, where they spread it on the floor next to the fire to watch *Breakfast at Tiffany's* while rain lashed the window and the gas flames licked hungrily at the decorative pebbles. The familiar surroundings, which had once felt so lonely, now seemed intimate and cosy. Often they would just lie and talk. Alex was a good listener, and she found herself opening up to him more and more, sometimes about incidents she had almost forgotten. One evening she told him about going alone to the cinema when she was a little girl. She intended the story to be funny, but Alex seemed to see past the humour.

'How long ago did your parents die?' he asked, when she had finished. They were lying naked on the settee, Kate's head resting in the crook of his arm.

She counted back, tracing a pattern on his chest. 'My mother died when I was nineteen. My father died a year before that, just after I went to university.'

'That was very young. For you and them, I mean.'

'They didn't have me until they were in their forties. I don't think I was planned.'

'Do you miss them?'

The question sobered her. She found she couldn't give a simple answer. 'I'd have liked them to meet you,' she said. Alex didn't comment. Kate watched the hairs on his chest spring back up in the wake of her fingers. 'No, I don't suppose I do miss them, in the conventional sense. Not in the way I'd miss someone like Lucy. I loved them, and it was a jolt when they died, but we didn't see much of each other once I'd left home. And we didn't know what to talk about when we did.'

'Didn't you get on with them?'

It wasn't something Kate let herself think about very often. 'It wasn't so much that we didn't get on. It was more that we just didn't understand each other. We didn't seem to have anything in common. I always felt I was never who or what they wanted me to be.' She gave a quiet laugh. 'I sometimes wondered if there wasn't a mix-up at the hospital and they'd been given the wrong baby. They'd wanted a boy, for a start, so I was a big disappointment all round.'

'Did they actually say that?'

'Not in so many words. But my mother sometimes acted like she resented me, because I wasn't the boy she'd wanted to give my father. Everything had to fall in with what he wanted. It was like there was only one person in the house who counted. He expected to have his own way, and my mother saw her role as making sure he got it. And I was expected to go along with that as well. It was probably a relief for everybody when I left home.' She looked up at Alex. 'What about you?'

209

'Me?'

'What was your childhood like?'

She felt him shift slightly.

'Nothing exceptional. Abroad every year for holidays, bikes at Christmas. Boringly normal, I suppose.'

'How about your brothers? Did you get on with them?'

'Most of the time. I mean, there was a bit of tormenting went on, with me being the youngest, but it was always good-natured. They were quite protective, really.'

Kate fingered the solid coldness of the St Christopher on his chest. She could feel it sometimes during their lovemaking, its coolness tracing rhythmic patterns on her breasts. 'Tell me about your grandmother.'

'My gran? What about her?'

'Just what she was like. You said you were close.'

Alex was quiet for so long she thought he wasn't going to reply. 'She was great. If I'd hurt myself, or got in trouble, or . . . or whatever, I could always go to my gran and tell her, and she'd listen. And when I'd done something wrong, she'd tell me, but she'd never get cross, or shout or hit me. She was always there.'

He stared at the ceiling. His eyes were bright.

'How old were you when she died?' Kate asked.

'Fifteen. She gave me this,' he touched the St Christopher, 'the week before she died. It'd belonged to my grandad. It was almost like she knew she wasn't going to be there to look out for me for much longer.'

He stopped. 'You were saying about your parents,' he went on in a brisker tone. 'Did you get on any better with your mother after your father died?'

Kate let him change the subject. 'Not really. I hoped she might come out of his shadow, you know? Start living her own life. But she never did. It was like she lost interest in everything. Every time I came home from university, I could see how she'd deteriorated. It was horrible. It was like she was winding down, as though she'd no reason to carry on living without him. She kept all his clothes and talked about him as if he was still there. She'd even cook his favourite meals, even things she didn't like, right up to when she died.' She paused, remembering. 'I still can't make up my mind if it was love or not. It never seemed healthy. I always told myself I'd never let anyone dominate me like that.'

'You nearly did, though.'

She glanced at Alex. Two patches of colour burned on his cheeks.

'You're not jealous of Paul, are you?' she asked.

He tried to sound dismissive. 'No, of course not.' He avoided her eyes. 'I just don't like to think of you with someone like that, that's all.'

Part amused, part annoyed, Kate wriggled around until she was facing him. 'That's not a very professional attitude, is it? I thought psychologists were above such things?'

'Perhaps I'm not a very good psychologist.'

She had the impression that he had changed his mind at the last second about what he was going to say.

'I'd have thought you'd be pretty good,' she said. 'You're a good listener. That's a lot of what psychology's about, isn't it?'

'Oh, yeah. There's plenty of listening, but that's about all. Psychologists don't actually *do* anything.'

His tone was uncharacteristically bitter. Wanting to pull him out of his suddenly dark mood, Kate bent her head and lightly nipped the flesh of his chest in her teeth.

'I'd better keep you busy, then.'

Lucy called later that same evening.

'Hi, Kate,' she said cheerfully. 'Just thought I'd give you a ring and make sure you weren't dead.'

Kate felt a prod of conscience. She hadn't spoken to Lucy since telling her she was meeting Alex for the final time. She glanced involuntarily towards the bedroom.

'Sorry, I've been meaning to, but—'

'I know, I know, you've got a lot on at work. Never mind. Anyway, what happened with Alex? Did you meet him?'

'Uh . . . yes.'

'How did it go?'

'Oh . . . OK.'

'So that's it, then? You told him you're not going to see him any more?' Lucy's disapproval was obvious.

'Er . . . actually he's here now.'

There was a pause.

'Oh, really? The farewell dinner didn't go quite as planned, I take it?'

Kate could almost hear her smirking. 'Not exactly.'

'Well, I *was* going to invite you over for lunch tomorrow, but I dare say now you'll be busy,' Lucy said sweetly. 'Unless you wanted to bring Alex as well?'

'Thanks, but I think we'll pass.'

'I thought you might. Well, give Alex my love – if you've any left – and I'll talk to you next week. Oh, and Kate?'

'What?'

Lucy was laughing. 'Don't forget to use a contraceptive.'

The irony of her timing wasn't lost on Kate. She wasn't sure if waiting until she'd started the donor insemination treatment before sleeping with Alex qualified as perversity or just karma. Whichever, it changed everything.

Kate knew there were issues that had to be faced: about the clinic, about her relationship with Alex. But she couldn't bring herself to worry about them. Her life, at last, seemed to have achieved its natural, preordained balance. She felt a *rightness* about it all, a certainty that this was how things were meant to be, that now everything would fall into place.

It seemed inevitable that she would miss her period.

She waited several days before mentioning it to Alex. 'You said when I first met you that you liked the idea of fatherhood without the responsibility,' she said. 'Do you still feel the same way?'

They lay folded around each other in bed. His arm was draped over her in the darkness.

'Why?'

She toyed with the St Christopher on his chest, winding the silver chain around her finger, then off. 'It isn't definite, but I went to the doctor's today for a pregnancy test.'

She waited for what seemed an age.

'When will you know?'

'In a few days, when the blood test comes back.'

She could have just bought a home urine-testing kit. But even if it had been positive, she wouldn't have entirely believed it. She didn't want to risk the disappointment of making a mistake. Having it confirmed by a doctor would somehow make it more official. More real.

Kate looked up towards Alex's face, almost invisible in the dark. 'I just want you to know that you're not under any obligation. This – us – doesn't change anything.'

'It does for me.'

His voice was throaty. Kate let go of the chain. Unable to speak, she laid her head on his chest, glad he couldn't see the dampness on her cheeks.

She was never sure why she didn't tell him exactly when the result of the test would be through. The doctor had told her which day to phone in, but something made her hold that back from Alex. She told herself that she wanted to surprise him, to let him believe they wouldn't know until later in the week. But she knew there was a more selfish reason.

She wanted to keep that much for herself.

On the morning she was to phone for the result they ate breakfast together at her cramped breakfast bar in the kitchen. Alex had to leave before she did, and Kate kissed him and watched him go down the stairs to the front door. At the bottom he turned and waved, and seeing him there, grinning, his dark hair tufted, Kate almost gave in and told him. Then he went out and closed the door, and the chance was gone.

She went to work in a strange mood of hope and near terror, the two blending until they became indistinguishable. She was hardly aware of her surroundings, getting on and off the tube automatically, letting her body take her through the familiar routine without consciously thinking about it. Only when she came up from the Underground into the morning furore outside King's Cross was she jolted from her internal world as a fire engine blared past in a cacophony of noise and colour. Looking after it, Kate felt a disquieting tug of déjà vu. But even as she tried to grasp the memory, it drifted out of reach, insubstantial as smoke.

She'd been told to call for the results after lunch. She waited until half past two and then phoned the doctor's surgery. The receptionist took her details and put her on hold. A reedy recording of classical piano came down the line. Kate tensed when it stopped, but it had only reached the end of its loop. A second later it started up again, as bland as the chime from an ice-cream van. The tune played through twice, then was abruptly cut off.

'Miss Powell?' the receptionist's voice broke in. 'Your test's positive.'

Kate's mouth had dried. 'Positive? So I'm pregnant?'

'According to this.' There was a pause before the woman added, 'Congratulations.'

It was said without real feeling, but Kate didn't care. She thanked the receptionist and rang off. She sat back, examining how she felt. No different and yet, at the same time, utterly changed. An emotion so strong rose up in her she couldn't have put a name to it.

All at once, the need to tell Alex was unbearable. Shivering with excitement, she phoned him and could have shouted with frustration when it went straight to voicemail. He was probably with a patient – he'd warned her he rarely answered his phone at work – but she was still disappointed. She hesitated, tempted to blurt out her news anyway, but she wanted to tell him in person. In the end she just said, 'It's Kate. Phone me,' before ending the call. Then, because she wanted to make really, really sure he got the message, she texted him as well.

She sat at her desk, chewing her lip. What if he left his phone turned off? Or was somewhere without any signal? She knew that texts and voicemail sometimes took hours to come through: she'd had to apologize to more than one client who thought they were being ignored. After ten minutes she gave in and called him again, with the same result.

She tapped his card on the desk. The only time she'd phoned the clinic where he worked was to check up on him after receiving his letter. He'd asked her not to, but this was different, surely. After wrestling with indecision she gave in and called the number.

A woman answered. 'Ferndale Centre.'

'Can I speak to Alex Turner, please?'

'Dr Turner's with a patient at the moment. Would you like to leave a message?'

If it hadn't been for the receptionist's snooty manner, the slight emphasis on the 'Dr Turner', Kate might have left her name, at least. As it was she coolly said, 'No, thanks, it doesn't matter,' and hung up.

There was one more thing to try. Grinning to herself, she went on to her computer and started composing an email. Typing in his work address from the card, she tried to think what to say. Nothing too specific. She doubted that anyone else would have access to his emails, but she wasn't sure of the office protocol in a medical clinic. The last thing she wanted was the snitty receptionist reading it first. Besides, she only needed to make him hurry up and phone her. She wanted to break the news herself.

After a moment she typed, 'Your grandmother's lucky St Christopher worked! Call me!!' and signed it, 'Love, Kate.' There, she thought. Cryptic enough not to mean anything if any of his colleagues saw it, but enough to get Alex scrambling for his phone.

Pleased with herself, she sent it off before she could change her mind.

Alex didn't call. Kate tried phoning his mobile and texting him again later that afternoon, each time feeling her frustration crank up a notch. When Clive and the others went home for the day and she'd still not heard from him, her impatience became tinged with anxiety.

She refused to acknowledge it. Alex had made it clear from the start that he couldn't take calls at work. Now she knew why: his phone was probably switched off while he dealt with patients. And he was a clinical psychologist, not an office worker. Who knew how often he checked his emails?

Resolutely ignoring the worry that had started to form, she stopped off on the way home and bought a bottle of champagne and some non-alcoholic elder-flower fizz. That was for her – she wouldn't be drinking now for at least nine months – but Alex would want to celebrate. He rarely arrived at her flat before half past seven at the earliest, so Kate turned on the oven while she prepared dinner and set the table with candles and a white cloth. Humming along to a Nina Simone album – one of Alex's favourites – she changed into a figure-hugging navy-blue dress. She smiled as she studied her flat stomach in the mirror.

'Make the most,' she said out loud.

It was almost half past seven. She turned on the heat under the vegetables and put the salmon steaks into the oven, trying all the while not to watch the clock or look over at her silent phone on the worktop. She made a minute adjustment to the napkins she'd already neatly folded, lit the candles, and then there was nothing left to do.

She sat down and waited for Alex.

The shrill beeping made her jump. For an instant she thought it was her phone before realizing it was the timer. The kitchen was full of steam as she turned off the oven and hob. There was a flat, bitter taste like copper at the back of her throat as she picked up her phone and tried Alex again. She could feel her heart bumping as it rang, and then the voicemail message cut in. It was a generic recording, not even Alex's voice. Kate waited for it to finish.

'Alex, it's Kate. Please call me, let me know where you are . . .'

There was a perfectly reasonable explanation, she

told herself as she ended the call. His phone might not be working, or there could be an emergency with a patient. He was probably on the tube right now, already on his way there. He couldn't have got her messages. Because if he had there was no way he wouldn't have called. He'd have guessed her news and be as thrilled as she was.

Wouldn't he?

She waited another half-hour and then phoned the clinic. She wasn't expecting anyone to answer, not this late, but there wasn't even a ring tone. The line echoed hollowly, and after a few seconds she disconnected and tried again. The same eerie silence greeted her then as well. Frowning, she tried calling Alex's home number. That at least rang, but no one picked up. Kate stayed on the line, willing someone to answer, before she finally hung up.

She turned on the lamp and felt an awful emptiness at the sight of the table, set for two. The candles had dripped wax on to the cloth. Kate looked down at the dark circles on the white surface, and then leaned over and blew out the flames. The wicks sent thick ribbons of smoke towards the ceiling. Its pungent, cloying odour filled the room.

The phone rang. Kate gave a start, then ran and snatched it up.

'Hello?'

'Hi, Kate, it's Lucy.'

The leaden ball settled back in her stomach. 'Oh, hi, Lucy.'

'Well, don't sound so pleased. What's the matter?'

'Nothing, sorry. Well, Alex is a bit late, that's all.'

Lucy laughed. 'Got to that stage already, has it? Rolling pin behind the door?'

Kate concealed her irritation. 'No. I'm just worried. He should have been here over an hour ago.'

'I wouldn't worry. He's probably stuck on a tube somewhere. So how's it going?'

'OK.' She felt no desire to tell Lucy she was pregnant. Not until Alex knew.

Lucy sighed. 'I can tell you're not in a chatting mood. Look, I'm sure he's fine. He'll turn up with some excuse. They always do.'

But he didn't.

By next morning Kate felt dulled with worry and fatigue. She had slept fitfully, sometimes jerking awake convinced that the doorbell or the phone had rung. Then she would lie with her heart thudding in the aftermath of the adrenalin rush, conscious of the cold space beside her in the bed as she listened to the meaningless night-noises of the flat.

She'd tried calling and texting him several more times before accepting that there was no point. If he were going to get in touch he would have by now. She'd considered calling a taxi and going to his flat: if nothing else it would have given her something to do. But if he was at home he'd have answered the phone. Kate could tell herself that his mobile or landline might not be working, but not both. And what if he arrived at her flat while she was out? Better to wait till morning, she rationalized, trying to ignore the small but insistent voice that reminded her that in all this time she'd never, not even once, seen where he lived.

She had tried calling Alex again first thing, without success. There was still a fault on the Ferndale Centre's phone line, and not knowing what else to do, Kate went into work. She told herself the clinic's phones would be repaired by then, and someone there would surely know what had happened to him. Would at least be able to tell her if he was all right. She hurried along the rain-drenched streets, driven by a fearful eagerness.

The door to the agency was unlocked. She opened it and backed in, shaking off the water from her umbrella outside. Closing the door, she turned and saw Clive looking at her. Two men were in the office with him.

'There's somebody to see you,' Clive said in a voice that was oddly flat. One of the men stepped forward.

'Miss Powell?'

He was a big, heavily built man in his fifties, with bristly grey hair thinning on top and startlingly thick black eyebrows. His overcoat smelled like a wet dog. The other man was younger and wore a blue waterproof jacket. He remained in the background.

Kate glanced at Clive, but his face was expressionless. 'Yes?' she said.

'I'm Detective Inspector Collins. This is Detective Sergeant Daikin. I wonder if you could spare us a few minutes?'

A hollowness had settled in her stomach. 'Come up to my office.'

She led them upstairs, remembering herself enough to ask if they wanted tea or coffee. Both declined. They sat opposite her across her desk, the older of the two opening his overcoat to reveal a creased brown suit. His shirt was stretched drum-tight across his heavy stomach.

The younger man took out a notebook and a sheet of paper from the folder he was carrying. He put the paper on the desk and pushed it towards her. The inspector watched as she picked it up.

'Can you tell me if you sent this?'

It was a copy of the email she had sent to Alex the day before. She fought down a rising panic.

'Yes, I sent it yesterday.'

'So you know Dr Turner?'

The hollowness in her gut had contracted, squeezing so she couldn't breathe. 'Yes. Look, what's happened?'

'What's your relationship with him?'

'I'm a – a friend. Please, is he all right?'

The inspector spoke matter-of-factly.

'I'm sorry. He's dead.'

It was as though the air pressure in the room had suddenly altered. There was a roaring in her ears. She saw the older man watching her, a concerned expression on his face, and realized she was swaying in her seat. She put both hands on the desk to steady herself.

'How?' She wasn't sure if she had spoken out loud, but she must have because the inspector answered.

'There was a fire last night at the clinic where Dr Turner worked. When the fire brigade went in they found him in his office. There were signs of a struggle and he'd been assaulted. We'll have to wait for the post mortem, but we think he was killed by a head injury rather than the fire. It looks like that was started

222

afterwards, probably to destroy any evidence. But it was a rush job, and the clinic's sprinkler system cut in before it could get hold.'

Kate felt strangely detached. There was no pain, no sensation at all. She wasn't really sitting here, hearing this. This wasn't Alex they were talking about, and when she spoke the words seemed unreal.

'Who did it?'

The inspector shifted in his seat. It creaked under his weight.

'We're not sure yet. But we know Dr Turner was staying behind to see a patient. Unfortunately, with the computers shorted out by the sprinkler system and the office in turmoil, everything's still a bit confused. We're hoping to have a better idea who it was later this morning.'

He nodded at the printed email on Kate's desk. 'We found a copy of that underneath him. The agency's address is printed at the bottom, so we thought we'd see if you know anything that might help us.'

Kate looked down at the piece of paper. '*Your grandmother's lucky St Christopher worked! Call me!! Love, Kate.*' She became aware that the policeman had asked her something.

'Sorry?'

'I said, can you tell me what it means?'

Kate felt as though she were trying to think through a fog. 'Nothing. It was just a joke. A private thing.'

'Can you elaborate?'

'It's a sort of . . . a lucky charm he wears.'

She had to force the words out, as though they'd

physical weight. The inspector nodded encouragingly. 'And why did you say it'd "worked"?'

'I . . . I'd had some good news.'

'Can you be more specific?'

'I'd rather not.'

She met the inspector's gaze, too numb to care what he thought. He pursed his lips but didn't press.

'OK, then, can you describe what this St Christopher looks like? Is it big, small, gold, silver . . . ?'

'Silver, about the size of a pound coin. He always wears it on a chain around his neck.' She saw the sergeant glance at his superior. The older man showed no reaction, but Kate belatedly made the connection. 'Wasn't he wearing it?'

'It's possible it could have come off in the struggle,' the inspector said blandly.

'You mean someone stole it?' The small violation pierced her daze in a way the larger loss hadn't.

'We're still examining the office. It might turn up.' He looked down at the email lying on the desk between them. 'You say he always wears it. How do you know?'

The question seemed senseless. 'Because he told me. And I've seen it on him.'

'How long have you known each other?'

'I don't know . . . Eight, nine months.' The numbers meant nothing.

'When did you last see him?'

'Yesterday morning. About . . . a quarter to eight. Before he left for work.' She remembered Alex grinning at her from the bottom of the stairs. How his dark hair had been tufted.

The inspector's eyebrows went up. 'Are you sure?'

'Of course I'm sure.'

'So you're saying he stayed the night with you. The two of you were sleeping together.'

'Yes.' She couldn't understand why that mattered. The younger officer looked at the inspector again, then quickly down at his notes. 'Why, what's that got to do with anything?'

'I know this is upsetting, but I need to know what your relationship was. I take it you and Dr Turner were having an affair?'

Affair. The word seemed wrong. Sordid. She rubbed her temples. 'If you like.'

'And you live alone? You're not married?'

'No, I'm not married. And, yes, I live alone.'

'Any boyfriends?'

She stared at him, wondering what he thought Alex was. Had been. Suddenly, she felt dizzy. 'No.'

As she said it, though, something occurred to her, a terrible possibility she didn't want to consider. Something must have registered on her face, because the inspector frowned.

'What is it?'

'Nothing, I was . . .' She shook her head. 'Nothing.'

He looked at her for a few moments but again let it go. 'So, you last saw Dr Turner yesterday morning. Did you talk to him after that?'

'No. I tried phoning his mobile a few times, but I couldn't get hold of him.'

'So that's when you sent the email.'

'Yes.'

225

'Can you tell me where you were yesterday evening?'

'I was at home. Waiting for Alex. I was . . . I'd cooked dinner.'

'Did you see anyone else during that time?'

'No. A friend phoned, but that's all.'

'What time was that?'

She tried to remember. 'I don't know. About half past eight?'

'And what's your friend's name?'

Kate realized that he was checking her out. It didn't seem to matter. She gave him Lucy's details.

The sergeant's pen scratched as he made notes.

'What did you do when Dr Turner didn't arrive?' the inspector asked.

For an instant she felt disoriented, as an echo of the fear she had felt the previous night overlapped with the impossibility of the present.

'I tried calling the clinic, but there was something wrong with the phone.' Comprehension came like a blow. She broke off, looking across at the policeman.

'The phones all went down when the sprinklers cut in,' he said. 'That was between half past seven and eight, as far as we can tell.'

He was already dead then. He was lying there, dead, when I phoned. The thought was too immense to take in.

'Did you do anything else? Phone anyone else?'

'After I'd called the clinic I tried phoning him at home. But there wasn't . . . there was no answer.'

The inspector's face was impassive. 'There wouldn't be. His wife was visiting her mother. Otherwise we

226

might have known he was missing sooner.'

Kate stared at him.

'His wife?'

He gave her a quizzical look. 'Dr Turner's married.'

She shook her head. 'No . . . No, he isn't.'

'I've just spoken to his wife, so I can assure you he is. I'm sorry, I assumed, as his mistress, you'd know.'

A wind of dizziness was blowing over her, like nausea. *Mistress.*

'He can't be!' The denial was wrung from her. 'I'd have known! I've been seeing him for – for *months*! He gave me his home telephone number! He wouldn't have done that if he was married!'

'What number did he give you?'

Kate struggled to concentrate as she went through her phone's contacts for Alex's numbers. She gave them his mobile as well, stammering it out as the sergeant wrote it down. He leafed through his notes before looking at the inspector.

'They aren't the ones we have.'

He avoided Kate's eyes. She turned back to the inspector.

There was something that might have been pity in his expression now.

'Did you ever go to his home?' he asked.

'No.' It was a whisper. 'He – he said he was living in a studio flat until he found somewhere to buy. He told me it was a dump, and he'd be embarrassed at me seeing it.' She remembered his reluctance, how he had always insisted on dropping her off first when they shared a taxi. It was a physical pain in her chest.

227

The scratching of the sergeant's pen had stopped. There was an uneasy silence.

'I'm sorry,' the inspector said. 'I know this must all have come as a shock.'

Kate didn't respond. She stared down at the surface of her desk. There was a dent in it she had never noticed before.

The policeman coughed.

'I don't suppose Dr Turner made any mention to you about who he was seeing last night?' he asked.

It was an effort to shake her head. 'He doesn't talk much about his work.'

Or anything else.

'So there was nothing out of the ordinary at all?'

She gave another shake of her head.

The inspector took out a crumpled handkerchief and blew his nose. The handkerchief was returned to his pocket.

'Can you think of anyone who might have had a grudge against him?' he asked. 'Dr Turner, I mean?'

'I thought you were looking for one of his patients?'

'We certainly want to question whoever he saw last night, but we're not ruling out other possibilities.'

Kate began to say no, but the awful thought she'd had earlier had returned.

'Yes?' the inspector prompted.

'There was . . . an incident with an old boyfriend in a restaurant. He hit Alex. But I don't think . . .'

'When was this?'

'About . . . about three, four weeks ago.' It seemed much longer.

'What's his name, please?'

'Paul Sutherland. Look, I don't want to cause any trouble for him,' she added, seeing the sergeant write down the name.

'Don't worry, we'll just check it out. Can you tell us anything more about him?'

Kate told him about the court case. The detachment had returned, sealing her off as she spoke. When she had finished there was a pause. The inspector rubbed his nose.

'There's one more thing,' he said slowly. 'The body hasn't been formally identified yet. His wife isn't really in any fit state to do it, so I wonder if you would?'

The sergeant glanced up from his book. He looked unhappy. 'We could ask someone else, couldn't we, sir?'

Collins gave him a look. 'We could, but now we're here I'd like Miss Powell to do it.' He turned back to Kate. 'If you don't mind.'

She answered from within a core of unnatural calm.

'All right.'

The mortuary was part of a 1970s concrete and glass building. Kate walked between the two policemen down tiled steps into the basement. The smell was similar to a hospital's, yet subtly different. They came to a row of plastic chairs in a corridor. Kate stayed there with the sergeant while the inspector disappeared through a nearby door.

She tried to remember the sergeant's name, but couldn't.

She could tell he was uncomfortable and felt distantly

sorry for him. But other than that nothing penetrated the numbness that surrounded her.

Only once had the fact of Alex's death seemed real.

During the car journey she had been sitting in the back, staring out of the window, when the knowledge had come crashing in. *Alex is dead.* There was an instant of appalling loss, but then the sense of unreality returned, putting an anaesthetizing screen between her and everything else.

She almost welcomed it.

Collins came back out. He spoke in a subdued voice. 'Are you ready?'

Kate rose to her feet. She moved towards the door he was holding open for her. She could see through into the room beyond. Facing her was a large window, looking into yet another room.

And suddenly it hit her. Where she was. What she was doing.

She didn't know she had stepped backwards until she bumped into the sergeant.

'Come on, love.'

He spoke softly and took her arm. Her legs were weak as she let him lead her towards the window. She kept her head down as she took the last few steps up to it. Her feet seemed a great distance away.

'All right.'

She wasn't sure who had spoken, but she looked up. On the other side of the glass was a steel table. A body lay on it, covered by a sheet.

That's Alex, Kate thought. *That's him, that's Alex.* She closed her throat on a moan.

The sheet covering the body was perfectly still, unruffled by breath. A woman in a white coat, whom Kate hadn't noticed till now, took hold of it at the top and pulled it back.

Kate looked.

The dark hair was singed and matted, clotted with blood. She could see where the skull under it had been crushed. One eye was swollen shut, the flesh around it discoloured, but the other was partly open, a thin sickle staring up at the ceiling.

Kate felt a pulse throb in her temple. She took a breath, forced herself to speak.

'No,' she said. 'That's not him.'

14

The police asked for a photograph of Alex. The only one she had was the one she'd taken on her phone during their picnic in Cambridge. She printed out a copy for them and agreed to email it later as well. She looked at the image before she handed it over, remembering how happy they'd been that day.

'We'll be in touch,' Collins said as he left.

She left soon afterwards herself. She needed time alone. The relief she'd felt at discovering it wasn't Alex's body had been replaced by reaction, and now she felt drained.

Clive made no comment when she told him she was going home, but she had seen the concern in his face. 'I know it isn't any of my business, but is everything OK?'

She began to formulate a polite response, then abandoned the attempt.

'No, not really.'

'Is it anything I can help with?'

'Thanks, but, no, I don't think it is.'

He looked at her, then nodded. 'Let me know if you want to talk about it.'

She said she would. When she got back to her flat, she stood in the lounge, unable to decide what to do. Finally, with the vague idea of making something to eat, she went into the kitchen. Without bothering to see what type it was, she took out a carton of soup from the fridge. It was only when she looked for a saucepan that she remembered they were still on the cooker from the night before.

Kate stared down at the cold vegetables, and then grabbed the pans and tipped them down the sink. The potatoes had dissolved into the water, forming a scummy tidemark on the stainless steel. She scooped out the congealed lumps that were too big to drain down the plughole and dumped them into the bin, then turned on the tap and rinsed the sink. Leaving the water running, she pulled open the oven door and pulled out the foil-wrapped salmon, dropping that into the bin, too.

The water had begun to run hot. Kate squirted washing-up liquid on to the saucepans and scoured them until her arms ached. When they were dripping on the draining rack, she looked around for something else. She took the heavy metal frames from around the gas rings and plunged them into the soapy water. Then she started on the cooker itself.

Doing something, anything, helped keep the fear and confusion at bay. She could feel it waiting for her, like dark water under thin ice. Only activity kept her from plunging through, so she scrubbed and wiped and polished, working her way from the kitchen to the bathroom, then down the hall to the lounge. She was vacuuming the carpet when the doorbell rang.

Kate froze, then switched off the vacuum cleaner. The doorbell rang again as it whined into silence. She ran out of the lounge and down the stairs, but the sudden hope died when she saw two figures through the stained-glass panel.

The inspector's bulk filled the top step when she opened the front door. This time he had a uniformed policewoman with him.

'Sorry to bother you again, Miss Powell. Can we come in?'

Kate led them upstairs into the lounge. They picked their way around the vacuum cleaner and sat down. All three sat on the edge of their seats. Collins told Kate the policewoman's name, but it made no impression. She wouldn't think about why he might have brought a woman officer with him this time.

The inspector sat with his meaty hands dangling between his legs. His stomach pushed out towards his knees.

'There've been some developments,' he said.

Kate couldn't wait any longer. 'Have you found him?'

There was a minute hesitation. 'No, no we haven't. But, first off, I owe you an apology. I wasn't being entirely honest earlier when I asked you to identify the body. There were other people we could have asked, but I wanted you to see it after you said Dr Turner spent the night at your flat.'

'Why? He did, I don't understand.'

'The thing is, his wife told us her husband spent the night at home. According to her she was with him the whole time until he set off for work at about eight o'clock yesterday morning.'

'I don't care what . . .' Kate couldn't bring herself to say "his wife", '. . . what anyone else says, Alex was with me. Don't you think I'd remember something like that?'

Collins made a placating gesture. 'I'm sure you would. But he could hardly be in two places at once, so when you couldn't identify the body we took one of Dr Turner's colleagues to the mortuary.'

He rubbed his hands slowly together. They made a dry, rasping noise.

'He positively identified him as Alex Turner.'

Kate struggled to make sense of what he'd said. 'He can't have.'

'He's known Dr Turner for ten years. He wasn't in any doubt.'

'I don't care how long he'd known him, that wasn't Alex! For God's sake, don't you think I'd *know*? You've only got to look at the photograph to see it was nothing like him!'

'Actually, we showed it to Dr Turner's colleague. I'm afraid he didn't recognize the man in it.'

'I don't understand. He must have!'

'After that we also showed it to Turner's secretary.' Collins's eyes were mournful as he looked across at Kate. 'She identified him as one of Dr Turner's patients.'

The ice broke. The waters closed over her.

'His real name's Timothy Ellis,' Collins went on. 'He's a schizophrenic. He's been Turner's patient for the past two years. Since the last time he was released, apparently.'

235

As if on cue, the policewoman pulled a large photograph from a file and passed it to Kate. It was black and white and divided into two halves, one a full-face picture, the other a profile. The man in it was younger, with shorter hair, but still recognizably Alex.

'He's twenty-nine and has had a history of arson since he was a kid,' Collins was saying. 'Which would explain the attempt to set fire to the office. We don't have full access to his psychiatric file yet, but we know he's had a police record as an arsonist since he was ten. He was recommended for psychiatric assessment when he was fourteen, after he set fire to his school. Can't have done much good, though, because a year or so later he set fire to his home. Killed his parents and two older brothers.'

'No!' The cry was wrung from her. 'No, his parents live in Cornwall! He told me!'

Collins looked almost regretful. 'Timothy Ellis's parents and brothers died in a house fire that he started. He's been in various institutions ever since. He came out two years ago, and since then he's been employed part-time in a computer repair shop through a community care programme. The latest psychological reports said he was adapting well.' He gave a wry grimace. 'They obviously got it wrong.'

There wasn't enough air in the room.

'No!'

'I'm sorry, Miss Powell—'

'Do you think I don't *know* him?'

'You know Timothy Ellis. You never met Alex Turner.'

'I don't believe you!'

236

'We checked the phone numbers he gave you. They both belong to Ellis. The landline's even listed under his name; you can look it up for yourself. He just told you it was ex-directory in case you checked and wondered why no one called Alex Turner lived there.'

Kate shook her head, denying it. But the policeman's words triggered a sudden memory of the ink stain she'd seen on Alex's jeans. How his face had drained of colour when she'd asked about it. *'Don't tell me they've got you changing the printer cartridges at the clinic?'* She didn't want to hear any more, but Collins was relentless.

'Alex Turner is dead, Miss Powell. You saw his body at the mortuary this morning, and it seems increasingly likely that Timothy Ellis killed him. We know now it was Ellis who Dr Turner was staying behind late to see. He told his secretary about it, and although he didn't say why, I think we can assume that it had something to do with the email you sent. We've also spoken to Ellis's boss at the computer shop. He's told us Ellis got a phone call yesterday afternoon, after which he seemed moody and upset. I think that call was from Dr Turner, telling Ellis he wanted to see him. Now one of them is dead and the other is missing, and we need to find out what happened. And I believe you can help us with that.'

She was suffocating. 'You think this is my fault?'

'No, I don't think that at all. But Ellis went to a lot of trouble to make you think he was Alex Turner. Dr Turner reported his wallet missing nine months ago, which I'm guessing is around the time Ellis first contacted you. Apparently Dr Turner suspected it might be one of his patients, but at the time he didn't know which one. None of the credit cards were ever used, so Ellis probably wanted it more for window dressing than anything else.'

Hoping to refute it even now, Kate tried to recall Alex paying for a meal or drinks with anything except cash. She couldn't. She thought back to how clever she'd felt at their first meeting, surreptitiously reading his name as he'd searched through his wallet for a business card. A business card belonging to the real Alex Turner, that conveniently gave only his work details. And all of it staged for her benefit, to make her believe he was someone he wasn't.

Collins still hadn't finished. 'I know this is difficult, but what happened yesterday seems to have been sparked by your email. We need to know why, so no matter how personal it is I'm going to have to ask you again why you sent it.'

Kate shivered. She folded her arms around herself. A signal must have passed between Collins and the policewoman, because now she stood up.

'Would you like a cup of tea?' she asked.

Kate shook her head.

'I can make one. It's no trouble.'

'I don't want a bloody cup of tea!'

The policewoman's face hardened. She sat down again.

Collins let out a heavy sigh. 'Look, Miss Powell, I know this isn't easy, but I'd like you to bear in mind that, while we're sitting here with you, Alex Turner's lying on a mortuary slab, and his widow is having to come to terms with the fact that their baby will be born without a father because he was killed by a man he was trying to help. So, while you have my sympathy, my main priority is locating Timothy Ellis before he hurts anyone else.'

He spoke in a tone of patient weariness, but Kate felt her face flush as if she had been rebuked.

'His wife's pregnant?'

'Eight months,' Collins said. 'That's why I didn't ask her to identify the body.'

The last of Kate's resistance leaked away. 'I didn't know.'

'No reason why you should have. I didn't see any point in telling you yesterday. But I thought it might help put things in perspective now.'

She nodded, chastened. 'I'm sorry.'

'No need to apologize,' Collins said. 'But I think it's time you told us about the email you sent to Ellis. Something important must have happened to prompt you to send it, and I need to know what it was.'

There was a last reluctance, a protest that these strangers should be the first to be told. Then it had gone.

'I'd just found out I was pregnant.'

The words fell into the room's silence. Collins turned to the policewoman.

'I think we could do with that tea now.'

'So. What are you going to do?'

Lucy sat with her legs drawn under her on the sofa, leaning back on Jack. The children were in bed, and the

239

three of them sat in the darkened lounge, close to the stove. Kate stared at the flames dancing behind the glass panel.

'I don't know.'

A bottle of whisky stood between them. Kate held a tumbler of it in both hands. Lucy had pressed it on her, but she hadn't drunk from it yet.

'Are they sure, though?' Lucy asked. 'I mean, it seems so . . . so . . . .' She threw up her hands, speechless.

'They say there's no doubt.'

'But how can they be certain he killed him? The psychologist, I mean. For all they know, it could have been, I don't know, a burglar or something. It might not have been Alex.'

'Ellis,' Kate said, not taking her eyes from the flames. 'His name's Timothy Ellis.'

Lucy didn't say anything to that. Jack sat, grim-faced, looking at his lap.

'No wonder he didn't look his age,' Lucy went on after a while. 'Not even thirty! I mean, it's the cheek of it that gets me!'

'I don't think "cheek" comes into it,' Jack commented.

'No, I know, but . . . Well, he just seemed so *nice*. Although, now you look back, you can see that some things weren't right, can't you? I always thought he was a bit shy to be a psychologist. And, when you think about it, it was pretty odd that he never let you see where he lived. Or that you couldn't find him on Facebook or anywhere.'

'The police say Alex Turner . . .' She faltered but

forced herself to continue, '. . . the real Alex Turner really didn't want to risk patients stalking him online.' At least there had been that much truth in the lies. Collins didn't know if the psychologist's aversion to social media was the main reason Ellis had chosen to impersonate him or just unlucky coincidence. Either way, it had made the task that much easier.

'God, talk about ironic. Still, at least he didn't get any money out of you,' Lucy went on. Kate wanted to shout at her to shut up. 'I bet he was pig sick that he couldn't cash your cheques. Makes you wonder how he could afford all those trips to Birmingham and everything, doesn't it? I mean, he wouldn't get much working part-time at a printer's, would he?'

Kate had to rouse herself to answer. 'The police say he was left some money by his grandmother. Not much, but enough to supplement his wage. And they found a cardboard sign for Birmingham in his bedsit, so they think he must have hitched.'

Lucy greeted the information with a snort. 'Well, to say he's supposed to be mentally ill, he'd got it all worked out, I'll give him that. Have the police any idea why he'd do something like this? I mean, he must have had a reason.'

Kate felt the question like a physical weight. Her chest ached as she answered. 'They don't know. But . . . I don't think he was making everything up. Not about how badly he wanted a child or how important it was to him.'

She could see him now as he sat across from her that first day in the restaurant, nervous and – it seemed – desperately sincere. *'I just can't see myself settling down*

241

and having a normal family. This is the next best thing.'
The worst of it was that, in a way, it made even more sense now, knowing who and what Timothy Ellis really was.

How could she not have seen that?

Lucy was looking at her with an expression that said she had something on her mind. 'So what are you going to do?'

'I don't know. I can't even think straight at the moment.'

'Yes, but you're going to have to decide soon. About the baby, I mean.'

'Lucy . . . ' Jack said, warningly.

'Well, she *is*.'

'Decide what about the baby?' Kate asked.

Lucy looked surprised. 'If you're going to keep it or not.'

The crackling of the fire seemed to grow very loud, blending with the rush of blood in Kate's ears. The room tilted, as if not even the floor were stable any more. She put her glass on the coffee table and gripped the chair arms, feeling a greasy slide of nausea. Lucy and Jack's voices went on around her.

'For Christ's sake, Lucy!'

'Well, she's got to face up to it!'

'Give her a bloody chance! She's had enough shocks for one day!'

Jack was crouching in front of her, raising the whisky to her lips. She could smell it, and the wave of nausea rose. Then it passed. She pushed away the glass without drinking.

Jack set it on the coffee table and went back to his seat. 'You OK?'

Kate nodded. She wasn't, though. She felt weak, as though she was convalescing from an illness.

'Look, why don't you go and see a doctor tomorrow?' Lucy asked.

'I don't want tranquillizers.'

'I don't mean that. I just think you need to talk to someone. Get some expert advice.'

'About what?'

Kate saw Jack give his wife an incredulous look. Lucy ignored it.

'You know what about. I'm sorry, Kate, but I think you've got to accept that abortion's a serious consideration now.'

'Oh, for Christ's sake, leave it alone, Lucy!' Jack snapped.

'No, I won't! I'm as pro-life or whatever as anybody, but there have to be exceptions. And, let's face it, being made pregnant by a deranged murderer has got to be one of them!'

Kate felt buffeted by the words. Lucy pressed on.

'You've got to face facts, Kate. I liked him too, I admit, but the man's a lunatic. Apart from anything else, he got you pregnant under false pretences. They do emergency terminations for rape victims, and I don't see that this is much different. But the longer you leave it, the worse it'll be. The sooner you—'

'Please, Lucy.' Kate shut her eyes. 'Just . . . don't. Please.'

'I know but—'

'Leave it, Lucy.' Jack spoke firmly, putting a restraining hand on her shoulder. Lucy hesitated, then sat back.

'OK.' She threw up her arms with a sigh. 'OK.'

Behind the stove's glass panel, the logs blazed, indifferent.

Kate sat with the laptop open in front of her. The remains of her dinner lay congealing and uneaten on the table nearby. She cupped a mug of coffee in her hands, staring at the website on the screen. The last time she'd been on it she'd felt almost euphoric with excitement. That seemed to have happened to a different person now, in a different life.

She'd been putting off doing this, frightened of what she might find. But the need to know had been building up ever since Collins had told her that Timothy Ellis was an arsonist. A fire-starter.

She realized she'd read something about that before.

When she'd arrived home that evening the light had been flashing on her landline. The display told her she had a single message. She stood by the phone, staring down at the insistent pulse, then set it playing. There was a bristle of static but no one spoke. The silence ran on for several seconds before whoever it was rang off. Kate played it again, trying to hear something more, but there was nothing. Just a cold-caller, she told herself, and quickly deleted it.

She undressed to take a shower. As she pulled a clean towel from the drawer something else flipped into view. The child's mitten was shockingly red against the white towels. Kate had forgotten all about it, and its appearance now seemed deliberately mocking. Snatching it up, she took it into the kitchen and threw it into the bin.

The shower was her third of the day, and as she stood under the stinging jet she tried to dismiss the nagging feeling that had taken root after talking to the policeman. She tried to ignore it as she cooked dinner, stubbornly trying to force interest and appetite in the food.

But she could manage neither. The pasta almost choked her after the first mouthful, and as she pushed away her plate the last of her resistance crumbled.

Stomach knotting, she opened up her laptop.

She'd had to subscribe to the psychological journal in order to read the whole article rather than just the abstract she'd seen – and overlooked – before. Now it waited on the screen in dense lines of text: '*Prometheus' Children: Case Studies of Pyromania*'. Underneath the title was the author's name, Dr Alex Turner.

Kate started to read.

It was heavy going. According to the article, Prometheus was a character from Greek mythology who stole fire from the Gods using a hollow stick. Pyromania was something called an 'impulse-control disorder', she read: an irresistible impulse to light fires and a fascination with watching them burn. The article explained that pathological fire-setters were often young males from troubled backgrounds who suffered from 'psycho-social disadvantages and feelings of inadequacy'. It claimed that a high proportion had some sort of minor physical abnormality, and went on to provide four case studies.

Kate skimmed the first two, but the third leaped out at her. No names were given, but it concerned a young white male known only as 'C'. Of above average intelligence, he was from a middle-class but dysfunctional and violent background.

As the youngest of three brothers, C was often subjected to extreme sibling bullying. At five years old he had his fingers put into a lighted gas fire by one brother. This would bear out Jackson's observation (1994) that some arsonists have been victims of fire themselves at some point. Although it is not possible to say if this was the direct cause of C's obsession, the trauma left him with a speech impediment in the form of a severe stammer, which added to his isolation and sense of personal inadequacy.

Kate re-read that part before continuing on to the rest.

The first police involvement in C's fire-setting was at age ten, when he burned down a shed in the local park, resulting in a recommendation for psychological assessment. There followed a period of relative stability, which coincided with C going to live with his paternal grandmother after his father was imprisoned on a fraud charge.

However, on C's return home the fire-setting resumed. At fourteen he burned down school outbuildings and was referred for psychiatric treatment, following which he was recognized as exhibiting negative symptoms of schizophrenia, such as withdrawal from social contact, intense apathy and being acutely ill at ease in the presence of other people. However, C's pyromania was ascertained to be primarily a pathological problem rather than a symptom of his schizophrenia. At no time did he claim to have "heard" voices telling him to start fires, or report any other delusional ideas, as is frequently the case when the fire-setting is the result of an organic psychiatric disorder. His compulsion to start fires, and the obsession with watching them, seems to have stemmed from an unconscious urge to purge himself of negative emotions. Increasingly, this would result in his setting fire to whatever object they were associated with (as with the school outbuildings, where he had been beaten by other pupils). C's subsequent guilt would then result in a further emotional downturn, and a corresponding need to start further fires.

The article said his schizophrenia had responded well to anti-psychotic drugs and that for a time the pyromania appeared to be under control. Then Kate came to a passage that made her breath catch.

The pivotal event in C's history seems to be the death of his grandmother when he was fifteen. This came shortly after an argument between his grandmother and C's parents in which his welfare was the central issue. On the night of his grandmother's funeral C set fire to his home, killing his parents and both brothers. Even now he appears unclear over his intentions, and it is possible that the fire was set with no real regard for the consequences. As usual, C was remorseful after the fact, and after pouring petrol over himself outside the burning house only the swift intervention of the emergency services prevented him from the act of self-immolation.

Now Kate had to force herself to read on. C had been sectioned under the Mental Health Act and transferred to a young person's secure unit. As well as continued treatment with anti-psychotics, he'd received speech therapy to help his stammer, and after eight years he'd been discharged into the supervision of a psychiatric social worker and a clinical psychologist. The final lines of the article brought a bitter metallic taste into her mouth.

C has adapted well to living in the community and responded positively to talking treatments, including cognitive behavioural therapy. There has been no recurrence of his fire-setting, and he expresses a strong understanding of his condition and a desire to overcome it. Although he remains under psychiatric social worker monitoring, and bi-monthly psychological assessment, there seems a good possibility that he will achieve this.

A wave of light-headedness swept over Kate. She gripped the edge of the table as the edges of her vision darkened. She felt as though she were being swept away, her entire life suddenly upended and torn apart. Her eyes went back to the text on the glowing screen. '*A good possibility . . .*'

She managed to make it into the bathroom before she was sick.

15

The receptionist tried to convince her to make an appointment for later in the week but finally relented and grudgingly told Kate that she could wait to see a doctor that evening. Kate sat on one of the hard plastic chairs in the waiting room, avoiding eye contact with any of the other patients. An elderly man sat wheezing opposite her, one leg held out stiffly in front of him. Next to him a teenager pored over a women's magazine in silent absorption. Nearby, a young mother read quietly to a pale-looking toddler on her knee.

Kate picked up a magazine from the table in the centre of the room, but the words and pictures made no sense. When she came to an article on miscarriages she put it down.

The waiting room was oppressive in its silence, so that the slightest sound was amplified. The young mother's voice murmured on in a deafening whisper. The old man's coughs boomed from the depths of his chest while the teenager's magazine announced each turned page in a rustle of glossy paper. Kate stared at the top of the receptionist's head, bent over behind the glass partition, and tried to think of nothing.

One by one the other patients were called in, until she was the last one left. The old man came out and walked stiffly to the door. It squeaked shut behind him, leaving Kate alone once more.

'Kate Powell.'

It was a different GP from the ones she had seen before. He was an elderly man, small, with grey hair and half-moon glasses. Without looking up from what he was writing he gestured for her to take a seat. Kate sat down and waited.

Finally, he gave a small sigh and looked up. 'What can I do for you?'

Kate had rehearsed what she would say. Now it all vanished.

'I want an abortion,' she blurted.

The doctor looked at her over the top of his glasses. He took a moment to read her notes on his computer screen.

'You're not quite five weeks pregnant. Is that right?' Kate nodded. The doctor pursed his lips and unhurriedly continued reading through her notes. She waited, her hands clenched and white on her lap. When he saw nothing that interested him he turned back to her.

'Why do you want an abortion?'

She told him. He listened without comment, legs crossed, hands clasped on his desk. Kate tried to keep the quaver from her voice, but by the time she had finished she was shivering uncontrollably. She had hoped that telling someone, from beginning to end, would prove cathartic. It didn't.

The doctor sat for a moment, saying nothing.

'And what does the clinic that carried out the insemination say about this? I presume you've told them?'

'They . . . they say it's nothing to do with them. When I asked them about termination, they said I should contact my own GP.'

Dr Janson had been appalled when Kate had phoned her, and while she had tried hard not to sound unsympathetic, it was obvious that her main worry was absolving the clinic of responsibility. The choice of donor had been entirely Kate's, she hastily pointed out, scrambling to distance the clinic from any hint of scandal. But Kate hadn't needed anyone to tell her where the fault lay.

The GP's expression was unreadable.

'So what you're basically saying is that, after going to great lengths to become pregnant, you've now changed your mind.'

His matter-of-factness took Kate's breath away.

'No!' she exclaimed. 'It's not like that!'

The doctor took off his glasses, letting them dangle on the cord around his neck.

'But that is, essentially, what you're saying, isn't it?' Taking a tissue from his pocket, he began wiping the half-moon lenses. 'I'm not unsympathetic. I know this must have been very traumatic. But what we've got to look at is why, exactly, you want to terminate your pregnancy.'

Kate stared at him. 'Isn't it obvious?'

He examined the lenses before letting the glasses hang on the cord again. 'It's obvious that you're very upset, which is understandable. What I'm trying to establish is whether you no longer want a baby. Or if you just no longer want this particular one?'

Kate opened her mouth to answer, then closed it. The doctor continued.

'It's only natural for you to feel confused and frightened. And angry, I dare say. You've been lied to, cheated, and found out in possibly the worst way imaginable that the man you trusted to be the father of your baby is not who he claimed. But perhaps you should be looking at counselling to help you cope with those feelings, rather than rushing into an abortion.'

'I don't want counselling!' The confusion she thought had been resolved surfaced again. She shook her head. 'I just can't go through with this!'

'Why can't you?'

'*Why?* Because he's mentally ill!'

'Is that the only reason?'

'Isn't it *enough*? He lied to me about who he was. He killed his own family! He's just killed somebody else, for God's sake!'

'The baby hasn't.' The doctor looked at her calmly. 'The child you're carrying hasn't done anything, except be conceived. Is it fair to blame it for something its father's done?'

Again, Kate couldn't answer. She hadn't expected an argument, and the issues the doctor raised penetrated her decision like spikes.

'But how can I have his baby now?' Her voice was anguished. 'How do I know it won't be like him?'

The doctor kneaded the bridge of his nose tiredly. 'If

every family with a history of mental illness passed it on to their children, sooner or later we'd all be affected.' He sighed. 'Yes, schizophrenia can sometimes run in families, but it isn't like eye colour. It isn't passed on directly. I think something like one child in ten may, *may*,' he stressed, 'develop it if one of its parents is schizophrenic. Which gives a ninety per cent chance that it won't.'

He put his glasses on again, with a tired air.

'As for the arson . . . Well, I'm not an expert on psychology, but I doubt very much that something like that is hereditary. I think compulsive behaviour of that sort is more a matter of environment and upbringing than inheritance.'

'So you're saying you won't recommend me for an abortion,' Kate said, on the verge of walking out.

'No, I'm saying it's a serious decision, and before I refer you to have your pregnancy terminated I need to satisfy myself that you're not doing it for the wrong reasons. I don't want you to do anything you'll regret.'

She remembered Lucy saying the same thing at the beginning, when the idea had seemed full of hope. It wasn't a welcome memory. The doctor watched her.

'No one would argue that it isn't an awful situation,' he said, when it was obvious she wasn't going to speak. 'This man is obviously a very disturbed individual, and you've undoubtedly suffered a type of abuse. Which is all the more reason why you should consider counselling. At the very least I suggest you wait a while before making any decision about your pregnancy.'

'I don't want to wait.'

The doctor inclined his head. 'It's your decision, but once you go ahead with this, it's something you'll have to live with for the rest of your life. You need to think carefully if it's what you really want.'

He looked steadily at her.

'Is it?'

Kate felt she wasn't really in the room, that this wasn't her abortion they were discussing. She gripped tight to her resolve. 'Yes.'

As she unlocked the door to her flat it began to rain, a fine drizzle that fogged the yellow glow from the street lights. She trudged upstairs, absently bending to stroke Dougal when he appeared and wound himself around her ankles. She went through the flat, turning on lights and lamps until there was at least the appearance of warmth. The television provided a background of noise and life.

She fed Dougal and made herself a cheese sandwich. The fridge was almost empty, she noticed. She supposed she would have to go shopping soon, but the thought lacked urgency. As she was about to close the fridge door, she saw the bottle of champagne, still waiting unopened. The sight of it brought a sudden pang, piercing the numbness that surrounded her. She picked it up and quickly dropped it in the bin. The cold, wet touch of the glass burned her hand. She wiped it on a towel until the sensation had gone.

Taking her sandwich through to the lounge, she saw the light flashing on her phone. There were two messages. The first was from Lucy, asking what had happened at the doctor's. The second was the low hiss of an open line before the click of disconnection.

Kate put down her plate. Her hands were shaking as she called Lucy. It went straight to voicemail, but Kate had only just started to speak when the phone was picked up at the other end.

'Sorry about that,' Lucy said breathlessly. 'We were halfway through tea, so we thought we'd see who it was before we answered.'

'I'll talk to you later, if you like.'

'No, it's OK. I want to hear how you got on.'

Now she had called her, Kate felt a reluctance to talk. 'I'm having the abortion.'

She heard Lucy breathe out, relieved. 'It's for the best, Kate, it really is. Do you know when?'

'Not yet. Soon, though.'

'You've done the right thing. I know it wasn't an easy choice, but—'

'Look, Lucy, I – I don't want to talk about it just now.' The urge to put down the phone was almost overpowering. 'I'm sorry, I'll give you a ring tomorrow.'

'Are you OK? Do you want to come over?'

'No. Thanks, I'll be fine, I just . . . I'll talk to you tomorrow.'

She hung up. The effort of communication left her exhausted. She looked at the sandwich on the plate, telling herself she should eat something. But as she went to pick it up the phone rang.

Kate stared at it. It rang again. She waited until the last second before the voicemail cut in, then picked up the receiver.

'Hello?'

There was a silence at the other end. She swallowed. 'It's you, isn't it?' Still no answer. 'For God's sake, *say* something!'

'*I'm sorry.*'

It was almost whispered. She leaned her forehead on the wall at the sound of his voice.

'Kate? A-are you there?'

'Yes, I'm here.'

'I phoned before. You w-weren't in.'

Kate wiped her eyes. 'Where are you?' she asked.

He didn't answer.

'I've seen the police,' she told him. She could hear him breathing. 'They told me what you did.'

Silence.

'Why? Why did you do it?' she burst out.

'I – I'm sorry.'

'*Sorry?*' The cry was wrung from her. She wanted to hammer the phone against the wall. '*Sorry?* I don't even know what to *call* you!'

'Kate ... p-please. I didn't m-mean this to happen.'

'You didn't *mean* it to happen? What the hell did you think was *going* to happen?'

'I – I'm sorry, I—'

'*Stop saying you're fucking sorry!*'

She stopped. She felt breathless, as though she had run upstairs. In a calmer voice, she asked, 'Why did you do it?'

The silence went on for so long she thought he wasn't going to answer.

'I saw your advert.' His voice sounded wet, as though he was talking through tears. 'I was in his waiting room, and it was in the m-magazine. And then, when I went in to see Dr T-Turner, he had to go out of his office and left his jacket on the back of his chair, so . . . I t-took his wallet.'

Kate sank down on to the floor, her back against the wall. '*Why*, though? I don't understand.'

She heard him sniff. 'I kn-knew you wouldn't want *me*! But if . . . if you thought I was somebody else . . . I didn't know it was g-going to go on for so *long*! I thought . . . I thought you'd n-never know, and that you'd have m-my baby and it'd be like *me* having a second chance!'

Oh, God. She caught her bottom lip between her teeth.

'But then I met you, and you told me it would t-take months . . . And I was glad. You looked so . . .'

Kate squeezed her eyes shut. *Don't. Please, don't.*

'I just wanted you to *like* me! I didn't kn-know it'd go on like it did. I . . . I kept *wanting* to tell you, but I couldn't. I knew you w-wouldn't want to see me any more . . .'

'Is that why you killed Alex Turner?'

It seemed strange, saying the name to him, meaning someone else. He didn't answer straight away.

'He saw your email.' He spoke softly. 'He phoned me and said it was important, and I'd g-got to go round straight after work.'

'After work? Do you mean the computer repair shop, or is this some other career you've invented?' She felt ashamed as soon as she'd said it.

He faltered, 'K-Kate, I—'

'Just go on.'

She heard him draw a shaky breath. 'Everyone else had gone home. When I went in, he showed me the email and said, "Who's Kate?" I – I just couldn't *think*! He said he'd thought I'd taken his wallet, but he hadn't been sure. Not until he saw what you'd put about my g-gran's St Christopher, because I'd told him all about her. And he said, "Tim, don't you think you'd b-better tell me what you've done?" So I told him, and all the time I k-kept thinking about you being pregnant, and that it was our baby, and – and I felt so *happy*!'

There was a pause. She could hear him breathing, reliving it.

'And then he said, "You've c-caused quite a mess, haven't you?" He told me it'd got to be sorted out, and he was going to have to t-tell you. I wanted to tell you myself, but he said n-no, it had gone too far for that. He w-wouldn't *l-listen*!'

His stammer had grown worse, like a machine shaking itself apart.

'He started telling me to c-calm down, but how c-could I when he was going to spoil everything? If he'd just let me *tell* you it would have b-been all right, but he wouldn't. He told me to sit down, and started saying everything w-would be OK, but I knew he was lying. Then he told me not to *push* him, but I *hadn't*, I – I'm sure I hadn't, and then he started going towards the d-door, and I knew if I let him I'd n-never see you again. I – I tried to *stop* him, but I just wanted to *explain*, to m-make him see, and then—'

He stopped. Kate was rigid, every muscle tense. She could hear his breathing, rapid and laboured.

'I didn't m-mean to,' he said. 'It was only because he was g-going to tell you, but there was so much *blood*. I just didn't want him to t-*tell* you, that was all, I couldn't stand the thought of what you'd think about me. Kate, I . . .'

Don't. She wasn't sure if she'd spoken it or not.

'. . . I l-love you, Kate . . .'

No.

'P-please, Kate, I'm s-sorry—'

'No.'

'Please don't h-hate me, I didn't m-mean to hurt anyone—'

'Shut up.'

'Don't be upset, I wouldn't hurt you—'

'Shut *up*!'

'I only did it because of the b-baby—'

'*There isn't any baby!*'

It was a reflexive cry. There was a silence.

'What do you m-mean?' She could hear the fear in his voice. 'K-Kate, don't say that!'

'I mean there isn't any baby!'

'There is, I saw your email, you s-said—'

'It's *dead*! I've had an abortion!'

Distantly, she felt herself recoil from the words, but there was a savage exultation in lashing out, in hurting him back.

'No.' The denial was hushed.

'I had it this morning.'

'N-no, I d-don't believe you!'

260

'They killed it.' The words ran away with her.

'You're lying!'

'They cut it out—'

'Oh, God, no . . .'

'—and then they threw it in the incinerator and burned it!'

She stopped, appalled with herself. She heard him moan.

'Don't,' she said. 'I didn't mean it.'

'No, no, God, no—'

'Listen,' she began, 'I haven't—'

'*No, no, no no nonono—*'

The sound of his pain cut through her own. 'Please, don't! You were right, I was—'

'*Bitch!*'

The word hit her like a fist.

'*M-murdering fucking bitch!*'

'No, listen to me—!'

'*I'll kill you! I'll fucking k-kill you, you murdering BITCH!*'

The line went dead.

The phone hummed in her ear. Slowly, Kate lowered it. She became aware of a weight on her lap. Looking down, she saw that at some point Dougal had come and sat on her knee without her noticing. She dislodged him and got unsteadily to her feet.

On the TV, the quiz show still buzzed with gleeful laughter. Kate walked away from the sound. She went downstairs and checked that both doors were locked.

Then she came back up and phoned the police.

16

It was nothing like the clinic in Birmingham. For one thing, she was fully clothed, sitting on a hard plastic chair instead of lying on a couch. The room was a dull cream colour, NHS instead of private, and lit by a harsh strip light that buzzed like a trapped fly. The doctor was short and plump, and the nurse's uniform nothing like so crisply ironed. But for all that, Kate couldn't help but be reminded of the other place. Perhaps it was because one had been a beginning while the other was an end.

She had come a full, futile circle.

Her hand went instinctively to her throat, feeling for the gold locket that was now in a drawer in her flat. She lowered it again.

'The procedure for an early medical termination's quite simple,' the doctor said, and again Kate was faced with a ghost of that other time, the other clinic. 'Effectively, what we're doing is inducing a miscarriage. The drug we give you basically stops the lining of your womb forming. You'll have to stay here for an hour after you've taken it to make sure there aren't any side effects, but there rarely are.'

The doctor gave a reassuring smile. She was a pleasant-faced woman in her fifties. 'After that you can go home again. Then you'll have to come back in a couple of days, and we'll give you a pessary to make you pass what's in your womb.'

'Will I be able to see anything?' Kate could hear the tremor in her own voice.

'You'll probably see what you pass, yes. But it won't be much different from a heavy period. There won't be anything recognizable, if that's what you mean. At this stage it's still only cells.'

Cells.

Kate pushed the image out of her mind. 'What . . . what happens to it? Afterwards, I mean. What do you do with it?'

Her eyes went to the yellow cardboard cylinder on the window ledge. It had stylized drawings of flames on it. The doctor saw where she was looking and gave an understanding shake of her head.

'That's only for wipes.'

She gave Kate a small paper container, like a miniature cup. In it was a single white pill. Kate looked down at it. The tiny object seemed bland and innocuous. The nurse held out a glass of water for her. Kate took it. The tremor in her hand caused a faint rippling of the water's surface. She raised the plastic cup with the pill in it to her lips. Over its rim she could see the doctor and nurse watching her. She held it poised, tensing herself. One swallow and it would be done. Seconds passed.

Kate lowered the cup.

'I can't.'

She shook her head. 'I'm sorry, I just can't.'

She held out the container, suddenly wanting to be rid of it. The doctor took it from her.

'That's all right, you aren't under any pressure to go through with this.'

Kate felt her eyes begin to swim. 'I'm sorry. I should never have come.'

'Don't worry. You're not the first one who's got this far and then changed her mind.' The doctor gave her a smile and patted her arm, although the nurse was stony-faced as she emptied the glass into the sink. 'Better to find out now than later.'

Kate felt weak and washed out as she went out into the corridor and down to the waiting area. Lucy looked up in surprise from a magazine.

'That was quick.'

'I haven't had it.'

Lucy lowered the magazine. 'Why, what's—?'

'Please, let's just go.' Kate glanced at the other women in the waiting room. They looked away but were obviously listening. 'I'll tell you outside.'

A thin skim of brown mush lay on the pavement from the snow that had fallen that morning. A few flakes still drifted down. They expired against Kate's cheeks like cold sparks.

'What happened?' Lucy asked, as they walked away from the hospital.

'Nothing. I just couldn't go through with it.'

'You mean you just walked out?'

Kate nodded. Lucy made an exasperated noise in her

264

throat. 'Kate, what are you *thinking* of? Look, perhaps if you went back in and—'

'I'm not going back.'

'Don't be silly. I know it's difficult, but you've got to face up to it sooner or later.'

'I have faced up to it. I'm going to keep the baby.'

'Oh, come *on*, Kate, be reasonable!'

'I am.'

'I thought it was all decided! You said yourself it was the best thing to do!'

'I changed my mind.'

They had stopped. The falling snow crystals had turned to sleet, speckling their hair with glistening beads. Lucy brushed a damp strand from her forehead.

'Look, let's get out of this muck and talk about it.'

'There's nothing to talk about. I've told you, I'm keeping it.'

'You *can't* keep it! Just think about what you're doing! The father's a raving lunatic who's on the run for murder, he's already threatened to kill you, and you're still going to have his baby?'

'It isn't the baby's fault. The doctor was right, I can't blame it for what its father's done.'

'And what if it turns out like him? And it might, I don't care what the doctor says. What will you do then?'

'I'll have to risk it. But it'll be as much me as him, and I'll do everything I can to make sure it has more chances than he did.'

'And it's that simple? You think it'll thank you when it's old enough to understand who its father was? What will you say?'

265

'I don't know, all right? I can't even think about what I'll be doing tomorrow, let alone God knows how many years from now! I just know that I'm not going to kill this baby!'

'For God's sake, Kate, it isn't even a baby yet! Don't be stupid!'

'I'm not being stupid.'

'No?' Lucy cast her eyes skyward. 'This is just so typical of you! You won't listen to anybody, will you?'

Kate's own anger had been waiting for a focus. 'If I'd listened to you I'd have been married to him by now!'

'Fine, I admit he fooled me as well, but I said from the start this was a bad idea, and you wouldn't take any notice! You were hell-bent on doing things your way, and look where it's got you!'

'So you think this is my fault?'

'Since you ask, yes! Nobody made you do it, it was what *you* wanted. God, I could shake you sometimes! I'd have thought you'd have learned your lesson by now!'

'What's that supposed to mean?'

Lucy's cheeks had flushed an angry red. 'Nothing. Forget I said it.'

'No, come on, I want to know what you mean.'

'You know what I mean. I mean Paul Sutherland. You should have walked out on him months before you did, but, no, you'd got to wait until he threw you out. I swear I don't understand you, Kate! It's like when things get bad you go out of your way to make them worse!'

'This is nothing like that!'

266

'Yes, it is, it's exactly the same.'

Kate's face was hot. 'Except this time only one of us has slept with him.'

She knew, as she said it, that she was moving the argument on to a different level, but by then it had developed a momentum of its own. Lucy glared at her, white-lipped.

'Oh, now we're getting to it! I wondered how long it would be before you threw that one back at me!'

'I'm not throwing anything back at you. I'm just reminding you that you're not as perfect as you think.'

'Perhaps not, but at least I'm capable of having a relationship without it turning into a disaster!'

'Oh, piss off!'

They stared at each other, wide-eyed at the suddenness of the breach. Their breath steamed in a cloud around them. All at once neither could meet the other's eye.

Lucy spoke first. 'All right, I will. But just don't come running to me and Jack in future.'

'Don't worry, I won't.'

They began walking in opposite directions. Kate half expected to hear Lucy shout after her, and half wanted to turn round and do the same herself. But Lucy didn't shout, and Kate kept on walking.

When she reached the corner and glanced back, Lucy had gone.

Morning sickness was a joy Kate hadn't counted on. She'd known, intellectually, that she could probably expect it, but she had found out that expecting it and experiencing it were two different things. She had put her earlier attack of nausea down to shock at first, until it happened again the next morning. Since then it had been a regular part of her daily routine: along with showering, getting dressed, going for the tube, she knew that at some point she would also have to incorporate vomiting into her schedule.

It wouldn't be so bad, she thought, if it came along at the same time every day. She knew that Lucy (although she tried not to think about Lucy) had been as regular as clockwork, making sure she was near a bathroom between eleven and twelve each morning. But Kate's own attacks were sporadic. The queasiness she would wake up with could linger all day, like a low-grade hangover. Or it could send her running for the bathroom before she left her flat in the morning. It was just something else she couldn't predict.

She felt the nausea begin to build as she sat on the tube.

Anxiously, she counted the stations still to go. King's Cross was several stops away. She sat perfectly still, trying not to dwell on it. The train lurched and whined to a halt in the tunnel. The sudden jolt made Kate break out in a clammy sweat, a sign she had come to recognize as meaning that vomiting was imminent. She prayed for the train to move again, trying to think if she had anything in her bag to be sick into. There was nothing except the bag itself.

She closed her eyes, but that only made her feel worse. The train jerked forward, and with relief Kate saw the lights of a platform appear outside the windows. Without caring which station it was, she hurried off and pushed through the crowd waiting to board. Breathing as steadily as she could through her nose, she ran up the escalators, eyes scanning desperately for a toilet sign.

There was one on the upper concourse. She had a bad moment when there was a queue, but then she was inside and bolting the cubicle door behind her.

The only thing to be said for it was that it was over quickly. Feeling wretched, but less so than before, she rinsed her mouth out at a sink and dried it on a paper towel. She looked at herself in the mirror above the taps. Her face looked pale, the skin under her eyes bruised.

You wanted this, she told herself. *Too late to feel sorry for yourself now.*

The sickness left her blood sugar screaming for renewal.

She debated whether to call Clive and tell him she would be late, but decided he would work that out anyway and went into a coffee shop just outside the station. She ordered a croissant and jam, and a decaf tea. The coffee smelled wonderful, but she'd found that she had no stomach for it any more. She wondered what else she would be giving up before the nine months were over.

She felt more like herself when she came out and went back down the escalator to catch a train. As if the break in her journey had set a precedent, she was in no rush now to get to work. It was almost eleven before she turned into the row of Georgian terraced houses. The light was on in the downstairs office of the agency, and through the window she saw Clive clutching a bundle of papers to his chest. She had time to notice the harried expression on his face before she opened the door and her greeting died on her lips.

The office was a shambles. The desks had been tipped over and the filing cabinet drawers pulled out and emptied on to the floor. Computer equipment lay among the papers that were scattered on the carpet like snow.

Kate found her voice. 'What's happened?'

'We've been burgled. Well, broken into, at least. There doesn't seem to be much missing.' Clive looked around wryly. 'So far as we can tell, anyway.'

She closed the door and walked inside, picking her way carefully through the turmoil. 'Have you called the police?'

'Yeah, they've been. For what it's worth. They want us to make out a list of anything that's been taken. They're sending somebody round to fingerprint, so we've got to try to avoid touching anything. But I thought we could at least start clearing up some of the papers.'

Kate stared at the mess. 'Why didn't you call me?'

Clive's face and tone were carefully neutral. 'I tried. Your phone was switched off.'

She resisted the temptation to close her eyes. She'd started turning off her phone outside work hours and had forgotten to turn it back on that morning. Not so long ago the idea of being out of touch would have driven her mad. Now there was no one she wanted to hear from.

'Looks like they forced the toilet window at the back,' Clive went on. 'The alarm went off but no-one reported it, so the police didn't come out until I called them. It didn't stop whoever it was from breaking in, but they think it must have panicked them, because they don't seem to have taken much. They just trashed down here and in your office.'

'How bad?'

'You'd better see for yourself.'

She went upstairs, Clive following her. If anything, the chaos there was even worse. She reached out for the broken fan, lying smashed on a shelf, then remembered she wasn't supposed to touch anything and let her arm drop to her side.

Clive pushed the door shut. 'Look,' he began uneasily, 'I don't know if I've done the right thing, but . . . well, the police were asking if I knew of anyone with any grudges against us, so I told them about Paul Sutherland.'

Kate looked around at the wreckage of her office. 'I don't think he did this.'

'If he was drunk he might have. He's got a big enough chip on his shoulder.'

Kate kept her doubts to herself.

'The only thing I can't find so far is the back-up hard drive from the filing cabinet. It's only an old one, don't worry,' Clive added before Kate could react. 'We've got other back-ups, so it isn't the end of the world. I just wondered if you'd moved it somewhere.'

'No, I don't think so.' She couldn't summon up the energy to care. The drive itself wasn't valuable, and there wasn't anything particularly sensitive on it. If it had been stolen it wouldn't be much use to anyone.

'Well, I thought I'd ask. It might still turn up anyway.'

Clive looked around her office. 'Do you want a hand in here?'

'No, I'll manage, thanks.'

When he'd gone back downstairs she ran her hand through her hair, glad she hadn't tied it back that morning. The beginning of a tension headache was forming at her temples as she regarded the mess and wondered where to start. The violence seemed aimless and wanton. Her reference books had been swept from the shelf. As she went over to them, something crunched under her foot.

She looked down.

It was a box of matches.

17

The crematorium chapel was modern and austere. The walls were a dull mustard yellow, with clear glass windows set high up near the ceiling. The pews were a pale oak, functional and straight-lined, like park benches. Hung on the wall at the far end, the bare wooden crucifix looked geometric and stark.

Kate slipped into an empty pew at the back. Most of those in front of her were full, lines of dark-clothed figures facing the plain pulpit that stood on a low dais. She thought of Miss Willoughby's funeral, where there had been only herself and a bored solicitor. To one side of the dais lay the coffin, surrounded on three sides by dark-blue curtains. No one looked round as she quietly took her seat. A Bob Marley track was playing through the wall-mounted speakers, helping to cover the echoing rustles and coughs. It faded as the white-surpliced vicar mounted the pulpit.

He was a plump, youngish man with prematurely greying hair. He stood with his arms held loosely by his sides, waiting until the last strains of the music had died before speaking.

'We're gathered here today to celebrate the life of Alex Turner.'

His voice carried clearly in the bleak room. A choked sob came from a woman in the front row. An older woman sat beside her, an arm around her shoulders.

'I know all of you here will have come with your grief, and your anger, at the manner of his passing. It is never easy when someone we love dies, and it is even less so when they are taken from us as Alex was, suddenly, and with violence. It is natural to feel shocked and bewildered. And it is easy to let those emotions give way to hate for the person who took Alex's life. But today, I want you to put those feelings aside. We should remember that Alex dedicated his life to helping others. For him to lose his life in doing so is a cause for sorrow, but Alex himself would have been the first to urge us not to condemn. But to try to understand.'

The woman sat with her head bowed. Kate could see her shoulders shaking. Further along in the same pew, an elderly man blew his nose and dabbed at his eyes.

'It is not always easy. We have lost a friend. A son. A husband. And a father, because the child that Kay, Alex's wife, is carrying will now never know him.'

For an instant Kate thought he had said her own name. She looked again at the woman in the front row.

'One of the tragedies is that neither will Alex see his child when it's born, a child that he and Kay have long wanted. For them to be finally blessed, only to have their happiness snatched away in a senseless act of violence seems especially cruel. Yet to give way to thoughts of bitterness, of anger and revenge, would be an even greater waste. Because to do that is not only to dishonour Alex's memory. It is also to refute everything he lived, worked and ultimately died for.'

A draught of cold air brushed the back of Kate's neck as the chapel door was opened. She looked round to see a man wearing a thick waxed coat easing it shut behind him. His shoes squeaked on the floor as he went to the end of Kate's pew and sat down. A bulky camera was slung around his neck. Kate looked away as he began to fiddle with it.

'I was privileged to know Alex through the work we both did in the community, and I can truthfully say I found him to be a patient and kind man, who genuinely cared for the people who came to him for help. So, as we pray now for Alex, I would like us also to pray for the tortured young man who took him from us so suddenly. And also for each other, so we can find the strength within ourselves to forgive him.'

Abruptly, Kate's eyes filled. She hung her head, letting the tears drop directly on to her coat, where they quickly soaked into the rain-damp fabric. In the general shuffling as the congregation prepared itself to pray, she took a tissue from her pocket and quietly blew her nose.

A noise from the end of the pew distracted her. Glancing up, she saw that the photographer was also bent over, but only to change the lens on his camera. He had a bag open on the seat next to him, and as he took one from it, he knocked another on to the floor. She heard its thin rattle, and the man's muttered 'Shit,' over the vicar's resonant voice.

The prayer ended. The vicar continued, but now Kate's attention was divided between what he was saying and the photographer's preparations.

The service was short. There was no hymn. Instead, they sat in silence as Elgar's cello concerto was played through the PA system. At the end of it Kate would have slipped out, but the photographer blocked the exit from the pew.

'It is our hope and belief that Alex's spirit will not have died, that the Alex we knew and loved still continues, apart from us, but still whole,' the vicar said. 'But Alex remains with us in other ways. He will always be a part of our hearts, always be in our memories. And he will continue in the child that Kay gives birth to, a living reminder of the Alex Turner whom we knew and loved, and to whom we now bid goodbye.'

The curtains closed over the coffin with a jerky rustle. As they swayed to a standstill, the vicar stepped down from the pulpit without another word. Kate looked over at the photographer again. He was poised on the edge of his seat, camera at the ready. She turned away, wondering if she could squeeze out at the other end, but the pew was pushed up against the wall.

She looked back in time to see the photographer bob up to take a couple of shots as the woman rose to her feet. Kate lowered her head as the mourners began to file out. She didn't want to draw attention to herself, but the exit was on her side.

From the corner of her eye she could see the woman

being supported by an elderly couple. Behind her followed the man Kate had seen wiping his eyes earlier. The widow walked slowly, like an invalid, and Kate had time to see the heavy belly under the black coat, the pale and tear-blotched face.

Kate kept her head down. She could hear the woman's stifled sobs and ducked her head further, tensing for the cry of accusation.

The door creaked open. The footsteps diminished and were drowned by the shuffling tread of the other mourners as they went out.

Kate didn't move. She kept her eyes on her hands, clasped tightly on her lap, as the procession dragged on. Finally, she could hear that it was coming to an end. The rest of the chapel was quiet as the stragglers made their way behind her to the door, and Kate prepared to leave.

'Hello, Miss Powell.'

She jumped at the sound of the voice. She looked up at the man standing over her, unable to think who he was. Then the bristly grey hair, the faintly mournful eyes under thick black brows slotted into place and she recognized DI Collins.

'I wasn't expecting to see you here,' he said.

The last of the mourners had disappeared through the door. They had the chapel to themselves.

'I wanted to come.' Kate looked over to where the coffin was hidden by the closed drapes. 'I thought it was the least I could do.'

A mechanical whirring sound came from behind the curtains. They swayed slightly.

'We'd better go,' Collins said. 'There's another funeral scheduled.'

Kate made her way along the pew. Collins waited for her.

He was wearing the brown suit and tweed overcoat that he always seemed to have on. He held the door open for her, and they went along the short corridor to the main exit.

Outside, the air was cold and sharp. The mourners were clustered in loose groups on the wide tarmac drive around the young woman. Kate looked away.

'I'd better go.'

Collins regarded her. 'If you want to hang on a second I'll give you a lift.'

'No, it's all right. Thanks.' She was suddenly in a hurry to get away.

'I'd like a word with you anyway. I won't be a minute. The car's parked at the other side.'

They moved around the mourners towards a line of parked cars. Then Collins stopped. She felt his hand on her arm, restraining her, and looked up to see him staring ahead at the photographer who had been in the chapel. The man's attention was on the central group around the widow as he took more shots.

'Let's go this way,' Collins said, taking her arm and leading her back the way they had come.

They went around the back of the chapel, coming out behind the photographer, so he was facing away from them.

'Why didn't you want him to see you?' Kate asked.

He glanced at her, then away again.

'It was more you I didn't want him to see. We've kept you out of it so far. I don't want the press to start sniffing around over some "mystery woman" at the funeral.'

The murder of a psychologist by one of his patients had made national news, but none of the reports had mentioned Kate's involvement. She was surprised by Collins's consideration.

'Thank you.'

'No need to thank me. The press coverage was bad enough when they thought it was just another failure of community care. They've lost interest now, but if they find out why Ellis killed him it'll turn into a three-ring circus. That won't help anybody.'

They reached the line of waiting cars. Collins went to a grey Ford. The sergeant who had been with him the first time he had visited Kate's office was in the driver's seat, reading a newspaper. He quickly folded it.

'We're giving Miss Powell a lift,' Collins told him, opening the rear door for her.

The sergeant grinned at Kate, then seemed to think that might be too familiar and looked more serious. He cast a glance at the DI, as Collins eased his bulk on to the back seat next to her.

'Where to?'

'The nearest tube station's fine,' Kate said.

The sergeant started the car. Others from the line were already pulling on to the drive.

'I've been in touch with the Wynguard Clinic,' Collins said, as they passed through the crematorium gates. 'Not that they were able to help much. Your Dr Janson's a worried woman. It seems the clinic never got around to checking with Ellis's GP. They didn't seem to think there was any real need, because you'd presented him to them as your "known donor". Is that the right term?'

Kate said nothing, remembering how Alex had claimed he'd forgotten his GP's address. How he'd specified he was doing this just for her, that nothing he donated should be used for anyone else. It had seemed touching at the time.

'Anyway, that's between you and them, but I wouldn't be surprised if you'd got a case for negligence. I doubt that Ellis knew who the real Alex Turner's doctor was, so if the clinic had tried to get hold of his medical records they'd have known something was wrong straight away.'

She shook her head. 'I can't blame them.'

Collins let the matter drop. 'The other thing I wanted to tell you is that Paul Sutherland's in the clear.'

'What for?' she asked, surprised.

'The break-in at your agency. He claims he can't remember where he was that night, but that's not hard to believe. When we questioned him we had to let him sober up before he could talk any sense at all. But his alibi checks out, so it doesn't look as though it was him.'

The car smelled musty. Kate wound down the window a little to let some air in. The breeze was cold on her face. 'I never thought it was.'

'No luck with fingerprints, either, I'm afraid.' Collins's knees pressed into the back of the seat in front. Sitting next to him, Kate felt like a little girl. 'Looks as though whoever did it wore gloves. Either they knew what they were doing or they'd got cold hands.'

'What about the matches?'

Collins turned down his mouth and shook his head. 'Doesn't prove it was Ellis, if that's what you mean.'

'So you don't think it was.'

'I don't think a box of matches proves anything, one way or another. It could just have been a burglar who smoked. We'll keep an eye on your office as well as your flat, but I wouldn't read too much into it.'

Kate gazed out of the window. 'Did you find out where he called from?'

'We traced the number to a public payphone near Oxford Circus, so evidently he's avoiding using his mobile.' Collins sounded disgruntled. 'Somebody like that won't be able to keep out of sight for very long, though. He's unstable, with no friends or easy access to money. And he's got nowhere to go.'

Kate supposed she should find his confidence reassuring, but she didn't take any comfort from it. She wouldn't feel safe until Ellis was in custody. And perhaps not even then. The sergeant pulled into the kerb. 'This OK? There's a tube station on the other side of the road.'

Kate said it was and got out. Collins climbed out as well.

'Don't worry,' he said, his hand on the passenger door handle. 'It's only a matter of time before we find him.'

The car sank down slightly as he eased into the front seat.

As it pulled away, Kate looked to see if the road was clear to cross.

Outlined against the grey clouds, the thin column of the crematorium chimney was poised like a rebuking finger.

That night she cooked herself a cheese and ham omelette, with Brussels sprouts and two slices of wholemeal bread. Sprouts weren't her favourite vegetable, but they were rich in folic acid. Even though she had no appetite, now she was pregnant there was an incentive to make an effort. Part of her noted the irony that she was finally able to eat as much as she liked without feeling guilty, but she wasn't able to enjoy it.

Kate found that she had moved to an acceptance of her pregnancy without really being aware of it. The thrill she had expected to feel seemed to have been lost in the larger emotional turmoil. At odd moments the knowledge would hit her, and there would be a vertiginous plunge. But even that was growing rarer.

She forced herself to eat the omelette and helped down the final bread crust with a glass of milk. Taking her plate and glass into the kitchen, she washed and dried them. When she had put them away she looked at her watch. Eight o'clock. She went back into the lounge and stared at the television until it was ten o'clock and she felt she could reasonably go to bed.

Sleep came hard. Often it was little more than a restless, half-awake state that would last until the early hours, leaving her grainy and listless when it was time to get up. It was like that now. Kate groped for the clock as the insistent beep of the alarm dragged her towards consciousness. She fumbled to turn it off before realizing that the noise was coming from outside her room.

She sat up. It was still dark, without even the subtle lightening that indicates dawn. Still hazy with sleep, it took her several seconds to understand what had woken her.

It was the smoke alarm.

She threw back the covers and rushed into the hall. The yammer of the alarm was immediately louder, and now she could smell the smoke that had triggered it. She switched on the hall light and blinked against the sudden brightness. There was a faint grey haze in the air, but no fire.

Kate ran to the lounge. It was as she had left it, dark and quiet. The smell of smoke was fainter. She hurried out to check the kitchen, noticing that the smoke in the hallway was already thicker. As she passed the top of the stairwell a noise made her look down.

Smoke was oozing from around the door at the bottom. The foot of the stairs was in shadow, but a bright glow came from the translucent cat-flap. It was bumping inwards as though blown by a wind, nudged by the heat on the other side. The plastic was already beginning to bubble.

Kate ran into the kitchen. She turned both taps full on to fill the washing-up bowl and then, leaving them running, dashed to the phone. Her hands were shaking as she called 999.

'Emergency, which service do you require?'

'Fire. My flat's on fire.'

She tried to keep her voice level but couldn't stop the tremor as she gave the details. The smoke alarm continued to shrill in the background.

'Is there anyone else in the property?' the operator, a woman, asked.

'No.' At least Miss Willoughby's flat was still empty.

'Can you go outside?'

'No, the exit's on fire, for God's sake!'

She heard the panic in her voice, but the operator remained calm as she told Kate to go to a room facing the street, close the door and put something at the bottom to block the smoke.

'Open the window and stay by it so they can see you,' the operator said. 'And hang a towel or something out of it as a marker.'

The smoke was already thicker, given a toxic bite from the melting plastic of the cat-flap. Coughing, Kate hung up and ran back to the kitchen. The washing-up bowl was overflowing and, without turning off the taps, she picked it up and staggered out with it. Water sloshed on to the T-shirt she wore to sleep in as she reached the top of the stairs and heaved the entire bowl towards the bottom. Without waiting to see what effect it had, she stumbled back down the hallway and into the lounge.

The air in there was clearer, and it wasn't until she had closed the door that it occurred to her that the room was directly above the fire. Belatedly, she wondered if the bathroom would be safer. But she balked at the thought of going back out into the smoke.

Putting cushions at the bottom of the door, she crossed to the window. It was a sash, and years of paint had stuck it together. Every summer since she had been in the flat Kate had meant to repair it, but never had. It slid open easily for six inches and then jammed. She struggled with it for a few seconds and then gave up. A bar of cold air breezed against her midriff. She had forgotten to grab a towel, so she stripped the cover off one of the cushions and draped that through the gap instead. Resting her head against the cold glass, she looked out. The street was empty, with no sign of the police patrols Collins had promised. The path in front of the front door was lit by a moving, multi-coloured light. Flickering patches of blue, red and orange danced on the garden as the flames shone through the stained-glass facets. A faint tinkling came to Kate as, one by one, they shattered, until the harlequin glow was a uniform yellow.

There was a movement in the shadows. She peered into them and saw Dougal sitting on the garden wall. The cat's eyes gleamed with reflected light as he watched the fire. Kate's breath misted the window, and when she wiped it clear Dougal had gone.

Dimly, in the distance she heard the wail of a siren.

Water dropped from the ceiling. A sooty pool of it scummed the floor, covering the cracked ceramic tiles. The walls and ceiling were blackened, the woodwork of the doorways charred and blistered. The welcome mat lay where it had been pushed into a corner by the pressure of the hose, a shrunken black square. Hanging over everything was a tickling charcoal reek.

The fire officer straightened. Behind him other uniformed men were coiling the hose and packing it away. Glass crunched under his feet. The bulb in the ceiling had shattered, but enough light came from the stairs to see by.

'We'll have to wait for the forensic results, but I don't think there's much doubt.' He was a stocky middle-aged man. His hair had been flattened by the yellow helmet he held under one arm as he nodded down at the cat-flap at the base of the door.

It had melted and congealed like candle wax, a surreal twin to the one set in the inside door.

'Looks like they poured petrol through the outside flap, then stuck a piece of cloth through and set fire to it.' He nudged with his foot at a charred fragment that could have been fabric. 'Whoever did it knew enough not to get their fingers burned by sticking their hand through with a match. You're lucky it was only in the entrance area. There's nothing much in here to burn. Still, it could still have been nasty if you hadn't got a smoke alarm.'

He looked at the stubs of smoky glass in the top half of the front door and shook his head. 'Any idea who might have done it?'

Kate hugged her bathrobe more tightly around her. The porch was dank from the water dripping from every surface but she shook more from reaction than cold. 'He's . . . uh, the police are already looking for him.'

The fire officer waited for her to say more, then looked around as a white patrol car pulled up in front of the red engine. 'I'll leave you to tell them, then.'

He stepped down on to the path. His boots splashed in the grimy puddles.

'One thing. I wouldn't have another cat-flap when you have the new door fitted. Whoever it was might make a more serious attempt next time. All it would take would be a length of pipe and they could pour the petrol straight into your flat.'

He stared at her, to make sure his words had registered, then winked.

'Puss'll just have to wait until you let him in.'

18

Kate's birthday was on a grey, windy day, when all the lights had to be switched on to counter the unrelieved twilight, and the approaching spring seemed like another country. She hadn't given much thought to it before; too much else had been happening to dwell on such irrelevancies. But that morning she woke up with the awareness that another year had been ticked off her life's calendar.

The post arrived before she left for work. She collected it from the cage covering the letter-box on her way out. The new front door had been fitted the day after the fire, a sturdy hardwood slab with a small frosted-glass window. The door to Miss Willoughby's flat had also been replaced, at the insistence of the estate agent. Ironically, her own only needed repainting, but the coconut mat in front of the other had acted like a wick, charring the wood deeply.

She left the junk mail inside and closed the front door, glad to be in fresh air. Several days after the fire, the stink of it still permeated everything. The painters were due at the end of the week, and Kate told herself that things would seem better when the flat smelled of wet paint instead of the oily reek of petrol and smoke.

A police car cruised by. Kate wondered if it was coincidence or evidence of Collins's assurance that they would step up patrols outside her home. The car went past without either of the occupants glancing at her, and she turned her attention to the post.

There were two birthday cards. One was from an aunt who lived in Dorset, while the other was from a girl she had been to university with, one of the few people she'd given her new address to when she'd moved and who kept in occasional touch. There was nothing from Lucy. Kate felt a skim of anger masking the hurt. They had never missed each other's birthdays before. She'd felt sure that Lucy would still send her a card and had already anticipated using it as an excuse to phone her again. Now, though, the snub only made her more resolved not to.

No one mentioned her birthday at work. Clive had usually remembered in the past, but obviously hadn't this time. Kate knew she was feeling sorry for herself and in danger of wallowing in it. *Stop being pathetic*, she thought angrily, and went up to her office and shut herself away.

It was almost lunchtime when Clive buzzed through on the intercom. 'There's somebody to see you,' he said. His voice sounded odd. 'Can you come down?'

'Who is it?'

'Er . . . I think you'd better see for yourself.' There was a hesitation. 'It isn't anything to worry about, though.'

He cut the line. More irritated than puzzled, Kate went downstairs. She opened the door to the office. A police constable was standing in the centre of the room.

'It's all right, there's no problem,' Clive said quickly.

Kate noticed him flash Caroline a glance, but her attention was on the policeman. He was young and good looking. He stepped towards her.

'Kate Powell?'

Her mouth was dry. 'Yes?'

In the background Clive was trying to smile reassuringly, looking worried at the same time. The policeman opened a notebook. 'Is today your birthday?'

'Uh, yes. Why, what's—'

'In that case I'll have to charge you with being thirty-four in possession of an eighteen year old's body,' he said, and tore open his tunic.

It came apart in a rip of Velcro, revealing a shirt and tie bib over a bare chest. He cast them flamboyantly to the floor with his helmet and ripped open his trousers. Underneath he wore only a black posing pouch, with a police badge pinned on the front. She heard Clive mutter, 'Oh, Christ,' as the young man kicked free of his trousers and began singing.

'Happy birthday to Kate, happy birthday to Kate, happy birthday dear Ka-yate, happy birthday to you!'

He ended with a flourish and grinned. 'Now I've got a surprise for you,' he said, and Kate took an involuntary step back as he put his hand into his pouch and began to pull something out.

'No!' she exclaimed, and then he was holding up a stuffed cloth truncheon. He waggled it at her.

'The sentence is a kiss, or I'll have to hit you with this,' he said, but before Kate could answer Clive had stepped forward.

'I think we'll skip that bit, thanks.'

The stripper gave them a quick look, then nodded cheerfully. 'In that case, have a happy birthday,' he told Kate. Scooping up his clothes, he dressed with practised efficiency and went to the door. He gave her a wink.

'I'll let you off this time with a verbal,' he said, and went out.

There was a silence. The alcohol scent of his after-shave lingered in the office.

'It, er, it was supposed to be a vicar,' Clive said, giving Caroline a hard look.

'They said they could only do a cop-o-gram!' the girl protested. 'It was either that or a gorilla!'

It was their anxious expressions that did it. The pressures that had been building up for days were abruptly lanced. Kate lolled back against the edge of a desk as laughter swept over her. There was an edge of hysteria to it, but it was no less purging for that. Wiping her eyes, she looked at the other three, whose own laughter was touched with relief.

'Let's go for lunch,' she said.

They went to an Italian restaurant that wasn't too far from the office. Clive ordered a bottle of wine, most of which Caroline and Josefina drank. He raised his eyebrows when Kate asked for mineral water but said nothing. After they'd eaten and had coffee, he surprised her by telling the two girls to go back to the office alone.

'We'll be along in a while,' he said.

They watched them through the window, leaning on each other and laughing as they disappeared from view. Clive shook his head.

'Somehow I can't see them getting much work done this afternoon.' His smile faded. He slowly stirred his coffee. 'Sorry if it was a shock, walking in and seeing a policeman. I should have known better than to leave it to Caroline to sort out.'

Kate smiled. 'Whose idea was it?'

'Hers and Josefina's. I went along with it, though. We thought it might cheer you up.'

She looked down at her glass. 'It's been that obvious, then?'

'I could tell something was wrong, let's put it that way. You've not been the same since the police came to see you.' Clive paused. 'Do you want to talk about it yet?'

Kate found she did. She glanced around. No waiters were within earshot.

'I'm pregnant.'

Clive didn't seem surprised. 'I did wonder.' He nodded at her mineral water. 'No wine or coffee. And you've started drinking herbal tea at work. Well, congratulations. Or is that the wrong thing to say?'

Kate tried to smile. 'I'm not sure myself, to be honest.' She felt her eyes filling up. She wiped them with the napkin. 'Shit. Sorry.'

'No need to be. If I hadn't wanted to know, I wouldn't have asked. So what's happened?'

She hadn't intended to tell him everything. But now that she didn't have Lucy to talk to, the need to unload on somebody was too great. He listened in silence until she'd finished, then sat back and gave a low whistle.

'Well, I was expecting boyfriend problems, but not quite like this.'

'Original, isn't it? And before you say it, if anyone else tells me I've been stupid, I'm going to scream.'

He shrugged. 'I don't think you've been stupid. You've been bloody unlucky, but that's all.'

'You don't think it's my fault, then? That I've brought it on myself?'

'How is it your fault? All you've done was try to be careful. I don't see how anyone can blame you for that.'

'Didn't get me very far, did it?'

'No, but how could you expect something like this?'

Kate had told herself that countless times, but a masochistic voice still whispered that she deserved it. 'So you think I'm doing the right thing, keeping the baby?'

'If that's what you want, yes.' He leaned towards her. 'Look, it's your life. You get one crack at it, so do what you want. If you felt you wanted an abortion, fine. That's your choice. But if you don't, then that's your choice, too. It doesn't matter what anybody else thinks.'

Kate smiled, watching her hands crumble a piece of breadstick on to her plate. 'Perhaps I should have listened to Lucy, after all. She said I should have asked you to be the donor.'

Clive didn't answer. She looked up, worried she'd been tactless.

'Sorry, I didn't mean to embarrass you.'

'You haven't. I'm flattered.' He cocked his head as he considered her. 'Not that I blame you, but just out of curiosity, why didn't you?'

'Working together afterwards would have been a little awkward, don't you think?'

'Yeah, I suppose. And it might have complicated things if the father was black and gay.'

'That had nothing to do with it,' Kate said. She hesitated. 'Actually, I didn't know you were gay.'

Clive gave a shrug. 'No reason why you should. It's not a secret, but I don't make a point of telling people. My life, my business.'

Kate raised her sparkling water. 'I'll drink to that.'

They chinked glasses.

'So,' he went on. 'What are the police doing about this character?'

For a moment Kate had almost forgotten her problems. Now they settled on her again. 'I don't know. They say they're keeping an eye on my flat and the agency, but all that amounts to is a patrol car going past every now and again. Other than that . . .' She let the sentence go unfinished.

Clive frowned down at his empty coffee cup. 'Perhaps you should keep away from your flat until this all blows over. All right, he probably won't do anything else, but I think you should still consider it. You're welcome to stay at my place. There's a sofa bed going empty.'

Kate had already thought about retreating to the safety of a hotel but had dismissed the temptation. She wasn't going to run away.

She reached across the table and squeezed Clive's hand. 'I appreciate the offer, but it's OK. I'll be all right.'

She stood up.

'Come on. We'd better get back.'

The old cupboards and filing cabinets were replaced with new fireproof ones, and additional fire extinguishers installed in every room. Kate bought one for her flat as well.

Short of fitting a sprinkler system at the office, which they couldn't afford, they had done as much as they could. The fact of doing *something*, other than passively sitting back and waiting, made her feel better. Even so, Kate found herself tensing for the sight of charred window frames and scorched bricks whenever she approached the agency. Each day she didn't, her relief added to a growing hope that the fire at her flat was an end, not a beginning. For the first time, she began to feel, if not actual optimism, at least that one day life might return to normal.

The feeling was reinforced when she went to the office one morning and saw that demolition work had begun on the burned-out warehouse. She would be glad to see it go, she thought, as the wrecking ball crumpled another section of wall and blackened timbers into a pile of dusty rubble. She reached the agency's street, relaxing a little when there were no fire engines parked in the road. As she searched in her bag for the keys, she noted absently that the bill posters had been active again. The abundance of boarded-up buildings provided a canvas for bands, clubs and political fringe groups to advertise. The constantly changing display was so much a part of the scenery that Kate rarely noticed it, and when she pulled out the keys and looked up, her first thought was that she had stopped in front of the wrong building. Then she looked again, and shock drained the use from her limbs.

The posters completely covered the ground floor, not just of the agency but also the buildings on either side. They were pasted on haphazardly, overlapping each other and crookedly running over windows and doors. Every one was the same, so that the entire terrace front was a jumbled collage of a single repeated image.

Kate felt the street swim around her. She clutched at a street light as the edges of her vision darkened. Then foosteps were running towards her and she heard Clive's voice.

'Kate? Kate, are you all right?'

She didn't answer. She straightened, though she still held on to the lamp post for support. Clive hovered beside her. She heard him say, 'Jesus!'

The posters were A3 size and full colour. They showed a naked woman having sex with a barely seen man, thighs spread wide in graphic display. But it wasn't the explicitness that was shocking. Smiling directly at the camera, Kate's own face stared back at her from every single poster. Her head had been photoshopped on to the woman's body, her laughing, happy expression blithely indifferent to the rest of the image. Across the base of the poster a sentence had been spelled out in bold red words.

KATE POWELL IS A MURDERING WHORE

She managed to lower herself on to the step before her legs gave way.

19

Collins's face gave no indication of his thoughts as he studied the poster. It had ragged edges from where it had been torn from the wall, but most of it was intact. From the street came the wet hiss of the steam cleaner as it blasted the front of the terrace. Even with the windows closed, the office was humid with the smell of damp paper.

The inspector put the poster down on the desk. 'Well, I think we can safely say he's putting his work experience with computers to good use.'

Kate looked away from the upside-down image in front of her. 'I'm glad you think it's funny.'

The chair protested as Collins tried to ease his bulk into a more comfortable position. He gave up and sat uncomfortably, his big hands resting slackly on his thighs.

'I don't think it's particularly funny, Miss Powell. Though I'd rather he occupied himself making posters instead of lighting fires. Upsetting, I know, but not as bad as burning the building down.'

Kate didn't answer. The fire at her flat had shaken her, but somehow this seemed worse.

'Do you recognize the photograph? The one of you, I mean?' Collins asked.

She nodded, still without looking at it. 'It looks like it's from Cambridge. From the same day as the one I gave you. I don't think he had any others.'

The memory seemed to belong to another person. It gave her a dull ache in her chest, like heartburn.

'He must have downloaded the main photo from some porn site,' Collins said. 'Could have been worse, I suppose.'

'Could it?' Kate heard the sharpness in her voice but couldn't help it. 'Anyway, I don't care where he got it from. How can he *do* something like this? I thought he was supposed to be on the run?'

The policeman rubbed the bridge of his nose with a thick finger. 'We can't be everywhere and posters don't take long to put up.'

'He managed to cover practically the entire building! I thought the police were supposed to be keeping a lookout? And what about CCTV? Didn't any street cameras see anything?'

'We're still checking footage, but even if they did they'll only tell us where he's been, not where he is now. Or where he'll be next,' Collins said reproachfully. He had a shaving nick on his jowls, she noticed. For some reason the sight of it made her feel bad for losing her temper.

'We kept a car stationed near your flat and the agency for several nights after the arson attempt,' the DI continued. 'I'm sorry this has happened, but we can't mount twenty-four-hour surveillance permanently. And

299

it's hard to know what someone like Ellis is going to do at the best of times. He's proved unstable enough even when he was supposedly on medication. If he's stopped taking it – which I think we can safely assume – then he's going to be more unpredictable than ever.'

Collins fixed her with a look.

'Especially now he thinks you've had an abortion.'

The pointed reminder brought colour to Kate's cheeks. 'I'm sorry,' she said, her anger snuffed out. 'I shouldn't take it out on you.'

'Don't worry about it. All part of the job.' He smiled and got to his feet, wincing as his knee joints cracked. He handed the poster to the sergeant, who had been keeping an even lower profile than usual. 'We'll take a look at this anyway, see if it tells us anything.'

He didn't sound hopeful.

Clive waited with her as she locked up that evening, insisting on walking her to the station. She had closed early, almost as soon as the steam cleaners had finished. The atmosphere at the office had been subdued all day. Caroline and Josefina had had to be given some explanation, and although there was a brittle attempt at normality whenever Kate went downstairs, she recognized it as a façade. No one knew quite what to say.

She set the burglar alarm and pulled the door shut, then stepped back and looked at the front of the building. The pavement was littered with scraps of paper left by the cleaners. Water dripped from the walls and pooled on the ground. The door and windows had been scoured clean, but tiny flecks of white still clung to the rougher surfaces of the bricks and mortar.

'Not too bad now, is it?' Clive said.

He didn't sound convinced. Kate shook her head, not trusting her voice. She tried to imagine the figure working in the darkness with its brush and paper. She wondered what had been in Ellis's mind as he went about his business, and realized with a jolt that she was now thinking of him by that name. Ellis. Not Alex. With a subtle tug of loss, she finally understood that Alex Turner was dead.

There was only Timothy Ellis now.

Kate turned away. As she did so she saw that a scrap of poster had stuck wetly to her shoe. She scraped it off with her other foot and stepped back.

'Let's go,' she said.

She left Clive at King's Cross and caught a tube to the health club. Although it wasn't far from her flat, she hadn't been since finding out she was pregnant. There had been other things on her mind.

She had packed her swimsuit that morning, intending to start a new regime, but now all she wanted to do was go home and lock herself in her flat. Which was all the more reason not to.

The health-club gymnasium was busy with the usual post-work crowd. Kate changed into her black one-piece costume and looked down at her stomach. She wasn't showing yet, and she put her bloated feeling down to lack of exercise and too much imagination. Eager now, she went downstairs into the low basement that housed the club's swimming pool.

301

Inside, the air was warm and moist, like a greenhouse. A few other swimmers were already in the pool, performing their laps with disciplined regularity. Obeying the sign not to dive, Kate lowered herself into the water. It was blood warm. She felt it wrap around her, comforting, and on impulse she closed her eyes and dipped her head below the surface.

The external world ceased. She let herself sink, giving herself up to the water. There was a roaring in her ears, like listening to the seashells she had found on beaches as a little girl. Through it came the deep, steady pulse of her heart. *Womb music. This is what it's like inside me. We're hearing the same sounds.*

Lulled by the sensory deprivation, she floated, suspended, until her lungs pulled for air. For an instant Kate felt an impulse to draw a breath and let the water engulf her inside as well as out. Then, opening her eyes, she kicked through the amniotic warmth for the surface.

She swam thirty laps before climbing out. Her body ached with the afterglow of exertion as she showered, then dressed and dried her hair. Luxuriating in the feeling, she contemplated getting a takeaway on her way home. The exercise had made her hungry but reduced her inclination to cook. By the time she came out of the changing room she had decided to indulge herself fully and eat out. She was dimly aware that the attendant on the reception desk gave her a strange look as she left, but was too preoccupied over whether to go for Italian or Chinese to pay much attention.

The club took up most of the first two floors and part

of the basement of a converted warehouse. Its entrance on the ground floor was a doorway set between a fruit shop and a chemist's. They had been open when she arrived, but both were closed now, with steel security shutters pulled down over their windows. As Kate came out she realized that there was something different about them. It was a second or two before she understood that the grey metal was flecked with specks of white.

She stopped. More aware now, she noticed the scraps of paper dotting the pavement in front of the shops. She looked back at the door to the club. The steel sheet that covered it had fresh scratches gouged in its surface, as though something had been scraped off.

Kate looked along the length of the other shops, but there was nothing to indicate that anything had ever been pasted on to them. She became conscious of a pain in her hands. Her nails were digging into the palms of her clenched fists. She opened them, turning away from the mottled shutters that didn't, after all, prove anything.

Her appetite had vanished. Intending to go home, she went to cross the road. A bus shelter stood on the other side, opposite the entrance to the club. She had passed it on her way in, walked right by without giving it a glance. Now, though, it was directly facing her.

The posters almost covered it.

Later, Kate told herself she should have expected what came next. There was an inevitability about it, as she of all people should have known. But even if she had, there would have been nothing she could have done to stop it.

During the next two days, it seemed that Kate saw the poster wherever she went. Her features smiled out from on top of a stranger's body all over the city. Sometimes there would be only one, slapped in a prominent position in the middle of a wall or window. At others there would be a cluster. Coming up from Tottenham Court Road tube station she saw a line of them running parallel to the escalators, raggedly pasted between and over the everyday advertisements. Most had been partially ripped off, but on some her face or name still remained. Kate ducked her head and stared at her feet as the escalator carried her past them. At the top she stumbled when she stepped off and saw one stuck to the floor. It was dirty and scuffed from the hundreds of feet that had trampled it, but still recognisable. KATE POWELL IS A MURDER— it said, before a missing corner obliterated the rest of the message.

Buffeted by the other people coming off the escalator, Kate walked over it. She felt exhausted by the time she reached the agency. All she wanted right then was to sit down at her desk and try to occupy her mind in work. But one look at Clive's expression told her that wasn't going to happen.

'What is it?' she asked, not wanting to hear.

His face was grim. 'Have you been on Facebook this morning?'

The message 'KATE POWELL IS A MURDERING WHORE' had been posted on the Powell PR Facebook page overnight, by a user calling themself 'Telleveryone'. Not just once but over and over again, each identical post accompanied by a miniature replica of the obscene poster image as its user's profile picture. Clive had removed them all but not before they had been noticed. The post had already been shared over a dozen times and prompted several outraged comments. Two visitors had even 'liked' it.

'I've reported the account it was posted from,' Clive told her. 'But even if it's closed down there's nothing to stop him from opening another.'

Kate was only too aware of that. As bad as the printed posters had been, she'd been able to take some comfort from telling herself the damage they could cause was limited. Ellis could only put up so many, and Kate knew from campaigns she'd run herself that posters tended to be invisible. Streets and tube stations were plastered with so many that most people walked past without really seeing them. Even an image as graphic and shocking as this would soon be lost, covered over by the next band, nightclub or activist that came along.

But online was different. Online there was nothing to hide behind, and gossip could be spread by a single click. The only consolation was that while Ellis might be familiar with computers, having spent much of his formative years sectioned and lacking family or friends, he'd little experience of social media. He had at least that much in common with the man he'd impersonated. Ellis's posts had been limited purely to the agency's Facebook page, which at least gave Kate a chance for damage limitation. Reluctantly, she told Clive to temporarily remove any details of the agency's clients from their website and social media pages. It went against all her normal instincts, but if Ellis were trying to publicly smear her she saw no reason to make it easier by supplying him with a handy list of targets.

It worked to an extent. No clients got in touch to complain that their own social media pages had been hit. But too many people had already seen and shared the obscene post, and it was only a matter of time before the connection was made between it and the printed poster that had been put up in prominent sites around the city. By that afternoon #whoiskatepowell had become a small but steadily growing trend.

'How can Ellis do this?' she protested to Collins. 'He's supposed to be wanted for murder! How can he go around sticking posters everywhere and . . . and starting a bloody *trolling* campaign against me?'

'Thousands of illegal flyposters go up all over London every day. We don't have the manpower or resources to police that sort of thing. As for him using social media, that's an unfortunate development—'

'Unfortunate!'

'—but you need to see it in perspective. It's better that he's attacking you like this rather than trying anything more direct. Given his track record we should be thankful for small mercies. And at least no one's made the connection between the posters and Dr Turner's murder so far. If that came out . . . well, then people would have a lot more to talk about.'

Kate felt as though she were falling. 'But can't you do something? He must be going online from somewhere. Can't you find him from that?'

'We're looking into it, but it's not that straightforward. Ellis has worked with computers, so he obviously knows enough to cover his tracks. And if he's using public or unprotected wifi networks, then he's going to be well nigh impossible to trace. He's evidently found somewhere to hole up, so all he'll need is a laptop and a cheap A3 printer and he's in business.'

'So you're saying there's nothing you can do.'

'No, I'm not saying that at all. Believe me, I don't enjoy having a murder suspect running round pulling stunts like this. We're doing everything we can, and we will catch him, I promise you that. But London's a big city and until we get a lead on whereabouts he's hiding we're going to have to wait until we get a break. Or he makes a mistake.'

Kate didn't think she could bear to just wait. Whatever anyone else said, she knew this was her fault. Not only because she'd lied to Ellis about the abortion, wanting to hurt him as he'd hurt her. But because she'd presented him with the means to do it. She'd told him herself how the art of publicity was to get people talking. And how important social networks were in doing that.

He'd obviously taken it to heart.

Although they'd sanitized the agency's website and social media pages to deny Ellis easy access to their clients, they couldn't prevent him posting his message and obscene image elsewhere. Inevitably, it wasn't long before the first bloggers picked up on the story. Kate found herself reduced to a bystander, forced to watch helplessly as rumours and speculation about her took on a life of their own. She even found herself Googling her own name – something she'd always scorned – in a desperate attempt to keep track. Her eyes hurt from peering at the bright screen as she systematically hopped from one site to the other, reporting offensive posts when she could and torturing herself over the ones she couldn't. Eventually Clive came into her office and stood in front of her desk.

'All right, you need to take a break.'

'Just a minute. I've started putting together a rebuttal I thought we could post.'

He took the mouse from her and moved it out of reach. 'Enough, Kate.'

'What? Jesus, Clive, you've seen what's going on, I can't just ignore it!'

'You can't stop it, either. You're going to make yourself ill. And it isn't just you any more, is it?'

He cocked an eyebrow at her, staring her down until she looked away. 'This is a nightmare,' she said, feeling tears closing in.

'No, this is an annoyance. And it'll pass, the same as everything else.'

'Yeah, right.'

'It will. You know what the best thing you can do now is?'

She was too exhausted to think straight. 'Not off-hand, no.'

'Nothing. The rest of us can keep an eye on social media, make sure anything inappropriate gets taken off. All this is right now is just a bit of minor excitement for a few sad bloggers and trolls with nothing better to do. If you ignore it they'll get bored and move on to the next juicy scandal. If you start getting involved, try to stop it, then you're only going to add fuel to the fire.' He winced.

'Sorry. That wasn't the best choice of metaphor, was it?'

She gave a sour laugh. 'I can't just pretend nothing's happened. Some clients are bound to see something, if they haven't already. What do I tell them?'

'That it's a crude smear campaign, the police are investigating, and meanwhile it's business as usual. But I don't think many of them will. Let's be honest, how many of our clients are going to be regularly bothering to look us up on Facebook or Twitter? Or scouring the internet for scandal about you? I know some bloggers have picked up on it, but it's hardly gone viral. And it won't if you let it run its course.' He gave her a smile. 'Come on, Kate, you know how these things work.'

Yes, but not when it's about me. She managed to smile back. 'I suppose so.'

For a while it seemed as though Clive was right. Kate took his advice and was surprised to find that online gossip wasn't half so disturbing if she didn't bother to read it. Only one client got in touch to say she'd seen the poster image, and her reaction was one of sympathy. Kate began to let herself hope that this might blow over after all.

And then she'd remember Ellis, and the lies, and her pregnancy, and the hope would turn to ashes.

Even so, when the phone call came from the Kingsmere Trust two days later, Kate wasn't worried. Out of all their clients, the Trust was easily the most old-fashioned. They were the least likely to come across the online rumours, let alone venture into the sort of areas where the posters had gone up. As Kate took the call she wondered what petty quibble the Trust had come up with now.

'Hello, Mr Redwood,' she said. 'What can I do for you?'

There was no reciprocal pleasantry. 'I expect you know why I'm calling.'

Even by Redwood's graceless standards, that was particularly blunt. Kate answered carefully. 'Should I?'

'It's about certain offensive material concerning you. I assume you know what I'm talking about now?'

Oh, God. 'Yes, but I can explain—'

'Good. Then perhaps you can tell me how the head of the PR agency the Trust instructed to develop a planned strategy – and I stress planned – to raise its profile has become involved in something like this?'

'It's hardly from choice,' she said before she could stop herself. She was still struggling to accept that her largest – and most conservative – client had found out so soon. Taking a deep breath she tried to sound calm. 'I apologize for any embarrassment this has caused the Trust, but this is obviously a crude attempt to discredit me. I assure you we are taking appropriate action against . . . against the person responsible.'

She grimaced at how awkward she sounded.

Redwood was unmoved. 'With all due respect, that's small consolation to myself or the other trustees. The fact is that disturbing material involving someone connected to the Trust is now in the public domain. That's hardly the sort of publicity we expected when we hired your agency.'

'And with all due respect,' she flashed back, 'this is a

310

personal attack on me. It has nothing to do with the Kingsmere Trust.'

'I disagree. Your agency is the public face of the Trust, so any adverse publicity reflects on us by association. As a publicist I would expect you to know that. I would also expect you to realize that we cannot continue a relationship with a company whose head is involved in some kind of sordid smear campaign. And I might add that we have no intention of doing so. Under the circumstances—'

'Under the circumstances you're not concerned that an associate of the "charitable" Kingsmere Trust is the victim of what's obviously a sick and malicious slander, is that right?'

She had spoken heatedly, without thinking, but it gave Redwood pause.

'Obviously, we're not unsympathetic,' he said cautiously, 'but our sympathies can only extend so far.'

'Obviously. But it wouldn't enhance the Trust's reputation as a humanitarian organization if it became known that it had treated the victim unfairly. Particularly not when the victim was a woman, the Trust is run by men, and the slander was largely sexual in nature.'

Redwood was silent. Kate gripped the receiver, forcing herself to wait him out.

'The Trust doesn't respond to threats, Miss Powell.'

'I wouldn't expect you to. I'm only telling you what would happen under those circumstances. As you say, I'm a publicist. I'm expected to know these things.'

She held her breath. Her knuckles on the phone were white.

311

'We'll let it pass this time, Miss Powell,' Redwood said finally. 'I wouldn't want to appear callous. But if there's any further . . . unpleasantness I'll have no choice but to terminate the Trust's association with your agency. And just so there's no misunderstanding, I'll notify you of that in writing.'

'Thank you. Again, I really am very sorry about this.' Kate paused. 'Just for reference, can you tell me where you saw the, uh, the image?'

'We received it this morning. And I have to say some of the older trustees were extremely upset.'

Redwood was sounding aggrieved again, but Kate barely noticed. 'Sorry, you say you *received* it? You mean someone sent it to you?'

'The entire board of trustees each received it in an anonymous email, as well as printed versions by post. And while you may believe that your personal life is your own concern, I might remind you that the Trust believes strongly in upholding Christian ethics, and that particularly includes the sanctity of life. Be it born or unborn.'

Kate felt control of the conversation slipping away from her. 'What are you talking about?'

'I'm talking about what the email and poster accuses you of. While we obviously don't accept the accusation at face value, nevertheless—'

An awful understanding was growing in Kate. 'What did it say?' she demanded.

'I hardly think there's any point in my repeating it—'

'Please! Tell me what it says!'

There was a silence, in which she could sense

Redwood's puzzlement change to comprehension.

'Perhaps you'd better check your own emails, Miss Powell,' he said, and hung up.

Kate's head throbbed as she turned to her computer. She'd already gone through her emails that morning, but as usual she'd ignored or deleted any that didn't seem important. She buzzed Clive on the intercom as she scanned her inbox.

'Has the post arrived yet?'

'Yeah, I'm just sorting through it now. I'll bring it up.'

There was nothing in her inbox, but she saw it straight away in the spam folder. It was from a Hotmail address that contained only random letters instead of the sender's name, but her name jumped out at her from the subject line: *The Truth About Kate Powell*. She hesitated, her mouth suddenly dry, then clicked on it.

There was no text, just an image pasted into the main body of the email. She didn't even have to open an attachment to view it. More chance of it being seen this way, she thought numbly. This time her head had been Photoshopped on to the body of a woman wearing a white nightgown. It was gory with blood and the woman's hands, held stiffly by her sides, were dripping and red. Written across the top in the same colour was a single sentence:

KATE POWELL KILLED HER UNBORN BABY

Clive came in holding a bunch of envelopes. He was smiling until he saw her.

'What's wrong?'

She shook her head, unable to speak. He set the envelopes down and came to see for himself.

'Oh, Christ. The sick bastard.'

Tearing her eyes from the screen, Kate grabbed the post and started shuffling through it. She stopped when she came to a large brown envelope. Her name and the agency's address were written on it in block letters. She ripped it open and took out the single sheet of paper. The poster was smaller than the first one, A4 instead of A3, but looked even more lurid in print than it had onscreen. She let it fall on to her desk.

'He sent it to the Kingsmere Trust.' Her voice sounded strange even to her. 'The whole board of trustees. Emailed and posted it to every one of them.'

'Shit. How did he get their details?'

Kate lifted her shoulders in an apathetic shrug. 'I used to talk about the Trust to him. If he remembered what they were called he could have got the rest from their website, or . . .' She broke off as an awful thought swept everything else away. 'Oh, God. The back-up drive.'

She saw understanding spread across Clive's face. The hard drive stolen in the burglary hadn't contained any financial information or sensitive details, and at the time, losing it had seemed little more than an inconvenience. But what it did have was a copy of the agency's address book.

'He's got our client list,' Kate said, the full enormity of it still sinking in. 'Names, email addresses. Everything.'

'We don't know that,' Clive said, but unconvincingly.

'Anyway, the drive was password protected; he couldn't just open it.'

'Maybe not, but it was ancient. How long do you think it'd keep out anyone who worked with computers? And the password was "Dougal", for God's sake! That's probably the first thing he'd try!' They'd only ever paid token attention to cyber security in the past: it hadn't seemed an issue until now. Kate threw a hand towards the image on the screen. 'He could have sent this to everyone!'

Clive held up his hands placatingly. 'All right, let's stay calm. Even if you're right, most people aren't going to take any notice of hate mail and crap sent through the post. It's obviously garbage; no one's going to believe it.'

'Really?' Kate's headache had bloomed into a full-blown migraine. 'Anyway, they don't have to believe it. A lot of people are going to feel the same way as the Kingsmere Trust. They won't want to be associated with anything like this, whether it's true or not. Christ, I should have seen this coming!'

This time Clive didn't even try to reassure her. 'What shall we do?' he asked.

'I've no idea,' Kate said.

20

'He's getting more circumspect.'

Collins set his teacup back in the saucer with a slight rattle. The chair creaked under the big policeman as he leaned forward and placed them on the coffee table.

'I don't see what's so circumspect about sending all the agency's clients a bloodstained poster accusing me of having an abortion,' Kate said.

When she'd answered the door to her flat that evening she had been surprised to find the DI standing outside. She'd spoken to him only that morning, when she'd told him about the second poster. Seeing him there had given her a start, but he'd quickly reassured her. No news, he'd said. Just an informal visit.

Kate had gone home that evening feeling numb: physically and emotionally drained. There was no longer any doubt that Ellis had access to the agency's client details. It wasn't just the Kingsmere Trust that had been sent the poster. Every client they'd ever had, past and present, had received both emailed and printed versions, and this time Ellis had been busy on their social media pages as well.

He'd evidently learned from his earlier mistake.

Collins settled back heavily in his seat, legs apart, meaty hands resting on his thighs. His brown suit looked even more rumpled than usual.

'I don't mean what's on the poster so much as what he's doing with it.' The DI shifted on the chair uncomfortably. 'Sorry. Got a problem with my back.'

'Would you like a straight-backed chair?'

'Oh, no, I'll be fine, thanks.' He stopped fidgeting. 'Ellis has obviously changed his approach. To start off with he took a lot of risks, physically putting up posters in high-visibility places like bus stops and tube stations. He's changed tack now.'

'He's got all our clients' details; he can afford to.'

'I'm not so sure he's thinking that logically,' Collins said. 'I don't think he's planned all this out, not to that extent. He's making it up as he goes along, using whatever comes his way.'

'Like our client list.'

He waved his hand, both conceding the point and dismissing it. 'I'm not saying he's stupid, and he's obviously intent on hurting you through your agency. And, yes, what he's done has been very effective. But the *tone* of his attack has changed. The first image was much angrier. He was hitting out, trying to degrade you by using a picture from a porn site. Now he's calmed down, and instead of plastering up posters willy-nilly all across London and attacking you through social media, he's targeting your clients individually. Even the picture he's used is less . . . well, less hysterical. More deliberate.'

Kate gave a weary smile. 'Is this supposed to make me feel any better?'

Collins reached out and picked up his cup and saucer again. They looked like a child's tea-set in his hand. 'No, just to remind you who it is we're dealing with. Ellis isn't some criminal genius, he's a disturbed individual with a grudge. You need to remember that.'

Kate looked down at her own tea. Hers was herbal, and untouched. 'You make it sound like he's building up to something.'

'I wouldn't like to say what he's going to do next, and I'm not sure he even knows himself. That's my point.' He flexed his shoulder and winced, careful not to spill his tea. 'Still, I think it might be a good idea for you to take a few extra precautions. Just commonsense things, really. Avoid anywhere quiet or isolated like car parks or empty streets, especially when it's dark. Stick to public places, and if you've got to go somewhere be sure to tell someone where you're going. Or even better, get them to go with you.'

'You think he might attack me?'

'I think you shouldn't take any chances. Maybe you should consider staying somewhere else until this blows over. Is there a friend's or relative's you could go to?'

Kate automatically thought of Lucy and Jack's. But she couldn't ask them. Not after how it had ended last time she'd seen Lucy. 'I don't think that'd make much difference. If he wants to find me he knows where I work. And I'm not going to be frightened off from my own agency.'

Collins sighed. 'Well, it's your choice. But bear in mind what I've said.'

'Have any more of our clients been in touch?' she asked, wanting to change the subject.

She'd decided that the best chance of limiting the damage done by Ellis was to confront the problem head-on. The rest of the morning had been spent contacting clients, explaining that the posters and emails were part of a campaign to discredit her personally, and asking that anyone who received them should forward them straight to DI Collins. After agonizing over the wording, she'd also posted a new message on each of the agency's social media sites.

Kate Powell is proud to announce that she's expecting her first child.

No jubilation, no emoticons or exclamation marks: just a simple statement of fact. Yet it gave her an odd thrill to see the words written down, and she'd posted it quickly, before she could change her mind.

The inspector took another drink of tea. 'Quite a few people contacted us, yes. The poster image is a fairly crude affair, the sort of thing anyone can knock up with basic software. The Hotmail account he used for the emails is a dead end, and the paper and envelopes are fairly generic. They all had a Central London postmark, which doesn't narrow it down very much.'

Kate tried not to show her frustration. 'Well, we weren't really expecting a return address, I suppose.'

'No,' Collins agreed. He made another attempt to ease himself into a more comfortable position. 'How have your clients reacted to all this?'

'Two cancelled their accounts this afternoon.'

One was a small publishing company that specialized in children's books. The other was a fine-art dealer, who used Kate to promote occasional exhibitions at his Covent Garden gallery. Neither were big accounts, or currently active, but the dealer's was a prestigious one, and Kate had enjoyed the contact with the rarefied art world. The publisher had been polite but firm when she had telephoned. The art dealer, a man called Ramsey whom Kate had always thought a little cold, refused to discuss it.

'No chance of getting them to change their minds?' Collins asked.

'No.'

She couldn't really blame them for wanting to distance themselves. She'd thought it was bad enough when Ellis had targeted the agency's Facebook page, but this was far worse. Given the speed with which the story was spreading, he must have sent his latest handiwork to the bloggers who'd picked up on the original poster as well. Or perhaps he hadn't had to: with its inflammatory message, the new image seemed to be provoking far more outrage than the first. As many people were dismissing it as some kind of sick hoax as taking it seriously, and most of the criticism on social networks was reserved for whoever had created it. But the image and its slogan had started to snowball, sparking online arguments about abortion that were now generating their own momentum. Kate had felt sick at the vitriol in some of the comments she'd read about herself. *But that isn't me. It isn't true*, she'd wanted to yell at the screen.

This time she hadn't needed Clive to tell her to stop looking.

'I'm sorry about the clients. As for the rest . . .' Collins tugged at his earlobe. 'It's probably not what you want to hear right now, but all this stuff he's doing . . . It's only words. It could be worse.'

He didn't have to say what he meant: at least Ellis hadn't hurt anyone else. Yet. Collins let that hang, then drained his teacup and set it down on the coffee table.

'Would you like another?' Kate asked.

'No, thanks. I'd better be off. My wife's expecting me.' He made no attempt to leave. He nodded at Kate's stomach. 'How's the, er . . .'

She glanced down at herself. 'Oh, OK. Thanks. It doesn't really feel like I'm pregnant yet. Apart from the morning sickness.'

'My wife was like that. Started early and went right on until she was eight months. Not that that means anything,' he added quickly.

Kate smiled. 'How many kids have you got?'

'Just the one. A daughter, Elizabeth. She's a doctor.' He said it with automatic pride.

'In London?'

'Manchester. Husband's a surgeon there.'

'Any grandchildren?'

'Two grandsons. They'll be six and four now.' His smile was fond and sad. 'Don't see much of them, but it's difficult, I suppose. With both parents being so busy.'

It had the sound of an old rationalization, used to brush over a lingering pain.

'How about you?' Collins asked. 'Have you any brothers or sisters?'

'No, there's just me.'

'What about your mum and dad?'

'They're both dead. But even if they weren't, I wouldn't go running to them for help now, if that's why you were asking.'

He didn't bother to deny it. 'Didn't you see eye to eye?'

Kate looked into the gas fire, trying to put the complex emotions into a simple sentence. She remembered a similar conversation with someone else, and the subject was suddenly uncomfortable.

'Not really,' she said. 'Anyway. Past history now.'

'But wouldn't you have liked them to see their grandchild?'

There was an intense curiosity about him, almost a bewilderment. *His daughter*, Kate realized. *He still doesn't understand what went wrong.* And all at once, as Collins sat there, she saw him as a father instead of a policeman, unable to fathom the hurts inflicted by his own blood.

Was I like that? She had only ever considered the pain and injustices she'd received, not any she might have caused. The thought was disturbing, and she pushed the doubts away from her. She had enough to think about with the present.

'All things considered, it's perhaps as well they can't,' Kate said, making light of it. 'They'd share your views on how I got it.'

The inspector looked down at his hands, smiling. 'It's probably an age thing.'

It was the closest they had come to acknowledging their differences. The concession made them awkward. Abruptly, Collins's stomach gave a rumbling growl.

He looked startled. 'Pardon,' he mumbled, patting it.

Kate was amused to see him blush.

'Well,' he said, putting his hands on his knees and standing up, 'I'd better be going.'

Kate walked downstairs with him. He examined the freshly painted entrance.

'Glad you got rid of the cat-flap,' he commented, tapping the new door. He went out on to the path. 'You remember what I said now. Watch yourself.'

She was surprised to find she appreciated his concern. She wanted to tell him she'd enjoyed talking to him, but the words wouldn't come.

'Goodnight,' she said, and closed the door.

The man was waiting on the other side of the road to the agency. Kate noticed him as she walked up the street, but after her first quick glance she paid him no further attention. Collins's visit the night before had left her in an odd mood. She had gone to bed and, unusually, fallen asleep straight away. Even rarer, she had slept right through to her alarm clock going off.

But she had woken with the fading memory of a dream in which her father had stood outside the ruins of a house and accused her of burning it down with her baby inside. Even though she could barely remember it, the dream had been upsetting, and she was still trying to shake off its pall when she became aware that the man across the road was openly watching her.

She looked across at him again, expecting him to turn away. He didn't. He was leaning against a street lamp with his hands in his pockets and his collar turned up against the morning chill. As she approached he straightened, breath steaming from his mouth, not taking his eyes from her.

Kate looked away. All at once she was conscious of how empty the street was. She began walking a little faster, hoping Clive had already arrived and pulling the keys from her bag in case he hadn't. The man started to cross the road. She reached the door. It was locked. She fumbled with the keys, trying to appear calm, and as she got the door open he came up behind her.

'Kate Powell?'

She turned, hand still on the door, poised to dart in and slam it. 'Yes?'

He looked in his early twenties, with long, reddish hair and a thick leather jacket. His eyes were very pale, a non-colour. He gave her a grin.

'Glad you've turned up. I was starting to freeze over there. My name's Stu Clark. Been waiting to have a few words with you.'

'What about?'

He nodded towards the half-open door. 'Be warmer talking inside.' His grin seemed a permanent fixture.

'Talking about what?'

'I've got a proposition for you. I think you'll be interested.'

'Tell me what it is, and I'll tell you if I am or not,' she said, her arm still barring the doorway.

'It'll sound better over a cup of coffee.'

'I'm not letting you in, so either tell me what you want or go.'

There was something about the way he looked at her that made his grin seem mocking.

'Have it your way, love. It's about certain posters that have been popping up all over the place. Very graphic ones, claiming all sorts of nasty things.'

Kate felt the shock run through her. She tried to brazen it out. 'I don't know what you're talking about.'

'I'm talking about this campaign someone's carrying out against you. Causing quite a stir, it is. All sorts of unpleasant things and pictures of you being circulated. Well, your face, anyway. I don't think the rest is you.' His gaze flicked down her body, then he held up his hands. 'Only joking, love, no offence.'

She stared at him. 'You're a reporter, aren't you?'

'Freelance journalist, actually. I work for whoever's paying. And I'm telling you, there'll be so much interest in a story like this that they'll be queuing up for it. There'll be something in it for you as well.'

'There isn't a story.'

'Oh, come on, Kate – can I call you Kate? A vicious smear campaign accusing a pretty young woman of all sorts of things? It's a great human-interest story.' He cocked his head to one side. 'Specially when I've heard it's the nutter who murdered that psychologist who's doing it.'

Kate felt her face drain of blood. 'Who told you that?'

'Sorry, love, I can't reveal my contacts. You know how it is.'

'Was it the police?'

She knew the leak had to have come from them, but the look of triumph in his eyes told her she had made a mistake.

'So it is him, then?'

'I'm not saying anything.'

She made to go inside, but he put his hand on the door, holding it.

'There's no need to get upset. I'm on your side. All I want is to give you the chance to tell your version.'

'Move your hand.'

'If it's a good enough story, you can probably name your price. Within reason.'

'Are you going to move?'

'Look, it's going to get written anyway. It's in your own interests to co-operate.'

She pushed on the door, barging his arm out of the way. He stood in the doorway, preventing her from closing it.

'So why's Timothy Ellis so pissed off with you, Kate? What's your relationship with him?'

The grin hadn't slipped from his face. Kate went to where the fire extinguisher was clipped to the wall.

'Did you get rid of his kid, is that it? Is that why he flipped and killed the shrink?'

Kate tugged the extinguisher free and turned with it. His grin dropped when he saw what she was holding. 'OK, OK, I'm going.'

He stepped backwards on to the pavement as she advanced, pointing the nozzle, and almost bumped into

Clive. Clive looked from him to the fire extinguisher in Kate's hands. 'What's going on?'

The journalist held up both hands, edging away. 'Nothing, just having a chat. It's cool.'

He reached the pavement edge. 'Thanks for your help, Miss Powell.'

Grinning, he walked across the road. Clive watched him go, then turned back to Kate. He nodded at the extinguisher. 'You're getting pretty handy with that.'

'I'm getting plenty of practice.'

She moved aside to let him in.

'So what was it all about?' he asked.

Kate dumped the fire extinguisher on a desk. 'He's a journalist. He's found out who the Kate Powell on the posters is.'

'Shit. How much does he know?'

'Enough. And it doesn't take a genius to work out the rest.' She pressed the heels of her hands into her eyes, struggling to deal with this new blow. 'Christ, this is all I need!'

'Calm down, let's think it through. Which paper was he from?'

'He wasn't. He said he was a freelance.'

Clive took off his coat and began preparing the coffee. 'That's not so bad, then.'

She lowered her hands and looked at him. 'Why isn't it?'

'Because freelances are ten a penny. He's still got to sell the story, and you know how hard that is.'

Kate did, from the numerous press releases she'd had

ignored by editors herself. But it was difficult to be objective when she was so intimately involved. It fogged her thinking.

The coffee machine gave a hiss as Clive poured water into it. 'Don't worry,' he told her, setting the jug to catch the drips. 'It'll probably never get into print.'

The story appeared two days later. Kate was sitting on the tube, on one of the long seats that face each other across the aisle. A man on the other side was reading a tabloid newspaper, folding its pages back on themselves, and she looked at it for a while without realizing what she was seeing.

Then, all at once, the words came into focus. Kate felt the carriage spin round her, but as though he'd been waiting for that moment the man turned the page, leaving her uncertain about what she'd actually seen.

Suddenly, the train was full of rustling newspapers. It slowed to a halt, and Kate stood up and got off. She was halfway up the escalators before she realized that it wasn't her stop.

She didn't know what the man had been reading, only that it was a tabloid. That ruled out the *Guardian* and *Daily Telegraph*, but that was as much as she could say. At King's Cross she picked up a free paper from the station concourse then went to a newsstand and bought a copy of every paper it sold.

'You setting up in competition?' the vendor grinned as she paid.

Kate didn't answer. She was dimly aware of his

muttered 'Yeah, and a nice fucking day to you, too,' when she walked away, but her mind was on the thick stack of newsprint under her arm.

Clive had already arrived at the office. His smile of greeting faded as he looked from her face to what she was carrying. Kate went straight upstairs. The newspapers made a heavy thud as she dropped them on to her desk and began to go through them.

She found it in the third tabloid she looked at. The article took up half of an inside page, topped by the headline she had seen on the train.

SUSPECTED KILLER'S OBSCENE REVENGE PLOT

The story was billed as an exclusive. It referred to Ellis as a schizophrenic wanted in connection with the '*frenzied killing*' of psychologist Alex Turner. It explained how, while still on the run from the police, he was carrying out an '*obscene hate campaign against attractive PR boss Kate Powell*'. The posters were described with relish, especially the first one, and the story dwelt on her refusal to comment on either her '*affair*' with Ellis, or if she'd had his '*love-child*' aborted. There was no mention of donor insemination. It ended with a quote from an unnamed source, speculating that Ellis could have murdered the psychologist because he was '*maddened with grief*'.

Inset in the article was the police photograph of Ellis and also one of the second poster, less lurid in black and white. Beneath it was a photo of Kate herself. It had obviously been taken outside the agency. She was caught

329

mid-step and had a harried expression on her face as she walked obliquely towards the camera.

I look old, she thought, with detachment.

There was a *crack*. Kate looked with surprise at the broken pencil in her hand. She couldn't remember picking it up. She dropped the two halves into the bin, then went to the window. A little further down the street, on the opposite side of the road, was an alleyway. The photograph could have been taken from there. Or from one of the deep doorways.

She turned away as Clive knocked and entered. 'It's in, then?'

Kate nodded, waving him to the newspaper still lying open on her desk. He read the article, then closed and folded the paper.

'He can't write for shit anyway.'

She had to smile. But not for very long.

The story wasn't in any of the other newspapers, but now it had appeared in one, the rest picked up on it. She didn't even bother looking online. The telephone rang repeatedly with requests for interviews, information. Kate didn't take any of them. Caroline, Josefina or Clive would politely say that no, she had no comment to make. Several journalists actually called at the office, where they were told the same thing. When she went to her window she could see a group of photographers idling on the other side of the road, looking cold but patient. Kate moved away before they saw her.

Collins was phlegmatic when she phoned him. He had already seen the article.

'It was bound to come out, the longer all this went on,' he said. 'We've been lucky to keep it quiet as long as we did.'

'What should I do?'

She heard him sigh. 'That's up to you. You could always go public. Tell them you're still pregnant, and hope that Ellis sees it and believes you.'

Kate doubted that would happen. He must have already seen her posts about the baby online: if he hadn't believed those nothing she now said would make any difference. And any inclination to trust the press withered when she remembered the mocking grin of the journalist who'd started all this. *So much for the great publicist.*

'I don't think I can,' she told Collins.

'There's your answer, then. Just keep your head down and keep saying, "No comment." The murder's old news now. They'll get bored if you don't give them anything new to write.'

The prediction proved accurate, and even sooner than the DI could have expected. In the afternoon Clive came up to tell her that the waiting photographers and journalists had gone. 'They just all took off at once,' he said. 'Something else must have happened.'

The incident was on the evening news: a block of flats had collapsed, providing scenes of carnage for the eager press. Kate was all but forgotten. Some of the papers ran small pieces on her the following day, but they were little more than recaps of the first and completely overshadowed by coverage of the more dramatic story.

The damage had been done, though. When she arrived

at work next morning, the post had already been delivered. There was no sign of Clive, and Kate huddled under her umbrella as she opened the mailbox and took out the selection of envelopes. She recognized the Kingsmere Trust's expensive stationery straight away. Unlocking the office, she left her umbrella to drip on to the floor and sat down behind a desk without taking off her coat or switching on the lights. The other envelopes were ignored as she slit open the thick white one with a plastic paperknife. Rain rattled against the window like hail as she withdrew the letter.

It was brief and to the point. The Trust regretted that, in view of the recent negative publicity received by herself and her agency, they were withdrawing their account. Such publicity was contrary to the Trust's interests, as had already been made clear to her. While not wanting to appear in any way judgemental, it was nevertheless felt that there was no option but to terminate the Trust's relationship with Powell PR & Marketing.

Kate could hear Redwood's desiccated voice as she read it. She reached for the phone, then stopped. Her umbrella dripped with the slow insistence of a clock. The window rattled as a gust of wind struck it. She lowered the letter.

The door opened and Clive came in. He closed it quickly against the blast of cold air and rain. Kate drew herself up, preparing to tell him, when she saw his travel bag. Then she noticed his face.

'Clive? What's wrong?'

He had made no attempt to take off his wet coat. He stood awkwardly, not looking at her.

'I've got to go up to Newcastle.' His voice was raw. 'My mum phoned last night. My brother's been in a car crash. He's, uh . . . he's been killed.'

'Oh, Clive, I'm so sorry.'

His Adam's apple bobbed as he swallowed. 'The thing is, I don't know how long it'll be. The funeral's got to be fixed, and—'

He broke off, covering his eyes. Kate saw his shoulders spasm. She quickly put the letter aside before he could see it and hurried over to him.

He returned her hug and wiped his eyes with the heel of his hand.

'I know it's come at a bad time. I'll get back as soon as I can.'

'Don't worry about that. Just take as long as you need.' She felt lost and inadequate. 'You didn't have to come here to tell me. You could have just phoned.'

He adjusted his grip on the travel bag. 'The train's from King's Cross anyway. There's one in half an hour that'll get me there just after lunch.'

'Have you got a ticket?'

'No, not yet.'

'You'd better go. I don't want you to miss it.' Clive didn't move. 'Go. I'll be fine,' she told him.

He nodded. 'I'll phone you.'

He went out. The umbrella still dripped on to the carpet but more slowly now. Kate switched on the lights and started the coffee machine, then went down to the kitchen and stood her umbrella in the sink before going back upstairs.

The letter from the Kingsmere Trust crinkled in her

pocket. She took it out and looked at the envelope without removing the letter. Abruptly, she tore it in half, ripping it into smaller and smaller pieces that she flung from her. They fluttered to the floor like dead moths. She sat down behind her desk but made no move to turn on her computer. She stared at a damp patch in a high corner of the wall without seeing it. Then, not letting herself think about what she was doing, she picked up the phone and entered a number. It rang several times at the other end before she heard Lucy answer.

'Lucy, it's Kate, look, I'm sorry—' she said in a rush, then broke off as Lucy's recorded voice continued. Kate listened to the message for a few seconds longer, then hung up.

Caroline and Josefina arrived downstairs. She heard them moving around, talking. Some time later the intercom beeped. Kate watched the light flashing on it, but didn't move.

Eventually, it stopped.

21

They lost several more clients in the wake of the newspaper story. One was a company that made maternity outfits.

Kate almost smiled at the irony of that.

She was aware that the agency was approaching the stage where it was more a matter of survival than of making a profit. She knew she should be taking a more aggressive approach, actively seeking out new clients as well as reassuring the remaining ones. But knowing it was one thing. Bringing herself to do it was something else.

Caroline and Josefina tiptoed around her at the office, hushed and deferential as nurses at a sickbed. They needn't have bothered. Nothing touched her. Even when the occasional client phoned to congratulate her on being pregnant, her pleasure was a superficial thing, short-lived and shallow. Her world had contracted to the journey between her flat and the office. She avoided the health club, no longer going anywhere unless she had to. She spoke to Collins every day, hoping for news but receiving none.

She couldn't avoid going online altogether, but she knew enough to be selective. News and social media sites had become a bottomless pit, a gateway to another universe in which her life was discussed, dissected and judged, all of it without her consent or participation.

But at least Ellis's attempts to smear her seemed to be dying down. No new posters appeared, and after a couple of days even the trolls and bloggers began to lose interest. Cautiously, Kate began to hope that Ellis was giving up.

Then the jiffy bag arrived in the post. She'd known who it was from as soon as she'd seen the handwritten address. Inside was a polythene bag containing a small pile of ashes and blackened paper. It was a burned poster, identifiable only because the flames had been extinguished to leave one particular section untouched.

Her face.

'It's a threat, isn't it?' she said when Collins arrived, hating the edge of hysteria in her voice. Even though she'd washed the ash from her hands they still felt unclean.

Collins seemed unperturbed. 'Just try to calm down.'

'Calm down?'

'He's trying to rattle you, that's all. He wants to scare you.'

'Well, he's doing a bloody good job!' She looked down at the plastic bag on the desk. Her own features stared back out at her, haloed by charred paper. 'It's like he's telling me what he's going to do. As if he's psyching himself up for it!'

'Look, Kate,' the policeman said, and the unexpected

use of her Christian name was somehow comforting. 'I'm not trying to kid you that Ellis isn't dangerous. But we're doing everything we can to find him, and the fact is he's running out of time. He knows he can't carry on putting up posters in the street without being caught, and he's already tried going after you online and telling your clients. And now the story's been in the press it's yesterday's news. He's shot his bolt, so sending you a burned picture is probably just a sign of desperation.'

'Doesn't that make it more likely he'll try to do something?'

Collins sighed. 'I wasn't going to tell you this, because I didn't want you to get your hopes up. But we had a sighting of Ellis last night. A transport police officer saw him at Piccadilly Underground. He was carrying a plastic bag full of posters and a tub of wallpaper paste. He dropped them and vaulted the barriers when the officer challenged him.'

'He got away?' Kate felt a strange mix of adrenalin and disappointment, as though the outcome were still in doubt.

'Unfortunately, but it proves my point. Every time he pokes his nose out now he increases the risk of being caught. And it won't be long now before he is.'

The thought buoyed Kate up for the rest of the day. When she finished work, for the first time since Clive had gone home she left the office without hurrying straight into a taxi. It had only been days, but it seemed much longer. The street seemed bigger than she remembered, terribly exposed under the grey plain of the sky. She looked behind herself repeatedly as she walked to

337

King's Cross, but with every yard her confidence grew. She caught the tube for the three stops to Oxford Circus. By the time she emerged from the Underground, a watery sun was shining through the cloud. Kate turned her face to it gratefully. People thronged past, intent on their own business. The rest of the world was still there, unchanged. She called in at a café and had a cup of hot chocolate. After drinking it she decided she was hungry and ordered a mozzarella and tomato sandwich. The taste of olive oil made her think of summer. It would soon be spring, she realized with surprise. The thought gave her a further boost.

Kate left the café and browsed outside shop windows. She stared into a display of baby clothes. There were tiny sweaters and jackets, miniature jeans and boots. She caught sight of her reflection in the glass and saw that she was smiling.

Everything passes, she told herself.

She wasn't confident enough to walk to her flat from the tube station, though. As the light fell, some of her earlier fears revived. Kate asked the taxi driver to wait until she had unlocked the front door. Dougal was waiting outside by the step. He yowled irritably when he saw her. Even though he had rarely used it, he seemed to have taken the disappearance of the cat-flap as a personal affront.

The tomcat ran upstairs ahead of her. There was always a moment of anxiety as she went from room to room, quickly drawing the heavy curtains before turning on the lights. But, as usual, the flat was empty.

She fed Dougal and grilled herself a fillet of sea bass. She baked a potato in the microwave, putting it in the oven to crisp while she chopped carrots into strips, then blanched them quickly in boiling water and drained them out on to a plate. Dougal showed more interest in her fish than his own food, and eventually she gave in and flaked a small piece into his dish so he would leave her alone.

She took her plate through into the lounge. Curling her legs under her, she ate with a fork while she read the brochures she had picked up earlier. They showed push-chairs and prams, cots and cradles. Kate felt almost intoxicated as she looked at them. This was the future, this was what she should be focused on, not the petrol fantasies of a disturbed mind.

When the phone rang she thought it would be Clive. He had already called once, briefly, to say he would be away longer than he'd expected. The date for his brother's funeral still hadn't been fixed, and she guessed he would call again soon, if only to say he still didn't know when he'd be back.

Setting her plate down on a shelf, out of Dougal's reach, she got up to answer the phone. 'Hello?'

'Kate?'

It was a man's voice, familiar but not Clive's, and she stiffened before she realized who it was.

'It's Paul.'

She put her head against the wall. Her heart thumped with anticlimax.

'Are you still there?' he asked.

Kate straightened wearily. 'What do you want?'

'Nothing. I just thought I'd phone, see how you are—'

'I've got nothing to say to you.'

She was already lowering the phone.

'No, wait! Please!'

It was that *please* that stopped her. She hesitated, then raised the phone again.

'All right, I'm waiting.'

She heard him breathing. 'Look, I'm – I know you don't want to talk to me, and I can't blame you. I just phoned because, well, because – Look, I'm trying to say I'm sorry.'

Kate was too surprised to answer. Paul waited a moment, obviously hoping she would.

'Kate? I said I'm sorry.'

There was none of the arrogance she'd come to expect. Even so, she anticipated some catch.

'You're sorry?' It was all she could think of to say.

'Yeah, I know it's a bit late in the day, but . . . I just wanted to tell you.'

Curious now, she tried to detect some hint that he was lying. But he spoke without any of his usual bombast.

'What's brought this on?'

'I've been doing a lot of thinking lately.' He gave an uneasy laugh. 'Spending the night in a prison cell for suspected burglary does that to you.'

With everything else that had happened, Kate had almost forgotten the police had questioned Paul about the office break-in. She tensed for the accusation. It didn't come.

'When I was arrested after I'd put the brick through

your window, I wasn't thinking straight,' he went on. 'I blamed you. You know what I'm like. It's always someone else's fault, never mine.

His tone was thinly jocular, but she could hear the edge to it.

'When they picked me up for the break-in, though, I was so drunk they had to put me in a holding cell to sober up. You wouldn't believe how bad it stank. All the winos in the other cells were yelling and crying. Christ, it was a fucking nightmare. I can remember hearing a couple of cops outside talking about this drunk they'd picked up for burglary. I didn't realize it was me until they unlocked the cell door. And then I sat up and saw I'd pissed myself and puked up all down my front.'

He broke off. Kate didn't say anything: if Paul wanted to get this off his chest she wasn't going to help.

'Anyway, in the end they managed to trace the cabby who'd taken me home that night. He remembered me because I'd argued with him and been sick in his cab. Good job, I suppose.' He gave a humourless laugh. 'They let me go, but when I got outside I realized I didn't have my wallet or any money to get home. And I started crying. Like a bloody kid. I just thought, "What the fuck am I doing?" Jesus, talk about low. So the first thing I did when I got back was bin all the bottles in the house. Every one. And then I called Alcoholics Anonymous.'

There was a dramatic pause. Kate couldn't help but wonder if he'd rehearsed this. When she didn't respond he cleared his throat and continued.

'I've been to quite a few meetings, and I've not had a drink since. There are twelve steps you've got to take. The

341

hardest one is accepting you've got a problem. That and apologizing to everyone you've been a shit to. Like you.'

Kate closed her eyes. It wasn't that she didn't believe him: just that none of it seemed to matter any more.

'I know I gave you a hard time,' he went on. 'Not just recently, I mean before as well.'

She tried to summon the energy to respond. 'It's a long time ago. Let's just forget about it.'

'No, I mean it. I was a bastard. I wish I could blame it all on the booze, but I can't.'

He sounded sincere. Pleading, almost. She sighed. 'I'm glad you're sorting yourself out, Paul.' And then, because she knew he expected more, she added, 'This can't have been easy.'

He laughed, sounding relieved. 'Hardest thing I've ever done. I came to the office this afternoon to tell you, but I couldn't bring myself to go in. After last time I didn't think I'd be welcome. And I saw your friend outside, so it didn't seem like a good idea.'

The change of tack threw her. *Lucy?* she thought.

'You know,' Paul continued. 'The guy you were with at the restaurant.'

Understanding came in a rush.

'Outside?' she said stupidly.

'On the other side of the road. He was in a doorway. I thought he must be waiting for you.'

'He was there this afternoon?'

'Yeah, about four o'clock, but—'

'What was he doing?'

'Nothing, he was just standing there. I couldn't place who he was at first. In fact, I thought he was a vagrant or something. He looked like he should have been begging.'

Kate didn't laugh.

'Yeah, well, he was in a bit of a state anyway. I wondered about going over and apologizing for . . . well, you know. But then he saw me and gave me this look, and I thought, *Maybe not*. I'd got myself into enough trouble, and if he'd had a go nobody'd believe I hadn't started it.'

A faintly aggrieved note had entered his voice, but Kate barely noticed.

'Did he do anything?'

'Not while I was there, but like I say, I didn't stay. I just got as far as your office and turned back. He was still staring at me when I left. Why, what's wrong?'

The words wouldn't come. 'The, uh . . . the police are looking for him.'

Distantly, she heard Paul exclaim, asking why, and her own voice answering. There was a roaring in her ears. When it passed Paul was shouting at her.

'Kate? Kate, you still there?'

'. . . Yes.'

'So this guy's stalking you, then?'

The effort to explain was too much. 'Sort of.'

'Christ! I wish I'd known! I've not exactly been following the news much recently, you know?' The familiar swagger was back. 'Are you by yourself?'

'Yes, but—'

'I'll come over.'

Kate felt herself teeter on the edge of acceptance. 'No, I don't . . .'

'I'll be there in about an hour. Don't worry, if I see him again you won't have any more trouble. Listen, have you eaten? I can stop off for—'

'*I said no!*'

There was a silence. Kate made an effort to stay calm, knowing her anger was directed at herself for being tempted. 'I don't think that's a good idea.'

'Yeah, I suppose you're right.' Paul sounded subdued. 'I can't really blame you. But the offer stands. If you need any help, just shout.'

The *thank you* lodged unspoken in Kate's throat.

'Well, then.' Paul seemed to search for something else to say. 'Look after yourself.'

She nodded, then remembered that he couldn't see her. 'I will.'

The connection remained for a few seconds, then the line went dead. Kate put down the phone, telling herself she had no cause to feel bad, and jumped at a sudden clatter from behind her.

Dougal leaped down from the shelf where she'd left her plate. It lay on the floor with the carrots and remains of the fish scattered around it. Kate stared at the mess without really seeing it.

Then she went to fetch a cloth.

22

The weak sun of the previous afternoon was stronger next morning. It gave a hard, clear-edged quality to the dead verges and the bare branches in the gardens. The streets seemed bleached out, so bright they were almost painful.

Kate watched them pass outside the taxi window. It dropped her at the tube station, and the sun touched her briefly as she stepped out of the cab. Then she was in the shadow of the Underground, where the crispness of the day was lost in the stale, subterranean air.

She was later than usual. The early-morning commuters had already gone, and the station looked abandoned in the post-rush-hour quiet. The dying rumble of a recently departed train was fading down the tunnel as Kate emerged on to the empty platform. She sat down on one of the plastic seats fixed to the wall.

Her eyes felt gritty with fatigue. She had hardly slept the night before. She had tried calling Collins but he wasn't in, so she'd left a message for him to ring her.

After that she hadn't been able to settle. She had gone downstairs to check the locks on the door and then turned off the lounge light and peered through the window. The dark street outside was empty and full of shadows. She had waited for one of them to move until her eyes hurt. When she had gone to bed, she had lain awake and listened to every creak of the cooling house.

The electronic noticeboard said a train was due in two minutes. Kate yawned. From the entrance to the platform came the echoing scuff of a shoe. Still yawning, she put her hand to her mouth and glanced around, expecting someone to appear.

No one did.

She was about to look away when she heard the scuff again. It was softer this time, but nearer. She waited, watching the opening in the wall.

The noise came a third time. Now it was from the other side. Kate turned. There was a second entrance on her right, this one only ten feet away. A faint squeak, like a rubber sole on concrete, came from it. But still no one appeared.

Kate looked quickly around. The platform was silent and deserted. Belatedly, she remembered Collins's warning. *Just commonsense things, really. Avoid anywhere quiet or isolated.* She stood up, gripping her bag in front of her. Slowly, she began to edge as quietly as she could away from the second entrance. She tried to visualize the layout on the other side, how far away the steps were. The scuff sounded again. She stopped.

She didn't know which of the openings it had come from.

Kate didn't move. There was no further sound. She

waited, then began to creep along the platform once more. The first entrance was twenty feet away, then fifteen, then five. She halted at the corner, listening.

A faint, rustling whisper from the other side, like blown litter. Or breathing.

I'm imagining it; there's nothing there.

The opening in the wall lay in front of her. Through it she could glimpse the bottom of the steps, disappearing upwards. *Just run.* She tensed for the effort, and then there was a noise behind her, and she remembered the other entrance.

She spun around, the scream choking off as the windows of the train flashed past, elongated squares of light framing faces and bodies. Kate sank back against the wall as it slowed and stopped. She looked back down the platform. It was empty.

The train doors hissed open, and people were stepping off. Clutching her bag, Kate ran to the nearest carriage and jumped in.

She watched, but no one else got on.

By the time she reached the agency, Kate had almost convinced herself that it had been nothing. A wind from the tunnel, a piece of paper, and her imagination. She actually smiled at the thought of leaping out to confront an empty crisp packet. Then she remembered Ellis standing in the doorway the day before, and her smile faded.

Even so, it was a good day. An importer of South American artefacts phoned out of the blue and commissioned her to handle the publicity for an exhibition of Mexican jewellery. She had been recommended by a friend, the man told her with a faint American accent. He had been out of the country for the past month and would be out again the following week, so he didn't have time to waste sifting through PR agencies. Was she interested?

She was.

The acquisition of a new client lifted her spirits. She was eagerly reading the material the importer had emailed over when Caroline buzzed through and said that DI Collins and DS Daikin were downstairs.

Kate told her to send them up. She wondered why Collins was calling in person. *God, please let them have caught him.* She felt a spark of hope.

But when Collins walked in she could see that they hadn't. The policeman looked tired. The chair creaked as he lowered himself into it. His sergeant gave her a smile, but his heart didn't seem in it.

'Did you get my messages?' Kate asked.

Collins nodded. He was about to say something, but Kate couldn't wait any longer to tell him her news.

'He was here,' she exclaimed. 'Yesterday afternoon.'

Collins came alert. 'Ellis? You've seen him?'

'No, but someone else did. I only found out last night, that's why I called you.'

'What time was this?'

'I think it was about four o'clock. Ellis was standing in a doorway across the road.'

'Who saw him?'

'Paul Sutherland. He's the one who was picked up for

348

the break-in. He phoned last night and . . . What's the matter?'

They were both staring at her. Kate saw Daikin glance at the inspector.

'What is it?' she asked. 'What's wrong?'

The sergeant dropped his gaze to his notebook.

Collins spoke gently. 'Paul Sutherland was killed last night.'

Kate felt herself blown back to another time, being told by the same two men of another death.

'Someone set fire to his house,' the inspector said. 'Poured petrol through the letter-box and then lobbed petrol bombs through the upstairs and downstairs windows.'

'Someone,' she echoed. She could hear Paul's voice, quite clearly. *He saw me and gave me this look . . . He was still staring at me when I left.*

Collins rubbed his eyes. His skin wrinkled up like old leather where his fingers pushed it. 'We haven't got a definite ID. But some neighbours heard the glass going and saw a man standing in the street outside as the fire started. They say he was just watching and only ran off when they shouted. We didn't get a very good description but . . . it sounds like Ellis.'

Kate closed her eyes. She saw flames, smelled petrol.

'You say you spoke to Paul Sutherland,' Collins said. 'Can you remember what time?'

'I don't know . . . not late. Eight o'clock, perhaps.'

'The fire was started just after three a.m. I only found out an hour ago myself or I'd have let you know sooner. There's supposed to be communication but

349

you wouldn't know it half the time.' He sounded apologetic.

Her stomach lurched as a thought struck her. 'Do you want me to identify him?'

Collins was startled. 'Good God, no! No, that's already been done. I just came to tell you, that's all.' He shifted uncomfortably in his seat. 'Well, that and to talk to you about personal security. Under the circumstances I think it'd be wise to take a few extra precautions.'

Kate's mouth had dried. 'You think he was planning to do something to me, don't you? Then he saw Paul and followed him home instead.'

'We don't know that,' Collins said firmly. 'But it wouldn't hurt to carry a personal alarm, if you don't already have one. We can look at rigging up panic buttons here and at your flat, although I'd feel happier if you'd reconsider staying somewhere else for the time being. Have you got any friends who'd put you up?'

'I don't . . . I need to think about it.'

'A hotel, then. Just for a few days.' His tone was almost gentle. 'I'd feel a lot happier.'

Kate felt like any sudden move would break her. She managed to nod. 'All right. But I'll have to pick up some things from home.'

Collins looked relieved. 'Good. We're probably being over-cautious, but you're doing the right thing. Let me know where you'll be staying, and remember what I said. Stay around other people as much as possible, and if you've got to go somewhere use a taxi rather than public transport.'

Kate nodded, not trusting herself to speak. Collins stood up, followed by the sergeant.

'I know it's easy for me to say, but try to keep your chin up.' He gave an unconvincing smile. 'We won't let him get to you.'

Caroline and Josefina were clearly surprised when she closed the agency soon after the two policemen had left, but Kate didn't offer any explanation. She booked a mid-priced hotel off Oxford Street and then took a taxi home. The streets that had been sunny that morning were now grey with the coming dusk. They hit a traffic jam, and Kate watched the meter ticking away as they sat among the fumes and car horns, wondering if she had enough cash for the fare.

Her conversation with Paul played in a loop in her head. Every nuance, every inflection sounded with a new and callous finality. She thought about the last thing he had said to her. *Look after yourself*. She hadn't bothered to tell him to do the same. *Be careful*, she could have said. *He's dangerous. He burns people. Look after yourself*.

But she hadn't.

It was growing dark when the taxi pulled up outside her flat. She paid the driver and climbed out. She meant to ask him to wait, but before she could he pulled away, leaving her alone on the pavement.

The street was deserted. Kate hurried up the path and let herself in. There was no sign of Dougal; she'd have to work out what to do about feeding him later. She switched on the light in the small entrance hall and cried

351

out as it burst with a blue flash. She sank back against the wall, her heart racing.

Stop it. It's only the bulb.

But she was still shaking as she went upstairs. She closed the door behind her, automatically drawing the curtains before turning on the lights. The silent flat confronted her, the brightness only seeming to underscore its emptiness. She took her weekend case down from on top of the wardrobe, but as she began to pack her chest was already starting to heave. She fought it, but her eyes blurred and then she broke down. Wracked, she stood by the half-packed case, unable to move as the sobs tore at her.

'Oh, G-God . . . oh, God . . .'

Suddenly, everything that had happened over the past few weeks seemed to crash down on her. Stumbling blindly down the hallway, Kate grabbed her phone and stabbed clumsily at the keypad.

She fought for control as it rang out at the other end. When Lucy's recorded message cut in it was almost too much. She could barely wait until the recording finished.

'Lucy, it's Kate, I'm sorry, please—'

The phone was picked up at the other end.

'Yes?'

Lucy's voice was inflectionless. Kate could have wept again, this time with relief. 'I . . . it's me. I'm sorry, I know I shouldn't just call you but . . . Please, can I just come over?'

There was no answer.

'Lucy . . . ?'

Another hesitation. 'OK.'

Kate managed a choked thanks and ended the call. Wiping her eyes, she called for a cab and hurried to finish packing. It was too much to expect to stay with Lucy and Jack, but she desperately wanted to see them before she went to the hotel. Even Lucy's censure was better than enduring more of this on her own.

She waited in the dark for the taxi to arrive, then ran out to it. The street lights had come on, casting deep shadows as she climbed in and mumbled the address to the driver. Then, huddling in a corner, she stared through the window at the normal world outside. The nervousness didn't start until the cab had dropped her outside Lucy and Jack's. It seemed an age since she had been to the big house. She hesitated with her hand on the gate. *I'm doing exactly what Lucy accused me of, running to them now I'm in trouble.* She didn't care how much contempt and blame Lucy heaped on her, though. Just so long as there was no rejection. She couldn't stand the thought of losing anyone else.

Kate wheeled her case up the path. She tried to compose herself as she rang the bell, knowing that she must look a mess. She heard someone approaching, and then Lucy opened the door.

They looked at each other without speaking. In the background Kate could hear the chatter of the TV, see the cheerful spill of light from the lounge and kitchen. It silhouetted Lucy in the unlit hall. Kate couldn't make out her expression.

Wordlessly, Lucy stood back so that she could enter. Kate couldn't look at her as she went inside. Lucy closed the door and followed her as Kate stepped around Jack's heap of boxes in the hall. The house smelled of food and dirty nappies. She went through into the brightly lit lounge.

The TV was blaring out some frantic children's programme. Jack and Emily were engrossed in watching it, their backs to Kate as they sat side by side on the sofa. They didn't turn around. Angus was in his playpen next to them, which surprised her since he had long since outgrown it. He began to cry when he saw her, holding out his arms to be picked up, and Kate instinctively went to him. The forced bright greeting was already on her lips when she reached the sofa and the words died.

Jack and Emily's mouths were covered with brown parcel tape.

Kate's mind refused to make sense of what she was seeing. There was a sound from behind her. She turned.

Lucy stood in the doorway. Her head was tilted up by the blade of the long kitchen knife held to her throat. Ellis stood close behind her. The hand not holding the knife was gripping Lucy's bare arm, fingers digging into the flesh above the elbow.

'*I'm sorry.*' Lucy's voice was a whisper. Her face was puffy and tear-streaked. Her eyes, as she looked at Kate, were terrified. '*I'm sorry.*'

No one moved. The moment stretched out, suspended.

Kate stepped backwards.

Ellis herded Lucy further into the room. He didn't take his eyes from Kate. They were bright and feverish, purple smears discolouring the pale flesh underneath. His face was gaunt, and his hair stuck up in matted tufts. There was a straggly growth of beard on his cheeks.

He looked like a stranger.

Lucy's chest was heaving. 'I'm sorry,' she whispered again, and now Kate took in her stained clothes and unwashed hair. She looked thinner. 'He threatened the *children*, Kate! He said if we didn't do what he wanted, he'd – he'd—' Her gaze flicked to Emily and Angus, agonized. 'We didn't have any *choice*! We tried, Jack—'

'Shut up!'

Lucy fell silent. Her mouth was trembling. Her chin was still held high, away from the knife, giving her a model's self-conscious pose. There was a muffled noise from Jack. Kate glanced at him and saw that his hands and feet were also bound. There was a yellowing bruise on one temple, and the look he gave Ellis was full of violence. Kate saw him straining against the tape, but it was wrapped around him too many times.

Beside him, Emily was similarly fastened. Tears were rolling down the little girl's face, and the sight of them filled Kate with outrage.

'You *bastard*!' she cried, turning back to face Ellis. 'What have they ever done to you?'

He blinked at her outburst but didn't take the knife from Lucy's throat. 'They're your friends!'

Kate forced herself to stare back at him. She pointed at Emily. 'She's a little girl, for God's sake!'

She strode over to the sofa.

'Hold tight,' she said, trying to smile as she took a grip on the tape covering Emily's mouth.

'D-don't!' Ellis said, as Kate pulled it off.

The tape came free with a tearing sound, leaving the skin red underneath. Emily began to cry.

'Happy now?' Kate demanded, glaring at Ellis. He looked confused, almost defensive. She went over to the playpen where Angus was also crying.

'L-leave him!'

She took no notice. Angus's feet were taped together so that he couldn't climb out of the pen. She bent to pick him up.

'*I said f-fucking leave him!*'

Kate froze. Ellis's eyes were wild, his knuckles white knobs of bone on the knife handle. Its point made a depression in Lucy's skin. Lucy had closed her eyes.

Kate straightened, her momentary outrage deserting her. 'All right. I'm sorry.'

'G-get away from them!'

She moved back into the centre of the lounge.

'I know you're angry with me, but don't take it out on them. Please. They haven't hurt you.'

'Shut up!'

'At least let the kids go.'

'I s-said shut up!'

'Look at them, they're scared to death! They're only children, for God's sake! How can you do this to them?'

'*Because my child's dead!*'

Kate flinched back from the shout. Ellis's face was contorted. But he didn't do anything else. She waited for her breathing to steady.

'I lied to you,' she said, as calmly as she could. 'I didn't have an abortion. I only said it because—'

'You're lying n-now!'

356

'No—'

'Fucking *liar*!'

'Listen to me! I haven't had an abortion—'

'Liar! Lying *b-bitch*!'

Kate recoiled, silenced by the hate in his face.

'He won't believe you.' Lucy's voice was quavering.

'Shut up,' Ellis said flatly.

Tears rolled down Lucy's cheeks as she stared across at Kate. 'I said – I told him you hadn't, but he wouldn't believe—'

'*Don't talk about me as if I'm not here!*' Ellis screamed, and Kate saw his arm tense. *No!* she thought as he pulled back the knife, but the blade was unbloodied as he shoved Lucy towards her.

Lucy stumbled forward and almost fell. Kate went to help her but stopped when Ellis pointed with the kitchen knife.

'Leave her!'

Lucy wiped her eyes with the palm of her hand. Her head was nodding, like a palsied old woman's. She was no longer looking at Kate.

'Sit over there,' Ellis told her. 'In the chair.'

Lucy did as he said. He turned to Kate.

'Get the t-tape.' He gestured to a roll of parcel tape on the coffee table.

'Listen to me—'

'Get the *fucking t-tape!*'

She went and picked it up.

'Wrap it round her ankles first, then her wrists.'

'Please, you can't—'

'*Do it!*'

357

Kate looked at where Jack was sitting bound on the sofa. His eyes stared at her over the brown strip, trying to communicate some message, but Kate didn't know what. Beside him, Emily's bottom lip was quivering. Only Angus was making a noise as he sobbed. Standing this close, Kate could smell the sour, unwashed odour of their bodies. On the floor around them were empty tins of food, some furred with several days' worth of mould. Wadded-up pieces of parcel tape lay among them, too many to count. Kate tasted bile in the back of her throat as she grasped the significance of what she was seeing.

How long has he been here? But she already knew the answer. *All the time.* Maybe even since killing Alex Turner. This wasn't just a place to hide, there was food and some money, Jack's printing equipment, a computer and internet access.

And people she loved, to hold hostage and punish instead of her.

'Ankles first,' Ellis said.

Kate kneeled down in front of Lucy. It felt like it wasn't her doing this, as if she was watching someone else. She pulled the end of the tape free with numb fingers but stopped as Jack gave a muffled grunt. She looked up at him. He was staring at her with a desperate intensity. He shook his head violently.

'Now!' shouted Ellis, and took a step towards where Angus was snivelling in the playpen. She saw him shift his grip on the knife. With a last glance at Jack, Kate wrapped the tape once around Lucy's ankles. The red marks from earlier strips formed bands on her flesh.

'Do it again. T-tight.'

She hesitated, then did as he said. The roll of tape dangled, still attached. Kate felt a weak hope. 'I've nothing to cut it with.'

'B-bite it.'

The hope went out. She tore the tape with her teeth.

'Now her wrists.'

She could feel the tremor in Lucy's hands as she bound them. There was no accusation in Lucy's eyes when they looked at each other, only fear.

'Put a strip over her m-mouth.'

'What good—?'

'Just do it!'

Lucy shut her eyes, compressing her lips as Kate stuck a piece of tape across them. Kate straightened and threw the tape down.

'Feel safe now, do you?'

Ellis stared at her, then pointed to a corner of the room.

'P-pick that up.'

In the corner against the wall were stationery and materials for Jack's business, a sprawling pile of cardboard boxes and containers. On top was a stack of posters. Kate wondered, almost absently, whether Ellis had gone there with the intention already in mind, remembering all the conversations he'd had with Jack about printing and publishing. Or if the idea had only come later, with Lucy and Jack bound and impotent under the threat of his knife, and everything he needed laid out for him.

But then she saw what Ellis was pointing at and forgot everything else. Standing by the posters and stationery was a red plastic petrol can.

She looked at Ellis, understanding now what Jack had been trying to tell her. 'No.' She shook her head. 'No, you can't . . .'

'P-pick it up.'

'Please—' She faltered over what to call him. 'Please, just think what you're doing.'

'Pick it up.'

'At least let them go! You've got me now, you don't need them!'

He advanced towards her. She backed away, but he stopped when he reached Jack. He put the knife against his neck.

'Pick it up.'

Kate slowly walked across the room towards where the petrol can waited. The sheaf of posters drew her eye. They were new ones. This time her smiling face had been planted on a journalistic photograph of a woman holding a dead child. It was black and white, obviously taken from some war zone, and flames had been super-imposed to make it look as if mother and baby were on fire. Five words were printed across the bottom.

KATE POWELL BURN IN HELL.

She looked away. The petrol can was at her feet. Next to it was a shallow cardboard box filled with cans of cleaning solvent. Beside that was a cluster of aerosol cans of spray adhesive. The *flammable* sign was printed on all of them. Kate reached down and took hold of the red container. It was heavy. A faint sloshing came from inside when she lifted it.

'T-take the lid off.'

Kate did as she was told. It felt greasy. The lid dangled from a plastic strip when it was unscrewed. The smell of the petrol was a sickly-sweet taste at the back of her nose and throat.

'P-pour it out.'

'Please, don't do this.'

Ellis took hold of Jack's hair, pulling his head back to expose his throat to the blade.

Shakily, Kate tilted the can. Petrol glugged out of the wide spout. It splashed over the boxes and containers of ink, ran down into the carpet. It ran across the image of her face that smiled up from the posters, pooling over the cold likeness of the flames.

'N-now the curtains.'

The heavy drapes were drawn across the French windows. Kate threw petrol on to them. The fabric stained dark where the fluid soaked into it.

'And the carpet,' Ellis told her. His voice sounded thick and drugged. The stammer had almost gone. 'Work your way over here.'

He stood back as she walked towards the sofa and chairs, sloshing liquid from the can as she went. It was more than half empty now. The room reeked of petrol.

'Pour it over them.'

Kate shook her head, mutely. Ellis put the blade back to Jack's neck. His eyes were bright. Kate could see that his pupils were black and dilated.

'Do it.'

Emily began to cry in lost little sobs, a counterpoint to Angus's huskier wails. The can felt slick in Kate's hands.

'I can't!'

Ellis's breathing was heavy. He held out his hand. 'Give it to me.'

Kate didn't move.

'I said f-fucking give it to me!' There was urgency in his voice now. 'P-please!'

She backed away from him.

'Remember what you said?' He was reaching into his pocket, moving away from Jack now. 'They threw it in the incinerator, you t-told me. Remember?'

He pulled out a box of matches.

'I'll show you what suffering is,' he said, and as he opened the matches Kate flung the petrol can at his face.

It struck his upraised arms, a swirl of liquid trailing in the air behind it, and then Kate was running past him. She felt a tug on her arm but didn't stop. She ran down the darkened hallway, careening into Jack's boxes and pushing them over behind her. She slammed into the front door. It was locked. Kate wrenched at it until she heard a noise from the lounge doorway, and turned to see Ellis coming after her.

She ran upstairs. The landing at the top was in darkness. A banister railing edged the open side where it overlooked the downstairs hall, and from it Kate could hear him blundering over the boxes. She pushed herself away, into the deeper darkness of the upstairs corridor. A pale square at the far end showed the window. By its faint light Kate began to make out the rectangles of doors in the shadows. They were all closed. Lungs burning, she ran past them until she reached the end of the corridor. Footsteps pounded up the stairs. Kate opened the nearest door and went in.

The room was even darker. She stood with her back against the door and faced the blackness. It was unrelieved by even a glimmer of light, but a sweetness of talcum powder and crayons told her she was in Emily and Angus's bedroom. She heard a door open further along the corridor.

Kate felt for a lock or bolt. There was nothing. She moved blindly into the room, hands outstretched in front of her. She tried to remember if there was anything she could use. Anywhere to hide. She jumped as she walked into a bed. Feeling her way along it, she came to the bookshelf.

And the wall.

She groped across its unyielding hardness. Her heart thudded when she banged her shins on the small table. She reached out to steady it and her hand hit a lamp, almost knocking it over. She grabbed at it, heart thudding.

A second door was opened.

She gently set the lamp upright and shrank back against the wall. She pressed herself into the cranny between the bookshelf and table, knowing the shelter was illusory. Her breath came in rasps. She tried to quiet it, listening for the sounds from the corridor. Another door opened, nearer.

There was a dull ache in her arm. She reached up to touch it and almost cried out at the sudden slash of pain. Biting her lip, she touched her arm again. This time she was more prepared when the petrol on her fingers stung the long cut above her elbow. She remembered the tug on her arm as she ran past Ellis, thought about the sharp length of the knife.

She felt sick.

The door of the next room along was opened. Kate squeezed her eyes shut. The cloying stink of petrol was nauseating. She heard a footstep outside and folded her arms over her stomach. She could feel her heart beating, banging against her ribs, and thought of the smaller one keeping time with it, a tiny pulse of innocence.

The door opened. It made a whispering sound of wood on carpet. Kate opened her eyes. She saw nothing, only blackness and fading sparkles of phosphene after-images. 'Kate.'

The word was like a shout in the silence. Kate pressed back against the wall. A dull glow came from beside her. She turned towards it and found herself looking at the lamp on the table. The room came into being around her as it grew brighter, small beds and cuddly toys. Mickey Mouse grinned at her from the lampshade.

Ellis stood in the doorway with his hand on the dimmer switch. His eyes were red from the petrol. She could see the dark splashes of it on his clothes. He stepped into the room, bringing a stronger reek of it with him. Kate stepped to one side, hoping to dart around him to the door, but he moved to block her. The knife was still gripped in his hand. Kate saw the dark smear on its blade.

She backed between the bookshelves and the table again.

Ellis stopped in the middle of the room. 'You shouldn't have done it.' He sounded calmer. Kate wasn't sure whether he meant she shouldn't have run, or had an abortion. She couldn't speak.

'You'd no right,' he said. 'It was my baby. You'd no right.'

She shook her head, but he wasn't looking. He was staring at her arm.

'You're bleeding.'

He sounded surprised. Kate looked down. There was a gaping slice in the left sleeve of her coat. Her arm was soaked in blood. She had forgotten about it, but now it began to throb again. The pain goaded her.

'What are you so upset about?' She wiped her hand on her bloody sleeve and held it up to show him. 'This is what you wanted, isn't it?'

A stricken expression crossed his face. 'I – I didn't mean to.'

'You didn't *mean* to? So what *did* you mean?' Suddenly, the weeks of fear boiled over. The sight of him infuriated her. She thrust out her injured arm. 'Did I make you cut me?'

'N-no, I—'

'So who did? Who made you do *any* of this? Who made you kill Alex Turner?'

He tore his eyes from her arm. 'I t-told you! I d-didn't want that!'

'He's still dead, though, isn't he? His wife was pregnant, did you know that?'

Kate could tell that he hadn't. He looked devastated.

'N-no!'

'She was eight months pregnant! She might even have had the baby by now, and Alex Turner's never going to see it! Because *you* killed him!'

'N-no!' He shook his head, violently. 'I-I didn't . . .'

'You killed him, and now you want to kill an innocent family as well!'

'Shut up!'

He took a step towards her, but she was reckless now. 'Why? You're going to burn me anyway! You've already cut me! What else are you going to do?'

'*I don't know!*' he shouted. 'Leave me alone!'

'Leave *you* alone?' Kate stared at him. 'For God's sake, just listen to yourself! Think what you're *doing*!'

His features were contorted with pain. Seeing him, the anger drained out of her.

'Put the knife down.' She almost called him Alex, and in her haste to cover it up she spoke without thinking. 'You need help.'

His head jerked up.

'Help? People asking stupid qu-questions, telling me what my fucking p-*problem* is? They don't want to *help*, they just want me to *behave*! So long as I don't b-bother anybody else, that's all they care about! Nobody cares whether *I'm* bothered! Nobody c-cares about *me*!'

I cared. The thought went unspoken.

'Lucy and Jack did,' she said instead.

'No, they d-didn't! I thought they did, but they didn't! That's why I c-came here, but they're like all the rest!'

'What about Angus and Emily? Are you going to kill them, too? Burn them, like you did your own family?'

He looked as though he'd been slapped. 'Who t-told you that?'

'Never mind who told me, it's true, isn't it?'

'N-no!'

'Yes, it is! You set fire to the house while your mother and father and your brothers were asleep, and then you stood and watched them burn!'

'It wasn't like that, it was an accident!'

'An accident that you set fire to the house?'

'Yes! No, I d-don't—' His voice was anguished. 'I didn't mean to *hurt* them! I just wanted them to *n-notice* me! They were always fighting, and leaving me with M-Michael and Andrew and – and they'd d-*do* things, hurt me, but my m-mum and dad wouldn't *believe* me! Even though I kept *telling* them, they wouldn't. And then my g-gran tried to help, she tried to t-tell them, and they started shouting, and – and then Gran was on the floor, all *blue*, her f-face was *blue*. And they said she was – she was dead, and nobody – nobody c-cared except me. So I lit the fire, and I thought, *N-now* they'll listen, *now* they'll know, they'll be sorry . . .'

His eyes were focused on something Kate couldn't see.

'I could see right into the flames, like it was another world. I watched them, and . . . and nothing worried me any more. They got bigger and bigger, until there wasn't anything else. They were beautiful.'

'But it isn't beautiful afterwards, is it?' Kate said.

His face clouded, losing its transcendent quality. 'No.'

For a moment he looked like a young boy, lost and scared.

'You didn't mean to hurt them,' Kate said.

'N-no.'

'Do you want to hurt Angus and Emily?'

He shook his head.

'Let them go, then! Please!'

'I c-can't.'

'Why?'

'It's too l-late.' It was a whisper.

'It isn't!' Kate almost shouted. 'It isn't too late! Think about it! Think about how you'll feel afterwards!'

He looked at her. 'There won't be any after.'

She had seen the same expression on his face when the man had thrown himself on to the bonfire. *Perhaps it didn't seem horrible to him.*

'This is what you want, isn't it?' she said, finally understanding. 'This is what you've always wanted.'

His gaze was still on faraway flames, but she saw his grip shift on the knife.

'It's g-got to be done.'

She could feel him retreating into himself again and continued desperately.

'Like killing Paul Sutherland, you mean? Did that "have to be *done*" as well?'

His eyes snapped back to her. 'He deserved it!'

'Why? Because he hit you? Are you really that pathetic?'

'No.' He had a sullen expression.

'Why, then? Come, on, what's your excuse? You've always got one, so let's hear it!'

He didn't answer. It took Kate a moment to realize why. *Oh, God.*

'You killed him because of what he did to *me*?'

Ellis wouldn't look at her.

'And what about what *you*'ve done?' she demanded.

'That's d-different!'

'How? How is it different?'

'Because you k-killed our b-baby!'

'*I haven't killed our baby!*' she yelled back at him. 'I haven't killed *anything*! I'm still *pregnant*, for God's sake! I've been sick every fucking morning and . . . oh, Christ!'

She broke off, putting her head in her hands. When she looked up, Ellis was still watching her. But now he had a strange, almost frightened expression.

'I lied about the abortion,' Kate said quietly. 'I wanted to hurt you. I'd been told you were dead and taken to see your body. And then found out you weren't Alex Turner, and . . . And I wanted to hurt you *back*!'

She felt tears closing in.

'Jesus Christ, after all that, what did you *expect*? I *loved* you!'

He was looking at her like a man woken from one bad dream only to find himself in another.

'You're still p-pregnant?'

Kate closed her eyes, nodded wearily.

There was an almost inaudible moan. She opened her eyes. Ellis was hugging himself, gently rocking backwards and forwards. Tears were trickling down his face.

'Oh, G-God.' He closed his eyes in anguish. 'Everything's gone wrong.'

Kate moved fractionally away from the wall. 'Just let

us go. You can do that now, can't you? There's no need to hurt anybody.'

He didn't say anything. Just rocked himself, crying quietly.

'You don't want to hurt the baby, do you?' Kate urged. 'Not after all this?'

Ellis shook his head.

'Let us go, then. Give me the knife and let us go.'

He didn't seem to have heard. He was still shaking his head.

'I'm sorry,' he said. 'I've made such a m-mess of things. I'm sorry.'

He was crying as he came towards her, and Kate was never sure if he was apologizing for what he had done or for what he was about to do. She saw the knife in his hand and instinctively swept the lamp off the table at him.

There was a *bang* as the bulb exploded. She cringed back, dazzled by the flash, waiting for the cut of the knife. Instead the darkness was broken by a new, flickering illumination.

The igniting petrol on Ellis's clothes filled the room with a sick light. Kate stared, rooted, as he beat at the flames on his arm and chest. The next moment they had spread to his shoulders and head.

There was a clatter as he dropped the knife. He cried out, taking wild swipes at himself as his hair caught fire. The light in the room was brighter now, more yellow, and the stink of burning hair and petrol made Kate gag as she ran to try and smother the fire leaping from Ellis's head. Her hands came away covered in blue gloves of

370

flame as the petrol on them caught. Panicking, she slapped them out against her coat, feeling the first sting of it, and then grabbed a quilt from the nearest bed.

She tried to throw it over Ellis but he reeled away, lurching first into the wall and then from the room. The flames threw a crazy light on the walls as he staggered blindly down the corridor, flailing at himself, and Kate knew what was going to happen an instant before it did. She shouted as he hit the railing at the end of the corridor, too far away for her to grab him, and in a swift, choreographed motion he toppled over.

There was a thud as he hit the floor below. Everything was suddenly dark again. Kate rushed down the stairs, not pausing to search for a light switch, and ran to the figure lying in the hall. Ellis had landed on the boxes by the cellar door, splitting them open and scattering paper over the carpet. Some of the flames had been snuffed by the impact, but he was still burning. Fire was already beginning to lick at the surrounding paper and boxes, less dramatic in the light from the open lounge doorway. Kate flung the quilt over him and beat at the motionless body, but a sudden pain in her leg made her cry out and jerk back. One corner of the quilt had been trailing in a cluster of burning papers and had caught fire. She snatched it away, trying to stifle the flames, before she saw it was starting to burn in other places as well.

Kate flung it against the floor, stamping and kicking at it. Something stung her cheek. She brushed off a glowing piece of ash. Looking up, she saw the hall was full of them. The stink of petrol from the lounge returned like a forgotten threat, and she turned in time to see burning scraps of paper drift like black leaves through the open doorway.

The light from inside suddenly changed.

Angus screamed.

'Oh, Jesus, no,' Kate breathed.

She dropped the smouldering quilt and ran past Ellis to the lounge. The heat struck her before she reached it. The room was full of fire. Flames clamoured from everything the petrol had touched. The carpet was awash with them. The curtains were blazing rags, while the stack of posters was a torch that sent waves of smoke and ash across the Victorian mouldings. Kate recoiled, but the children's screams were a stronger spur. She could see beyond the flames that the area around the leather sofa and chair was still clear, and without waiting she pulled her coat around her head and darted through the doorway.

Hot hands patted her back and nipped her legs, and then she was through. She kept to the side of the room away from the windows, where the fire had yet to reach, and ran to the sofa. Jack was ducking forward, thrashing his head around, and she could see how the back of his hair was singed and smouldering. A yard or two behind him the remains of the petrol can was a roaring yellow beacon that flared to the ceiling. He had managed to pull Emily so she lay across his lap, shielded from the worst of it, and Kate slapped at his hair, feeling the bite of the sparks on her already burned hands. Across from her Lucy's eyes were frantic as she sat bound and gagged in the leather armchair, protected so far by its high, winged back.

Jack pulled his head away, lifting his chin for Kate to remove the tape from his mouth.

'Get the kids out!' he gasped, when she yanked it off.

'What about you?'

'No time! Just do it!'

Kate wavered, knowing she would never get back in time for Lucy and Jack. It was already like trying to breathe in the open door of a furnace. The room was filling with smoke as the flames spread, crowding the enclosure formed by the chairs and sofa. Kate looked across at Lucy. Her blue eyes were wide and tearful over the tape as she nodded.

Kate snatched Angus from the playpen and grabbed up Emily from Jack's lap. Emily began screaming, 'Mummy! Mummy!' as she carried them away. Kate saw Jack gnawing at the tape around his wrists, and suddenly she went back. Still holding the children, she awkwardly kneeled in front of him.

'What the fuck are you doing? Get out!' Jack shouted, but she had already bent to take the tape binding his ankles between her teeth. She tugged and worried at it, then it ripped and with a jerk he pulled his legs free.

'Right, now go!' he shouted.

She stood up, hoisting Angus and Emily into better positions, her wounded arm throbbing under their weight. Jack was on his hands and knees, biting at the tape binding Lucy's feet, pulling at it with his still fastened hands as Kate struggled to carry the two children to the wall furthest from the flames. She flinched at a pop from overhead as the bulb burst, but its light was hardly needed now. Squinting against the heat, she pressed their faces into her coat as she edged past the blazing petrol can and then stopped.

Through the smoke, she saw that the doorframe and the carpet in front of it was engulfed.

'Jack!' she shouted.

She heard him swear, and then there was a sudden clatter. She turned and saw him dragging the rug from the floor, his wrists free and bleeding now, tipping the coffee table from it. He lurched towards her, wincing and clumsy with the pain of returning circulation, while behind him Lucy hobbled and almost fell. Kate started forward to help, but hot smoke suddenly took the air from her lungs. Coughing and fighting for breath, she turned her face and buried her mouth and nose in her coat as Jack pushed past and began to lash with the heavy rug at the flames around the door. Lucy made it to her and half collapsed on Kate's shoulder, chest heaving as she struggled to draw in air with her mouth still covered by tape. She tried to peel it off, but her wrists were also bound, and a sudden choking spasm doubled her up. Kate supported her as best she could, unable to do anything more with the children clinging to her. The skin of her face felt tight as they staggered after Jack. She could smell her hair beginning to burn. It was difficult to see through the heat and smoke. She ducked as a sudden bang from the far side of the room threw a punch of white-hot flame at them. It was followed by more as the aerosol cans exploded. Cowering against the wall, Kate could hear a metallic pinging even above the roar of the fire and remembered the tins of cleaning solvent. So did Jack, because she saw him dart a glance towards that corner before turning to where she and Lucy were huddled.

'Come on!' he shouted, and swept the thick rug over them like a man sheltering under a jacket. 'Move!'

They stumbled towards the door. The carpet in front of it was still on fire, but Jack had beaten it down enough to pass, and the tented rug shielded them from the burning doorframe. Kate felt the hot lash of flames on her legs, and then they were out in the relative cool of the hall.

Ellis still lay face down. His clothes had largely burned away, and most of the papers and boxes around him had caught on fire. Kate faltered, but Jack draped the rug between them and Ellis's pyre, blocking it from view as he herded them past.

Further along, the quilt was blazing where Kate had left it, lying across the width of the hall. Jack stepped forward and flung the rug over it. It landed with a heavy *whumph*, snuffing the quilt's flames like a candle. They hurried over it to the front door. The smoke was suffocating as Jack struggled with the lock. Then it snicked free, and he pulled open the door and ushered them out into the night's sweet, cold air.

They staggered down the path supporting each other, not halting until they reached the gate. Kate looked back. Smoke was billowing out through the open door, and without thinking what she was doing she set down the children and ran back to the house.

She heard Jack shout, then she was in the hallway and the thick heat and smoke closed around her again. Holding her breath, she ran to where Ellis lay, barely able to see as she kicked aside the flaming papers and took hold of his feet. His raw ankles looked bony and pathetic above the scorched training shoes as she dragged him backwards. After a few steps she stopped, pulled her coat over her mouth and nose and took several quick breaths. She was reaching down for his feet again when the tins of cleaning solvent exploded.

There was a noiseless flash, and a hot pressure knocked her sideways. The hall was instantly an oven. She felt the skin of her face flayed and knew her hair was on fire. She drew breath to scream but choked it off as the overheated air scorched her throat and lungs. Blinded by pain and smoke, she floundered, and then something slammed into her.

She was enveloped in darkness as the rug smothered the flames. She felt Jack pull her towards the front door, but broke away, emerging from the rug to seize one of Ellis's ankles again.

She saw Jack mouth curses at her, but her head was full of ringing from the explosion. She shook her head anyway and carried on pulling, and a moment later he threw the rug over them both and took hold of Ellis's other ankle.

Together they dragged him towards the front door, stumbling backwards over the smoking quilt as fast as they could. She nearly fell down the step, and then Ellis bumped down over it on to the path. Kate felt a dim nudge of memory, but it was gone before she was really aware of it.

They pulled him to the gate before they stopped and shucked off the smouldering rug. The cold air was like a balm on Kate's skin. She sucked it down into her lungs, wincing with the pain of it. Through streaming eyes, she could see that Lucy was sobbing as she tried to hug Jack with her still-bound hands.

Kate turned back to Ellis. He lay half on his side, almost in the recovery position. Kate had avoided looking at his face, but she did so now. His hair had gone, and the skin was cracked like overdone meat. She nearly gagged on the smell. She felt sure he was dead. She didn't know herself why she had gone back for him. Then his eyes flickered. Most of his eyelids had been burned away, and Kate knew he must be blind. But his eyes moved, as though he were searching for something. His hands weren't too badly burned, and Kate gently took hold of one.

Her throat felt as though there was broken glass in it when she tried to speak. She tried again.

'I'm here.'

The grating voice wasn't hers. It echoed, hollow and distant, through the ringing in her ears. His eyes fixed on the sound of it. She could feel quivers running through him. His mouth opened slightly, and with a sure intuition Kate knew what he wanted.

'I've still got the baby,' she croaked in a whisper.

He continued to stare towards her, his sightless eyes looking slightly to one side. But he didn't move again.

She set his hand down and stood up. The house was blazing fiercely now. Smoke gouted through the doorway and windows. She became aware that the pain from her burns was growing. She went over to where Lucy and Jack were standing with the children.

Lucy's hands and mouth were free from the tape now.

She was still crying. She and Kate looked at each other, then stumbled into a hug. Kate felt her own tears begin to rack her, and the two of them clung to each other and sobbed as the house burned and sirens began to sound in the distance.

Epilogue

The hospital smell is cooked dinners and antiseptic. She cries out as the pain clubs at her. It seems as if it will never stop. Then, at last, it does. She sinks back.

Her short hair, still growing back, is plastered to her head. Below one sleeve of the white cotton gown, the pink line of a newly healed scar shows. As the pain ebbs, she raises her head as a white-smocked woman approaches, holding something wriggling in her arms.

The woman smiles. 'It's a boy.'

Acknowledgements

The original version of *Where There's Smoke* owed thanks to Dr Sheila Cook and the team at the University of Sheffield's Department of Obstetrics and Gynaecology, Jessop Hospital; Dr Gwilym Hayes, Consultant Forensic Psychiatrist at Wathwood Hospital Regional Secure Unit; and Judy Winter, then head of Student Services at the University of Derby. A long-time friend, Judy sadly passed away in April 2015. She will be very sadly missed.

The article on pages 247–249 refers to Faulk, M. (1988) *Basic Forensic Psychiatry,* London, Blackwell Scientific Publications, and Jackson, H. F. (1994) 'Assessment of Fire-setters' from *The Assessment of Criminal Behaviours of Clients in Secure Settings*, eds McMurran, M. and Hodge, J., Jessica Kingsley Publishers.

Thanks also to John at John Highfield PR, the HFEA press office, and Ben Willis and Lizzy Goudsmit at Transworld. Finally, thank you to my wife Hilary for working on this with me.